"With heart, wisdom, and a quartet of unforgettable protagonists, Cecilia Galante deftly examines the ways in which the sense of community created by profound friendships can act as a salve on even the deepest of wounds. Gripping and heart-rending, *The Invisibles* will—warning!—keep you up into the wee hours, hungry for just one more page."

—Meg Donohue, *USA TODAY* bestselling author
of *All the Summer Girls* and *Dog Crazy*

"In *The Invisibles*, Cecilia Galante artfully reminds us that even the most carefully constructed facade doesn't stand a chance against the healing power of true friendship."

—Zoe Fishman, author of *Balancing Acts*

"Cecilia Galante tells a difficult story with sensitivity and grace . . . Fraught with pain but quietly hopeful, *The Invisibles* is a moving tribute to the strength of female friendship."

—*Shelf Awareness*, starred review

"Galante's first adult novel is one of letting go of your past, allowing others to love you and, above all else, forgiving yourself. For readers who like a story of healing and the power of friendship."

—*Library Journal*

"Galante displays the same sensitivity and insight shown in her children's and YA fiction . . . in this moving story of reconciliation and renewal."

—*Booklist*

"[A] lovely, poignant book about female friendships and making your own family . . . a compelling, powerful summer read, *The Invisibles* is a page turner that is perfect for a rainy beach day."

—*Times Leader*

Also by Cecilia Galante

The Invisibles

The Odds of You and Me

The Odds of You and Me

Cecilia Galante

WILLIAM MORROW
An Imprint of HarperCollinsPublishers

This is a work of fiction. Names, characters, places, and incidents are products of the author's imagination or are used fictitiously and are not to be construed as real. Any resemblance to actual events, locales, organizations, or persons, living or dead, is entirely coincidental.

P.S.™ is a trademark of HarperCollins Publishers.

HarperCollins books may be purchased for educational, business, or sales promotional use. For information, please email the Special Markets Department at SPsales@harpercollins.com.

FIRST EDITION

Designed by Diahann Sturge

Library of Congress Cataloging-in-Publication Data has been applied for.

ISBN 978-0-06-243485-2

17 18 19 20 21 RRD 10 9 8 7 6 5 4 3 2 1

For my mother, who stayed awake with me all through that dark, terrible night as the winds howled and the snow fell— and gave me the courage to pursue a bright, new world.

Two possibilities exist: either we are alone in the Universe, or we are not.

Both are equally terrifying.

—Arthur C. Clark

The Odds of You and Me

Chapter 1

B ird?" Mrs. Ross, all blond hair and wide, kohl-rimmed eyes, beckons from inside the probation office. "Hi, hon! Come on in." She holds the door open and strides ahead of me, winding her way through a maze of pale brown cubicles. It's impossible not to stare at her legs; encased in a pair of mustard-yellow tights and spiky black pumps, they demand to be noticed, dare you to look away. Even without heels, Mrs. Ross has got to be at least five-ten, most of it from the waist down. Her black skirt, white silk blouse, and matching black jacket lend an air of confidence, decorum, and smarts, all at the same time. Things I will never have—at least not in this lifetime. "So, how are things?" The question is tossed over her shoulder, both a propriety and an afterthought. "Everything all right?"

"Yeah." I trot a little to keep up with her. "Things are fine."

She indicates the empty seat next to her desk with an out-stretched palm, and then settles into her own chair. A cloud of something sweet drifts out from under her—a blend of Ivory soap and roses and maybe a little bit of cinnamon, too. When she crosses her legs, she has to move them to one side, since they don't fit under her desk, hooking one ankle around the other. The wheels on her chair make a small screeching sound, like the brakes in my car. "Okay, now." She taps her keyboard, glances at the computer screen. "Let me just get you caught up here and then we can talk."

I sit back as her fingers fly over the keys and glance at the familiar items lined up along her desk: the black-and-silver placard that spells out ALLISON ROSS, PROBATION OFFICER in neat, shiny letters; a blue coffee cup with the message 40 IS THE NEW 20; a varied assortment of red-and-black ballpoint pens, neatly rubber-banded and stashed inside a narrow black container. Next to it is a withered plant inside a terra cotta pot, the only indication of Mrs. Ross's fallibility. The purple flowers are wrinkled and dry as old Saran wrap, the leaves almost brown. Along the corkboard walls of her cubicle are thumb-tacked photographs—mostly of the same two kids, blond, gap-toothed, their arms flung around Mrs. Ross, a snowman, each other. There is one of the three of them in a pool, with just their heads peeking out of the water. Mrs. Ross is shielding her eyes against the glare of the sun; drops of water bead her forearms. Even with her hair slicked back, and no makeup, she is beautiful.

Next to the photographs, encased in a plastic frame with faux wood edging, is a college diploma announcing her bachelor's degree in criminal justice from Wheaton University. I've never heard of Wheaton University, but then I haven't heard of a lot of colleges. I was never one of those people who planned on going to college, especially since I barely even made it through high school. Whenever I come here, though, I find myself thinking about it, wondering what kind of school I would have been in-terested in if I had ever taken the time to look at any, if I would have actually studied something, or just screwed around, the way I did during my last two years of high school. There was a time when I'd toyed with the idea of becoming a nurse, especially right after Dad died. Something about all those life-hinging moments interspersed between the ordinary hum of daily activity; what other kind of work granted such a thing? I was good at biology, too—one of the few subjects that ever held my interest in school, and even when I was younger, things like blood and innards had never freaked me out. Of course, you needed good grades to get into nursing school—good grades and money, too; neither of which I had. And so life took a different turn, veered around another bend. Which is part of the reason I'm sitting here right now.

"Hoe. Lee. *Cow*," Mrs. Ross says suddenly, squinting at the screen. "Do you really only have two more weeks left, Bird?"

"Thirteen days actually."

She taps a few more buttons on the computer, narrows a neatly edged brow. "Wowzer. Now, where did *that* time go?"

"Oh, you know." I stick a piece of hair behind my ear. "Time flies when you're having fun."

Mrs. Ross turns all the way around, done with the computer, and settles her folded hands into her lap. Her fingernails are beautifully manicured—small and square, painted the palest pink. The large pear-shaped diamond looks perfectly natural adorning her fourth finger, expected even. "And these last two weeks will fly by, too. Boy, before you know it, Bird, you and I will go back to being strangers again."

Except that we weren't ever friends. I smile, shrug, look away. People like Mrs. Ross always think they're friends with every-one. Especially people like me who they think don't know any better. I wait as she riffles through a stack of manila files on her desk and then pulls one out.

"Okay, here's the letter I got from the manager at Super Fresh last week. He said he received your last payment on . . ." She pauses, her eyes scanning the note. "February twenty-second. And today's April sixth, which means you're a few weeks ahead of schedule." She lets the file drop again into her lap. "Wow. You're all paid up with time to spare. Good for you, hon."

I nod, although she doesn't have to remind me. The little notebook in my top dresser drawer has a list of every payment I've made over the last eighty-nine weeks—thirty-four dollars every Monday—until the six hundred dollars I wrote in bad checks eighteen months ago plus restitution fees, which added up to a grand total of twenty-four hundred dollars, was paid off. The debt has been front and center in my life for so long that making that last payment felt like I had won the lottery, or as if someone had just let me out of jail. It was a good feeling knowing that—at least financially—I had made things right. Now I was at the starting line again. Maybe, after a little more time, I could even get back in the race.

"So, how's everything else going?" Mrs. Ross adjusts her ankles, settling in for an extended conversation. "No problems at home or anything?"

She means home with Ma, where I've been living since I got into trouble with the checks. I've made the mistake of admitting once or twice how trying the whole setup can get sometimes, how often I have to bite my tongue with my mother, who is not only the polar opposite of me but has also made it her life's mission to change that. Now I wish I hadn't said anything. Mrs. Ross never fails to bring it up when I come in, almost as if she is expecting me to break down and confess one day that I lost my temper and took a swing at her.

"Nope, no problems," I say lightly. "Everything's good."

"You sure?"

"Positive."

"You're still working with her, right? Cleaning people's houses?"

"Yup."

"And how's that going?"

"It's work." I shrug. "It pays the bills."

Ma's been cleaning houses for as long as I can remember, but I only started last year, after I moved back in. When I was younger, she only took jobs during the day so that she could be there for me when I got home from school. But after Dad died, she started working night shifts, too. I was in high school then, but for a long time, I barely saw her at all, just for an hour or two after school, which we usually spent arguing about my poor grades or my even poorer choice of friends, before she had to leave again to work through most of the night. She didn't have a choice, of course. It was the only way she could make ends meet. But her absence created another layer in the shaky foundation that had become our new, two-person family, infusing the holes with a loneliness I hadn't yet known existed.

Most nights, unbeknownst to Ma, of course, I'd head out to meet up with my best friend, Tracy. We'd go sit behind the old water tower a few blocks away and smoke a few joints or nurse a bottle of vodka Tracy had stolen from her parents' liquor cabinet and stagger back home at midnight. It was always a relief to realize that I had once again successfully killed the string of empty hours behind me, but no matter how drunk or high I got, I could never fell asleep until Ma returned, until I heard the click of her key in the front door, the familiar gait of her footsteps on the stairs. I swore to myself back then that I'd never go that route, that I would never get myself into a position where I was so hard off financially that I had to clean other people's houses.

Until the day came when I did.

Mrs. Ross sits back, her face softening. "It's hard work, I'm sure."

"Nothing wrong with that."

"Oh, not at all! Hard work is the best work there is." She pauses, adjusting the hem of her skirt. "And how's Angus?"

I grin when she says my little boy's name, despite the fact that he told me this morning he never wanted to speak to me again after discovering that I put his magic sneakers in the washing machine. *("You'll wash all the magic off, Mom! Jeez! Don't you know anything?")* "He's great," I reply. "Getting big."

"Four now, right?"

"Five in a few more months."

"Wow. Five years old." Mrs. Ross shakes her head. "You still don't look old enough to have a five-*month*-old, Bird."

I bristle a little when she says that, although I know she means well. She probably even thinks it's a compliment. People say things like that all the time when they find out I have a child, especially women. I think it's because, with my small frame and pale, unremarkable features, I look a lot younger than my twenty-five years. One woman, a cashier at the super-market, actually reared back when I told her Angus was mine, and said, "And *how* old are *you*?" When I told her, she shook her head and clicked her tongue against her teeth, as if having a five-year-old child at my age wasn't just an impossibility but an atrocity, too. I doubt getting pregnant a few months shy of your twentieth birthday is part of any lucid woman's plans. But it happens sometimes. Sort of like other things you don't plan on happening.

"Well, you've been doing everything exactly the way you're supposed to." Mrs. Ross smiles fondly at me, a mother hen whose chick has just learned to use her wings. "You're paid up on the bill, you've come in again for your biweekly report, and things are almost completely settled in your file. Now we just have to wait until this probation clock of yours stops ticking, and then all of this will be behind you." She hitches both hands around the top of her knee and arches the shiny black pump on her foot. "Have you thought about what you're going to do next?"

"Well, I'll move out of my mother's house for starters. Get my own place. For Angus and me. I've been saving."

Mrs. Ross nods. "What're you thinking? Downtown, maybe? Or over on the east side?"

"No. God, no. I've lived here in town all my life. I hate this area." I glance up quickly. "No offense to you or anything. I mean, if you live here. In the area."

Mrs. Ross smiles faintly. "None taken."

I withdraw a small newspaper photograph from my back pocket and unfold it carefully. The crease in the middle is practically a slit now, the edges of the paper curled and worn. I lay it down flat on Mrs. Ross's desk, tap it lightly with my fingers. "I found this place, right on the lake. There's an apartment on the second floor—two bedrooms, an eat-in kitchen, a full bathroom. It's perfect for Angus and me. I've been putting a little aside for weeks. Five or six more days, and I'll have the full security deposit, and then Angus and I can move in."

Mrs. Ross wrinkles her forehead, studying the picture. "Is this out at Moon Lake?"

"Yeah." I point to the peaked roof on top of the house, and draw my finger down the inverted side of it. "Can you see the skylights on top? Those are in the bedroom where Angus'll be. He'll be able to look up every night and see the stars. The snow, too." I lean in a little, grinning. "Can you imagine lying in bed and staring up at the snow falling above you?" I've done it hundreds of times already, usually when I'm knee-deep in the grime around the base of someone's toilet, yellow rubber gloves slick with suds, the knees of my pants damp and reeking of bleach: imagining a cocoon of Angus and me, beneath his *Toy Story* comforter, staring up at the whiteness above us, the glass window dotted with pale, sugary stars, the downward, rushing movement of them a tiny heaven all its own.

"Wow. That'll be beautiful." Mrs. Ross's voice is soft. "Have you seen it in person? You're sure it's okay?"

"Oh, yeah. It's great."

I'd actually driven up to the property two weeks earlier on a whim, not expecting much to come of it, just to look around for myself. I almost hoped something *would* be wrong with it, a hole in the kitchen wall that might suggest mice, or a perpetual leak in the bathroom. Anything that might make me second-guess my decision, or even make it for me. But the place—a pale yellow house with two large bay windows and a dried rosebud wreath on the front door—was perfect. The upstairs, where Angus and I would live, was more than I could have hoped for, with its hardwood floors, smooth, clean walls, and kitchen with a tiny breakfast nook built into one corner. And when the owner of the place, a short, gray-haired woman named Mrs. Vandermark, not only turned out to be close friends with a client whose house I used to clean but also decided on the spot that such a happy coincidence qualified me as her next renter, I felt something shift into place. She didn't even protest when I told her I had the first and last month's rent, but that I needed a few more weeks to get the security deposit together. "I understand completely," she said. "No one's making millions cleaning houses these days, although you should be, in my opinion, with all the horrible things people make you do." She clucked her tongue. "I've heard stories." I smiled and nodded as she patted me on the back. "You take your time with the security, dear. I'll be in Florida for the next few weeks anyway. This place isn't going anywhere." It was as if it had been waiting for me. As if something had drawn me there, knowing somehow that this was the place. This was home. Finally.

Mrs. Ross slides a paper clip along her desk with the tip of her index finger, as if trying to follow a wayward thought in her head. "How do you think your mother's going to take you leaving?"

"Oh, she'll be fine." I fold the picture up and slide it back inside my pocket. "My coming home was always just temporary anyway. She knows that."

"Yes." Mrs. Ross nods thoughtfully. "But she has gotten particularly close to Angus over these past few years, hasn't she?"

"Well, yeah, but it's not like we're leaving for California. Moon Lake is only twelve miles outside of New Haven. She'll be able to see him whenever she wants."

"And you?" Mrs. Ross asks gently. "Will you take him down to see her . . . if he asks?"

"Of course." Something inside me bristles again. Mrs. Ross is my probation officer, not my therapist. There's no need for all this personal probing, these extra questions. And I don't owe her any of the answers.

I stand up, inserting my hands into my back pants pocket. On the wall behind me, the crackle of static bleeds out from a police scanner, followed by a male voice: *"Shoplifting suspect in transport. All stations ready."* The ticker tape of criminal activity in New Haven seems to run on a never-ending loop; whenever I am here, at least, there is always something being reported. On my last visit, I listened as the chatter reported a robbery at one of the local mini-marts. The suspect had used a plastic squirt gun hidden beneath a denim jacket, and managed to leave with twenty dollars in cash and six boxes of Ho Ho cupcakes. That little detail sums up New Haven perfectly: a desperate blend of insolence and stupidity that I've been saturated in all my life. Getting out can't come fast enough.

"Okay, well, good, good." Mrs. Ross flattens her palms against the top of her skirt, and slides them briskly to the tops of her knees, as if everything is all settled. "You know, it sounds as if once all of this is over, Bird, you'll really be starting a whole new chapter."

"That's the plan." I fasten a few snaps on the front of my coat, look down at my watch quickly. "So we're okay, right? I really have to get back. Angus has to be in preschool at nine, and then I have a house to clean at nine-thirty."

"Go, go," Mrs. Ross says. "You're all set. Last and final check-in will be April eighteenth." She closes my file once more and slides it back in the pile. "Don't get into any trouble before then. You know the rules."

I cock my head as she winks at me. "See you, Mrs. Ross."

"Take care of yourself, Bird." Her voice lilts gently behind me. "See you in two weeks."

Chapter 2

The sun looks like a washed-out slice of lemon hidden behind a gauze of clouds. The air, still tinged with a latent winter chill, refuses to soften, even around the edges, and the sky is a flat sheet of gray. I shiver getting behind the wheel of my car, which is parked in the first row of the probation office parking lot, and start the engine. Mrs. Ross's words reverberate in my head as I sit there for a moment, waiting for the heat to kick in: *Once all this is over, Bird, you'll really be starting a whole new chapter.* Whole new chapter, my ass. I'm out here trying to start a whole new *life.* I know a lot of people don't get second chances, but mine is right around the corner, hovering there like one of those brass rings you get to snatch off a merry-go-round. And there's no way I'm not going to grab it when it comes within arm's reach—and then run like hell.

Things weren't always this hard, of course. Or quite so dire. Ma would say my problems started after I fell in with Tracy and the rest of the headbanger crowd during my junior year of high school, but she's way off, the way she is about most things. It was the headbangers, with their black leather boots, dirty T-shirts, and oddly mournful music, that kept me afloat after Dad died that year. They were the ones who not only understood my new "screw the world" attitude, but embraced it. Encouraged it, even. The days when I got to school on time, accompanied Ma to church on Sunday mornings, and did my homework every night became a thing of the past that year, although I was diligent about my required good-night call to Ma so that she wouldn't suspect anything and come looking for me. I saw even less of her on weekends; if she found me at home at all, it was just to grab clean clothes, or to scavenge a few dollars from the bottom of the sugar canister she kept in the pantry to contribute to Tracy's growing pot fund. I pierced my nose, developed a perpetual, cloying scent of weed and corn chips, and turned a deaf ear to Ma's constant ranting and raving.

Which was not difficult to do. With his soft-spoken voice and gentle mannerisms, Dad had always been the parent I related to, not Ma. Never Ma. Her voice went up an octave after Dad died, settling at a decibel far above anything I'd ever thought humanly possible, but even before that, she was a yeller. A nagger. The proud owner of a nothing's-ever-good-enough personality that made me want to go hide in a corner when I was younger and put a bag over my head. Being left alone in that house without Dad felt at times as if I'd been abandoned in the worst way. Betrayed, even. For years I would wake up and stare at my door, waiting for his head to poke in suddenly, listen for the light clicking sound of his wedding band as he tapped his hand against the doorway, for the singsong lilt in his voice as he called, "Rise and shine, little bird! Up and at 'em!" Dad possessed an innate sort of lightness, a steady level of calm that settled the rapid knocking pace my heart acquired whenever Ma came around. He used to say that it was their differences that made their marriage work, but I never believed him. I think he was just too nice of a guy to ever leave her.

Every once in a while, I let myself go back to that night in the hospital, watch as my mind's eye drifts over that picture again: Ma and me on either side of the gurney, Dad's face, nearly unrecognizable after his car was smashed from behind and he was thrown headfirst through the windshield. His skin was a mottled eggplant shade, the shape of his head so swollen that it could have been a balloon someone blew up, a child's plaything. Pieces of glass stuck out of his hair; a shard the size of my thumb was lodged beneath the skin on his forehead like a misplaced seashell. The surgeon, a small Indian man with dark hair and neat fingernails, had already told Ma and me that his internal injuries were so severe that there was nothing anyone could do, except to keep him company while he died. "I can't say if he can still hear you," the doctor said. "But he might respond to touch."

"Pray," Ma said, staring at me across Dad's still-heaving chest. Her fingers were entwined with his, fear etched on her face like the cracks in an eggshell. "Pray with all your might, Bernadette. Like you've never prayed before."

I did, of course, closing my eyes, and bending my head over my father's battered body, whispering fervently. Back then, I believed in things like that. Like praying. Pleading with an omnipotent, invisible force to keep my father's breath in his body did not seem so unusual. It was what we did. What we had always done, whether for a simple request, like finding more work for Ma, or the life and death situation we found ourselves in now. We prayed, we begged, we beseeched. *Pleasepleasepleaseplease.* Of course, whether or not God decided to grant our wish was another thing entirely. That was up to Him. It had nothing to do with us, or how badly we wanted—or even needed—the thing. The ball was in His court. Always.

Slowly, like some sort of strange evaporation, I watched the life leave my father's body that night, felt his hands grow more and more limp in my own, until the one I was holding slipped out altogether, and hung there like a gutted fish. The machine he was hooked up to made an ominous sound, a single unabbreviated beep, and a nurse took us out of the room, ushering Ma and me into the hallway just outside. Ma wept silently beside me, her face in her hands, her shoulders rising and then falling again, and I leaned into her, wrapping an arm around her back, and pushing my face into the sleeve of her itchy winter coat.

I didn't cry, a fact that stunned me afterward, and filled me with guilt, as if I had betrayed my father with my lack of emotion. I felt numb instead, as if I was watching everything from overhead, as if it might be happening to someone else instead of us. I stared at the floor for a while, watched the lines in the neat squares beneath me blur, come back into focus, and then blur again. A movement inside the room next to Dad's made me lift my eyes, and I looked at a nurse holding an old man's wrist between her thumb and middle finger. She was dressed in pink scrubs, her blond ponytail anchored high on the back of her head like a tail. Her eyes watched the clock on the wall as she counted his pulse, and her lips moved just the slightest bit, keeping time with the beats. Pieces of the man's white hair were splayed out above his head like a split milkweed pod, and even from where I sat, I could see the papery quality of his skin. His face was tilted up to the ceiling, as if searching for light or a long-lost scent. When she was finished, the nurse put his hand back down among the folds of his blanket, and reached around behind her for a plastic cup of pills. She waited as the man swallowed them, and then arranged his neck carefully in her palm as he gulped a chaser of water.

The scene looked like some sort of a painting—framed by the white slats of the doorway, a pale afternoon light touching the nurse's blond hair, her shadows thrown across the man's bed as she moved quietly around his room. I didn't want to look away, could not bring myself to turn back to my mother, still weeping violently into my shoulder, or even to my father, not ten feet away, already growing cold and stiff. It occurred to me instead that I might do that sort of thing someday, that I was the kind of person who could get through a day intermittently pocked with the beginnings and endings of life. It was a relief of sorts, knowing this, a reminder that some things would go on, even as others ended.

Which they did, of course. Not the way I planned them, not even the way I had hoped. Since nursing school was out of the question, or at least out of my immediate grasp, I found other work after graduating from high school, waitressing at a place called the Burger Barn, and began saving up for a place of my own. It didn't take long, especially since another waitress named Jenny expressed an interest in sharing a place with me. I was nineteen when I moved into a tiny dismal apartment with her, the ceilings so low that you could reach up and touch them, carpeting that smelled like cat urine, and a leaky shower. But the rent was cheap, and it was two towns away from New Haven—six whole miles from Ma—which, when all was said and done, had been my only real requirement in the first place.

It didn't take long for me to get into trouble, and I'm not even talking about the positive pregnancy test I found myself staring at six months later, or how Angus pushed his way into the world with a cry that broke through the haze of pain between my legs and made me sit up straight. The fact that his father was not in the delivery room, and would probably never be in the same room as his child, was not so much a concern to me at the time either, nor was the fact that my new life as a single, working mother was so exhausting that some nights I literally fell asleep standing in front of the microwave, waiting for Angus's bottles to heat up.

It was the money that got me in trouble—the pediatric bills that began to pile up over the next year and a half as Angus's ear infections worsened, the cost of day care, and, of course, rent and utilities and diapers and food. I didn't set out to engage in deliberate criminal activity. But I was too proud to apply for government assistance, and there was no way I was going to approach Ma, who was still aghast at the "predicament" I had gotten myself into. I hadn't even realized I'd overwritten the first check until I sat down and balanced my checkbook that night. I was terrified at first, but when nothing came of it, and another week went by without any problems, I wrote another very small one. The scary thing was how easy it was. I over-wrote four more checks to Super Fresh, loading up on milk and Pull-Ups and orange juice and bread like Angus and I were getting ready for Armageddon, before anyone caught on. By then, I was six hundred dollars in. And if it had taken someone a while to figure things out in the beginning, the legal notifi-cations started coming in fast and furious once they did.

Two weeks later, I was summoned to court, where I was sentenced to repay the cost of the checks, plus three times the total amount in restitution. Since it was my first offense, I also received eighteen months of probation and was introduced to Mrs. Ross, who would be my very own probation officer. It was Mrs. Ross who encouraged me to move back in with Ma so that I could set up a payment plan without having to worry about additional financial obligations, and of course Ma herself who, in a sudden burst of maternal sanity, insisted. What else could I do? The choice would have been an easy one if I hadn't had Angus to think about.

He was two and a half years old by then and just starting to make the transition to big-boy underpants. I was twenty-two and just starting to figure out that maybe I hadn't ever learned how to make the transition to big-girl underpants.

And so, broke, shamed, and out of options, I moved back home.

For all my misgivings about it, though, living with Ma again hasn't been as terrible as I thought it would be. A lot of people would say that I'm lucky. Blessed, even. (Well, that's the word Ma uses.) And I guess I'll give her that. She didn't *have* to take me back in after I got in trouble, especially the kind of trouble that drove her to her knees, reciting novena after novena for my jeopardized salvation, which, aside from my obvious illegal activity, was in even direr straits since I'd obviously slept with someone out of wedlock. Having unmarried sex, according to Ma, had always been the sin equivalent of murder. ("You might as well just be tossing your body into a gutter, treating it like that," she liked to say. "A woman's body is for her husband to enjoy, only. No one else.") She got me involved with her whole house-cleaning business, too, which, while not my life's goal, has turned out to be much more lucrative than I ever realized.

I even have a few steady clients of my own now—Mr. Herron, who lives over on the south side of town, and Mrs. Livingston, both of whom expect me to be punctual and do good work. I do, too, cleaning behind the furniture and scrubbing down the baseboards, even when it's not expected or asked for. Working hard is more important than ever, especially now that I have Angus. I want to set a good example, let him know that being tired at the end of the day because you've worked your tail off is nothing to be ashamed of. Even if you've spent it on your hands and knees, scrubbing other people's toilets. Or silently begging forgiveness.

What's made things most tolerable, however, has been how much Ma has taken to Angus. She has a habit of nitpicking at the little things he does, and insists on calling him Gus, which is a direct passive-aggressive jab at me. But it's obvious that she adores him, pampering him in a way that both astounds and delights me. For someone whose idea of fun used to be taking me out to buy new socks, Ma rolls out the red carpet when it comes to my little boy. She takes him everywhere—to the park, the zoo, the movies, even the mall, which she hates, so that he can ride on the merry-go-round in the food court.

And yet, it's the big things that continue to amaze me. For as long as I've been alive, Ma has been what I consider a SuperCatholic. Someone whose answer to every question I've ever asked has eventually, somehow, turned out to be about God or Jesus or the Blessed Virgin Mary. Since my own religious beliefs have been challenged over the years, I informed her in no uncertain terms when we moved in that she was not allowed to talk about God or church with Angus, that his religious upbringing was my responsibility alone. It pained her enormously to have to agree to this, mostly because my religious sensibilities, which have continued to be nonexistent, are the singular bane of her life. For the most part, however, she's kept her end of the bargain, although she doesn't hide her displeasure about having to.

To be fair, Angus is so young that it hasn't even really come up much. Except once, just a few months ago, when he asked me who made the sky and the dirt and all the earthworms in the world. Ma stopped chewing, her eyes locking with mine over the dinner table. I could tell she was holding her breath, waiting for my answer, which would inevitably fall short of whatever one she would offer. I dropped my eyes and speared a green bean. "Well, the world was created a long time ago, buddy. You know, back when there were dinosaurs."

"I know *that*," Angus insisted. "But who did it? Who *made* it?"

Ma's eyes were boring a hole into the top of my skull, daring me to omit God from the equation. I inserted the green bean into my mouth and chewed slowly. "No one created it," I said finally. "It just sort of created itself. See, there was a big explosion once—"

The sound of Ma's chair scraping the floor made me wince even before I lifted my eyes. She glared at me, snatching her plate off the table as she walked over toward the sink.

"You mean, like a bomb?" Angus breathed, undeterred.

"Yeah, sort of like a bomb." I stared at the veins along the side of Ma's neck as she stalked out of the room, green and rigid against her pale skin. She yanked her cardigan sweater around her, and I caught sight of a hole in the bottom of it, near the hem. "Except much, much bigger than a bomb."

Later that night, after I'd explained the Big Bang Theory another three times to Angus and had tucked him into bed for the night, she appeared in my doorway, just as I knew she would. I lifted one of my headphones from my ear and raised an eyebrow, feigning surprise. "What's up?"

"You're not going to teach him *anything* about God?" she asked.

Robert Plant was still moaning in my other ear about needing every inch of his love. I switched it off. "Not yet."

"Well, when?" She crossed her arms.

"When it feels right. When it comes up naturally. When he asks me about it."

"*Him*, Bernadette, not it. God is not an 'it.'" Her nostrils flared white around the edges. "And what do you mean, 'when it feels right'? To you or to him?"

I shrugged. "To both of us, I guess. I haven't really thought about it."

"Maybe you should. Giving him some cockamamy story about a star exploding in the universe—"

"It's not a cockamamy story, Ma." I struggled to keep my voice level. "It's science, okay? And why are we arguing about this? You seem to forget that—"

"I haven't forgotten anything," she said. "And don't use that tone with me, please. I'm still your mother." She raised an eyebrow. "In case *you've* forgotten."

I tipped my headphones back over my head as she closed the door and turned the volume up to a near deafening level. "Whole Lotta Love" bled into my ears again like a salve. I closed my eyes and let the music fill me. It wasn't difficult. Robert Plant had a voice that was alternately orgasmic and abrasive, often at the same time. Right now, the combination of his words—"way down inside, girl, you need it"—and the pitch at which he delivered them stirred something in my belly. My aggravation about Ma began to dissipate, hovering along the very edges of Plant's groaning and shrieking until, with one final wail, it disappeared altogether.

Now, though, that part of my life is over. I've served my time. In a little less than two weeks, I'll be able to start clean. No more probation, no more Ma, no more anything hanging over me. It'll just be Angus and me inside the tiny apartment on Moon Lake. A fresh start. Maybe even new dreams.

Two weeks. Thirteen days. Three hundred and twelve hours to freedom.

Some days, it feels like forever.

Chapter 3

Everything go all right with Mrs. Ross?" Ma turns around from the stove as I walk inside the house. Her apron is tied around her waist, the sleeves of her denim shirt rolled up to her elbows. The thick scent of coffee and melting butter mingles in the air.

"Yeah, same old stuff. Where's Angus?"

"Still in bed." Ma traces the bottom of the pan with a pat of butter, moving it around in a figure-eight shape.

"Still in bed?" I drape my jacket over the back of one of the chairs. "Ma! Come on! It's almost eight!"

"There's no need to shout, Bernadette. And believe me, I tried. He would not get up for me. I mean, he absolutely refused. He has the will of a goat, that child. An absolute goat."

She is still muttering as I dash upstairs to Angus's room, peek inside. It's empty. "Angus?" I see the lump in my bed across the hall before it moves, and squish in tightly against the sack of warm knees and elbows. He reaches up from inside the covers, his tiny starfish hands feeling around for my face.

"What's the deal, O'Neil?" I ask, lowering my head. "Why didn't you get up for Nanny?"

"I'm tired!" The voice comes through the covers, small and muffled. "I didn't sleep good!"

"Why not?"

He throws back the covers, gazing up at me. "I had bad dreams." He reaches up with his hands and squeezes the hollow part beneath my cheeks as if emphasizing this statement.

"Again?" I stare down into the small, rumpled face looking out at me, searching for signs of distress. He has eyes like blue bottle glass, skin like a ripening peach. On any given day, at any given moment, his beauty astounds me. "Why are you having bad dreams, Boo?"

He shrugs just as Ma appears in the doorway, wiping her small hands on the corner of her apron. "I wanted to ask you, Bernadette, before I forget—" She breaks off suddenly, spotting Angus. "Angus *Connolly*! What are you doing in your mother's bed again?"

Angus ducks back under the blankets, clutching them tightly around his head.

I rest my hand lightly along his back. "Don't, Ma."

"How many times have I told you not to let that child get in bed with you, Bernadette! The longer you perpetuate this kind of dependence, the harder it will be for him to—"

"*Ma!*" My voice is sharp. "He just came in a little while ago. He was in his bed when I left this morning, and he spent the whole night in his room. Now stop, okay? I mean it!"

She stares at me for a moment, a look she has given me so many times over the years that sometimes I see it in my sleep. It's a pitiful expression, mixed with a vague sort of terror. I am too far out of her reach; she cannot save me, nor by extension Angus, no matter how desperately she continues to pray, or how often she attends morning Mass. I reach over, brush the edges of her fingers with my hand. "C'mon, what were you about to say?"

"I left my sweater at church yesterday." Her voice is quiet, still hurt by my reprimand. "And I was wondering if you could go pick it up for me this morning on your way to Mr. Herron's. It's on the way, and I have to go to the Reynoldses' house, which is on the other side of town." She looks down, brushes a crumb off the front of her apron.

"Sure. I can do that."

"I shouldn't be more than a few hours at the Reynoldses' place," she says. "I'm pretty sure she doesn't need me to do any laundry today. I can come help you finish at Mr. Herron's, if you want. Just in case he gives you any trouble about being late. You know how he can get."

It occurs to me to ask why, if she can come help me at Mr. Herron's house, which is just a few blocks away from the church, she needs me to go pick up her sweater. Why can't she just swing by herself and get it? Have a little chat with Father Delaney, the pastor, while she's at it? Maybe talk to him again about how to save my soul? But then she raises one of her hands to brush a wayward curl off her forehead. Her fingers are thick and calloused from years of scrubbing other people's floors, the knuckles swollen so badly on her left hand that she cannot wear her wedding band anymore. Some nights when she comes home after working all day, she falls asleep in her chair. And that's before dinner.

"No, there's no reason to do that." I put one of my hands over hers. "Getting your sweater won't take me more than ten minutes. Besides, I don't want you doing any more than you're already doing."

She gives me a weary look. "It does get done faster if we do it together."

"Don't worry," I say, patting her hand. "I'll be fine."

"You sure?"

"Absolutely."

"All right, then." Her eyes flit over the front of the Metallica T-shirt I am wearing, and she makes no attempt to hide her disgust. "Oh, Bernadette. You didn't just wear that to the probation office, did you?"

She shakes her head slowly. "Would it kill you to at least *try* to look like you're turning over a new leaf?"

"Because I have a *Metallica* T-shirt on?" My voice is already rising. "Are you serious? Do you really think—"

"Never mind, Bernadette." She cuts me off with a brusque wave of her hand. "I don't want to start."

"Then don't."

"Father Delaney asked for you again," she says wistfully. "Yesterday, after morning Mass."

"That's nice." I look over at Angus, hoping he's still breathing okay under all those sheets still wrapped around his head and that maybe, somehow, he is not listening to our conversation and will not pop his head out and ask who Father Delaney is. I know Ma will be all too thrilled to tell him that he is the pastor at Saint Augustine's where, when I was a little girl, I used to go every Sunday morning with her and Dad. She'll probably even launch into the story about the horrible nickname he dubbed me with—Bunny-Bernie—because I used to wiggle my nose when I got nervous.

"You know what he told me?" Ma asks.

"What?"

"That every single time he says Mass, he looks out over the congregation for you." She opens her eyes wide at me. "*You*, Bernadette."

I throw the covers off, walk over to my dresser, and pick up my hairbrush. A few years ago, I might have thrown the brush across the room when Ma started talking like this. Now, I just yank it through my hair, static crackling angrily. "Well, next time Mr. Delaney says something like that, tell him he's wasting his time."

Ma looks startled. "*Father* Delaney, Bernadette. And when you speak to him, you must use that formality. It's not *Mister*. It's never *Mister*. Father only."

I whirl around, brush in my hand. "When am I going to speak to him, Ma? I don't go to church, okay? And I'm not going to go to church. I haven't been inside a church in almost ten years."

Her eyes are piercing blue, the color of a gas flame. "I'm talking about this morning. He'll be at the church. To give you my sweater. I've already talked to him about it."

Oh. Well, of course she has. This whole conversation "asking" me to go get her sweater has just been a formality. I was one hundred percent right to think of questioning her opportunity to retrieve it later. Everything has already been set in motion. Her way. Father Delaney will give me her "forgotten" sweater, while taking the rare opportunity to ask me how I am, what I have been doing, and why he doesn't see me around anymore. Why am I surprised? It's the way she's always done things, will probably be the way she does things for the rest of her life. Dad used to call it using the back door to get out the front, which I'd never under-stood until I got older. Now the phrase reverberates like a bell inside my head.

"Okay, Ma. Fine. Whatever." I lean over, pat the blankets with my free hand. "Let's go, Angus! You have T-ball practice tonight, too, which means we have to pack your uniform. C'mon, now. You have to get dressed."

Angus's voice comes out from beneath the covers. "I don't wanna go to T-ball practice! I *hate* T-ball!"

Ma presses her lips together. "You do not *hate* anything, Gus, especially T-ball. You just had a hard time with it last week because of all that sneezing you were doing. It was hard to focus. You'll do much better this time, now that your cold is gone. I promise."

Angus shoves the blankets off with a few rapid scissor kicks. The top of his Thomas the Train pajamas are twisted around his belly, exposing a smooth, half-moon of skin. "But I sneezed two times yesterday! How do you know I'm not going to sneeze today?"

"You'll be just fine." Ma heads downstairs, dismissing Angus's concerns with a wave of her hand.

"You won't be fine. You'll be *awe*some!" I jump on the bed, tickling Angus's tiny rib cage. He shrieks and flails, laughing in the kind of way that makes me feel sometimes that nothing will ever be wrong with the world again.

"More!" he screams breathlessly.

"Nope. You have school in less than an hour, and Mom and Nanny have work. C'mon, let's get dressed and then go downstairs. I bet if you ask, Nanny will make you peanut butter pancakes."

"Yes!" Angus bellows, zooming into his room across the hall. "Peanut butter pancakes *rock*!"

Inside his room, Angus is struggling with his shirt; it's on backward, and he already has an arm in the wrong sleeve.

"Hold on, Boo." I kneel down in front of him. "You're going to pull a muscle in your neck if you keep doing that." His arms fall limp as I help him out of the shirt. It's his favorite one—

yellow, with little green turtles all over it. He wore it yesterday. And the day before that, too. He scratches his belly button, watching me. "Getting dressed looks easy, but it's really not."

"I know." I squat down, smooth my hand over the pale arc of his stomach. When he was an infant, the thought of dressing him almost gave me a panic attack. His arms were like pipe cleaners, his wrists the circumference of a Magic Marker. What if they broke off when I tried to bend them through the tiny armholes of his clothes? What if they accidentally snapped out of the sockets? They didn't, of course, thanks to the odd rubbery quality of his limbs, which were a marvel all to themselves. I touch him all the time now, cupping a cheek against the inside of my hand while he sleeps, tracing my fingertips along the length of one arm. He's put on weight, but his skin is still as smooth and pale as marble, his knees as perfectly shaped as keyholes. "You know, I had an awful time learning how to get dressed when I was little, too."

"You did?" Angus's eyes open wide. "How come?"

"Same as you. I had a hard time with arms and getting things turned the right way. And I *always* put my shoes on the wrong feet." His right arm goes in, then his left. There is a stain on one of the turtles, right at the hem of the shirt. Barely noticeable.

He grins, showing the hole in his mouth where his front tooth used to be, a tiny, cherry-stained cave. "Did you walk funny?"

"You bet I walked funny." I imitate a duck, walking across his room with my toes spread wide. "I walked like a dorky little duck!"

Angus's laugh slows suddenly. "Did the other kids make fun of you?" He is doing that thing to his neck, pulling at the soft skin of it with his fingers until little red welts appear.

Sometimes, when he stands in front of the T-ball mound, he will do that. It makes me crazy to see that kind of nervousness in him. I'll look around from my seat in the bleachers, trying to figure out who might be responsible: the coach, maybe, who has a voice like a megaphone? Or could it be that bigger kid, the six-year-old, whose father screams from the bleachers? Maybe it's from Angus's own father, who I didn't know very well when I got pregnant, at least not well enough to pick up on little details like that. It's hard to tell. Sometimes, I mentally will him to stop; from my seat behind the mound, I will close my eyes, concentrate on sending him good energy: *Mom loves you Angus, no matter what. Please stop doing that thing to your neck. Everything's going to be okay.*

But it doesn't work. Every time I open my eyes again, his fingers are still working the soft skin, his eyes large and fearful. He gets it from me, that inner anxiety. He must.

I walk back over to him now, drop down to eye level. "No, no one made fun of me back then. Why? Is someone making fun of you at school?"

He shakes his head slowly. His fingers have dropped away from his throat.

"Are you sure?" I rub my hand in slow circles over the small of his back. "Angus? You can tell me."

"Bernadette! Gus! Time for breakfast!"

"Pancakes!" Angus shouts, bolting from the room. "Let's go!"

And like a shot, the moment is over.

Chapter 4

The kitchen smells like warm peanut butter when I come back downstairs. Ma is at the stove, poking at two pancakes with a spatula and fiddling with the TV channel with the other hand. Angus is standing atop one of the kitchen chairs next to the stove. He is on his tiptoes, leaning precariously over Ma's arm. A tuft of hair sticks out from the back of his head like antennae.

"Angus," I say. "Get away from the stove."

He pulls back, whines. "But I'm watching Nanny cook the pancakes! She said I could look for the bubbles!"

"Right now."

Ma looks over at me, annoyance knitted across her face. "I'm right here next to him, Bernadette. He's fine."

"You're not even watching him!" I nudge her hand away from the TV. "What channel do you want?"

"Twelve. The news."

"Angus." I use my warning tone, still flipping the channel. He whines, louder this time, and does that droopy thing with his eyebrows. "Do not make me say it again. A*way* from the stove."

"Oh, Bird." Ma whispers her disapproval as Angus gets down slowly and drags his chair back over to the table.

"Don't 'oh, Bird' me." I yank out a chair across from Angus, give him my best I'm-still-in-charge-here-buddy stare as I sit down. "I'm his mother, Ma."

"I know, I know," she says, managing to sound agreeable and dismissive at the same time. She slides Angus's plate in front of him and leans in for a kiss. He gives her a big one, right on the cheek, while staring pointedly at me. Traitor.

I get up to pour myself some coffee, concentrate on keeping my voice casual. "So I'm going to be working some double shifts over the next few days. Get a little extra money. Mr. Randolph said he could use me one day this week, and I'm going to ask Mr. Herron . . ."

"Doubles?" Ma interrupts, flipping another pancake. "Why? You don't need to do that."

"Well, the opportunity's there, Ma. It's stupid not to take advantage of it. It's more money." What I don't say, of course, is that the extra money will be going toward the new apartment. The only thing that Ma knows about my future plans right now is that I'm "saving up." She has no idea about the place on Moon Lake or that in less than two weeks, Angus and I will be moving out of here for good. It's shitty of me, I know, especially because the reality is that our leaving—or at least Angus leaving—is going to be hard on her. I hadn't wanted to get into it with Mrs. Ross earlier because, frankly, it was none of her business, and also because it would have extended a conversation I didn't want to have, but now I feel the same twinge of guilt I did in her office. Ma hates being alone, has always hated it, especially in this house. Even before Dad died, she used to make sure she was out doing something at church or at a friend's house if she knew neither of us would be home until later. And having Angus in the house has brought a level of joy into her life that I don't think anything else has been able to after losing Dad.

But I can't stay. And I'd rather not face that hurdle until I absolutely have to.

She turns back to the stove, and then leans in suddenly, staring at the television next to it. "Is that James Rittenhouse?"

"James who?"

She points at the screen with her spatula. "James Rittenhouse. His father owns a construction company, doesn't he? Or at least he used to. He worked on our house a while back, when the roof needed to be retiled. Or maybe it was the chimney." She squints again at the television. "*Is* that him?"

A flash of white heat travels through my belly as the image of a slight, scruffy-looking man dressed in a green T-shirt and brown cargo pants appears on the screen. He is being led down a set of steps by two grim-faced policemen, each one holding an elbow. His hands, cuffed at the wrists, hang down awkwardly in front of him, and his head has been shaved smooth as a pool ball. Behind him, the sky is the color of a bruise, the sun still hours away from rising.

"Oh my God," I say. "That *is* James."

"You know him, too?" Ma asks.

"I used to work with him. A long time ago. At the Burger Barn."

"You never told me that." Ma puts a hand on her hip. "How did I never know that? I came over to see you at that place a number of times. I never saw him anywhere."

"He was the cook." I am still staring at the screen, my words coming from some small, faraway place inside. "He worked in

the back. You wouldn't have seen him." He looks older somehow, although how is that possible? It's only been six years
since I spoke to him last. I move closer, trying to discern his
features. But he is looking down at the ground, shying away
from the camera, as if the light is hurting his eyes. He walks
with a shuffle, as if his feet are bound, but there is nothing
around them, no chain or rope in sight.

"Well, what happened?" Ma has turned back to the pancakes, flipping them deftly. "What'd he do? Are they arresting
him?" Ma has always been a huge fan of local gossip, although
she tries hard not to indulge in it, especially during Lent.

"Shhh!" I turn up the volume as a female reporter begins
speaking:

*"Police arrested James Rittenhouse early this morning after an
altercation at a local bar led to a man being seriously wounded. The
victim, whose name is not being disclosed pending further investigation,
is currently in the critical care unit at New Haven Hospital with severe
head injuries. Police say James Rittenhouse, who was heavily intoxi-
cated at the time, has admitted to the crime and will be held at the
county prison until formal charges can be filed . . ."*

My mouth falls open, listening. Critical care unit? Severe
head injuries? *James?*

The television camera pulls away as one of the patrolmen
leads James toward the back of a police cruiser. Just for an
instant, he lifts his head. He has the same narrow nose, although the ridge of it has a wound across the top, dark and
thin as a parenthesis, the same flat cheekbones and deep-set
eyes. But they look exaggerated under his bald head, larger
somehow than the rest of him. And why is he bald? Where has
all that beautiful reddish-brown hair gone?

*". . . Police say Rittenhouse will be held in the county jail without
bail until his arraignment . . ."*

"Holy *shit*." I put my coffee cup down, shake my head. "Without bail?"

"Holy shit!" Angus yells, grinning widely.

"Angus!" It's hard to say his name sharply when I am stifling a giggle. "Don't. That's not a good word."

He looks at me defiantly. "Then how come *you* said it?"

I make a point not to look at Ma, who is standing both arms akimbo in front of the stove, glaring at me. "Well, sometimes grown-ups say things they shouldn't."

"Like when we were coloring in my *Nemo* book and you said, 'Fuck'?"

Ma gasps. Her back goes rigid. "Jesus, Mary, and *Joseph*, Bernadette!" Then she turns on Angus. "You listen to me, young man! If I *ever* hear you say that word again in my house, you will stay in your room for a week! Is that understood?"

Angus's hand goes up to his neck; his fingers start pinching the smooth skin, and his eyes well with tears.

James is momentarily forgotten as I come around quickly to his side of the table, and pick him up. "Don't lay into him like that, Ma. That was my fault."

Ma's face is set tight. "Well, somebody has to."

"*Ma.*"

She looks at the clock. "You're going to be late dropping him off."

I shift Angus against my hip. He has buried his face into my neck, arms clasped around my shoulders, away from Ma. "Come on, Boo. We have to go." On the TV screen, the police cruiser, which looks like some kind of enormous white fish in the darkness, drives away. It's impossible to see anything inside the dark windows, but knowing James is in there leaves a bitter, coppery taste in the back of my mouth. For some reason, I wonder if he is hungry.

"Wait!" Ma says as we head for the door.

"What?"

"I just want to get him a clean shirt. There's a huge stain on the hem of the one he's wearing now."

She's halfway up the steps by the time we make it out the front door. I catch a glimpse of her again only when I adjust the rearview mirror of my old Toyota Camry; she is standing in the doorway, waving something furiously above her head.

From the distance, it looks like a white flag, almost like a tiny peace offering.

Except that I know better.

Chapter 5

I was nineteen and working the morning shift at the Burger Barn the first time I met James Rittenhouse. Technically, the morning shift began at eight A.M., but every two weeks, someone was assigned to come in at six A.M. to do prep work, mindless, necessary chores that involved wiping down and refilling all the condiment bottles (ketchup, mustard, salt, pepper, malt vinegar, mayonnaise, and horsey-sauce tubs), making sure the tables and booths were spotless, stocking the napkin and silverware holders, slicing fifty lemons into eight precise wedges for the iced tea orders, and preparing the coffee urns, which gurgled endlessly throughout the day. Prep work was so detested by the waitress pool that we actually drew straws to see who would be assigned to it. I was one of the few, however, who didn't mind when my turn came around. I'd never had trouble getting up early, and it was easy, if monotonous, work, something that had never bothered me.

I sped through the litany of chores that week, pausing after I'd dusted the silk orange lily bouquets on each table to pour myself a cup of coffee (my first of six or seven before noon), before starting on the lemons. I always saved the condiment task for last, since I had to empty out the condiment holder—a rectangular, boat-like structure that sectioned off the various packets and bottles—and then hose it down in the alley behind the restaurant. Not only was hauling the thing out there a pain in the ass, but the awkwardness of the container, combined with a spitting, leaky hose, never failed to soak my shoes, a detail that set me on edge for the rest of the day.

It was still early when I went out back that morning, the pale summer light hovering over a distance that encompassed a pair of old railroad tracks, waist-high field grass, and beyond that just the yellow tips of a McDonald's arches. The handle on the container—which Charlie, the manager, had promised to fix three days ago—slipped as I turned it over, and gobs of ketchup, mustard, and mayonnaise spotted the tips of my sneakers. "God*damn* it." I threw it to the ground and leaned over to pick up the hose, pausing when a movement caught my eye.

Sitting on a small cement stoop just around the corner with a cigarette between the thumb and forefinger of his left hand and a small book perched open in his right was James. Up until that point, I'd never really seen him up close, since he was always rushing around inside the kitchen alongside Lionel, the other cook, a white apron tied around his waist, his head wrapped in a blue kerchief, bent over something behind the small window that separated us. Now he was casually dressed in jeans, heavy work boots that came up around his ankles, and a gray T-shirt; I could see the outline of his biceps beneath the thin material. His hair, loose and untethered, was the color of deer hide and curled lightly along the tops of his shoulders. High cheekbones curved in dramatically when he inhaled on his cigarette, and his lips were dry and cracked. He was staring at something inside the little book with such concentration that I wondered if he even knew I was there.

"Oh, hi," I said anyway, shoving the container to one side with the tip of my shoe and grabbing the hose. "Sorry, I didn't even see you there."

It was impossible, given the enclosed vicinity of our surroundings, that he had not heard me push open the door and throw the plastic tub to the ground, but he had not moved an inch. Now, I wondered if he was deaf, as he did not indicate that he had heard anything I'd just said either. I stared at him a moment, once again admiring the smooth line of biceps under his shirt, and then turned back to the hose. Whatever. It was just as well. I was a little behind this morning anyway. There wasn't any time for small talk. I winced as I turned on the hose, water spitting out left and right.

A voice sounded behind me, and I turned, startled.

James was still staring at his book.

"Did you say something?" I asked.

"Turn the nozzle all the way to the right." His eyes were still fixed on his book, but he spoke loud enough this time that I could hear him. "It won't leak that way."

I did as he said, twisting the rusty metal ring to one side. Almost immediately, the water began to flow in a smooth, fluid arc. "Shit," I said. "Finally. Thanks."

James shut his book and put it down next to him. He studied the tip of his cigarette for a moment, as if waiting for it to say something. "You're Bird, right?" he asked finally.

"Uh-huh." I angled the stream of water along the inside of the plastic tub. Blobs of red and yellow began to bleed against the plastic, dissolving into an orange swirl.

"That your real name?" He lowered his cigarette and looked at me. A thick, crescent-shaped scar traveled down between his eyebrows, sloping over the bridge of his nose and ending just at the center of his right cheek. The mark was pale enough that it might have passed as just an odd section of skin, but the thickness of it, combined with a strange, ridged pattern along the edges, gave it a menacing quality, something that made my breath catch tight in the back of my throat.

"My real name's Bernadette," I said, hoping the expression on my face didn't convey the vague revulsion I felt inside. "Bird's my nickname. My dad made it up when I was younger. He said I used to look like a—" I stopped talking and stared down at the stream of water still gushing from the hose. What the hell was I telling him all this for? I didn't even know the guy.

James nodded slowly, as if the unfinished explanation—or maybe my reason for leaving it that way—made perfect sense. "You date Charlie, right?"

I blushed, although there was no reason to. It wasn't any secret that Charlie and I had been together for a few months now. It wasn't serious, but still, I didn't have anything to hide. Except possibly the fact that I already knew he wasn't what I wanted. "Yeah."

"I thought so." He nodded once, reaching up to pull on his earlobe. "I'm James," he said. "If you didn't already know."

I ignored the comment, glancing instead at his book, small and compact on the stoop next to him. It was red, with gold lettering on the front. Various pieces of paper stuck out from the top, like jagged leaves. "What're you reading?" I asked.

James glanced down at the book, and then flicked his cigarette into the distance. It bounced along the hardened dirt like a small caterpillar and then rolled to a halt. *"Curious Facts and Data,"* he said finally.

I stared at him. Curious facts and data? At six A.M. behind the Burger Barn? Was he for real?

"You want to hear one?" He was looking directly at me again, shading his eyes with the back of his hand, which softened the appearance of his scar. He had small teeth, and too many of them, the ones in front crowded and overlapped like kids pushing in line.

"One what?" I asked.

"Curious fact."

"Um . . . okay." I watched as he opened the book and slid his hand down the width of the page.

"Here's one of my favorites," he said. "One-sixth of our entire lives will be spent on a Wednesday." There was a pause as he waited for me to absorb this information and then, when I didn't say anything, he shrugged. "You don't think that's kind of interesting?"

I guessed it was kind of interesting; mostly, I just thought it was weird. Was this how this guy really spent his time, besides frying up burgers all day long? What did he do after work, go look for unusual bugs along the riverbank? "That's what it says, huh?" I asked finally. "Wednesdays?"

James nodded, flattening the pages with one hand so that the book would stay open. "That's what it says. This guy who wrote it is some kind of a fact person. You know, like into numbers and stuff. From MIT. He's got hundreds of these kinds of things in here. I don't know how he figured them all out, especially the Wednesday one, but he did."

"How do you know he's right?" I turned off the hose and kicked the rubber tubing to one side. Despite the adjustment of nozzle, my shoes were once again saturated. Perfect.

"It's in the book." James held it up, as if I needed proof. "You can't publish something for people to read unless it's true."

"You sure about that?"

"Well, not statistics," James argued. "Not facts."

"How do you know?" I picked up the container, adjusting it awkwardly against one hip. The handle slipped, and I grabbed for it.

James shielded his face again with his hand, although there was no sun in sight. "That's common knowledge. You can't publish known facts unless they're already proven. It would be irresponsible." He paused, watching me. "You want me to fix that handle for you?"

I gave the canister a final swing against my hip. "Charlie said he would do it."

"Well, until he does . . ." James stood up. He pulled something out of his pocket, kneaded it between his hands for a moment, and then flattened it beneath the loose handle. His hands were large, the knuckles rough and worn, but his fingernails were surprisingly neat, smooth, and clean around the edges. "Silly Putty," he said. "Just for the time being."

I smiled. "You find out how to do that in that book?"

"No." He shook his head. "I do carpentry work, too. Just a little on the side. I know some things."

"Oh." My cheeks flushed hot for some reason, as if I'd insulted him. "Well, thanks."

"You're welcome."

I went back inside.

I was on prep for the next two weeks, and during that time, I saw James every morning. It was always the same scenario with him sitting on the cement step, smoking a cigarette and reading his little red factoid book, while I came out to rinse the condiment holder. Every day, he gave me some piece of odd, random information, like how a year on Venus is shorter than its day, or how the Greeks used to dip their children in olive oil after they were born so that they would not get too hairy throughout the rest of their lives. I learned that human feet had 250,000 sweat glands, that if you threw a snowball hard enough against a wall it would completely vaporize, and that our solar system's biggest mountain was on Mars. It was bizarre, obscure, completely random information. And for some reason, I began to look forward to hearing it, found myself getting up even earlier to share this odd space of time that had morphed somehow from an awkward, slightly suspicious rapport into strangely comforting company. More often than not, I just smiled and nodded at the bits of information; sometimes I balked at their validity, but a few times, they led to brief discussions. He'd mentioned something about sleep, for example, that gave me pause one morning, something about ninety percent of our dreams being forgotten within ten minutes of waking up.

"Ninety percent?" I repeated. "Out of how many dreams—a thousand?"

"Actually, it says here that we only have five or six dreams a night," James answered. "So that means we only remember one of them. And only a little section of it, at that." He had already tied his blue bandanna around the top of his head. Thick pieces of hair snaked out beneath the back of it, some slightly curled at the tips, as if shyer than the rest.

This couldn't be true, I told myself, even as I was trying desperately to access the image of Dad I'd had that morning. I didn't dream about him very often, but when I did, it was always vague and peripheral, as if he wasn't too sure whether or not he wanted to enter my consciousness. The one I'd had that morning, though, was markedly different. Dad had been standing in a field of waist-high grass, both arms over his head, waving to me. His mouth was open and his lips were forming words, but there was no sound coming from them. The only thing I could hear was the force of my own breathing as I raced toward him, the distance between us shortening with every step as I got closer and closer until I could see the soft lines in his face, the sporadic patches of gray in his hair. And then suddenly, with five or six feet to go, he began to retreat, fading into the horizon like a mirage, a watercolor, until there was nothing there at all. That was disconcerting enough, but now I was struck with another thought: What if the other four or five dreams I'd had that night had been about Dad, too? And what if they had been different from the one I remembered—he hadn't faded from sight, I'd gotten close enough so that he could wrap his arms around me, whisper into my ear what he'd been trying to shout across the grass. If I couldn't remember them, did that mean they were lost forever? Or worse, that they hadn't happened at all?

"You remember any of your dreams from last night?" James asked suddenly.

"Nah." I pressed my thumb over part of the nozzle so that a stream of water shot out with dangerous force against the plastic condiment holder. "I'm not a very good sleeper. I don't think I even have dreams."

"You do lose consciousness at some point, don't you?" James's voice was dry. "Or are you an insomniac?"

"I sleep some, I guess. It's just not very restful."

"Yeah." He nodded, running the edge of his thumb down the spine of his book. "I know what that's like."

I glanced over at him, wondering briefly what his life was like outside of this tiny part of the world we inhabited. Did he live alone? With a girlfriend? I imagined him heading straight for the refrigerator when he got home from work, twisting a can of Bud Light out from the plastic rings. Maybe he'd kick off his sneakers as he gulped from it, sit down for a while on a couch to watch TV. Or maybe he was one of those guys who kept a change of clothes in a Nike bag stashed in the back of the car, and then went straight to the gym after his shift. It was hard to guess.

"You don't sleep?" I asked.

"Some." He shrugged. "Like you. In and out. Not very restful."

What did he wear to bed? I wondered. Boxers? Briefs? Nothing? "Why not?"

He shrugged again and reached into his shirt pocket for another cigarette. "Lot on my mind, I guess."

I nodded, looking away as he perched the cigarette between his lips and reached for his lighter. With his face in profile, his scar hidden on the other side, he could definitely pass for a decent-looking guy. Maybe even handsome.

"What's your excuse?" he asked, exhaling the smoke between his lips.

"Oh, I've never been a good sleeper," I lied. "Even when I was younger. I'd stay up until three or four in the morning."

"So you *are* an insomniac." His cheekbones appeared as he inhaled on his cigarette.

"Yeah," I concurred. "Maybe I am."

"You don't have bags under your eyes." He was looking right at me. "Or dark circles or anything."

"I guess I've got youth on my side." I turned off the hose, slightly unsettled that he had noticed such a thing. Or was that pleasure? "At least for now."

"How old are you?"

"Nineteen."

"Wow." He nodded, looking at something in the distance.

"Wow?" I repeated.

"You've got your whole life before you," he said. "The world is your oyster."

I considered this for a moment. I might have had my whole

life before me, but if the world was my oyster, I was definitely looking at things just now from inside the shell. "How old are you?" I asked.

"Twenty-four." There was a heaviness to his voice that hadn't been there before, a sort of weighted resignation.

"You make it sound like you're ninety."

He stood up, crushing the half-smoked cigarette under his shoe. "Ninety and counting," he said, giving me a small smile. "Come on. We've gotta get going."

Another morning, I spoke up first, before he had a chance to give me a factoid. "Why are you always here so early?" I asked. "Lionel doesn't even roll out of bed 'til nine-thirty, and he does just as much work back there as you do."

"Lionel does half the work I do." He was wearing a blue plaid shirt with the sleeves rolled up to his elbows. Pale veins stood out along the tops of his arms like green tubing, and a large blister, soft and nearly collapsed in the center, had appeared on the knuckle of his thumb. "Besides, what do you care if I'm here?"

I glanced quickly at him, stung by his curtness. "I was just wondering. You don't have to be rude about it."

"I'm sorry." He shook his head, as if trying to realign something inside, and then reached inside his pocket for a cigarette. "The truth is, I have a nightmare situation back at my apartment. I try to get out of there as quickly as I can."

I could feel myself tense inside. I'd asked the question because I was genuinely curious. There was more to this guy than his cigarettes and factoid book suggested, and I wanted to know what it was. Or did I? A nightmare situation at home could mean anything. Maybe he lived with his mother, who was sick, elderly, an invalid who begged him to wash and feed her every morning. Or worse, a girl he loved who didn't love him back. They'd stopped talking finally, and neither of them could find the words to make the break, so he was doing what he could to endure it, leaving early in the morning, coming home late at night.

"I've got a pair of screamers upstairs," he said, rolling his eyes. "Every morning at five o'clock. No matter what."

"They fight?" I asked, feeling something drain inside. There was no mother. No girlfriend. At least, not yet.

He shrugged, a dry smile inching up at one corner. "I'm sure it's gone down that road a few times, too. Mostly it's just a lot of moaning and groaning, though, until they both lose it completely and start screaming like a pair of banshees."

The understanding of what he was saying hit me all at once, and when it did, I could feel my face flood with heat. I burst out laughing and shook my head. "Oh my God, no wonder you leave. I would, too. Jesus." The image of the people upstairs led to another image—this one of James in bed with some faceless woman, his lean body arched over hers, the muscles in his back contracting and then tightening as he moved in and around her. I became aware of a faint heat emanating from the skin on my neck, and I swallowed, as if doing such a thing might make it disappear.

"Do you mind that I'm here?" James asked.

"Mind?"

He shrugged. "Technically, I really shouldn't be, I guess, until my shift starts." He inhaled deeply on his cigarette, cheekbone blades appearing. "You're not going to tell Charlie or anything, are you?"

I drew back, as if tasting something bitter. "Why would I do that?"

"I don't know. Just wondering. He'd have a problem with it, you know."

"You think?" I asked, although I already knew the answer.

Charlie treated me fine (if carefully), but I'd heard him rip into the cooks and the other waitresses for sundry benign offenses: coming in five minutes late, or forgetting to offer a customer her complimentary onion rings with the Big and Meaty Meal. He'd screamed at Lionel once for having to leave early so that he wouldn't miss his kid's Little League game. "It's the championships," Lionel had said, putting on his baseball hat and heading for the back door. "And my kid's pitching. I told you about it two weeks ago, Charlie. I gotta go, man. My kid'll never forgive me if I miss it."

"Well, don't expect any fucking forgiveness from me!" Charlie screamed as the door shut in his face. "You're done man, you hear me? You're *done!*"

His threat was an empty one; the fact that Lionel had told him earlier about the game prevented Charlie from doing anything and both of them knew it. Lionel showed up wordlessly the next morning and got to work frying up a vat of onions— but to this day, Charlie treated him coldly, daring him to make another wrong move so that he could fire him for good.

James turned to look at me, drawing the edge of one thumb along his eyebrow. "Oh, I know he'd have a problem with it," he said. "That guy's a ticking time bomb."

I looked away, the weight of what was not being said hanging heavily in the air between us. Why was I with someone like Charlie, who treated people so carelessly? What did that say about me?

James stood up and crushed his cigarette out under his boot. "You didn't answer my original question," he said, inserting his hands inside his jeans pockets.

"What was it?"

"Do you mind that I'm here?"

For a split second we locked eyes, and I wondered if there was anything in his factoid book about how far or fast unspoken thoughts traveled. What explained the strange, liquid sensation that moved under one's skin in certain situations, or the faint twist of longing that somehow found its way into the pit of a stomach and then lodged there, silent as a sleeping animal?

I dropped my eyes, staring at the wet pavement beneath my feet, feeling James's still-steady gaze along the top of my head.

"Bird?" He took a step toward me.

I raised my eyes, but only to his knees. "No," I said too quickly, already hearing the dismissiveness in my voice. "No, I don't mind at all. It's fine."

He nodded, took a step back. "Okay," he said. "Well, okay, then."

TWO DAYS LATER, Jenny took over the prep shift, my two-week obligation finished. And for a little while, that was the end of my conversations with James. Once, during a lull in the restaurant, I leaned over the window that opened up into the kitchen and asked him for a factoid from the book. But he shook his head and turned away, almost as if he didn't know me, or even what I was talking about. In fact, inside the restaurant, James was an entirely different person—mute, withdrawn, and reserved almost to the point of rudeness. Another time, when I was working night shift and came back to ask him if he needed help cleaning up, I found everything dark and locked up. I hadn't known he'd left, hadn't even heard him go out the back door.

He came in, did his work, and then left again.

If he could, I thought, he would have disappeared altogether.

Chapter 6

Angus and I usually talk for the six or seven minutes it takes me to drive him to preschool, me eyeing him in the rearview mirror as he responds, just so that I can watch the way his face breaks open into a smile suddenly, or how his tiny eyebrows will knit themselves together in a small, worried line. Today, though, I am so distracted by the news about James that we are less than two blocks away from the school before I realize we haven't exchanged a single word. We've even passed the little green house on the corner, the one with the seven gnomes planted in the front yard, without saying hello to the one Angus has dubbed Dopester.

He throws his arms around me when I kiss him goodbye, and hugs me so tightly that even though I still have to stop at the church for Ma's sweater, which will make me late for Mr. Herron, who will not only dock my pay but make me feel guilty, too, something inside me says, *Wait*.

"Hey, Boo?" I say as he bends down to straighten the laces of his magic green-and-purple sneakers. They have to be just right, the laces, or the magic won't work. "I know something is bothering you. What is it?"

"Nothing." He does not lift his head.

I stare down at the dark whorls along his scalp, remember how I used to trace my finger over the tiny pulse-point at the top of his skull when he was first born, how the softness of it frightened me to death and fascinated me at the same time. It was like being able to see that tiny heart beat from the inside out. I lift his chin. "Angus. Come on, honey. It's just me."

His lower lip quivers as he avoids my eyes. "It's hard sometimes to be brave," he says.

My heart swells. I push his hair off his face, cup my fingers around the curve of his chin. Angus has my father's chin, slightly pointed at the tip, with just the hint of a cleft in the middle. A small miracle, I sometimes think, in the midst of such chaos. A gift. "What do you have to be brave for, sweetheart? Is someone being mean to you? Here at school?"

He shakes his head.

"Then what is it?"

"Today is Something Special Day." A single tear, fat as a pearl, slides down his cheek. "And I don't think Jeremy is going to think my magic shoes are special."

I kiss away his tear, tasting the salt on my lips, and keep my mouth close to his ear. I want to tell him to tell Jeremy to fuck off. Jeremy is a pain in the ass, a first-class brat who stomps his feet and holds his breath until his face turns blue when he doesn't get his way. But he is also Angus's best friend. I have come in many times at the end of the day to find the two of them playing with rubber dinosaurs, growling at one another, their faces flushed with joy. And so I hold Angus close instead and say as confidently as I can: "But I already know Jeremy will think your shoes are special."

Angus pulls back. "How?"

"Because they're magic! Everyone knows that magic sneakers are the coolest things in the entire world!"

Angus's hopeful face falls again. "But I already *told* him they were magic. And he didn't believe me."

"Well, that's his problem if he doesn't believe you. He'll be the one missing out."

"Yeah." Angus doesn't look convinced.

"What is it that your magic shoes can do again?"

"They can make me jump superhigh and run superfast." He looks disappointed that I haven't remembered. "You already *know* that, Mom."

I dig in my pocket, hold up a quarter. "What if they made money disappear, too?"

Angus leans forward, his excitement palpable as I show him the trick, which involves chewing and then attaching a tiny piece of gum to one side of the quarter and then stomping on it. "Okay?" I ask, showing him for the second time how the quarter sticks to the bottom of his shoe. "You think you can do it?"

He nods eagerly, throws his arms around me once more. "Now my magic shoes will *really* rock."

I brush his hair to the side, kiss his cheek. The light on his face right now makes his skin look translucent, the green veins beneath like rivers on a map. "They will totally rock. I'll see you at five, baby. And then T-ball practice! Don't forget."

I stand up as his teacher comes out into the hallway, blow him another kiss as she takes him inside.

If Jeremy gives him even a sidelong glance after his Something Special presentation, I'll wring his neck.

I don't care how old he is.

How is it that a person's life can skid so quickly off the tracks? And who am I to even think of asking such a question?

"There's a place called Rome on every continent," James had said one morning, a month or so after our initial meeting.

"Oh, I don't know about that one." I was sitting on the cement block a few feet away from him, my back pressed against the wall of the restaurant, hands draped over the tops of my tented knees. I'd rigged the last straw-drawing pool among the waitresses after Jenny's turn had ended, poking a pin through the shortest one so that I'd know which one to pull, and they'd all laughed when I held it up, and said, "Ah, Birdie-Bird, you have the worst luck!" to which I'd only nodded and shrugged, feigning exasperation. But when I'd come outside this morning with the condiment holder and seen him sitting on the stoop, the anxiety I hadn't known I'd been holding in my chest, worried that he wouldn't be there, eased and then disappeared. There was no other place I wanted to be. Charlie wouldn't be in for at least another hour.

James sidled a glance at me, his hair obscuring most of his eyes. "Do you realize that you argue with almost every piece of information I give you?"

I shrugged, chewed on my thumbnail. The summer sky was a faint peach color above us; a small flock of sparrows hopped and twittered just a few feet away.

"Do you enjoy arguing, or are you really just that naturally suspicious?"

I crossed my arms, sidestepping the question. "How about Antarctica? There can't be a place called Rome in Antarctica."

James looked back down at the page for a moment, then read: "The Filchner-Rome Ice Shelf is located in Antarctica."

"An ice shelf?" I repeated. "That's not a place. That's a thing."

"A thing called Rome," James said, looking back down again at the book. "Well, technically it's called Ronne, but a lot of people pronounce it as Rome. Including the author of this book."

"That doesn't count. It's hyphenated, it's a thing, and the word 'Ronne' doesn't even come close to Rome." I slid my knees down until my legs were straight out in front of me. We had to wear blue pleated shorts in the summer months, horrible things that gaped open along our thighs and ended just above the kneecap. My legs, which had always been too skinny, looked shapeless to me now, two soft, slightly stubbled breadsticks. I drew them back up, and wrapped my arms around the front of them, holding them against my chest.

James snorted softly. "You even have a problem with even the basic, biological stuff, like how our hearts beat up to 100,000 times a day. Someone somewhere must have counted a heart beating, Bird, in order for it to be in this book. Why don't you just take it for what it is?"

Something inside skipped as I heard him say my name aloud, which was ludicrous. Yes, something was pulling me toward him. Yes, I'd even fixed things so I could see him—alone—again. So why did the thrill of hearing him say my name frighten me at the same time? And why did I still keep my eyes fastened to the left side of his face when he looked at me, as if his horrible scar might come to life and rub off on me?

"Take it for what it is?" I repeated. "What is it?"

"Information. Facts." He shrugged. "I'm not telling you things that people *think*, or hope, or believe in. These are real. They're already proven."

"But how do you *know*?"

He smiled at me then, holding my eyes—*onetwothree*—and shook his head.

What had he thought of me at that moment that he had not said aloud? I wonder now, backing the car out of Angus's day care. Did he think I was impossible? That my need for proof of things just made me an argumentative, self-righteous pain in the ass? It wouldn't surprise me; it was this attitude of mine that had always been—and still was—at the root of Ma's and my strained relationship. She took things on faith, simply because, long ago, she had decided to believe. That wasn't enough for me. If I was going to believe in something, if I was going to stand in awe of a fact, I wanted to know that I was doing so for a logical, defined reason. That it deserved to be believed in; because it was not only worthy of, but merited, my awe.

So far, there hadn't been anything that came close to doing either.

The vestibule of Saint Augustine's is empty, except for the two marble statues flanking the inside doors: one of Saint Augustine himself, dressed in purple robes and a bishop's hat, the other of the Blessed Virgin, holding the Baby Jesus in her arms. I used to love looking up at the Baby Jesus when Mom and Dad and I would come here to Sunday Mass together. With his bare feet and lightly tousled hair, He seemed cherubic and adorable. Now, He looks oddly doll-like, the features of His face too mature for such an innocent age.

"Hello?" I call softly. "Father Delaney?"

No answer.

I open the doors leading into the church itself. It's been about a decade since I've been inside here, but everything comes back in a rush: the faint smells of incense and old-lady perfume, the countless rows of wooden pews with their smooth, curved armrests, scarlet and indigo stained-glass windows, the narrow red carpet leading up to the white marble altar. Behind the altar, the wooden cross, at least two feet tall, bearing the hideously draped figure of Jesus, hanging by His nailed hands and feet. When I was little, I used to stare at the cross during Mass and wait for Jesus to come down off it. I pictured Him shaking his arms—which would be stiff from being out straight for so long—maybe massaging the wounds in His hands, and doing a few deep knee bends. He'd look over the congregation until He saw me, and then move in my direction. When He got close, He would reach out and take my hand, say something like, "Hi, sweetie. I'm starving. You want to go get something to eat?" It didn't seem so strange to me. Ma was forever saying that God could do anything and Jesus was God's Son, so why not?

"Hello?" I call out again a little louder this time, wincing as my voice reverberates throughout the empty building. It feels sacrilegious to be speaking so loudly, but how else am I going to find Father Delaney? This *is* where Ma said he was going to meet me, right? Or did she mean the vestibule in the rectory next door? I head back through the doors again, glance impatiently over to my left at the set of winding stairs that lead up to the choir loft. Wow, the choir loft. It's hard to believe that I used to sing up there when I was younger, that between the ages of eight and twelve I spent half of every Sunday singing the Mass and then, afterward, practicing for next week. I didn't care much about the songs, or even about being up so high. The best part about the choir loft was climbing up and down those stairs. They could make you dizzy if you went up fast enough, take your breath away by the time you reached the last step.

"Father Delaney?" I call out again. "Hello? Are you here?"

A rustling sound overhead makes me glance up. It's highly unlikely that Father Delaney would be up there, since Ma's told me at least a hundred times that Saint Augustine's hasn't had a choir for the last four years. Still, I move over to the bottom step, rest my hands on either side of the wall, and call up into the void. "Father Delaney? It's Bird—Bernadette Connolly? My mother forgot her sweater and she said . . ."

Oh, for God's sake. Abruptly, I stop talking and start up the steps. I have to place my hand flat against the wall as I make my way, since the steps are smaller than I remember, and much more narrow. Toward the top, they are tapered so much that I actually have to turn to the side, placing my feet sideways, so that I won't fall. Plus, I am panting a little. Ma is definitely going to hear about this.

"Father Dela . . ." My voice trails off as I see the figure in the corner, huddled next to the enormous organ. His legs are stuck out in front of him, but the left one is splayed at an awkward angle, as if someone took it and then bent it in the wrong direction. A large, gaping wound is still bleeding on one side of his shaved head, and he is holding a gun. Pointed at me.

It's like time has stopped, as if I am watching a movie unreel itself in front of me. My feet are nailed to the floor, my breath a hollow ball in the back of my throat. A ticker tape flashes along the inside of my head: *This isn't real. This isn't real. This isn't real.* Except that it is real. It's James, the cook from the Burger Barn. James, who told me once that elephants can spend up to twenty-three hours a day eating. James, who was on the morning news this morning, being led down the front steps of the old apartment building in handcuffs after putting someone in the critical care unit of the hospital. He's right here somehow, right now, right this minute, sitting less than six feet away from me in the choir loft of Saint Augustine's Roman Catholic Church, pointing a gun at the middle of my chest.

Run! Run! Run!

I take a step back with feet that move with a mind of their own. First my right, then my left. Without dropping James's gaze—which is boring into me with an electric heat—I reach out behind me for the wall; when I feel it, I will turn around and run down the staircase, even if I fall, even if I roll down the length of them. James's eyes shift downward, following my feet, and then move back up again. His eyes are glossy with exhaustion, wide with fear. Purple cuts ribbon the sides of his wrists, and for some reason, the gun looks too heavy for him to be holding. He lets it fall suddenly, settling it on his right leg. His hands are shaking. "Bird?" he says. "Is that you?"

I take a few more steps back, terrified suddenly that he recognizes me, that he remembers my name. This is big. Too big. Yes, I knew James once—but this, I don't know what this is. This is like reality TV gone awry. A bad episode of *COPS*. I don't belong here. I have to go clean Mr. Herron's house. I have to get Ma's sweater. I have to find out what happened during Something Special Day and then make sure Angus gets a snack before he goes to T-ball practice. Behind me, the wall comes into contact with my hands, smooth-cool to the touch.

"Bird," James says. "It was an accident. What happened at the bar. It was an accident."

I don't care if it was an accident. And even if it was, why does he feel the need to tell me such a thing? Actually, I didn't even hear him say that. No, this is just a dream. I am just imagining this. My feet continue to move with a will of their own, as my hands feel their way along the wall. Just a little bit more, and I will be at the top of the stairs.

"You won't tell anyone I'm here, will you?" James's voice is ragged, his eyes enormous. Maybe the fact that there is no more hair on top of his head makes the white scar across his face look so awful. So permanent for some reason, as if such a thing has never occurred to me before. Or maybe it is just the gun, lying there on his lap like a dirty pipe. Whatever it is, I almost start to cry.

No. Focus, Bird. Focus. Right foot, left foot. Right foot, left foot.
"Bird?"

I scream so loudly as Father Delaney's voice comes up from the bottom of the steps that the priest rushes halfway up by the time I turn around and descend the first section of stairs. We meet in the belly of the stairwell, his eyes wide and fearful under a thatch of white hair. "Bird? Are you all right? What's the matter?"

I hold on to his arms for a moment, stare into his pale eyes. *Just say it. Just tell him. Whisper it, if you have to. Make signs with your hands. James Rittenhouse, who was just arrested this morning for assault and battery, is hiding upstairs in your choir loft, bleeding. Call the police.*

"You scared me!" bursts out instead. "I didn't hear you."

Father Delaney glances up the rest of the steps. Jowls under his chin sway a little as he moves; the white space along his black collar juts into the soft skin. "What were you doing in the choir loft? Didn't your mother tell you I would meet you in the sacristy?"

I nod, still gripping his arm. "I came in and you weren't there. I went all the way to the back, even. I was calling you, but there was no answer. I thought . . . I guess I thought maybe you would be in the choir loft for some reason. I'm sorry."

"Oh, no." Father Delaney shakes his head. "No one goes up here anymore. It's very sad. We haven't had a choir in years, and the organ is completely unusable. It's actually hollow now."

I laugh then for some reason, but it comes out weird, almost like a cry. "Do you have my mom's sweater?"

"Right down here." Father Delaney leads me back into the

vestibule. He is tall and very lean; his black pants hang off his backside like a paper sack. I'd guess he's in his sixties by now, but Ma says he still runs a few miles every day. It shows. He picks up Ma's sweater from the floor, swats at it with his free hand.

"I'm sorry if it's dirty." He holds it out to me, gives me an apologetic grin. "It's not every day you hear someone scream inside a church. I must've dropped it."

I take the sweater from him and hide my hands inside it. They are shaking. "It's okay. Ma won't mind." My heart is still hammering inside my chest; my mouth feels dry. What is James going to do? How long will he be up there until someone finds him?

"Are you okay, Bird?" Father Delaney is looking at me with a peculiar expression. "You look a little pale."

"Oh, yeah, I'm fine." I head over quickly to the door. "I just have to eat breakfast. Get my coffee, you know?"

He smiles, showing new lines around his eyes, his mouth. "Oh, I know all about that. I have to have a cup every morning before I run or my legs won't even think about moving under me."

I push the door open. "Good to see you, Mr. . . . I mean, Father Delaney. Thanks for the sweater."

"Bird."

Shit. He knows. He can tell I'm hiding something. They always know. Even in confession he knew when I was holding back. *Is that everything now, Bird? Are you sure that's all you want to tell me?* I turn back around. "Yeah?"

"Don't be a stranger." Father Delaney slides his hands inside his pockets, rocks back on his heels a little. "We're always here."

"Right." I nod uncomfortably. This is Ma speaking through him, what she'd asked him to say. "Thanks. But it's not really my thing anymore." I shake my head, try to smile amicably. "I'm sorry."

"Okay. Well, just so you know, we're starting a Forty Hours service tonight, which means that the church will be open until Saturday night. You can come anytime, Bird. Even if it's five o'clock in the morning and you just want to sit. It doesn't have to be for a service or anything."

"Uh-huh." I think back, trying to remember what Forty Hours is, but nothing comes. And what the hell would I want to just sit in the building for? Especially with that creepy crucifix staring down at me? And James Rittenhouse hiding in the choir loft upstairs? "Okay. Thanks. I appreciate it."

"Give my best to your mother!" His voice follows me eagerly as I race down the front steps. I raise my arm in response, throw the car into gear, and step down hard on the gas.

Chapter 7

T hat was James," I say aloud, slowing the car in front of a stop sign. "That was *James!*" I pause, looking out wildly at the street, as if he will suddenly appear at my passenger window. "He was on the news this morning. He was being taken to . . ." My brain races, struggling to remember. "Court? Jail? The magistrate's office? He was put in a police car. I *saw* them put him in a police car. And then . . . *what*? What happened? Did he escape?"

I can hear the words coming out of my mouth, but it is as if someone else is saying them. They hang around me in the small space of the car, like fragments of barbed wire. My fingers are trembling; something that tastes like bile is pooling along the insides of my cheeks. The light behind the windshield is sharp as glass, the leafless tree branches stark as ribbon. Behind me, a car leans on its horn. I startle out of my thoughts, pushing down hard on the accelerator.

What was the chain of events between James's arrest early this morning—less than three hours ago—and now? How in God's name did he become an escapee? Did he just run off?

Break out of his cell? He couldn't have broken out of a cell. They have bars. They're iron. They're *built* to hold people *in*. I pause, thinking of all those escape sequences on *COPS*, the way some people just snap sometimes and then bolt. Years ago, a story ran in the local paper about a lady who was being arrested in front of the pharmacy for stealing a CD player. Somehow, just as the policeman cuffed her and was trying to get her in the cruiser, she broke away from him, ran across two lanes of traffic, and jumped off the side of the Market Street Bridge. It was front page news, that picture, the dead woman lying in a puddle of blood on the riverbank, both arms twisted horribly behind her, her neck splayed at an impossible angle. There was an uproar, too, that the paper had run it; people by the hundreds canceled their subscriptions, called the newspaper en masse to voice their disgust. Ma was one of them.

I raise myself up in the seat, as if I will be able to see across town to the county jail, which is less than a mile from here, set back on a deserted stretch of the city. Where, at least, are the screaming sirens, the policemen running down the street? Shouldn't they have those special dogs out, the ones that sniff an article of clothing and then locate the missing person minutes later? I glance down both sides of the street at the next stop sign—empty, except for the usual houses and yards. There are a few cherry trees trying valiantly to bloom, their pink-and-white blossoms like fragments of a cloud suspended on the branch tips. But no people. No police.

I direct the car toward Mr. Herron's place across the river, head down a street with a pothole so big that I have to swerve so that I don't put a hole in my tire like I did last year. I am breathing in shallow gulps, as if my lungs are already filling with liquid. The image of James slumped in that corner keeps returning—the outstretched arm, the gun, the huge eyes underneath the white scar. He'd looked terrified. In all the time I'd known him—and it hadn't been so long, only a few months, really—I'd never seen him look frightened. He hardly even seemed capable of making any real noise, let alone inflicting harm on someone.

I turn the car down Cherry Drive where Mr. Herron lives, take a breath, stare out at the street. This part of the city is especially ugly, and this time of the year doesn't help things. Empty garbage pails lie along the sidewalks; lawns are muddy and unoccupied. There are a few blobs of green here and there—a promise of something to come—but they are small and infrequent as to be almost nothing. Just a few weeks ago, right at the end of March, we had a massive, freak snowstorm. Sixteen inches. There are still vague remnants of dirty snow lining the edges of the sidewalk, a few icy puddles here and there, and although things are finally starting to warm up, it still hasn't gotten over fifty yet. It won't get anywhere near the seventies until June.

My attention shifts to a man walking by briskly. With his lean frame, hunched shoulders, and fists shoved into his jacket pockets, he reminds me suddenly of Charlie, my old boyfriend. Another man I haven't thought about—at least consciously—in years. Another person whose face crowds the inside of my head like too many people in the same room.

I DIDN'T FIND Charlie, tall, with pale skin and a dead front tooth, particularly attractive when we first met, but he had a few other things going for him. He was the general manager at the Burger Barn for starters, which, at least in my mind, already set him apart from everyone else. He'd risen above the lowly ranks of the rest of us, had elevated himself to an administrative position, far from the humble, static plane we would probably occupy for the rest of our lives. I'd noticed him looking at me out of the corner of his eye a few times as I stood behind the register, clearing his throat as if he wanted to say something, but I didn't think anything of it. No one really looked at me. Not that way at least. I'd dated a few guys before Charlie came along, and was not a virgin, but at ninety-eight pounds with a head of dry brown hair and teeth that could stand not only to be straightened but spaced a little better, too, I was never going to win any beauty contests. If men showed an interest in me, I was grateful, not flattered, as if they'd done me a favor. When Charlie looked at me, though, it was as if I was the only person in the room—and he was hoping to keep it that way.

It was his dream of owning his own restaurant that really reeled me in, as if I might somehow get closer to actually *being* someone if I was with a person who had his own aspirations. He'd even told me about it once: a small corner place with hand-rubbed pine floors, strings of dried garlic hanging from the walls, and red, dripping candles on every table. It would garner a reputation for its homemade pasta, real minestrone soup, and broad, impressive wine list, and Charlie would be at the door every night, dressed in a dark suit and good shoes, welcoming the regulars back in. I liked it, too, that he was older than me—almost nine years, in fact—and that when he smiled, his green eyes lit up in a way that took me by surprise.

One night after work, he asked me to go with him to Dugan's, a corner bar a few blocks away from the Burger Barn. Dugan's had a perforated tin ceiling that was turning green around the edges, and shabby bar stools. It served all the local drunks, boasted a Friday night dollar draft special, and had a wooden floor that smelled like wet peanuts. Best of all, Big Ed, who stood behind the bar, never asked for ID.

Charlie bought me a beer, and then another. I listened as

he complained about the other employees: Laurie who took a bathroom break every half hour so that she could reapply her makeup, and Jenny, my roommate, who rolled her eyes at the customers when they waited too long to order. He didn't trust Lionel as far as he could throw him, but he thought James (who I didn't know yet) was an okay guy. He definitely knew how to make a decent hamburger, and people went crazy for his coleslaw, which he secretly peppered with chopped jalapeno. He'd never once come in late, and he kept the kitchen pretty clean. But for all the time he'd worked there, Charlie said, he'd never heard James say a single word to anyone. Half the time Charlie didn't even know when the guy had left for the night. He'd come in the back to check on things, and find everything turned off, including the lights.

"He could at least say good *night*," Charlie said, looking at me with slightly lidded eyes. He was on his third beer. "I mean, it's weird, you know? He's always slipping in and out that back door without a sound. Loners like that freak me out."

After our fourth drink, Charlie stopped talking about everyone else. Instead, he sat next to me and began whispering in my ear. When I felt the heat of his breath against my neck, everything inside me quivered and then jumped. It was as if someone had plucked a moth off the wall and cupped it in his palm. Maybe even blew on it a little. My brown, papery wings stretched, fluttered, and took off. All the way home with him.

It was not my first time. But it was the first time I'd been with someone in a real bed, inside a real apartment, like a real grown-up. Up until that point, my sexual experiences had been either in the backseat of a car, or on someone's floor with a set of sleeping parents upstairs. They'd been wordless, awkward, and much too brief. None memorable. None I ever found myself recalling later. For all the beer I'd downed that night, I still wasn't drunk enough to forget the sensation of Charlie's arms around me, the faint scent of peanut shells emanating from his skin as he pressed and squeezed me against him like a rag doll. We kissed briefly before he led me over to his bed, shoving his hands up my shirt as he pushed me down on the mattress. I remember feeling disappointed—*Already? It's going to be over so fast*—but staying quiet. He was the older one, obviously more experienced than me, and he knew what he wanted. Right now, he wanted me, which was all that mattered.

"Oh my God," he said a few minutes later, his body shuddering like a violin. "Oh, Jesus." I stared up at the ceiling as he collapsed against me, trailing my fingers absently through his hair the way I'd seen a girl do in a movie. She'd seemed blissful, though, caressing his scalp, her other hand resting lightly against his shoulder. I just felt lonely.

A few weeks later, Ma stopped into the restaurant to say hello. She did this every so often, claiming that she'd had a "sudden hankering" for a burger, a statement we both knew was a lie. Ever since I had moved out, she needed to lay eyes on me in person, liked to amuse herself, I guess, by keeping tabs on my whereabouts, even from afar. Charlie walked out from his office just as she was ordering, and I introduced him as my new boyfriend. She smiled and shook his hand, and we made small talk for a few moments. Afterward, I watched as she took her tray with the same single burger and small coffee she always ordered over to her favorite corner seat by the window. My heart sank as she sat there and ate silently. I already knew. But she called me later that night, just to confirm it.

"I don't like him, Bernadette," she said bluntly.

"You don't even know him, Ma."

"I don't have to," she said. "It's a feeling. In my gut."

"Based on what?"

"His eyes," she said. "He didn't look at me once, the whole time we talked. Anyone who avoids looking at you directly like that is always hiding something," she said. "Always."

I hung up on her.

NOW, A LITTLE girl across the street catches my eye. She can't be any older than two or three, her springy red hair held in tight ponytails, the hem of her pink spring jacket flapping open over a red T-shirt and pink pants. Her father's index finger fits neatly inside her whole fist as she walks along the length of the sidewalk curb, sliding off after a few feet, then getting back up, and sliding off once more. The father laughs every time she falls, lifts her back up with a raise of his arm, says, "Whoopsie-daisy!" He has a full head of brown hair, cut short around the sides, longer in front, and is dressed in a dark blue sweat suit. Sneakers, too, with green stripes on the sides. Handsome, in an off-kilter sort of way, with a nose that's too big and thin lips.

I take the key out of the ignition, slide a glance at the clock on the dashboard. It's well after ten A.M. I'm already later than Ma probably told Mr. Herron I would be, but I still can't make myself move. My shoulders are hunched up almost to my ears, my toes curled up inside my shoes. I bring my gaze back to the little girl, watch as she gets to the end of the sidewalk and then hops off with two feet. The father grins, holds out his hand for a high five, and then scoops her up. His arms are huge around her, and he holds her close, protecting her from everything harmful in the world.

I blink a few times as they disappear around the corner and then rub my eyes. What the hell is wrong with me? What am I doing, sitting here like some kind of zombie?

I have work to do. Money to make. A security deposit to pay. A life to start living.

I yank open the car door, slam it shut.

Bite my lip to hold back the tide of tears behind it and head across the street.

Chapter 8

Mr. Herron is eighty-one years old. He lives in a two-story, four-bedroom house that looks like it is about three hundred years old. Shingles are falling off the roof, and one of the window shutters is missing. He's got a rocking chair on the porch, and a rusty horseshoe nailed to the front door. An old welcome mat that used to spell HERRON looks as if a rodent of some kind has chewed through either side of it, so that only the letters ERR are still decipherable. Mr. Herron has lived in this house for over fifty years; it was where he and his wife raised all their children and, he told me once, where he would die and be buried.

Ma and I used to clean Mr. Herron's place every two weeks, just like all our other clients, until we got a call from his son Arthur, who lives out in Arizona. Arthur told us that his father's diabetes was causing him to lose his eyesight—the doctors said it wouldn't be long before he was completely blind—and that Mr. Herron had refused to be placed in a nursing home. Could we go over once a day to "straighten up, make sure the place wasn't turning into some kind of den?" He would cover the cost, whatever it was, and mail us a check twice a month from Arizona. He does, too. Arthur's checks are never late.

Now, I walk up the rickety front steps, and reach for the doorbell, which sticks half the time because it is so old. "I'm at my job," I say to myself. "I'm at my job, ready to do my work, so that I can make money for my security deposit, and that's all there is to it."

I ring the doorbell, stand back, and wait. The paint on the outside of Mr. Herron's house is chipping badly; the flaky curls remind me of the way Angus's sunburned skin sheds in the summertime. When he lets me peel it off, they make a little pile on the corner of the kitchen table, like insect wings.

I ring the doorbell twice more, and then try the door. It's unlocked.

"Mr. Herron?" I call down the hallway. No answer. A sharp, acrid smell fills my nostrils as I walk through the house. Something's burning in the kitchen. The lights are off—the lights are always off—but I can make out a dark plume of smoke rising out of a pot on the stove. "You've got something burning out here, Mr. Herron!" I turn off the burner under the pot, look inside. Whatever it was, it is indistinguishable now—just a bunch of black lumps at the bottom. I put the pot in the sink, squirt some detergent in, step back as an angry geyser of steam rises.

"Mr. Herron? Are you here?" A wave of fear washes over me. What if he has collapsed on the toilet? Fallen down the basement stairs? Then I catch sight of the top of his graying head through the kitchen window. He's outside in the yard again, on his hands and knees, fiddling in the garden. Rain or shine, snow or wind, Mr. Herron is always in the garden.

"Mr. Herron?" I push open the back door, squint a little against the pale light.

He straightens up, fastens his gaze in my direction, squints a little. "Bird? Is that you?" He's dressed in a gray cardigan over an old white T-shirt, dark blue pants, and leather moccasins. The closely cropped hair on his head is almost all white; only a few thin threads of gray peek out along the sideburns.

"Yeah, it's me. I've been calling for you in there." I start across the tiny backyard, stepping over pockets of dirty slush. "Did you know you had something burning on the stove?"

A shadow flits across his face; his bushy eyebrows narrow. "Ah, shit." He sits back on his heels. "You take it off?"

"Yeah, I put it in the sink so it could soak. Whatever it was, it's ruined now. What were you making?"

He shakes his head. "Just some applesauce. Lucille says I should be eatin' more fruits and veg'tables."

Lucille is one of Mr. Herron's home nurses. I've been here a few times when she comes in to give him his insulin and check his blood pressure. She's nice enough, although she uses a whiny, high-pitched kind of voice when she talks to him, like he's about two years old.

"You didn't smell it burning?" I ask.

"No, I didn't smell it *burning*," Mr. Herron says. "I'm out here, checkin' on the garden! If I smelled it burning, I woulda come back inside and turned the damn thing off!"

"Okay, okay. No need to get excited. But you know, it's probably not a good idea to put something on the stove if you're going to come out here and work."

He snorts and turns back around. "Now you sound like Lucille. Always naggin'."

"Did my mother call and tell you I was going to be late?"

Mr. Herron nods his head, turning over the dirt. "Yup. Said she'd asked you to stop in at the church to pick up her sweater? That right?"

"Yeah." What would he say if I told him? What if I just blurted it out: *I ran into someone I used to know, Mr. Herron, who just this morning was being taken to jail after putting someone in the hospital and then escaped somehow. He's at the church where my mother left her sweater! The one she asked me to go get! Can you believe it? When I saw him, he pointed a gun at me, and asked me not to tell anyone. He's still there, hiding in the choir loft, right next to the old organ. I think he's hurt, but I don't know for sure. How long do you think it'll be before they find him? And what will happen to him when they do?*

"Gotta tell Arthur to dock you," Mr. Herron says, shaking his head.

"Even though my mother called?" I look at him, trying to hide my annoyance. "Mr. Herron, it's not even ten o'clock yet."

"Job's a job." Mr. Herron shrugs. "You come in late, you get docked."

You're a cheapskate, I feel like saying. *An old, crotchety pain in the ass. You're lucky we come at all, with all the complaining you do, all the mistakes you try to point out even though you can't see half of them.*

"What're you planting today?" I ask instead, looking over his shoulder at the lightly packed dirt piles around several small plants. Last summer, before his eyesight really started to go, Mr. Herron made me come out every other week to look at something else that was blooming. I didn't know what the names of anything were, but for months, the small plot of ground was awash in a sea of colors: peach and magenta, dark purples and yellows. Now, there is a multitude of stems, leaves, and tightly closed buds but no color. Not yet.

"I'm not *plant*ing anything." Mr. Herron feels the ground under a wide plant with silvery buds. His fingertips feel their way up to the stem, inching gently out along the leaves. I swear his fingers have their own set of eyes. "I've already *done* the planting. I's checking on my dianthus and my tangerine parfaits. They'll be bloomin' soon, and I need to make sure they don't need any extra help sittin' up straight."

"Tangerine parfaits? That sounds like some kind of dessert."

"Mmm, they look good enough to eat, too, once they flower." Mr. Herron smiles with satisfaction. "Deep, deep orange. Like sherbert. Prettiest little things you ever saw."

"When will they bloom?" I wonder if he'll be able to see them at all by the time they bloom this year.

Mr. Herron reaches out again, feels around until his fingers come into contact with a stem and then make their way up to a tight, barely visible bud. He caresses it for a moment, thinking. "I'd say 'nother month is all. They late-spring risers. Like the dianthus. Pretty soon, this whole front section be drippin' in orange and purple."

"That'll be pretty." I look back toward the house. "I'm gonna get started inside now, okay? You want me to put some more apples on the stove while I clean?"

"Nah, forget it," Mr. Herron says. "Stuff tastes like baby food anyway."

"You sure? It's no trouble. I could slice some up right now, put them in with some cinnamon sugar . . ." I stop talking as Mr. Herron shakes his head vehemently.

"Didn't even want the stuff in the first place. I'm tellin' you. Just Lucille buggin' me. Forget it."

"All right." I head toward the back door. "I'll be inside if you need anything, okay?"

He grunts without turning back around, his fingers still exploring the ground beneath him.

THE NICE THING is that even though he can't see more than a foot in front of him anymore, Mr. Herron is still a pretty neat guy. Basically, I just cover the essentials when I come over: dusting, vacuuming, sanitizing the bathroom. (He does miss the toilet seat quite a bit now.) Sometimes he asks me to fold his wash, but not often. And unless he complains about the way I've made his bed, or how I forgot to Windex the TV screen, I'm almost never there for more than two hours. It's pretty easy work for a steady paycheck.

I put in my headphones as I start on the kitchen, nod my head along with AC/DC's opening riff of "Back in Black," and settle into my usual routine: counters first, then the sink, the front and very top of the refrigerator, and inside the microwave. Afterward, I will water his kitchen plants, sweep and mop the floor, and then, while it dries, move on to the downstairs bathroom. Except that despite turning the volume up as high as it will go, and bobbing my head along to "It's a Long Way to the Top," which has one of the single best guitar riffs ever written, nothing about me is settling in. My hands shake as I spray the counters, and when I get up on the little stepladder to water the ugly plant Mr. Herron keeps near the window, my legs feel so rubbery that I almost fall off.

Is James in pain? That foot injury—whatever it is—looked pretty bad. And the cut on his head was bleeding. Not gushing blood or anything, but still. It looked deep. His wrists, too. He probably needs to see a doctor. Go to the hospital. Maybe I should make an anonymous call to the police station, say something like, "Go look in the choir loft at Saint Augustine's. There's a man there. He's hurt." Except that they can trace things like that, can't they? I've seen it on those cop shows. Which means that then they'd come looking for me. Start asking questions. If I have a record now, God only knows what would happen if I got involved with something like this. One thing's for sure: I could kiss the apartment at

Moon Lake goodbye. And that's not going to happen. Not now. Not ever.

With the downstairs bathroom finished, I head upstairs to start on Mr. Herron's bedroom. The perimeter of his wide mahogany dresser is lined with a collection of Happy Meal toys from McDonald's: Strawberry Shortcake, Shrek, Hello Kitty, Minnie and Mickey Mouse, Goofy, even a Build-a-Bear one. He keeps them around for when his grandchildren come to visit. In all the time I've been working for him, though, they've never come to New Haven. Not once. Still, he tells me to keep them clean, to dust them daily. Just in case, I guess.

I accidentally knock Hello Kitty and Shrek over with the duster as I start moving it. And then, when I bend over to pick them up, I sit down with my knees folded under me, and stay there, tracing the edges of the figurines, as if I will find something that I am not sure I am looking for somewhere in those big plastic eyes.

"It says here that one out of every eight people in the United States will have been employed at a McDonald's at some time in their life," James said one morning. "Don't you feel kind of gypped that we only made it to the Burger Barn?"

I'd smiled when he said that, picked up the dead cigarette butt he'd crushed on the cement block next to him, and tossed it at his foot. It was the third morning of the week I'd purposely drawn the prep work slip just to see him. I still didn't know why I'd done it exactly. I knew I wanted to be near him, but when I was, like just now, a nameless, inexplicable uncertainty still filled me like water.

He rolled his shoulder back with a fluid movement and then inhaled. "Ah, well. I only got a year left here anyway, and then I'm heading out."

"To where?"

"Somewhere else. Anywhere else." He looked at me. "You're not staying, are you? I mean, this isn't gonna be one of those lifer jobs for you, is it?"

"God, no." I looked down, picked at the skin around my fingernails until one of them started bleeding. "I'm saving to go to nursing school." It was the first time I'd said anything regarding nursing school aloud to anyone, and while I knew it would take months, maybe even years, before it would actually come to fruition, in that moment, my dream became real—almost as real as James, who somehow, in the throes of these peculiar morning meetings, had morphed from a ghost into a real person.

"Oh, yeah?" James tapped another cigarette out of his pack, held it between two fingers. "That's great. My mother was a nurse."

"She was?"

He nodded, cupping his hand around the tip of the cigarette as he lit it. "Best woman in the world, my mom. Hell of a nurse, too. When I was real little, she used to take me into the hospital with her during her shift when she couldn't find anyone to watch me. I'd sit on one of those blue chairs by the nurses' station, and she'd me give me a *Reader's Digest* to look at, but I never did. I watched her instead. She was the head nurse, so all the rest of them on the floor were constantly asking her things or bugging her about some patient or this medicine." He took a drag on his cigarette. "She never lost her cool, never got upset, never once raised her voice. One time, even though I wasn't allowed, I stood in the doorway of this old guy's room and watched her lead a team of them as he coded, right there on the bed. She was amazing. Cool, confident, knew exactly what she was doing. They brought him back, even before the doctor on the floor got there. *She* brought him back."

I thought about telling him about the nurse I'd seen the night my father died, how tender she'd been with the old man across the hall, how gentle her movements, as if he was the most important person in the world. But the thought passed. What would he care? Besides, that was my memory, my night. There was no reason to share it with anyone.

"Wow," I said instead. "Does she still work there?"

"She's been dead almost ten years now." James's voice flattened, and he stared at something in the distance. What, I couldn't see. But as I pulled my legs up and settled my chin on my knees, I had the distinct feeling that there was someone else in the world who not only lived in the same country that I did, but also knew the language. It stilled me, this knowledge, as if it might leave again if I did not hold it close. And so that morning, I did not say anything else.

MR. HERRON IS SITTING in his easy chair in the living room, "watching" a John Wayne movie on TV, and eating a plate full of salami and saltine crackers. He's got a can of Bud Light cracked open, too, with a straw inserted into the top of it. Okay, so maybe Lucille's on to something about him needing to eat more fruit. For a moment, I'm tempted to ask him to turn the channel—"How about we just check the local news, Mr. Herron? Can we? Just to see if anything's going on?"—but the urge passes. He'd start asking questions.

He looks up at me, mouth moving.

I pull out my earphones. "Sorry, what?"

"You sick or som'thin'?"

"No, why?"

"Usually you rushin' around this place like you need t'get outta here yesterday. I can hear you up there today, draggin' your feet like you got stones attached to 'em." His voice is louder than usual, but then again, so is the volume on the TV. "You trying to figure out how to make my bed the way I like it?"

"No, just thinking." I take my feather duster out of the back of my jeans and start in on the front of the TV. Two cowboys are rushing across the screen, yelling about a ruckus in the saloon. One of them snatches the gun from inside the holster around his waist, holds it in his hand as if ready to shoot. I pause, watching for a moment. How many people have actually had a gun pointed at them? At close range? I have no idea what kind of guns policemen carry these days, but from what I can recall, the one James was holding looked like this one on the TV. Maybe a little smaller. I don't think the barrel was quite so long either.

"Whatchou thinkin' about?" Mr. Herron sounds bemused. "You got a hot date or somethin' after this?"

My face flushes, as if Mr. Herron has caught wind of my thoughts. "No, I have another house to clean today. You know that."

Mr. Herron grunts, takes out a handkerchief from his back pocket, and blows his nose. It's a loud, gurgling sound, followed by copious wiping. I look away. "Where else you goin'?" He asks me the same question every time I come over.

"Same as yesterday. The rich lady with all the kids. Over near the Grand Union."

His face eases a little. "The one with all the *kids*," he says. "Yeah."

I move soundlessly around the room, but his eyes follow me everywhere. It used to freak me out a little, him watching me like that, until I realized he just needed to know where I was. I guess if I was almost blind, I'd want to know where someone in my house was, too. "She just had another one, too, didn't she?" he asks.

"Little girl, two months ago." I move the feather duster along the edge of his bookshelf. *Moby Dick.* A Hardy Boys set. Sherlock Holmes. His kids' collections from way back when. I wonder why he still keeps them around. He's certainly not reading them.

"Well, she better get someone to tie them knees together," he says. *"Shit."*

I bite my tongue so I don't laugh out loud and keep dusting. It occurs to me suddenly that Mr. Herron has had sex, an obvious fact, of course, since he has children, but one that settles along my shoulders curiously for a moment, as if I'm discovering something unusual about him. The china cabinet, an enormous, cherrywood monstrosity, still filled with all of Mrs. Herron's china, needs to be wiped down and dusted. The dishes inside are white with a blue border, a picture of a house and a lake in the middle. Pretty stuff. I doubt Mr. Herron ever uses it now, but he expects me to dust it. I wonder if his wife pulled it out for special occasions—Christmas, maybe, or even Sunday dinners. Maybe Mr. Herron stood at the head of the table, the way Dad used to, slicing up a pork roast, while Mrs. Herron passed around bowls of glazed carrots and mashed potatoes.

Mr. Herron holds out his plate. "You want some salami? It's the good kind—with all them peppercorns in the middle."

"No thanks." I finish dusting, keeping rhythm to the staccato burst of gunshot on the television. "It's still pretty early for salami, Mr. Herron."

Mr. Herron pops another piece into his mouth. "Never too early for salami, Bird. Never."

"Well, I'll stick with cereal before noon. Maybe an egg sandwich if I have a few minutes."

"Man, I used to make a mean egg sandwich," Mr. Herron says, chewing slowly. "My men used to go nuts over 'em."

"Your men?"

"In the army. Korea—1950. I was the cook."

I stop dusting. "You were a cook in the army?"

"You bet your ass I was. Damn good one, too. Boys said I could make an egg sandwich that brought tears to their eyes."

How is it that things come out when they do? Who chooses how and when certain information is relayed between people? I've been cleaning Mr. Herron's house for over a year. Every day now—except weekends—since January. And this is the first time he's ever told me such a thing. "Wow" is all I can bring myself to say. "That's kind of amazing."

"What is? That I was in the Korean War, or that I can make an egg sandwich that'll bring tears to your eyes?"

I smile then, maybe for the first time since leaving Angus this morning. "Both," I say. "Both actually."

Mr. Herron chews thoughtfully for a minute. "Maybe someday I'll tell you 'bout it." He nods. "Got a lot a stories from back then. A *lot*."

"That'd be nice," I say, although I don't really mean it. As interesting as they probably are, I don't have time to listen to fifty-year-old stories about Mr. Herron's past. I barely get through the work I have to finish here before I have to rush over to my next job.

"You'd have to keep workin', though," Mr. Herron says. "I mean, while I'm talkin' to you. Don't expect to sit around here with your feet up while I'm telling you things."

"Oh, I'd never do that." I roll my eyes as I head for the basement, where I will start his laundry.

"And don't think I didn't see that little eye-roll, young lady."

I stop short. "What?"

"Fine." Mr. Herron pops another piece of salami into his mouth. "Maybe I didn't see it. But I felt it." He wags his finger in the air. "Don't think you gettin' nothin' past me, Bird."

"Oh, I wouldn't dream of it, Mr. Herron," I say, turning around again. "I know you better than that."

Chapter 9

It's noon when I leave Mr. Herron's house, which means I have just enough time to stop at Rensack's Deli to get a sandwich before heading over to Jane Livingston's. My stomach is growling, and getting stuck at Jane's house with a day's worth of work and an empty stomach is not a good combination. I get mean when that happens.

In the car, I turn the radio on and flip through all the music stations. My heart skips a beat whenever I hear something that sounds like a newscaster, but everything comes up empty. Or at least there's nothing on about James. The streets are still quiet, too—no sirens of any kind, no dogs or police officers running around. I don't get it. How can people not be aware of what's happened? Has James's escape even been noticed yet? Is it still too early? Or does it just not matter? Could it be that it's not really that big of a deal?

At Rensack's, I order a large turkey sandwich with provolone cheese, tomato, and spicy mustard, grab an extralarge bottle of water out of the cooler, and toss in a bag of potato chips. "Eight dollars," the woman behind the counter says, ringing me up. She's tall, with an obscenely large chest and a sweet smile. "You interested in any lottery tickets today?"

I shake my head, scanning the stack of newspapers on the floor next to the register. There's nothing on the front page about James's arrest. Maybe inside. "Just this," I say, putting one of the newspapers inside the bag. An elderly man gets in line behind me, holding a gallon of iced tea.

"Eight fifty," the woman says, punching a few more buttons on the register. Her skin is oily, the cheeks pitted as if someone has taken an ice pick to them.

"Did you hear anything weird on the news today?" I ask, digging into my purse for my wallet. It just comes out, a blurt, before I can stop myself.

"Weird?" the woman repeats. "Weird, how?"

"Oh, you know. Anything that might've happened this morning." I'm backpedaling now, furious at myself, but unable to stop. "I usually listen to the news, but I slept in today and missed it. I was just wondering if anything interesting happened today that I didn't know about." God, I sound like an idiot. A moron.

The woman nods slowly toward my newspaper, which is still sticking out of the bag. "You did just get a newspaper," she says slowly. "Stuff'll probably be in there."

I laugh lightly. "Yeah. But just yesterday's stuff." I bite my bottom lip. "I was talking about today. You know. This morning."

"Uh-huh." She takes my money, glancing at the man behind me, and scratches the edge of her ear as the register dings open. There's a tiny tattoo on the inside of her wrist: a roughly drawn diamond with a circle in the middle. It doesn't look professionally drawn; I wonder briefly if she did it herself. "You know, now that you mention it," she says, "I think I did hear something about one of Oprah's dog's passing away. Real early. On *Good Morning America*. I think they said it choked on a sandwich. Isn't that sad? She got those real small dogs, you know? Them miniature ones. I don't know why anyone in their right mind would be feeding it a *sand*wich, but that's what—"

"I mean locally," I interject. "Here. In New Haven. This morning."

"Oh." The woman hands me my change. "Locally? Well, no. But then, nothing ever happens here." She pauses. "'Cept for maybe a few car accidents."

"Yeah." I nod in agreement. "Well, thanks." I grab the bag, adjust my purse strap over my shoulder. "Have a good day now."

"Try WALL radio," the man with the iced tea says suddenly as I push the front door open. "It's an AM station, on at noon every day. They've got an hourly update on things going on in New Haven. Mostly traffic and stuff, but—"

"Oh, yeah?" I clutch the paper bag more tightly, as if it might fly out of my arms if I don't. "W-A-L-L?"

The man nods, slinging his gallon jug on the counter. He's wearing a tweed cap turned backward, the visor just barely brushing the back of his neck. "AM," he says. "Not FM. I got it on all the time."

THERE'S NOTHING IN the paper about James, but the guy at the deli was right about WALL. The station is right in the middle of a noon broadcast by the time I find it, and when I hear James's name, uttered by a slightly frantic male voice, I almost drive off the road.

"*. . . Rittenhouse, who just this morning was arrested on assault charges after the near fatal beating of another man, was being taken to the county jail where he was going to be arraigned. Police say that at* *around 8:05 A.M., while the cruiser was at a red light, Rittenhouse managed to kick his way out of the back of the patrol car, not only injuring the police officer, but also absconding with his firearm. He was last seen on foot, running toward Interstate 81. An all-points bulletin has been set up and police are currently in the process of issuing a city-wide search, since Mr. Rittenhouse is armed and considered dangerous. Police have also advised that Rittenhouse may be injured as a result of the physical altercation and might be in need of medical attention. Anyone with information about his whereabouts is asked to call the New Haven Police Department immediately at 567-9043."*

My hands are gripping the steering wheel so hard that the knuckles are turning white. You can bet your ass he's armed and dangerous. Three short hours ago, I was staring down the barrel of the gun he was holding. I guess I'm lucky to be alive, when I think about it. What if he hadn't recognized me? Or what if he had shot first and then looked?

A car swerves past me on the left. The driver leans on his horn, reaches out his window, and holds up his middle finger.

I glance down, eyes scanning the numbers behind the wheel. The speedometer says thirty. I'm in a fifty-mile-an-hour zone. I speed up, trying to focus. An advertisement for a morning TV show fills a billboard on the side of the road. The woman is blond and impossibly gorgeous, a smile so wide across her face it looks as though something might break, while the man sitting next to her appears comfortable and sophisticated, his arms crossed across the front of his chest. Behind it is another billboard, this one for K-Y warming oil. The nearly naked couple is clutching each other; the woman's leg, draped in purple silk, is raised across the man's bare thigh, his hand positioned behind the small of her back.

For a while, that was all we did, Charlie and me. Sex, sex, and more sex. Mostly whenever Charlie wanted to, and always at his apartment. I never turned him away, but after a while, I found that I could have done without the actual physical part of things. Sex for me had just become a way to get to the company that came afterward. Or at least the company I dreamed of coming afterward. I had notions of lying there face-to-face, propped up on our pillows after the physical act was over. I would trace the outline of Charlie's top lip, which was shaped like a slightly crooked parenthesis, and he would push the hair off my forehead. We would talk about our lives, our days, about things that had happened, people we had seen, until we drifted off to sleep.

But it never happened. Mostly because right after sex Charlie always fell asleep. I would come out of the bathroom after cleaning up, and find him snoring away, facedown in his favorite green pillow. I'd sit there for a while, waiting, hoping, and then I would wrap a blanket around my shoulders, and walk into the living room and sit in one of his windows. Staring out into the starless night, I would think about all the things I would have told him if he had stayed awake. Like how much I loved the bouquet of red roses he had brought to work the other day, just because. Or how grateful I was when he'd finally relented at the movies, agreeing to the one I'd been dying to see for weeks, instead of his first choice. We could have talked about how cold he got all the time, despite the fact that winter was still months away, and why, although he wore an extra T-shirt under his uniform at work, he still rubbed his hands together throughout the day to get warm.

I might have asked him why he thought the lady with the huge yellow hat who came into the Burger Barn every day and ordered the same double burger with extra pickles hadn't come in yesterday. Was she sick? She coughed sometimes, sitting there in the corner booth all alone, bringing a handkerchief to her lips and blotting them gently. Did he think she'd died, maybe, the way I did? Or did he think she'd be back tomorrow? Maybe I would have told him that I was starting to save for a biology class at the community college so that I could apply to nursing school, or even about the last fight Ma and I had had on the phone, especially since it had been about him. Specifically, about my having sex with him. She'd asked me point-blank if we were sleeping together, and out of spite, because I knew it would hurt her more than anything else I had done up to that point, I told her the truth. "Of course we're having sex, Ma. We've been dating for months now. That's what adults do." She'd caught her breath, the way I knew she would, and paused. I imagined her sitting on the old velour couch at home, the arms worn shiny with use, and pressing her fingertips against her lips, forcing back tears.

"Isn't it bad enough that you're wasting your time with this guy?" she said after finally finding her voice. "Do you think so little of yourself that you would go and *sleep* with him, too?"

"He's not just a *guy*, Ma." I stood up, stalking around the apartment as I talked. "He has dreams, you know. Real ones. He wants to open up his own restaurant. He wants to be someone."

"What about you?" she asked. "Who do you want to be?"

The question was so blunt and I was so unprepared for it that I stopped midstride and just stood there looking out the window. I could have told her about wanting to be a nurse, but I didn't. Maybe I wanted to keep it to myself. Or maybe I was afraid she'd say something like, "A nurse? Really?" Something she would insist later had been an innocent question, but one in which I had only heard uncertainty, especially since I'd never mentioned it before and my grades in high school had been so terrible. "Leave me alone, Ma," I said finally before plunking the phone back down in the cradle.

Later, when the prep mornings started with James, along with my strange, inexplicable feelings for him, these silent conversations I imagined in Charlie's living room turned to him. I could not imagine James falling asleep after sex, and although I did not let myself envision the two of us engaging in the actual, physical act, I felt my skin growing heated and the familiar stirring of pleasure as I pictured him stretched out naked in bed next to me. Maybe he would give me a factoid; maybe, more likely, he would not say anything at all, running the tip of his finger along the curve of my eyebrow instead, and then drawing it down along the edge of my hairline, tracing the outline of my ear. I closed my eyes, thinking of it, feeling something in me fill and pulse and hold, and when I opened my eyes again, whatever it was had emptied, and tears slid down the side of my face because I knew such a thing would never happen, at least not in this lifetime, not to someone like me.

BEHIND ME, ANOTHER horn blows. A woman leans out the window, her brown hair whipping around her face. "Get off the damn road if you can't drive!" she screams.

I speed up again, pull onto a side street with no traffic, and then position the car on the side of the road.

Leaning forward, I let my head rest against the middle part of the steering wheel, close my eyes.

I have to stop this.

I have to put this whole thing out of my mind, forget it ever happened.

I do.

I have a little boy who is depending on me. *I* am depending on me. I've had a rough go of it, a few false starts. I've wasted enough time screwing around, making bad choices, messing up the game. I'm sorry things happened the way they did back then, and I'm sorrier still that James has found himself in a bad place right now; I truly, truly am. But enough is enough. I pulled myself back up out of a bad time. And not just once either. If I can do it, then so can he.

And that's the end of it.

Chapter 10

Jane Livingston became a daily client of ours just a few months ago, after giving birth to her fourth baby. Ma and I had been switching off, one of us coming to clean her place every two weeks, until Jane's husband took us aside and admitted that he was afraid Jane was starting to feel a little overwhelmed, especially since Genevieve, the nanny who supervised the three older children, did not do a very good job keeping house. "Jane likes it clean," Mr. Livingston said, fiddling with a large gold watch on his wrist. "She *needs* it clean. Every day. Having things ordered and neat really seems to calm her down."

The Livingston house is on the opposite side of the river in the wealthy section of New Haven. It's one of those two-story English Tudor monstrosities with a pale stucco exterior, wood trim, and steeply pitched roofs. Inside there are six bedrooms, three bathrooms—one with a steam room and sunken marble tub—and a fully furnished basement. A brick path winds its way up to the front, and there is always some sort of seasonal wreath on the door: maple leaves for fall, dried sunflowers for summer. The three older kids are usually gone when I arrive, whisked off to whatever afternoon activity Genevieve has taken them on, but Jane is always home. Always.

Today, she greets me at the front door, the baby tightly swaddled in a blue gingham sack across the front of her chest. "Hiiiii, Bird! How are you?" Jane is blond and pretty, even with no makeup, although every time I come over, the circles under her eyes look a little darker. Despite having given birth so recently, she is achingly thin, as if she has been subsisting on air. I would guess she is in her early thirties, although she could be older. I've never seen her dressed in anything but the same black leggings, shiny ballet flats, and starched, button-down white shirt. The requisite pearl studs are in her ears, a thin gold Rolex on her left wrist.

"Hey, Jane." I always call her by her first name, since she had a fit the first time I addressed her as Mrs. Livingston—"Oh God, don't call me that! It makes me sound so *old*!" I peek inside the little baby hammock, touch the edge of the baby's fist with my fingertip. "How's Olivia doing?"

"Oh, fine now." Jane sighs, stepping back to let me into the black-and-white tiled foyer. "She was up most of the night, though. I swear I don't even know what day it is anymore." She watches me take off my shoes (her rules) and set them neatly next to the doormat. I get the weird feeling that she is studying me again, looking for something. It makes me nervous.

"Is there anything special you need done today?" I always start by asking this, since Jane's cleaning requests are so erratic. Some days she just wants me to do the older kids' rooms—other days, only the basement. Once, I spent three hours cleaning every single crystal on the large chandelier in the dining room. Today, it could be the outdoor patio, or even the two-car garage. I never know.

"Just a general pickup around the house today, I think."
Jane pauses. "The kids have been so messy lately. Just throwing
everything around. They're so careless, you know?"

"All right." I'm careful not to answer her question. There's
never any reason to get too personal with clients. Especially when
it involves family stuff. "No problem. I'll start upstairs, then."

Jane looks down at the baby, nods. "Everything's where it
usually is. Don't mind me. I'll just be in the kitchen."

I head upstairs, grab Jane's bucket of cleaning supplies out of
the hallway closet, and let myself into the master bath. Jane buys
the good stuff—real Windex, Murphy's Oil soap, and Magic
Eraser sponges—which makes the work so much easier. Most
of our clients—Mr. Herron included—skimp on the cleaning
supplies they are required to provide. I guess they think we can
make do with the store-brand window cleaners and scratchy
paper towels, but we really can't. Junk like that makes the job
twice as hard—since it doesn't work the first time—and just
leaves Ma and me exhausted.

I spray down Jane's black marble tub and the walk-in
shower, then mop the black-and-white tiled floor and empty
the garbage, which is full of pink, balled-up tissues. I pause,
the way I always do when I move over to Jane's vanity, and
just look. It's an enormous, richly veined marble countertop
with his-and-her sinks. Above it is a three-way mirror lined
on either side with grapefruit-sized lightbulbs. I push gently on
the corner of her side of the mirror until it springs open, and
then stand there, gazing.

If Ma has told me once she's told me a hundred times to
keep away from closed doors. "People have a way of knowing
if you've been in their things," she warned. "Especially medicine cabinets. And once they find out you're a snoop—even if
you haven't taken anything—you're done. They'll never ask

you back." I'd never take anything from anyone, but God, it's fun to look. Especially at rich people's things.

The bottom shelves of Jane's side of the mirror are filled with expensive skin serums and facial creams, undereye treatments and body masks. There's a blue rubber thing with the eyes cut out, I guess for putting over your face, and a wide, round tub of something called "caviar-infused body butter." Orange pill bottles line the top shelf, tallest to shortest, a small army of medicine; beneath it are the more practical items: Vaseline, rubbing alcohol, tweezers, even a tube of Preparation-H.

Mr. Livingston's side contains his own neat alignment of aftershaves and razors, dental floss, and a small drinking glass with three gold condoms inside. I take one of the condom pouches out, glance at the writing on the package: *Extra thin for superior comfort.* I wonder if Jane insists on them now, or if they were put here so long ago that he's forgotten they're still here. I place it back carefully. On the top shelf is one of those soap-on-a-rope things that looks as if it's never been touched, and a square glass bottle filled with blue fluid. I take it out, uncap it gently, and sniff the nozzle. It smells like eucalyptus and musk and something I can't place. Oranges, maybe. Lemons? No.

James.

It smells like James.

WE WERE ON the stoop again, a flush of morning light in the distance, the blurry sound of the occasional car passing on the street behind us. He hadn't had a cigarette yet for some reason, a detail I thought both interesting and odd, and his bandanna was missing. But he had his book. And when I finished hosing out the condiment holder and came to sit beside him the way I had taken to doing, he smiled at me and pointed to a line on one of the pages.

I leaned in and read: *"Although it's been proven that all human beings possess their own distinct scent, some researchers hypothesize that there are only seven primary odors: musky, putrid, pungent, camphoraceous, ethereal, floral, and minty."*

"What's a camphoraceous smell?" I asked, straightening up again.

"Like mothballs," James answered. "I think."

"And ethereal?"

"Dry cleaning fluid. I think."

"Hmm." I tapped the back of my heel against the edge of the stoop. "I've never actually taken the time to think about it, but I doubt I smell like either of those. Or any of the other ones they mention." I laughed. "Actually, I don't smell like anything, really."

"No, you're wrong." He had closed the book, was looking at me with a vague sort of intensity.

"I'm wrong?" I laughed again, but it was bubble-thin this time, settling at the back of my throat. "About what I smell like?"

There could not have been more than six inches between us, but the time it took for him to move his face close to mine seemed to take minutes. Hours, even, as if he was moving in slow motion. I could feel the heat from his face as he held it there without moving, and it occurred to me that if I moved my head ever so slightly, our noses would bump and my mouth would brush up against his. I stayed very still, every cell thrumming beneath the surface, hardly daring to breathe.

"You smell like rain," he said finally, his breath warm against my ear. "The kind of rain that comes after a long stretch of hot, dry weather." I could not bear the weight of his eyes against my face at such a close proximity; it felt somehow as if I were being held, not by arms and hands, but by longing, and I was afraid to give in to it, afraid of what might happen if I turned and met his gaze. Not to him. To me.

"I don't know what that smells like," I heard myself whisper.

"No?"

I shook my head.

He still hadn't moved, and for a moment I wondered what it might feel like if his eyelashes brushed the side of my cheek. "It smells like relief," he said. "Like liberation."

I turned then, not consciously, I don't think, but because I had no choice, and looked into his face. His words, like his presence, demanded something of me, the very least of which was acknowledgment. Up close the scar across his face did not look ugly or menacing; it looked perfectly natural, as if it had belonged there from the beginning. I could smell, too, the scent of his skin; it was warm and blue and slightly citrusy, as if he might have been eating a lemon, and I wanted to say that I knew exactly what he meant about relief and liberation, because it was what he smelled of, too, but I was afraid that if I opened my mouth, the emotion inside it would spill out into tears and stupid, meaningless words. I leaned in instead as he met me halfway across that infinitesimal space, his hand cupping the side of my face and then sliding back behind my head so that he could pull me closer, all without ever taking his mouth off mine.

And then I pulled back, hard and fast, as if an electrical current had shot up between us. I jumped to my feet and raced inside.

IT TAKES ME over an hour to finish the children's rooms, and when I come back downstairs, Jane is still in the kitchen, sitting in a window seat opposite the blue tiled butcher block. She is biting her nails ferociously; Olivia is asleep on her lap. "Okay, so the upstairs looks good." I speak softly, so as not to wake the baby. "I'm gonna start on the basement, and then come back up and finish the first floor, all right?"

Jane startles a little at the sound of my voice and drops her fingers. "Sure, that's fine." She blinks. "Boy, it'd be nice to get things done as quickly as you do. The other day, I started folding the kids' laundry and it took me almost an entire hour to finish it." She laughs softly, showing small, square teeth. "Of course, I like to get my seams straight. All those little armholes lined up."

"Yeah." I try to laugh, but it comes out awkwardly. "I know what you mean." Except that I don't know what she means. I never match up seams or armholes when I fold Angus's and my clothes; it's enough most of the time that they are clean and in the right drawers. Jane has a tendency to talk to me like I'm an old high school girlfriend. And even though I am not her friend, even though I am not even in the same league as her, I always feel as though I have to respond. That if I don't, she will get angry. Or maybe even fire me.

"Bird, can I ask you what kind of laundry detergent you use?" Her pretty face has taken on a look of intensity; it's a serious question. "I mean, for your son's things. Do you use a different kind of detergent for him when you wash his clothes?"

"No." I shake my head. "Not really."

"How about when he was a baby?" Her forehead is furrowed. "You know, they have all those detergents now without dyes—they're supposed to be so good for newborn skin. Did you ever use any of those?"

I shrug, embarrassed not to have known—or even heard of—such a thing. "No."

Jane's face falls. "No?"

"No. Just Tide, mostly."

"Tide." Jane says the word slowly, rolling it around in her mouth like a marble. "Yeah."

I point to the door that leads to the basement downstairs. "I really . . . I'm going to get started downstairs now, okay? I just don't want to run out of time."

"Sure. Go ahead."

I grab the bucket of cleaning supplies, head for the basement.

"Bird?" Jane calls.

I wince, back up a few steps until I can see her again. "Yeah?"

"Can I ask you something?" She pauses, ducking her head. "It's sort of personal."

No. "Okay."

Jane looks down at the sleeping baby in her lap. "Do you like being a mother?"

I glance sharply at her. Jane and I have only ever talked about Angus in passing—just the formalities, really, when she hired me. I tell all my clients that I have a child, in case I ever have to leave suddenly, or if there's some kind of emergency. Jane doesn't even know Angus's name. "Yeah," I say cautiously. "I do."

Jane nods, as if trying to catch up to the racing thoughts inside her head. "Can you . . . I mean, can you tell me *what* you like about it? Specifically, I mean?"

Now my own thoughts are racing. No one's ever asked me such a thing before. "Well . . . he's my little guy." I shrug, embarrassed again. "I just . . . I don't know. I love everything about him."

Jane keeps nodding. She gets up, walks over to the butcher block in the middle of the kitchen, leans one hip against the edge. A long, odd moment passes as the two of us watch her trace her finger around one of the blue squares. Her other hand rests protectively around Olivia. "God, I'm sorry," she says, looking up finally. "I can't believe I just asked you that. I must sound like some kind of crazy person."

"No, no." I am struggling to understand and then, just as quickly, let it go again. There's nothing about this woman that I can relate to, and her oddities don't seem worth any anxiety on my part. "You have a lot to deal with every day, having four. I only have the one."

She smiles. "Did you ever tell me his name?"

"Angus."

"*An*gus!" Her whole face brightens. "Now that's different! Where'd you come up with that one?"

"Oh, it's an old family name." I glance toward the basement door again, try to imagine the look on Jane's face if I told her about my AC/DC infatuation. She probably listens to Mozart in her spare time. Or Josh Grobin.

"I love old names," Jane says. "I was named after my grandmother. You have an interesting name, too, now that I think about it. Is Bird a family name?"

She startles, as the sound of children shrieking is heard outside the front door. "Oh, no!" She grabs my hand, just before racing upstairs. "Tell them to be quiet!" she begs. "Please! Tell Genevieve to take them downstairs! They'll wake the baby!"

And before I have a chance to answer, she disappears, bolting upstairs with the still-sleeping newborn in her arms.

AN HOUR OR so later, while I am wiping down the patio furniture on the back deck—black wrought iron with blue-and-white checkered seat cushions—Jane emerges again, holding a small paper bag. Olivia has been put down upstairs for a nap apparently, and Jane has arranged her hair in a ponytail. She's changed into a new, pale pink shirt, too, with the sleeves rolled up, and taken her shoes off. Her toenails are painted a bright fuchsia color. "Hey," she says, placing the bag down on the patio table. "I've been doing some spring cleaning of my own upstairs, and I came across a ton of these sample size beauty products that I thought you might like."

I straighten up, glance self-consciously at the bag. Does she suspect me of looking through her beauty cabinet? Or maybe she just thinks I need beauty products?

Jane withdraws a few plastic tubs, studying the front of them, and then begins to line them up on the cloudy glass counter-top. They're all white, miniature-sized, and covered with black writing. "There's some kind of body butter, a deep condition-ing treatment, some shampoos, body wash, cuticle cream." She looks over at me. "Do you ever use cuticle cream?"

"What is it?"

She laughs. "Well, I guess that answers that question. You know, *I* should be using cuticle cream. Maybe it would help me not to bite my nails so much." She takes a few more items out of the bag. "This stuff for undereye circles works like you wouldn't believe. I've been using it for years. I love it." She glances up. "Not that you have to worry about stuff like under-eye circles yet. But, you know, I thought you might want it anyway. Just to have. And these scented body wipes are great, too. I threw in a whole bunch for you. You can use them in a pinch if you get really sweaty and just want to wipe off a little. They're really small, but they smell so good, like spearmint and lavender. I always keep a handful of them in the glove com-partment, just in case."

I pick up a small tube, read the writing on the front: Chanel Enzyme Facial Scrub. I've heard of Chanel, seen the brand in magazines. It's expensive. So why is she giving them away? Jane leans over my shoulder, examining the tube, too. "Oooh, their enzyme facial scrubs are heaven! Have you ever used them?"

I shake my head, grin a little. "I don't even remember what an enzyme is."

"Oh, it's just some fancy kind of exfoliant," Jane says. "You know, to slough all the dead stuff off your skin. It'll make your whole face glow. Seriously. Promise me you'll try this tonight. I'm telling you, you'll see a difference in the morning."

But I put the tube back in the bag, pick up my cleaning cloth again. "I don't . . ." I start, shaking my head. "I mean, I appreciate you thinking of me, but I really wouldn't use this stuff."

"*Any* of it?" Jane looks as if I've just told her I quit.

"Well, no. Not really."

"How about your mother?"

I stare down at the table. I know she's trying to be nice. But can't she see how weird this is? How uncomfortable I feel? I'm already her cleaning lady. I wipe the inside of her toilets, get down on my hands and knees and scrub her bathroom floors. Does she really expect me to accept her leftovers, too?

"Please," Jane says. "Just take them."

"Um . . ." I say stiffly. "Okay."

Jane starts putting the items back in the bag. Her ponytail swings lightly, and she's holding her bottom lip with her teeth. "I hope I haven't been out of line or anything. It's not that I think you *need* any of this stuff. I really just thought you might like it."

I take the bag, give her a small, apologetic smile. "It's okay. I didn't think that."

"Okay." Jane turns to leave, sliding the heavy glass door. She's so small that she has to use both hands, pulling back with her whole weight to get it open. "I hope your mother enjoys them, too."

"Thanks," I say as she steps back into the house. And then: "Oh, Jane?" She turns, fingering one pearl stud. "Would you happen to have any more work I could do in the next few days?"

"More work?" Jane's brow furrows. "You mean than you already do?"

I bite the inside of my cheek. "Yeah. I need to make a little extra money by Thursday, and I was hoping I could pick up a few extra cleaning jobs." I shrug. "Do you have anything extra you need done? After hours, maybe? Or even at night?"

Her face creases into another thoughtful expression. "You know, it's funny you ask actually. We just had a new play set delivered for the kids the other day, but the guy couldn't stay to put it together. He said he could come back next week, but I was actually going to give it a go myself so that they could start enjoying it now." She cocks her head. "How 'bout it? You game for a few hours of huffing and puffing, trying to get a plastic playhouse together?"

I grin. "That sounds great."

"It'd have to be late," Jane says. "After the kids go to bed, since I want to keep it a surprise. Can you come tomorrow night at seven? I don't know how long it'll take us, but I would count on staying at least a few hours."

"That's perfect," I say, giving her a nod. "I'll be there."

Chapter 11

I have until five o'clock to pick up Angus from the after-school program; after that, they start charging by the hour. Twenty dollars an hour, to be exact, which I can't afford. T-ball practice starts at five-thirty, and since I forgot to pack a change of clothes for him this morning, I have to swing by the house first, too, so that I can grab all his gear. I am in a state of near panic as I leave Jane's at 4:50 and hightail it downtown. And yet, as I race along the quiet side streets and take a short-cut through the parking lot at Walmart, I find myself thinking about her again. Maybe I'm being too hard on her, criticizing her generosity, thinking her desperate questions about motherhood a sign of weakness or, worse, instability. She did just have a baby, after all. The first six months after Angus was born, I was so tired all the time that my brain felt like pudding. Watching TV didn't help; not even the funny stuff on the late-night talk shows seemed to register. Whole days seemed to come and then disappear again without my even knowing it.

I'm no expert, but maybe Jane is having problems inside her marriage, too. It's possible. We've never talked about it, of course, but I get the feeling that her husband isn't around all that much. And I'm guessing that being alone all day with three kids plus a newborn and waiting for someone to come home could make you a little batty. She probably needs a break. Just a chance to go do something on her own or with a bunch of girlfriends who require nothing from her except her presence. God knows I've felt that way over the last few years. Every once in a while, when it gets to be too much and I feel as though I might start gnawing my own arm off if I don't get out of the house, I'll kiss Angus good-night and tell Ma I'm going out.

"Oh?" she always asks, not taking her eyes off the TV. "Where to?"

I wish I could tell her that I'm meeting my friends down at the corner bar for a drink, or that we're all heading out bowling, but she knows I don't have girlfriends, that ever since I got in trouble I dropped the few I had in exchange for a life of restitution and solitude. It wasn't a huge sacrifice; the friendships I'd made after moving out of Ma's, including my roommate, Jenny, were shallow and tenuous, nothing to speak of. I'm also not permitted to set foot inside a bar, since one of my probation stipulations forbids me to "enter or frequent any establishment whose primary income is derived from the sale of alcoholic beverages." But when I get antsy, I'm usually not looking to tie one on anyway. Mostly, I just walk.

Just a few months ago, after putting Angus to bed, I went out and bought a package of cigarettes—even though I hadn't had one since I found out I was pregnant—and walked to the playground over on Cedar Avenue. Just a few blocks away from our house, it had, for a while at least, been one of Dad's and my "places," a tiny section of the world reserved only for us. When I was little, he would take me down for an hour before dinner and swing me on the rubber bucket swings or ride the seesaw with me as the sun began to drop low in the sky. As I got older, though, we would find ourselves drifting over to the wooden benches underneath the maple trees on the other side of the playground to talk. Teachers, middle school boys, the scab on my knee, nothing was off-limits.

"Do you love Ma?" I asked him once. I'd heard them arguing that morning while I was brushing my teeth, had felt my hand tighten around my toothbrush as I heard Ma call him an imbecile. "Even when she's mean to you?"

I expected him to look at me sharply; Dad was Ma's greatest defender, her stalwart companion even in the worst of situations. There was always an explanation for the sharp things she said to him: the words had come out of her perpetual state of exhaustion; she was Irish and had a fuse like a spark plug; she had always possessed, for as long as he'd known her, a naturally defensive personality. But he only sighed this time, linking his hands behind his head, and looked up at the light sifting through the leafy canopy above us. "Yes," he said. "I love her even when she's mean to me."

"How?" I pressed, wanting to understand. "How can you still love her when she says such awful things? I mean, she can just be so rude."

He nodded, not disagreeing. "She can be tough. But your mother loves us both very much. Her anger comes from places that have nothing to do with me. Or you."

I considered this, picking at my big toenail. At twelve years old, I already knew that Ma had had a life before us, and that with a father who had walked out on the family when she was eight years old and a mother who drank herself unconscious every night, it hadn't been all sunshine and roses. Still, it hardly seemed like a valid enough excuse to call her husband names, especially when he was so empathetic toward her past—and her present behavior. "You always make excuses for her," I said.

"Do I?" He put his hand on my knee.

I looked up, searching his face for some sign of condescension, but he only looked tired. "Yes. You do."

"Well." He shrugged. "Maybe that's just part of how things work. She makes you mad sometimes, doesn't she?"

I rolled my eyes. "That's the understatement of the year."

"Well." He squeezed my knee. "You still love her, don't you?"

"I guess." I looked down, aggravated by how simplistic he made it seem. Deep down, I knew there was nothing simple about it at all; Ma and I were as opposite from one another as two people could get. But the truth was, I spent so much time feeling angry at her that I'd never even stopped to think about whether or not I still loved her. Did I? I wasn't entirely sure.

"Of course you do." He hooked a finger around mine. "Even if you don't feel it. It's there, Bird. It's always there."

MY ANXIETY LEVEL soars as traffic on Market Street, which is the only street that leads to Angus's school, becomes more and more dense. The clock on the dashboard reads 4:56. I have four minutes before the overtime clock starts ticking. Just when I decide that there is some sort of external force deliberately working against me, I see the red-and-blue glare of the siren lights cutting through the sky, the faint sound of a megaphone up ahead. People are getting out of their cars; police are checking the backseats, opening up the trunks. My heart speeds up, a rapid knocking behind my ribs, like one of those rubber pink paddle balls. It's got to be because of James. Which means they haven't found him yet. Which also means he could still be up there in the loft. I think about cutting out of line, swerving the car over to the far left lane, but that would just look suspicious. I don't have anything to hide—except my conscience, which I'm pretty sure no one has found a way to tap into yet. I dial Angus's school number on my cell phone, listen as it rings loudly in my ear.

"Little People After Care," a voice says after four rings.

"Oh, hi, this is Bird. Angus's mom? Is this Molly?"

"Yes! Hi! Are you on your way?" With her reddish-purple hair and thin silver ring clipped in the middle of her nose, I would guess Molly to be only about eighteen or nineteen years old. On any given day, there is an innate frantic quality about her, as if she's just slugged four or five espressos, but right now she sounds borderline manic.

"Yes, I'm on my way, but I just wanted to tell you that I might be a few minutes late."

"You know we're on lockdown, don't you, Mrs. Connolly?" Molly never fails to call me "missus," no matter how many times I have told her that I am not married.

"Excuse me?"

"We're on *lock*down," Molly repeats. "Mayor's orders. There's some maniac out there who escaped from a cop car this morning with a gun and—"

"Wait, what?" I interrupt.

"I'm telling you," Molly says. "There's some psycho out there—"

"I got that part." The edges of my face feel warm. "But why is the day care on lockdown? Have they seen the guy around there?"

"Well, no. They haven't seen him *any*where." Molly pauses dramatically. "But the escape took place right here. At the red light on the corner of South and Market. Which means that he could be anywhere."

I inhale slowly, pulling at the skin on my neck, and then exhale again. "Well, I'm stuck in traffic right now, because the police are checking everyone's cars on Market Street. I just wanted you to know that I'll get there as soon as I can."

"The police are checking everyone's cars?" Without waiting for an answer, Molly leans away from the phone and yells, "Hey, Carol! The police are checking everyone's *cars* now!" Then she's back. "Okay, Mrs. Connolly. Well, get here when you can, I guess. Thanks for calling."

"Will you tell Angus—" I start, but there's only a dial tone. I click the phone shut, move the car toward an officer who is beckoning me forward.

"Hi, Officer." I roll down the window, rest an elbow casually on the edge of the door. "What's going on?"

He puts a hand on my door and leans in, glancing first at the front of the car, and then the back. Small wiry hairs jut out from inside his nose, and his breath smells like sour coffee. "We have to check your car, ma'am."

I put the car in park. "For what?"

"We had a prisoner escape this morning." His voice is brusque and tired; he's already answered this question a hundred times. "Pop your trunk, please, and step out of the vehicle."

I get out and step to the side as the policeman opens the backseat, and leans in, swiping a hand carelessly under both seats. Behind my car, another police officer is doing the same thing to a Ford Taurus pickup truck, the back of which is covered with an enormous black tarp. The woman who has stepped out of the Taurus is wearing denim overalls and a Yankees baseball hat. She looks like she's about to kill someone. "It's fertilizer," she says, rolling up the sleeves of her blue-and-green checkered shirt as if getting ready to take a swing. "For my garden. And no, there's no one *hid*ing in it.

Have you ever tried to hide in a pile of fertilizer? You'd smell like shit for about six months straight, for one thing. And you wouldn't be able to breathe."

"Sorry, ma'am. We got orders." The police officer walks away from her, rips off the tarp, and then heaves himself up to one side of the truck.

"Well, hey," the woman says, watching as the cop plunges an arm into the dry mixture. "Go right ahead, then. Knock yourself out." The cop turns his face as a smell like raw sewage drifts out from the truck, but keeps digging.

I look back over as the cop slams down the hood of my car. "Okay," he says, giving the trunk a few taps. "You're good."

I drive the rest of the way feeling suspended somehow, as if my body is outside of myself. It is such an odd feeling that I reach up and slap myself across the face—anything to snap me out of it. But it doesn't help. Something is making me think about that day, niggling around the edges, forcing me to re-member.

I MADE IT a point to stay away from James after the kiss on the back step, telling myself that I didn't want to turn into one of those people who cheated because I didn't have the guts to break up with my boyfriend. The truth was more complicated. James was shy and kind and quite possibly the most fascinating person I had ever met. He was almost ethereal, I sometimes thought, as if he'd been dropped down from another galaxy, and he possessed an inexplicable, innate knowledge about the world around us, including me. The secret tendril of feeling I harbored for him kept me awake some nights, poking insis-tently like some distant tapping underground. But it worried me, too, and I was not exactly sure why. Maybe it was because I sensed a goodness about him that did not match my own, an integrity that I had long since disposed of myself. Plus, he was so intellectually curious, his knowledge of things so captivating. I was nothing like that. I would never be able to catch up, to sustain his interest the way he did mine. If I let myself fall for him, something would go inevitably, irretrievably wrong, and it would be my fault. No, it was better to keep my distance, to not take that chance.

But things were starting to go undeniably sour with Charlie. In fact, unless he was trying to get me into bed, he barely talked to me at all. The roses stopped, we hadn't been to the movies in months, and even the talk about his future restaurant plans—at least with me—had come to a halt. And I'd begun to notice that his temper, which he had never directed toward me, began to sneak out around the edges. One day after I stuck my head into his office and asked him how things were going, Charlie reached over, grabbed the stapler off the desk, and flung it across the room. "Like *that*, okay?" he said, as if the thud of the instrument against the wall was enough of an explanation. "Now leave me alone and get back to work."

He didn't take the breakup well. We were in his office when I told him I didn't want to see him anymore, and after a few sputtering requests to reconsider, he threatened to fire me. When I told him to go ahead, that the answer was still no, he came out from behind his desk and grabbed me around the jaw. With his face centimeters away from mine, I wondered briefly how I had never noticed the constellation of blackheads scattered across his nose, or the way the celery-green color inside his eyes went flat when he got angry.

"You listen to me, you little shit," he said softly. His fingers were squeezing the bones behind my cheeks so hard that I thought they might crack. "People like you don't *get* to say no to people like me. Do you understand?"

There was a sound in the doorway and then the movement of a shadow across the floor. Charlie let go of my face and took a step back as James walked into the room. "What the hell do you want?"

"Don't you ever touch her like that again." James's face was flushed from standing over the grill, but I could see a muscle pulsing in his jaw.

"Who the fuck do you think you are?" Charlie was sputtering now, apoplectic. "Get the hell out of my office! Now!" He glared at me. "And you, too! Before I fire both of you!"

I slipped out, ducking my head as I passed James, ashamed that he had seen me in such a compromising situation and felt the need to come to my rescue. I didn't need his help. If he hadn't come in when he had, I would have shoved Charlie's hand away from my face and stalked out on my own.

I know I would have.

EVENTUALLY I MAKE it to the day care, park the car along the curb with the same precision that I usually use, and remember to turn the engine off. The lights, too.

My heart is still hammering away inside my rib cage and there is a rushing sound in my ears. But when I open the door to the after-care room and see Angus, everything falls away, the way it always does.

"Mom!" he yells, hurtling full speed across the room. I catch him under the arms, lift him up, hold him close.

Sometimes, like today, I can't hold him close enough.

Chapter 12

Once, a few days after Angus and I moved in with Ma, I woke up early and came down to the kitchen. Ma was sitting at the table, drinking a cup of coffee and reading the newspaper. It was spread out flat in front of her, her palms pressed down on either side, as if it might fly away otherwise. Her green bathrobe—the same one she's had for the last fifteen years—was double knotted around her waist, and tufts of her plaid nightgown peeked out from the opening around her throat. The ceramic cow-shaped salt and pepper shakers that Dad had given her for Christmas one year were in their usual place, just in front of the blue plastic napkin holder, and outside the window, behind her, I could see the aluminum siding of the old shed Dad had used to store his tools.

For a split second, I felt the familiar thrum of our lives humming around me as if it had never left; Dad was right up-stairs again, tuning his little transistor radio to the morning news station as he got ready for the shower, and I was running around, rummaging through the laundry hamper, looking for a matching sock. Any moment now, Ma would get up and take the eggs out of the refrigerator, grab the bag of bread out of the bread box, and drop two slices into the toaster. Dad liked his eggs over easy; I needed them scrambled and superdry. We all had toast, lots of it, and as the kitchen filled with the scents of Dad's Old Spice cologne and melted butter, he would reach over and poke me in the arm. "You wanna walk today or you want a ride with me?"

And I'd say the same thing I always did: "Ride with you."

The moment was so real that when it left again, and I found myself standing in the doorway, staring at Ma—and no one else—I couldn't speak, as if the memory itself had taken my voice along with it.

TONIGHT, THE HOUSE smells like meat loaf. Angus runs into the living room and turns on cartoons, while I walk into the kitchen and drape my coat over the back of a chair. Ma's at the stove, stirring something in a pot. She turns, wiping her hands on the edge of her apron. "Were you able to get my sweater?"

"Hello to you, too, Ma."

I head to the refrigerator, still distracted by Angus's response on the way home when I asked him about Something Special Day. He'd looked out the window, said, "It was okay," which meant obviously that it did not go well at all. Angus is the type of kid who cannot hide his happiness. It bursts out of him in an explosion, like the river of candy pouring out of a split piñata. If things had been wonderful, if the kids had leapt up and screamed and clapped the way I was picturing they might have, he would have said so. Loudly, while jumping up and down. His barely audible response made my heart sink.

"How about the coin trick?" I'd asked, pulling into the driveway. "Did the kids like that one?"

He shrugged again, opened the door. "It was all right."

Fucking Jeremy. He said something. I could feel it in my bones. But I left it alone, the way Dad used to do with me. It'd come out eventually. It always did with Angus, just as it had with me. And when it did, when he was ready, I'd handle it then.

"Hello, hello." Ma nudges me gently with the handle of her spoon. "Were you able to get my sweater?"

"Yes, I got your sweater. It's still in the car, though. I'll go out in a minute and get it."

She rakes a handful of fingers through her hair and turns back to the stove. "Did you see Father Delaney?"

"Uh-huh." I open the fridge, stare inside. Milk. Orange juice. A bag of green apples. Twelve plastic sleeves of neon-orange cheese squares. Strawberry Danimal yogurts for Angus, and six containers of plain vanilla yogurt, which is what Ma eats. What am I doing? I'm not even hungry.

"You're not thinking of eating, are you?" Ma asks. "I have a meat loaf and baked potatoes in the oven. They'll be ready in about twenty minutes. And I'm making a green bean cas-serole, too."

I grab one of the vanilla yogurts and take a teaspoon out of the drawer. "You know I don't eat meat loaf, Ma."

She sits down across from me, folds her hands neatly in front of her. "What did Father Delaney say when he saw you, Berna-dette? I bet he was shocked, wasn't he? I mean, you're so much older now." She raises her eyebrows, giggles a little.

It's the occasional moment like this—with Ma so obviously delighted with herself—when I sometimes think I catch a glimpse of who she really is. Or was, before the rest of the world got in there and mucked it all up. Her eyes get very bright, as if she's managed to retain a secret right up until the very last minute, and

her whole face softens like a child's. There is no sign of the hard-
ness in her jaw, and her pinched lips, usually set and pursed like a
dried plum, ease again. If there is any part of my mother that I am
aware of loving, it is this one.

She watches me giddily as I peel off the yogurt's foil top and
set it to the side. "Bernadette?"

"I guess he was a little surprised. He didn't really say anything about me looking older."

"Well, he wouldn't." Ma pulls at the cuffs of her sleeves—
first the right, then the left. "He's a gentleman. Did you talk
about anything?"

"No. I had to get to work. I took the sweater and I left." I
put a spoonful of yogurt in my mouth. When was the last time
James ate? He must be starving. And thirsty. My God, he's
probably so thirsty.

"He didn't *ask* you anything?" Ma is leaning forward on the
table, her head tilted slightly to the right. "Nothing?"

"Ma, come on." I put the spoon down slowly. "Gimme
a break with the games here, okay? I know you forgot your
sweater on purpose."

She unclasps her hands, sits back in her chair. Fiddles with
the hem of one sleeve.

"Didn't you?"

"Oh, Bernadette." She stands up, grabbing the yellow oven
mitts hanging on a hook next to the stove. "Don't use that tone
with me. It's not like I did anything wrong."

"You did too! You lied!"

She whirls around, mitts on her hands now, both anchored
firmly on her hips. "I did no such thing! I asked you to go get
my sweater . . ."

"Which you *pur*posely left behind, just so that I could 'run' into Father Delaney!" I use my fingers to make air quotes around the word "run." "That was completely dishonest, Ma, and you know it!"

Ma steadies her lower lip with her teeth. "Father Delaney is a good man."

"That is not the point, and do *not* do that."

"Do what?"

"Change the subject like you always do, so that you don't have to take responsibility for anything."

"Just what are you accusing me of?" Ma's eyes are flickering now, the edges of her nostrils turning white. I know that if I say what's really barreling through my head—that she is a scheming, calculating busybody—things will erupt into a full-blown war. It's not worth it anymore; I never win these kinds of arguments, and more importantly, Angus is around. He doesn't need to hear either of us spewing our vitriolic statements at one another. We're supposed to be role models here, not bad influences.

And so I take a deep breath, attempt to navigate the conversation in a different direction. "Do you seriously think I'm just going to start going back to church because I happen to say hello to a priest I once knew as a kid?"

"Nothing happens by accident," Ma says.

"Ma, come on! What is the *matter* with you?"

"There's nothing the matter with *me*," she snaps. "And lower your voice. Gus is in the next room."

"I know exactly where Angus is, Ma. And I have no intention of getting into a screaming match with you. But, *please*. For the thousandth time, please just stay out of my life. Especially when it comes to stuff like church and all that. Okay? I don't know how many times I have to tell you that I am not interested in any of it anymore. It's not for me."

She opens the oven door and sets the steaming pan of meat loaf on the counter, touching it lightly with the pad of her index finger. Then she looks up. "Well, Saint Monica never gave up on Augustine." Her voice is unnervingly steady. Like steel. "And I'm not going to give up on you."

If Ma has told me the story about Saint Monica and her son, Saint Augustine, once, she's told me a thousand times. Augustine's road to sainthood was an exceptionally long one. For years, he partied and slept around, leaving mounds of debt and bastard children in his wake. All the while, his mother, Monica, prayed for his conversion, begging God to help her son see the light. He did, of course, after hearing a voice directing him to pick up a scroll of sacred text and read it. There's always a voice that descends from a cloud in stories like these—always. Soon afterward, Augustine went home and made amends for all the sins he'd committed, eventually becoming one of the greatest bishops in the Catholic Church. Monica was ultimately made a saint, too, since her son's conversion was considered a direct result of her prayers.

I shake my head, draping both arms over the top of my head. "Oh my God, Ma. Why can't you ever listen to the things I try to tell you? It's like you don't even have *ears*."

"Don't you shake your head at me." Ma's voice is still hard, but she's losing ground, too; I can hear it in the tremor of her voice. "I'm not the one who's throwing her soul away."

She's thrown the last dart, aimed directly for the jugular. Everything for Ma comes back to the soul, which she considers our true, eternal essence. We all have one apparently, some fluttery thing inside of us that never dies, a kind of eternal flame that we are responsible for keeping sterile and smudge free. When I was younger, I used to imagine my soul as a little white butterfly that lived beneath my rib cage. It slept when I slept, flittered around when I was awake, and smelled like me in the summertime—a combination of warm grass, peonies, and Dial soap. When the time came for me to die, I pictured it drifting out of my mouth and floating around the world, trailing my scent behind it. That scent would be my mark. My stamp on the world.

For a split second, I feel genuinely sorry for Ma. I stopped believing in all that hokey stuff years and years ago. Aside from it being completely weird, it doesn't even make sense. Butterfly souls? Eternal scents? But she believes in the Catholic faith so desperately, even though she's never stopped to question any of it, not once, that it makes my heart break to think about it. Because what if she's wrong? What if Father Delaney and the Catholic Church and Saint Augustine got it all wrong and there is no God, there is no soul, there is no anything except this, right now? What happens then? Where does that leave her?

"The only part of my soul I've thrown away," I say slowly as the moment passes, "is the part of it that's gotten *gang*rene from listening to all your crap. Which is why, in thirteen days, Angus and I are moving into our own place at the lake."

Ma opens her mouth to say something, but shuts it again when I point my finger at her. "I've told you this a hundred times since we've been back, Ma, and I will say it one final time. Stay. Out. Of. My. *Life!*" I scream the last word, which causes Angus to come running in, eyes wide, looking first at me and then at Ma.

"What's wrong?" he asks. "Why are you yelling at Nanny, Mom?"

Everything inside that raised its head just moments earlier about not making a scene in front of Angus flies out the door. All I can see now is red, like an EXIT sign flashing on and off in front of me.

"I'm yelling at Nanny because she's out of her fucking mind!" I'm already at the stairs, and I take them two at a time, moving like a bull, as if the soles of my feet have springs attached to them. "And she's about to make me lose mine!"

I SLAM MY bedroom door behind me and then sink against it, still holding on to the doorknob. It's been a long time since I've said anything that harsh to Ma, and realizing just how harsh it was makes me wince. It hurts, feeling that way about her, even if it's true. I'm ashamed of myself, too, and sorry that Angus had to see me like that. I know better, of course; I always know better. Now if I could just get to the part where I *do* better. Ma reminds me all the time that I'm an adult now—a mature woman with real responsibilities. But the truth is that I don't feel like a woman; I don't think I ever have. Not even giving birth helped me turn that corner; in fact, the primary reminder reverberating through my head afterward was how young I was to be having a child, not that my female body had just created and nurtured a human being for the past nine months. When I think of real women, I think of Mrs. Ross at the probation office. Or Mrs. Vandermark, who owns the house out on the lake. And Jane Livingston. Each of them possesses a surety about themselves, a kind of innate self-knowledge that I don't have, that I might not ever have. Sometimes it feels like everything just stopped at fifteen, after Dad's car accident. Like the world around me—and inside me—shut down at that moment and never started up again. And it's never more apparent than now, when shit like this happens and I fly off the handle and start screaming like a bratty teenager.

I fall down heavily on my bed, push my face into my pillow. I kick the mattress hard with the tip of my foot, lift my arm, and punch the space next to my ribs. One, two, three, four. Pause. Five, six, seven, eight.

"Mommy?" Angus's voice, small and worried, slides under the door. "Are you okay in there?"

I flip over, stare at the ceiling. I'm panting a little; a buzzing inside my head goes on and on like an irritated fly. But I'm okay. I have to be okay. My boy needs me.

I get up and unlock the door. "Hey, Boo," I say softly.

He scrambles up from his place on the floor and brushes a stray curl from his forehead. "Are you okay?"

I pull him into my lap, drape his legs over my thigh. "Yeah, I'm okay. Don't worry." He nestles in, fitting his head under my chin, pressing his tiny form against mine. I push my nose into his hair, inhaling the faint scent of his coconut-scented shampoo. Close my eyes. "I'm sorry you had to hear that, Angus. I really am. I shouldn't've yelled at Nanny the way I did. It wasn't nice."

"Were you crying?" Angus asks.

I open my eyes again. "No. I had my face in the pillow because I was frustrated. But I'm okay. I promise."

Angus twists his head then, looking up at me. "What's 'fustrated'?"

"Oh, it just means I was feeling sad. And mad, too." I brush my fingers across the space between his neck and shoulders. It is the color of vanilla pudding and just as soft. "Do you ever feel like that? Sad and mad at the same time?"

"Yes." Angus kicks one of his magic shoes. The laces have come undone; his little white socks droop around the ankle. "Today I did."

"Today? When?"

"I don't want to talk about it, really."

"Okay." I squeeze him with both arms. "When you're ready, you tell me."

He doesn't say anything right away. Then: "Nanny's crying, too. Downstairs."

Shit. It takes a lot to make Ma cry. The last time I saw her get anywhere close to it was at the beginning of Dad's funeral, when a lady started singing some song about angel's wings. It was just a single tear, too, which she wiped away quickly with a piece of blue tissue. For the rest of the day, her face stayed dry. "She is?"

Angus bobs his head up and down, just as concerned about Ma right now as he is about me. It's one of about ten million things that I love most about him. "I heard her. She went into the potty and blew her nose, even. It was really loud."

"All right." I lift him off my lap. "We should go down and cheer her back up, then, don't you think?"

"Yes." Angus reaches out with both hands to pull me up. I play along, letting him think that he is lifting me off the ground, and stagger back up to my feet. "Come on. Let's go quick."

But Ma is putting her coat on when Angus and I come back downstairs. She's applied fresh lipstick, too, and is tying a red silk scarf around her throat. She raises her eyebrows at Angus, giving him a quick smile, and then turns back around, pointedly ignoring me.

"Where are you going?" I ask.

"To church." She snatches her purse off the table in the hall, yanks it up along her shoulder. "There's a service tonight. I'll be back later. The meat loaf and potatoes are staying warm in the oven, if you're interested."

Whoa, whoa, whoa. I grab Ma's arm. "What service? They don't have church services at night."

Ma looks at my hand on her arm until I release it again. "They do when they're having Forty Hours."

Forty Hours. That's what Father Delaney was talking about earlier. *The church will be unlocked until Saturday. You can come any time, Bird, even if you just want to sit.* Should I let her go? Is it safe? Maybe James isn't even there anymore. He can't be. It's been at least nine hours. He's had to have found a way out, if only to get water. He wouldn't stay there in the loft. Would he?

"You know what?" I grab my coat off the back of the kitchen chair, reach for Angus's, which is still on the floor. "I think we'll go with you."

Ma looks startled for a moment, and then her face hardens. "Why?" she asks.

"What do you mean, why?" I stammer. "I thought you'd be happy!"

"I don't need you to do any favors on my account." Ma levels her gaze with mine. "And I certainly don't want your pity."

"This has nothing to do with favors or pity." I grab Angus's jacket from the hallway. "Father Delaney said something earlier about just coming in and sitting, and that's all I'm going to do." I shove Angus's arms into the sleeves of his jacket. "Angus, too."

She still looks suspicious, but a softness has emerged from behind the creases in her eyes. I have to shove her a little to get her out the front door. "*Go*, Ma. Come on."

I get Angus in his booster seat in the back, then come around and slide in the front.

I'll just go to make sure Ma is safe. That's all.

In the car, Ma reaches over and squeezes my hand. Then she lets go again—quickly—as if I might swat her.

But at the stop sign, I reach over and squeeze it back.

Chapter 13

The front three rows in the church are packed. And despite the fact that we stopped at a McDonald's on the way over since Angus hadn't eaten yet, and we are a good fifteen minutes late, Ma strides directly up the middle of the aisle in full view of everyone and sits down. If she had a fur, I think to myself, she would toss it over one shoulder, wave to her adoring crowd. It's no secret that Ma is beloved in this congregation; aside from being a faithful parishioner for almost thirty years, she has also been part of every planning committee from picnics to the annual garage sale fund raiser, and her one night out on Wednesdays is spent in the basement here, playing bingo with her fellow churchgoers.

I follow grudgingly, holding Angus's hand, and stare straight ahead. People are probably wondering who the hell I am. Or more likely from the knowing looks they are giving Ma, they already know who I am and are sending her eye messages that say: *"See? We told you! That Saint Monica can do anything!"* Father Delaney is up on the altar saying Mass. He's dressed in white-and-gold robes that come all the way down to his feet, but when he sits down, I can see the tops of his black sneakers. The light from the candles flickers across his face and the rich, spicy scent of incense hovers in the air.

I don't dare look behind me. Or up. I don't *dare* look up. If James is still in the choir loft he's got to be freaking out with all these people so close by. Crazy thoughts start flying through my head: What if he stands up when Father Delaney lifts the Eucharist and shoots him? Ma told me about something like that happening once to a priest down in Ecuador. Shot right through the heart as he lifted the host. A martyr for God on the spot.

Or what if James comes down and orders all of us down into the basement? There are only about fifty people here, maybe less. Most, if not all, of them look to be around Ma's age or older. He could hold all of us hostage easy. Especially with that good-looking gun of his. I shake my head. Ma's the one who loves martyr and criminal stories; there's no need for me to get carried away.

Angus tugs on my arm, and points at Father Delaney, who is swinging the incense chamber around a large gold cross on the altar. "What are they doing?"

Ma moves his finger away—gently, deliberately—and then leans over, putting her lips to his ear. "They are venerating the Host, Gus." She says the words with such seriousness that I almost laugh out loud. Angus has never been inside a church before. Does she really think he knows what she's talking about?

"What's 'venerating'?" Angus whispers loudly.

"Shhh . . ." Ma says. "No talking in church. I'll tell you later."

Angus sits back quietly and then wrinkles his nose. "What *stinks*?"

Ma looks over at me aghast, like it's my fault that Angus has asked such a question. I take a deep breath, exhale. "It's just a spicy kind of perfume, Boo. Don't talk anymore, okay? It makes Nanny upset."

He glances up warily in Ma's direction, and then settles back in against my arm. The next twenty minutes tick by, slow as syrup. I'd forgotten how long Mass can be. Especially, apparently, when it's kicking off an adoration service. After the incense swinging, Father Delaney takes a seat. Then another guy—dressed in green robes and a flat, multicolored scarf—comes out from the back and starts talking. I catch something about the Eucharist being exposed for the next forty hours and how Jesus Himself is really inside that tiny chamber over there in the corner, waiting for us to come over and say hello, but my head is upstairs in that damn choir loft. I can't help it. He's so *close*. If he's still up there, I mean. I have to find out. I have to at least see if he's okay. And if I don't do it now, I won't get another chance.

I reach over, tug on Ma's sleeve gently. "Bathroom," I mouth. "Be right back."

"Now?" Ma looks horrified.

"I want to come!" Angus says loudly.

Two elderly women look over their shoulders at us, then turn back around. Ma stares straight ahead. A vein in her neck quivers.

I shake my head quickly, push Angus back. "Stay here with Nanny. I won't be long."

The stairs to the choir loft are just to the left of the outer vestibule; on the other side is another set leading downstairs to the bathrooms. I pause, my hand on the railing. Am I really going to do this? I don't have to. I could just cross over to the other set of steps, run downstairs, pee, and flush. Come back inside like nothing ever happened. My eyes flick back and forth, coming to rest finally on the basin of holy water at the feet of the Blessed Virgin. I stare at it for a few seconds, then start up the choir loft steps on tiptoe, holding my breath and the front of my purse at the same time. Holy shit, I think to myself. What the hell am I doing?

I use my free hand to guide myself along the wall, turning sideways again when the steps become too narrow at the top. The church itself is already dim, since the only light is coming from the candles on the altar, but up here it's so dark that it's like being at the bottom of a lake. Pitch black. It takes my eyes a full minute to adjust; after a while, I can make out the organ across the room, a few overturned chairs along the tiered steps. Wait. Were those chairs overturned this morning?

I crouch down, staying as close as possible to the wall that stretches out over the pews below, and start crawling. I can feel the velvety skin of dust against my hands, the scratch of grit against my knees. The faint smell of mildew comes out from somewhere—the cloth-covered pews, maybe?—and for some reason, it's freezing. If I could actually make anything out up here, I'm sure I would see my breath. Downstairs, the other priest is still droning on: *"I myself am the living bread come down from heaven. If anyone eats this bread, he shall live forever; the bread I will give is my flesh for the life of the world."* His voice blurs against the microphone; the *s* dragging in static. Palm, palm, knee, knee. I am getting closer and closer to the organ. Another moment and the enormous instrument is right in front of me. I stop crawling. Wince, as if getting ready for a foot or a fist to come flying out. Then: "James?" The word comes out so softly that, for a moment, I wonder if I've even said it. There's no answer. I creep forward again another inch or so. "James? Are you there? It's Bird again."

A rustling sound comes out from behind the organ and then quiets again, but I freeze, every nerve poised. Was that him? Or a mouse? Father Delaney did say it's been at least four years since anyone's been up here. And the place is covered with dust. It could definitely be a mouse. Maybe a whole nest of them. I saw a mouse once at Mr. Herron's place. It was outside, scurrying under the metal fence that separated the back of his yard from the neighbor's, and so small that if I had stepped on it, I might not have even felt it beneath my shoe. But I screamed like I'd just seen a cobra and ran back inside the house. Mr. Herron laughed about it for weeks afterward, but I didn't think it was funny. Mice make me crazy.

"Bird?" My name drifts out from the corner, faint as a shadow.

Oh my God. That was his voice. He's still here. This is still real. "Yeah. It's me."

"What are you doing here?"

Good question. Great question actually. I reach around my shoulder for the cross strap of my purse, lift it off as softly as possible. "I just. . . . I wanted to make sure you were okay."

Downstairs, the priest's voice rises: *"In the name of the Father, and the Son, and the Holy Spirit,"* followed by a murmur of amens. I scoot forward a little more as the collective movement of people rising to their feet sounds below. And all at once, there he is—right in front of me, so close this time that I can reach out and touch him.

Even in the dark, I can see that he is still in pain. His face, damp with sweat, is clenched in a grimace; the edges of his jaw are set tight. He's leaning against the wall, back arched, the green veins in his neck exposed, as if an invisible foot is pressing down on his chest. On the floor next to him is the gun. "You got any water?" he whispers.

The congregation downstairs begins chanting: *"We believe in one God, the Father Almighty, maker of heaven and earth . . ."*

Water? My hand moves inside my purse; something like relief floods over me as I pull out the half-empty bottle I bought for lunch earlier. James's eyes, slack and hooded, open wide at the sight of it; he reaches out instinctively, a man dying of thirst. Which, watching his Adam's apple pulse up and down the length of his throat as he swallows, he may very well be at this point. He drinks the whole thing in less than ten seconds, and then lets his arm drop, panting softly.

"Are you hurt?" I whisper.

He nods, the back of his head sliding up and down the wall.

"Where?"

He points to the lower half of his leg.

"Your leg?" I ask. "Or your foot?"

"Both." He pauses. "I tripped running up these steps and fell halfway back down the staircase. I can't believe I made it back up again. I heard something snap. I literally had to drag myself."

"Do you think it's broken?"

"Probably. I don't know. The whole thing just hurts. Bad. I can't move."

". . . We believe in the holy Catholic Church, the communion of saints, the forgiveness of sins, the resurrection of the body, and life everlasting. Amen."

I stare at him, not knowing what to say next. What the hell am I trying to do here? Be a hero? A friend? And how long have I been gone? Ma and Angus are going to start getting antsy, wondering where I am. One of the priests starts singing a hymn; other voices join in haltingly, gaining strength. "What are you going to do?" I ask.

"I don't know yet. I'm trying to figure that out." James lifts his head a little, looks straight at me. I don't recognize anything in his eyes anymore. They're blank, empty as tombs. "You tell anyone I'm here?"

I shake my head.

"You gonna?"

I look at the floor, stare at a dark, kidney-shaped stain on the carpet. Is it blood? Urine? I look back up. Shake my head again, no.

"Come back, then," he says. "Bring more water."

"I can't. I'll get in trouble."

"Please. Just for the water. I won't make it without water, Bird. Please."

I hesitate for a second. It wouldn't take long. Just another ten minutes. Maybe I could drop in quick tomorrow morning, before I go to Mr. Herron's. But then I think of Angus. The apartment with the skylight. And the security deposit. Thirteen more days until I never have to set foot in Mrs. Ross's office again. I shake my head. "I have a little boy now, James. And I'm already in trouble. I'm on probation. I can't do anything that'll get me in more trouble. I just can't. I'm sorry."

The last of the hymn drifts down the empty back of the church, a lost kite searching for the door.

"*You're* on probation?" James whispers. "For what?"

I drop my eyes, embarrassed. There is nothing he knows about me anymore either. We are two strangers, isolated by life and circumstance and the heavy hand of fate. So it goes. "I wrote some bad checks. It was stupid. I was desperate."

James studies me for a moment, is still studying me when I lift my eyes again, and for a moment I think of that day on the step when he leaned in, how, with his breath in my ear, every cell under my skin felt as if it were alive and singing. My heart pounds as I catch sight of the crescent moon scar along his eyebrow. It looks smaller somehow, and fainter, too, as if someone took an eraser and tried to rub it off his skin.

"Okay," James says. "Don't worry about it, then. I understand. It's okay."

It is? Yes, it is. Maybe he has help elsewhere. Another plan in place. He can't stay here forever. "You're not gonna stay here, are you?"

He looks down at the floor.

"Maybe you should just turn yourself in."

"No." He looks back up, shifting a little, his face wincing with pain, and then settles back against the wall. "No, I'm already looking at jail time for the fight. It'll be twice as much now that I've done this. I'll figure it out."

I nod, as if convincing myself that this is exactly what I want to hear. He will figure it out. This is his predicament. He's the one who's gotten himself into this. He'll have to be the one to figure out how to get himself back out of it. I crawl back toward the steps, start my way down, when I hear my name whispered again.

"Bird!"

"Yeah?"

James is leaning to one side, eyeing me carefully. "You hear anything about the other guy?" He hesitates. "That I hurt in the bar? Is he still alive?"

Alive? Jesus, what did he *do* to him? I stare at the floor, my brain racing. "I don't know. I haven't really been . . . listening to the news or anything. I haven't heard."

James tilts his head back, exposing his Adam's apple again. It is as large as a walnut, the skin over it rough and prickly. A sigh of resignation—or maybe just hopelessness—comes out of him. "Okay," he says. "All right. Thanks."

Chapter 14

The rest of the service is interminable, made even longer by the fact that I know James is less than fifty feet away, suffering hideously. The weird thing, though, is that knowing this doesn't make me want to go back up and help him. It just makes me want to run out of there as fast as possible, get as far away from the whole thing as I physically can. Forget I ever saw him, or that I just went back up and gave him water and admitted that I wanted to see how he was doing. Because now—whether I like it or not, whether I admit it or not—I've gotten involved. However extraneously, however unwillingly, I have crossed the line.

It's amazing how attractive my regular, humdrum life looks to me suddenly, how my plans for going to Target on my lunch break tomorrow—just to walk around the home section and look at curtains and bedsheets—have acquired a whole new appeal. The last time I was there, I saw a Ninja Turtle comforter with matching green sheets and a pillowcase. I was going to put that on layaway for Angus, along with some new pots and pans, maybe even a microwave. Those are the kind of boring, wonderful things I want to do tomorrow. Not this. Not now.

Not ever.

FATHER DELANEY IS thrilled to see us when the service finally comes to a close. He's out in the vestibule, saying good night to everyone, moving in for his signature hug as people file past. Everyone's still whispering since the tabernacle holding the Holy Eucharist is open, exposed for adoration over the next forty hours. Father Delaney and Ma exchange a knowing look before he grabs both of her hands and pulls her in. Then he turns to me. "It's wonderful to see you here, Bird." I smile and nod, watch as he gets down on one knee in front of Angus. "And you must be Gus. Your grandmother has told me all about you."

Angus looks up at me, a question mark on his face.

I put a hand on his shoulder. "This is Father Delaney, Angus. He's in charge of everything here."

"Oh." Angus looks down at the floor, shy suddenly. "Hi."

"You look just like your mother," Father Delaney says.

Angus looks up, horrified. "I do not! I'm a *boy*!"

Ma and Father Delaney laugh.

I squeeze Angus's shoulder. "It's okay, Boo. He means it as a good thing." I purse my lips together, look down at the floor.

Father Delaney looks over at me and pats me on the side of the shoulder. "I can't tell you how nice it was to look out and see you sitting there again, Bird."

"Thank you." I stare at his black sneakers, wonder if James can hear us down here, chatting away like old friends. Just another night at the neighborhood rectory. "Is the church open for the whole forty hours?" I hear myself ask suddenly, glancing back up at the priest. "Like . . . the whole time, I mean?"

"Well, it used to be," Father Delaney says. "That's the

whole point of the service, of course, for someone to be present during the entire forty hours. But we've had a few unfortunate incidents over the years, a break-in once, and then another very distressing one that involved an act of vandalism."

"Oh." I grimace in accordance with Ma, who murmurs something inaudible and shakes her head.

"So now we have to lock the church between midnight and five A.M.," Father Delaney continues. "Just for safety purposes." He beams in Ma's direction. "There are always a handful of people waiting at the doors when I unlock them in the morning. Always."

Ma looks down modestly at her shoes.

"I want to go home," Angus says, pulling on my hand. "I'm tired."

I could kiss him, right there, in front of everyone. "Me, too," I say. "Let's go."

I START COUNTING silently after we get back in the car, waiting for Ma to start in. It only takes her until seven. "So what did you think?"

"About what?"

"About the service." She looks out the window casually, adjusting the lapels of her coat, brushing at invisible crumbs with the back of her hand. Just a light conversation between mother and daughter.

"Not much, really. I don't remember much about the Forty Hours thing, but it seems to be like everything else. Nothing's changed."

She fiddles with the scarf around her neck, yanks the edges of it a little too roughly. "Meaning what?"

"Meaning nothing's changed, Ma. It's the same old story that it always was. Same prayers, same songs."

"And that's a bad thing?"

"What do you want me to tell you, Ma? That a bolt of lightning hit me during the homily and caused me to see the error of my ways?"

"That would be nice," Ma says dryly.

"Not gonna happen."

She shifts her purse onto her lap, touches a piece of hair lightly along the edge of her face. "So, where is this new place you and Angus are moving to?"

I rearrange my hands on the steering wheel, stare at the tail-lights of the car in front of me until they blur into puddles of red. "It's up at the lake."

"Moon Lake?"

"Mmm-hmm."

"How can you afford a place out there? The rent is astronomical."

I brake in front of a stop sign, look both ways. "It's an up-stairs apartment in a house. The people downstairs are renting it. It's not so much."

"How much?" Ma demands.

I shoot her a look that says *Stop* and *You're being rude* and *If you keep going like this, we are going to end up fighting in front of Angus for the second time in one night*, all in one slight creasing of my eyebrow, the twitch of my left eye, but she only cocks her head and says, "You don't want to tell me?"

"I can afford it, okay?" I step down on the gas. "I've already done the numbers. Don't worry about it."

Ma glances back at Angus, who is doing loop-de-loops with his plastic motorcycle along the edge of his booster seat, oblivious to our conversation. Small motor noises are coming out of his mouth; his brow is furrowed in concentration. "Is your seat belt on, young man?" Her voice is too harsh.

I sit up, look at Angus in the rearview mirror. His hands are still, the motorcycle forgotten. He is watching Ma anxiously. "Put your seat belt on, Boo. You know better." I watch as he sits back, his lower lip pushed out now, listen for the click of the belt.

"He knows about the apartment?" Ma asks in a low voice.

"Well, yeah," I lie. "Of course."

"He's seen it and everything? He likes it?"

"He hasn't seen it yet." I'm speaking with the least bit of volume necessary to make myself heard. "But I know he'll like it. He'll love it. It's on the lake, Ma. What's not to love?"

Ma rests an elbow on the window ledge, stares straight ahead. The windshield turns slick as a light rain begins. I click on my wipers. For a long moment, the only sound is the creak and sigh of the blades moving across the glass. "Two weeks?" she asks finally. "Is that when you said you'd be leaving?"

I nod, lick my lips. Why do I feel as if I am betraying her? It didn't feel like this when I left the first time. Back then, it was: *Good riddance. See you when I see you. Whenever that might be.* Which, in a way, is still how I feel.

Except maybe not as much. Maybe not as intensely as before.

"You can come visit us," I say, looking over at her. "I didn't really mean it, you know, when I said that earlier about staying out of my life. I was just angry."

"Oh, I know." Ma folds her hands, regarding them in her lap like little Easter eggs. Then she looks out the window. "I know."

Chapter 15

Angus's bedtime routine rarely, if ever, deviates from the following: a long, sudsy bath that involves me sitting at the edge of the tub for the first twenty minutes as he plays with his fleet of plastic tugboats, followed by the non-negotiable three-minute warning, after which he will scream and wail as I wash his hair and pour small buckets of water over his head to rinse him clean. After his bath I clean his ears gently with three separate Q-tips, count aloud to sixty as he brushes his teeth, and tuck him into bed before reading his two favorite books: *Curious George Goes to the Library* and *Imogen's Antlers*. Tonight, he reaches up as I close the second book and touches the edge of my face. "Mom?" he asks.

"Hmm?"

"Do you think Dopester is sad that we forgot to say hi to him this morning?"

I lean down, kiss him hard in the space between his ear and neck. "Maybe. But I think he gets a lot of hi's in the morning. From all different people. Besides, we can make it up to him tomorrow."

"How?"

"We'll pull over and wave at him. And yell real loud so that we make sure he can hear us. Okay?"

Angus's eyebrows are high on his forehead, his little fists tucked tightly under his chin. "Yeah. That'd be awesome."

"Okay." I smooth the lip of covers under his chin, kiss him once more. "Sweet dreams, baby."

Afterward, I slip into my room and lay down on my bed. Usually once he goes to sleep, I'll go downstairs and sit with Ma and watch TV for a while. She likes *Dancing with the Stars*, but she'll sit with me through an episode of *Law & Order*, too. Tonight though, the possibility of another tense or unkind word between us feels like too much. I just want to be alone.

Except that as soon as I get into bed and pull up the covers, all I can think about is not being alone. I swore off men after everything happened with Angus, telling myself that it would just be a lot of heartache for a little bit of pleasure. (And sometimes, not even that.) It wasn't that big of a deal for the first year, and maybe even for part of the second. Between taking care of Angus, working full-time, and then trying to get things straightened out with the probation office, there wasn't any time to bemoan the fact that I wasn't going out on any dates. Plus, if I did have any latent sexual desires lingering around, moving in with Ma definitely killed them off. Even if she was one of those progressive thinkers, Ma still wouldn't be the kind of person you could sit around and talk about getting laid with. When we rent the occasional movie, she'll jump up as soon as a woman starts unbuttoning her shirt in front of a man and disappear into the kitchen. Her aversion to anything remotely sexual both fascinates and infuriates me. It's like watching a child walk by an enormous chocolate cake and not only denying herself a piece of it but also refusing to acknowledge its existence. Once, a few months after Angus and I had moved in, I asked her if she'd ever considered dating again after Dad died.

"Of course not," she said, yanking at a piece of yellow yarn in her lap. She was knitting a sweater for Angus, yellow with blue trim around the neck.

"What do you mean, 'of *course* not'?" I pressed. "You're allowed to date, you know."

She glanced over at me with a bemused expression. "I know very well what I'm al*low*ed to, Bernadette. I'm just not interested."

"But . . ." I looked away, picked at a piece of lint on my jeans. "Don't you ever get lonely? Don't you ever want to be with someone again?" I stopped myself before I said "that way," or anything else that remotely hinted at a sex life, which I knew she would consider grossly disrespectful.

"Not particularly." She shrugged. "I have my friends at Saint Augustine's. We do a lot together."

"Yeah, but I'm talking about someone special. You know, someone who—" I stopped talking as Ma began shaking her head. "What?"

"I had someone special." She flicked her eyes over at the photograph of Dad on the mantelpiece. It was my favorite picture of him, dressed in a brown-striped, three-piece suit and straw hat. He was standing at the bottom of the front steps, his arm draped around Ma, who was bedecked in her Easter regalia: a light yellow dress with a lily corsage pinned just below her left shoulder, cream-colored pumps, and white wristlet gloves. They had only been married three years; it would be six more years before I came along, and they looked young and happy and confident with their place in the world. With each other. "He was all I needed."

"But he's gone, Ma. I'm talking about now. And all the years ahead."

"He was all I needed," she said, and just like that, I knew the conversation was over.

It was not that I ever looked for advice from Ma, but occasionally, as was the case just now, I was genuinely interested in trying to understand how she navigated the details of her own life. Not because I wanted to follow suit, but because I thought it might help me see her in a kinder, more appreciative light. But the information she did volunteer was so foreign to me that it just left me frustrated. Who in their right mind would willingly spend the next fifty years of their life celibate? And *why*?

Some nights—like right now—the thought of having to go another ten minutes without sex creates a physical desperation in me that is so intense I feel like I might cry out. The longing to be touched is so palpable that I can feel it in my groin.

Instead, I turn over in bed, reach for my earphones, and put them in. "Back in Black" blares so loud that I can feel my eardrums buzz. I stare up at the ceiling, as Angus Young starts screaming about how long it takes to get to the top, and lay there for a long time, listening to the whole album. In between songs, I close my eyes and fantasize about a man undressing me, one article of clothing at a time—shirt, bra, pants, underwear, socks—until I am completely naked. He sits on the edge of the bed, pulls me toward him. I am still standing as he leans forward, his lips moving over the outside of my ribs, his tongue circling my nipples, the outer rim of my belly button. His hands snake around the back of me, sliding up until they reach my shoulders and then settling in the small, hollow spaces of my collarbone. They drop lower, over my breasts, lingering, kneading, and then move down to the outside of my hips.

I can't see his face, but it doesn't bother me. He can remain faceless forever, as long as he keeps touching me, as long as his skin stays warm against mine, his arms around the small of my back, lifting me up.

Higher.

And then higher still.

"MOM!" I SIT up, startled, as Angus calls my name from down the hall. "Mommy! *Please!*"

I tear the covers off, race into his room. He's sitting up in bed, tears streaming down his cheeks, his hands like outstretched stars. "Here I am, Boo," I say, gathering him into me. "Here I am." His little body is warm and trembling. "What's wrong, baby? Are you sick?"

He shakes his head, pulls away from me. "I was calling you for*ev*er. But you wouldn't come."

"Oh, Angus, I didn't hear you, honey. I was sleeping. Why didn't you just come into my room?"

He looks down fearfully at the rug. "I was scared."

Scared? Of what? The only thing Angus has ever been scared of was the pool last summer after he accidentally fell into the deep end. After that, he didn't go near the water, not even when I bought him a life jacket. "What scared you?" I ask. "Did you have another bad dream?"

He shakes his head, embarrassed. "The dark," he says. "It's so . . . dark."

I pull him in again, closer this time, stroke the sides of his hair, run my finger over the tip of his ear. "Okay, baby. It's okay."

Two parallel lines of pain in the back of my throat begin to ache as I hold him close. Is it possible to protect him against everything out there? From everything in here? His heart flutters beneath his thin pajama top, a tiny, trapped bird.

"Can I sleep with you tonight?" Angus asks, his mouth

buried against the side of my shoulder. "Please? Even though I'm big, and Nanny gets mad, and . . ."

"Yes." I slide my hand back inside his. "Come on. You absolutely can."

Angus falls asleep immediately, but I lay there for a long time, just looking at him. The hair around his ears is a little shaggy and some of the curls in the front need to be thinned out. I'll have to take him back to Kuts for Kids where he sits in the snail-shaped chair, and Randy the beautician gives him Tootsie Rolls afterward. There's a scratch behind his ear that I haven't seen before; it's an angry red color, and deep, too. Where did that come from? Is someone being rough with him at school? Jeremy? I'll kill him. I will. Or at least get Angus switched out of his classroom. No one's going to screw with my kid.

Why has he started to be afraid of the dark? Could it be that the anxiousness he has been feeling about Jeremy is manifesting itself this way? Maybe he will start to wet the bed next. Or have those night terrors I heard about once. I sit up suddenly. It was James who told me about night terrors one day, after admitting that he'd had them as a kid. We were behind the Burger Barn again, in our usual place on the step, the sky awash with a thin, lemony light.

"What are they?" I'd asked. "Like nightmares?"

"Sort of." He shrugged. "Except that nightmares happen during the real deep stage of sleep, where you dream. Night terrors actually happen while you're moving from the light stage of sleep into the deep one. So technically, you're still asleep, but awake, too." He nodded toward the small book next to him. "At least, that's what this book says."

"If you were asleep," I'd asked, "how do you know you had them?"

"My mom told me. She was really concerned about it. Plus, my pajamas would be soaking wet from all the sweating I did. She'd have to change me out of them, give me dry ones so that I could go back to sleep."

"God," I said. "That sounds really intense. What were you afraid of?"

He stared at something in the distance for a moment. "My dad, mostly. He was hard on my mom and me. Too hard. I was terrified of him, growing up. Which led to a lot of other fears, I guess." He withdrew his cigarettes from his back pocket and snorted softly. "I'm still afraid of the dark."

I almost laughed, and then caught myself. "Not really, though, right?"

He looked over at me with an expression that I could not read—disappointment, maybe? Sadness?—and bent over to light his cigarette. "Not like I used to be," he said finally. "I don't have to sleep with a light on or anything. And I can walk down a dark street, of course, or any alleyway. But nighttime in general still freaks me out a little. I think it's because that's when my father used to start in on us. He'd come home from the bar every night just as the sun was starting to set, and, like clockwork, all hell would break loose. He'd start yelling, screaming, throwing things." James reached up and fingered the scar along his eyebrow. "Got this one night after he threw a chair at my mother. A piece of the leg splintered off and cut me in the face." He shrugged, as if brushing off the memory. "I don't know. Even now, when it gets dark, it feels sometimes like I'm still waiting for all that chaos to start up again." He inhaled deeply on his cigarette, and this time, when he exhaled, I noticed that his lower lip trembled slightly. "It's not rational, of course. I know that." He shook his head. "The mind is a funny thing. The things it holds close, the things it chooses to forget. There's no rhyme or reason to it, when you think about it."

We sat there for a moment, the two of us, James smoking, me nibbling at the edge of my thumb. It occurred to me that he had just shared an incredibly intimate detail with me, an extraordinary gesture, really, when I thought about it, like a secret shared between best friends, or something a husband might tell a wife. It felt almost like a gift, and yet I had not even known I wanted it until this very moment. I wondered if I'd ever be brave enough to return the favor.

"You have a nice father?" he asked suddenly, looking at me out of the corner of one eye.

"Real nice." I nodded. "Too nice."

James smiled. "Too nice? How is that possible?"

"He's dead," I said flatly. "Dead people are always too nice."

He turned and looked at me then, really looked at me, while bringing the cigarette to his lips again. I stared right back at him, wondering if his mother had taken him to the hospital after his head had been split open, or if it had had to heal on its own. Why couldn't I bring myself to ask him? What was it that I didn't want to know?

"You're a really unusual girl," he said finally.

I blushed and looked down again at my boots, fingering the dirt lodged alongside the heel. His words felt like a slap, something Ma might say to me, but wrapped in a compliment, too. Or maybe it was just the tone of voice he'd used—a mixture of curiosity and bemusement. We hadn't kissed yet—that would happen the following week—but I could already feel myself being drawn to him in a magnetic, almost mysterious way.

"I don't mean it as a bad thing," James continued. "I think unusual is great actually. It sure beats being a conformist. And it's a hell of a lot more interesting."

"You can say that again." I nodded.

"And it's a hell of a lot more interesting," James repeated.

We laughed at the same time and I realized as he opened his mouth and tipped his head back that it was the first time I had heard him do such a thing. Laugh, I mean. It was a beautiful sound, flush with feeling, and I carried it around with me for the rest of the day like a tiny stone in my pocket.

NEXT TO ME, Angus breathes deeply, his nostrils flaring slightly with the intake of each breath. I reach over, tuck a curl behind his ear, and then slide my hand under my pillow. "I'm going to go help someone tomorrow, Boo," I whisper. "He's trapped, and he's afraid of the dark, and I'm going to go help him."

Chapter 16

I get up early the next morning before Ma gets back from her hour of reverence at church, grab an old backpack from my closet, and start stuffing it with items from the refrigerator. A few apples, lots of bottled waters, a couple of yogurts. I cut the remaining three-quarters of Ma's meat loaf into thick slices and wrap them in Saran, slap together six peanut butter and jelly sandwiches, and throw in two more bottles of water, just to be safe. I pause before tossing in Dad's big green flashlight, which is still hanging on a hook in the pantry. It's got to be pitch black up in that choir loft at night, especially after Father Delaney turns off all of the overhead lights. But with the Forty-Hour service in full swing, a light this big would be too much of a risk. I leave it on the hook and root around in the kitchen drawer until I find what I'm looking for: two of Angus's toy flashlights that Ma got him for Christmas last year. They need batteries, but they are small, the size of cigars, and the light they provide is pale and watery. Perfect for the choir loft.

I've decided to leave Mr. Herron's place early, and call Jane

to tell her I'll be a little late. I'll be back over at her place tonight anyway, helping her with the play set, so she shouldn't
mind. In between, I'll sneak into the church and give James
the water and food. I have no idea how many people will be in
the church itself—do they have to sign up for something like
this? Fill out a chart to make sure all the required hourly spaces
are filled? —but hopefully no one will be lingering anywhere
near the vestibule. That's all I need: some old geezer stuffing
the novena box, pestering me with questions while I'm trying
to angle my way upstairs.

Ma rushes in through the front door, just as I'm zipping
everything up. Her face is pale, the whites of her eyes shot
through with little streaks of red. "Oh my goodness, Bird! Did
you hear the news about that man you used to work with at the
Burger Barn?"

My heart thumps in my ears. They found him. "No," I say
carefully. "What news?"

"He es*caped*! From prison!" Ma takes off her coat as she
talks, hangs it up on the hook in the hallway. "Well, she didn't
actually *make* it to prison. They're saying he escaped on the
way. That he got out of the *car* somehow. Can you imagine?
He just kicked his way out of a police vehicle and ran off! With
the officer's gun, too! And no one's been able to find him since!"

"Wow." I walk over to the front door to put the knapsack
down and then, thinking better of it, sling it over my shoulder.
My hands are trembling. "Are you sure it was him?"

"Oh, I'm positive." Ma heads for the coffeepot, starts measuring grounds into the white paper sleeve. "To think that he
worked here in this house, and at that burger place, too, *inches*
away from you!" She turns to look at me, the edge of an ac-
cusation in her voice. "What's his name again?"

I adjust the backpack against my shoulder again. It's surprisingly heavy. "James."

"Right." Ma turns back to the coffee. "James Rittenhouse." She shakes her head. "That man just about murdered some helpless drunk in a bar and now he's on the run. Unbelievable. Well, he's never going to last out there. You know how these things end."

"How what things end?"

"Oh, these 'men on the lam' kinds of things. These es*cape* ordeals. They always end badly."

"Since when have you ever seen something like this *end*, Ma?" I demand. "Has there ever even been a prisoner escape in New Haven before?"

Ma stops pouring water into the coffeemaker, turns around and looks at me. "Don't get de*fen*sive about it, Bernadette."

"I'm not getting defensive about it. It's just that you always act like you know everything, when you don't know anything about it at all."

She flutters her eyes at me, turns back to the coffeepot. "I'll have you know that I got the entire story firsthand from a reporter who was out in front of the church this morning."

A flash of heat travels up my arms. "A reporter? At the church?"

Ma nods vigorously. "From the *Times Leader*. He was interviewing all of us there, even Father Delaney."

"Why?" The question comes out in a squeak. I clear my throat. Someone's seen something. They must have. "Why would a reporter be looking for information in a church?"

"*I* don't know. Maybe because we're the only people a*wake* at this hour. Actually, they were talking to the people in the doughnut shop across the street, too, and then they came over when they saw us walking down the front steps of the church.

Don't ask me what they were doing with the people at the doughnut shop—half of them don't have *teeth* in their head, much less a brain—but what do I know? My *point* is that the reporter has been on the case since it broke yesterday. He's been asking everyone." She makes a clucking sound along the roof of her mouth. "It's just so sad. The whole thing. It's so awful."

"Did you tell the reporter anything?"

"Me? What would I have to say? That was the first I'd even heard of it! I don't know any of the details." She shakes her head. "Although Mona did say that her sister-in-law told her that the victim's in pretty bad shape."

A flicker inside. "Do they know who it is? The victim, I mean?"

"No names released," Ma says importantly. "The papers always try to protect the privacy of victims, you know."

"But he's still alive?"

"I think so. Although they're saying it's touch and go. He's still in intensive care, I think, and he'll have to undergo surgery, I'm sure. If he dies, that Rittenhouse boy is really going to be in for it. I mean, he'll be looking at a murder charge!" She punches the little red button on the coffeemaker, grabs the newspaper off the counter, and sits down in one of the kitchen chairs. "Just goes to show, you never really know someone, do you? Even if you did work with them. My *good*ness."

I roll my eyes, move toward the steps. "I'm gonna go wake up Angus."

"You want me to take Mr. Herron for you today?" Ma calls out behind me. "And Jane? Just to switch things up?"

"No." I whirl around, one foot on the bottom step. "No, I'm fine doing them today. Plus, Jane wants me to come back tonight and do a little extra work around her place. Whose place are you scheduled to do?"

"Violet Manning's," Ma says. "Over on the east side. What extra work does Jane want you to do?"

"She's putting together a play set for her kids. I told her I'd help her. She's paying me extra. You okay with Violet? She's an easy one, isn't she?"

"Oh, yeah." Ma's eyes scan the contents of the paper, glossing over the headlines. "All she ever wants me to do is re-arrange her good china. I think she's getting a little bit of the Alzheimer's. Poor soul."

"I'M READY," ANGUS says on our way over to preschool.

"Ready for what?"

"To tell you about Something Special Day."

I bite down hard on my bottom lip, glance at him in the rearview mirror. He looks so adorable dressed in the little white-and-blue striped polo shirt and navy pants Ma got him a few months ago. His dark hair is swept to one side, and a tiny curl like an apostrophe sits just above his eyebrows. Even the green-and-purple sneakers—which clash with everything—give him a certain level of panache. Nothing bad—nothing even remotely negative—should be allowed to come anywhere near this level of perfection.

"Okay," I say hopefully. "Go ahead."

Angus inhales, raising both shoulders as he does, and then sighs so deeply that I almost drive off the road. "It wasn't *terrible*," he says finally. "Jeremy didn't *laugh*."

"Okay. Well, that's good, right?"

"But he didn't pay at*ten*tion." Angus is wringing his hands, kneading them into the front of his blue pants like they are some kind of bread dough. "He stared out the window the whole time. And he picked his nose."

"Ewww . . ." I say, trying to catch his eye in the mirror:

Please laugh, Angus. "He picked his nose? That's so gross!" Angus doesn't laugh. He doesn't even crack a smile. "How about the gum trick?" I try. "Come on. Tell me that didn't blow his mind!"

"He didn't care," Angus says softly. "At *all*."

I stare at the dirty rear window of the car ahead of me as it brakes for a red light, the digital clock on the bank building, which reads 8:56, the green-and-white street banners fluttering in the breeze. On the corner, a woman in pink sweat pants and a white T-shirt is dragging a screaming child down the street. The child is very young, two or three at the most, dressed in denim overalls, a yellow T-shirt, and miniature sneakers. Her tiny pink face, contorted into one extended howl, is a map of anguish, and even behind my window, I can hear her sobs. I look away, close my eyes, remember the rage that used to build inside me like a growing storm when Angus's cries reached that level, and nothing I did could assuage them. More than once, I'd had to leave him screaming in his crib and shut the door while I stepped outside, my hands gripping the black railing of the fire escape outside my apartment until they stopped trembling. It was the helplessness imbued within that type of cry that unglued me, the helplessness, and the recognition, as if something very small and distant within myself remembered it and understood that until I learned to fend for myself, it would get me nowhere. Even now, the sound can create a wave of despair. I step on the gas as the light turns green and take a hard left at the corner, leaving the child and mother behind.

"Oh, honey," I say. "I'm sure he cared."

"He didn't." Angus is resolute. "Not even one little bit."

I pull over then as the green house on the corner comes into view, and edge the car along the curb until the gnomes can be seen from the backseat.

"Well, did anybody pay attention?" I ask, putting the car in park and turning around in my seat.

Angus's dour expression softens slightly. "Miss Annie did," he says. "And Raymond, too."

"Well, there you go! And did they think your shoes were cool?"

"Yeah." He sticks his legs out straight and taps the sides of his shoes together. "Especially Miss Annie. She said they were radical."

"Radical? *Radical?* Are you serious? Do you even know what radical *means?*"

"It means amazing!" Angus's face has finally split open into a grin; his tiny white teeth look like fat pieces of rice.

"Triple amazing!" I lean over, squeeze his knee. "Like a hundred *times* triple amazing!"

Angus moves over until his nose is pressed up against the window. "Can we go into the garden this morning, Mom? Just to say hi? Since we forgot yesterday?"

"No, Angus. That's someone's house. They wouldn't like it if we started walking around in their garden. But you can lean out the window. Yell superloud, too, so Dopester can hear you."

He gets up on his knees carefully as the window goes down, clutches the edge of the door with small pink hands. "Hi, Dopester!" he yells, waving to the plastic garden figurine. "Hope you have a good day outside!"

I let him go on a bit—he launches into a short anecdote about Miss Annie and the Lego set at school—before tapping him on the shoulder again. "Okay, that's enough. We have to go."

"Mom?"

"Yeah?" I buckle him back in and pull the car out into traffic again.

"Do you think Dopester knows it's me? I mean, when I yell? Do you think he knows my voice?"

"I do." I nod my head somberly. "I absolutely think he knows."

Angus sits back against the seat, folding his hands in his lap, and sighs contentedly.

When we get to preschool, I lift him out of the backseat and then straddle his legs around my waist as I walk into the building. He's way too big to be held like this, but I don't care. I carry him all the way to his classroom.

He lets me, too.

IT'S WARMER TODAY than it was yesterday, although the sun has disappeared behind a sea of metallic clouds. I take my jacket off in the car, throw it in the passenger seat next to my knapsack. I still haven't come up with an excuse yet for my planned early departure from Mr. Herron's, and it's making me nervous. You wouldn't think someone like Mr. Herron could get me anxious; he's nice enough. And hell, he can't see anything. But he can get ornery. Mean, even, on occasion. It's a meanness that comes out of nowhere, too, a thorn suddenly beneath a carpet of petals. Like the one morning last year when I had to leave less than an hour after arriving at his house because the preschool called to tell me Angus had a fever. I could've called Ma. She would have left the place she was working in a heartbeat to go pick him up. But Angus acts very particular when he gets sick. He clings to me like a little koala, nestling his head along the inside of my arm and drifting in and out of sleep until the end of the day when I finally put him down in his own bed. I couldn't bear not to be the one to give him that.

"You shouldn't be workin' at all, if you gotta run out like that," Mr. Herron said when I explained the situation to him.

"I have a little boy," I said, putting my coat on, searching for my gloves. "I explained that to you when I first started. He's sick. I have to go pick him up. I'll be back tomorrow to make up my work."

"Have someone else get him," Mr. Herron said. "His father."

"His father isn't around." I yanked on my other glove, reached for my bag.

"Ah. You one of those loosey-gooseys." It was a statement, not a question. I stared at him for a moment, disbelieving what he had just said, watching the torrent of profanity stream like a black ribbon through my head. *Youfuckingjudgmentalasshole.* I opened my mouth to say it, too. And then I closed it again and walked out the front door. We never spoke of it again. But there's that side to him—a thin, dark side—that I know is in there. And I have to be careful.

He's in the kitchen today, fiddling around with that ugly plant in the corner, when I come in. "Bird?"

"Hey, Mr. Herron." Nothing on the stove today, thank God. But the radio is on, tuned to a talk show, the volume bracingly loud. It's impossible not to listen: *". . . I won't even take my children to the park!"* It's a woman's voice, slightly frantic. *"The police keep saying they're doing everything they can, but I want to know what that means exactly. Where are they looking? What's the next step?"*

"Well, Amy, I know you're not the only person out there who feels this way," a male voice concurs. *"We all want answers. If a scumbag like James Rittenhouse can kick his way out of the back of a police car and then somehow disappear for the next twenty-four hours with a gun, what does that say about the capabilities of our police department? Just how safe are we in New Haven?"*

I lean over, turn down the volume.

"Hey!" Mr. Herron says. "I was listening to that."

"I know. I just need a second." I pull out a chair, sit down on the other side of the table. "Listen, I have to leave a little early today."

He frowns, the lines on both sides of his face sliding down, as if pulled by a string. "How early?"

"An hour."

"How come?" A pile of dead leaves is lying on the table next to the pot; his fingers are moving inside the plant, feeling, reaching, plucking.

I think fast. "I have to take my mother to the doctor."

"She's not feeling well?"

"No."

Mr. Herron nods. "Okay," he says. "I'll have to tell Arthur to dock you, though."

I sigh, pressing my hands flat against the table and stand up. "Well, I was thinking I could come back. And work a little extra, even."

"Extra?" Mr. Herron repeats. The pile of leaves on the table is getting bigger. They're dry and crinkled looking, like forgotten cocoons. "For what? You got some kind of nervous energy you need to burn off?"

"Bills actually." I stand up. Talking about finances is one of my least favorite things to do. Especially with a miser like Mr. Herron. "I have one that's due on Thursday, and I'm trying to get it covered."

"What kind of bill?"

"A security deposit. For a new apartment."

Mr. Herron's fingers stop moving. "You moving out on your mother?" He loves Ma, mostly because she makes his bed the way he likes it, with the corners pulled extra tight, a lip of blanket folded over at the top. I forget little details like that sometimes. Ma never does.

"Well, yeah." I rub my finger absently along the grain of the table. "You know. I've been living with her for a while now. I'm twenty-five years old. It's time."

Mr. Herron doesn't say anything. He puts his hands back inside the plant and resumes plucking. "I got a few odds and ends you could help me with," he says finally. "Out in the garden. You interested?"

"That's perfect." I push my chair back in, reach over, and turn the volume back up on the radio.

"*. . . and I think they should look into bringing the National Guard in or something.*" Another irate female voice from the radio. "*I mean, come on, people! We're talking about a friggin' psychopath here! He stomped some guy nearly to death, kicked his way out of a law enforcement vehicle,* and *stole a gun! What the hell are we* doing?"

I bolt out of the kitchen, out of hearing range, and head upstairs to start cleaning.

Any more talk like that, and I'll change my mind again.

Chapter 17

Cleaning Mr. Herron's bathroom can be tricky, since I have to take care not to touch any of the numerous bottles of medication lined up haphazardly along the sink countertop. I made the fatal mistake once of pushing them all to one side, aligning them neatly against the wall beneath the medicine cabinet—and heard about it for weeks afterward. "You don't touch the meds," he'd said on my following visit. "Don't ever, ever touch the meds. I know exactly where they are at all times." Now I spray around them, aiming the nozzle awkwardly in and among the tiny bottles, and wipe it down as best I can. His bedroom is next, an easy job since he moved into the spare bedroom a few months ago. He doesn't like the big bedroom he used to share with his wife anymore, he told me once, without elaborating further. Maybe it's too big. Maybe it makes him sad, thinking of the space she used to occupy next to him. I make the narrow twin bed, pulling the sheets tight and smoothing down the top cover, which is a soft gray color like the sky outside.

Dusting comes next, which goes quickly, too. Aside from

his bed, the only other items in Mr. Herron's room include a rectangular bureau centered with a mirror, a small, sturdy rocking chair, and a bedside table, each of them as pristine as a monk's. With the exception of the Happy Meal toys, lined up like a weird little army along the far edge of the bureau, the room is devoid of any personal items. No book or water glass on the bedside table, not even a pillow in the rocker. "Fuss free," as Ma would call it. An in-and-out job. Still, I move the feather duster slowly, careful to avoid the Happy Meal toys. God only knows what he'd say if he knew I knocked two of them over yesterday. Probably dock me another hour's pay.

The radio is still playing as I head downstairs for the vacuum. Some lady is shrieking about the security of the prison systems. *"I mean, don't we pay enough taxes to expect that our basic safety in this town won't be compromised?"* Mr. Herron is sitting in one of the kitchen table chairs, gazing out the window.

"You're still in here?" In all the time I've been working for Mr. Herron, I've never known him to sit down at the kitchen table and listen to the radio. How long does this program run anyway? "I thought you'd be out in the garden."

The vacant look in Mr. Herron's face eases, as if coming back from somewhere far away. "I been sittin' here listening."

"I can see that." Behind the kitchen curtains, the light is opaque, like milk.

"Amazing how sure people think they are about things."

I nod, tap the wall lightly. "Yeah."

"And when they find that sonofabitch, they should throw him into solitary," the woman says. *"I'm serious. Teach him a lesson about following the laws in this country. Maybe then he'll learn how to respect authority."*

"Amazing." Mr. Herron snorts and shakes his head. "I'd like to see her try to spend ten *minutes* in solitary."

The vacuum is all the way at the other end of the hall, and I still have the entire downstairs to tackle before I head out to Jane's house, but something about the pensiveness in Mr. Herron's voice makes me pause. Linger, even.

"The Koreans had a special kind of solitary," Mr. Herron says.

I lean against the doorjamb, stare at the wiry strands of white interspersed throughout his gray hair, try to imagine what Mr. Herron might have looked like in an army uniform. Tall, straight, dark, neat. Clipped fingernails. Maybe a mustache. A cap fitted just over his ears.

"We were caught in a surprise attack at the Chosin Reservoir. Winter of 1950. Damn near froze our balls off waiting for them to advance, and then the bastards came up from behind."

"I thought you said you were a cook." I bite the skin along the edge of my thumb. "What were you doing fighting if you were supposed to be in charge of the meals?"

"You think the Koreans cared if I *cooked* or not when they took all of us prisoner?"

My hand drops from my mouth. "*You* were a prisoner?"

"Three months. Just inside the 38th parallel. Pyoktong Camp. Don't talk about it much. Not real pretty stuff." He stretches out his hands, displaying them for some reason, as if he can see them. The knuckles are dry and gnarled like miniature tree trunks.

"Holy shit, Mr. Herron." I move out of the hallway, sit down in the empty chair across from him. "What was *that* like?"

He doesn't answer right away and I wince, thinking I've crossed a line. Or that he's annoyed I've taken a seat when I'm supposed to be working. "I'm sorry," I start, getting back up. "I shouldn't—"

"Oh, sit down," he interrupts. "Hell, I brought it up."

I sit back down.

"They were a sadistic bunch. Got their rocks off listening to us scream. Beg. Cry for our mothers. For mercy."

I bite my lower lip, watching him.

"They didn't separate us right away. Shoved me and another guy named Randy Cutlass into a hut with a dung heap for a floor. Randy was hysterical, crying and screaming. He was convinced that we were minutes away from being executed. He was just a baby. I don't think he'd even reached his nineteenth birthday yet. He'd joined the army right after graduating from high school. Everyone called him Randy-Kid." Mr. Herron stops for a moment, tapping his middle finger against the tabletop.

One.

Two.

Three.

"I got him to calm down a little. I kept telling him that the more noise he made, the quicker he was gonna piss off the guards, and the more trouble we'd be in. He quieted down some, but he never, not once, for the entire three days we were in that shithole, stopped crying. I mean, it went on and on . . . This goddamned whimpering, these whispery *sobs*, like he was choking on something. It was like being trapped in a cage with a sick cat. I was starting to lose it. And one day—it was probably the third day—I just hauled off and decked him." He pauses, gazing past my face at something only he can see. "Screamed at him to shut up. Split his lip right down the middle. There was blood all over the place."

"Oh, Mr. Herron."

"Don't 'oh, Mr. Herron' me." His face darkens. "I'm telling you this because it's what happened. Because people don't know and maybe they should." He runs his hand along the surface of the table. His wedding ring makes a faint scraping sound, an echo from the past.

"Did he stop crying after that?" I hesitate to ask the question, but I want to know.

Mr. Herron shakes his head. "He just stared at me afterward with these big, leaky eyes. Like he couldn't believe I'd actually hurt him, you know? I was s'posed to be on his side, not the other way around." He takes a deep breath, exhales loudly through his nose.

"They brought us out of the hut not too long after that, led us into a big room with white lights, a long table. A bunch of Korean officials sat on the other side of the table, waiting. Bunch of candy-ass pricks. They wanted to know our battle plans. What we would've done if they hadn't captured us. Randy-Kid didn't know how to handle it. He just started blabbing all over the place, telling them everything he knew, which wasn't a hell of a lot, really, since he was just a private. They didn't believe him, prolly 'cause he was crying so hard again they couldn't understand nothing. They gave him a hard time about it, too. The crying, I mean. Kept beatin' him around the head, poking him with a sharpened bamboo stick, to get him to stop. He just cried harder, though, said all he wanted to do was go home to his mother. I kept looking at him, trying to get him to look at me, so I could tell him to shut up again, but he was gone. I mean, the kid was in no-man's-land. The things coming out of his mouth weren't even making sense. Finally they dragged him out back. I could hear him sobbing and screaming and then a gun went off and everything was quiet."

I press the side of my fist against my mouth.

"I went ape-shit after that." Mr. Herron's lined face hardens. "My hands were tied with wire behind my back, but I hauled

off and kicked one of the guards in the face. I prolly broke
the bastard's jaw in three different places. The guy was on the
floor, screaming. They took me out back, too, after that. And
you know what? I didn't care. I was sure they were going to
kneel me down the way they'd made Randy-Kid kneel there
in the mud and shoot me in the back of the head, but I didn't
give a rat's ass. Getting killed didn't seem so terrible anymore.
Not after what had just happened."

I hold my breath, waiting for what will come next, wondering if I want to know. My breathing is shallow, the edges of
my face hot.

"But they didn't kill me. Obviously. They put me in solitary.
A hole in the ground, way the hell outside of camp, no wider
than two or three men. Board on top, nailed down shut. I don't
know how long I was down there. Three, four weeks, maybe
more. I tried to keep track of time by looking at the slats of
light through the board when the sun came up. Slept standing
up, leaning against one side of the hole. Meals were a dry bun
that they threw down once a day. If they remembered. Sometimes they didn't. It rained once for an entire day and night
and the hole filled up to my knees with water. All the skin on
the bottom of my feet came off. I got dysentery, a fever so bad
I thought my skin might split apart from the heat beneath it.
But that wasn't the worst part. The worst part was the silence.
For as terrible as Randy-Kid's crying and screaming had been,
I would have traded it quicker'n anything for that silence. It
was like being suffocated by something that didn't even exist,
living in that hole, inside that silence. Like the whole world,
even God, had forgotten about me."

He jerks his chin toward the radio in the corner. "I don't
blame that guy out there one bit for runnin'. There's nothing
worse than being locked up in some cage like an animal. Even

if you do deserve it. Nothin' worse in the world." He taps the side of his head with a finger. "That boy knows that. That's why he's runnin'. Not 'cause he thinks he's innocent. 'Cause he don't want to lose his dignity. His humanity."

Neither of us says anything for a moment. The only sound in the room is the squeak of Mr. Herron's chair as he leans back on it.

It takes me a while to find my voice. And when I do, it comes out high-pitched, like a little girl's. "How'd you get out of the hole?"

"American troops came in and razed the camp." His voice is tighter than twine. "Killed every one of 'em bastards. You know, that was probably the moment I was most scared."

"When you were getting rescued?"

"Waiting to get rescued. I could hear everyone running around in the distance, the sound of guns firing, bodies falling, and I screamed and screamed from the bottom of that hole, but no one came, not for a good ten minutes or so. Damn if I didn't die of a heart attack right then and there, thinking they were all goin' to head out and leave me behind." He inhales. Deeply, like a man coming up from the bottom of the ocean. "But they heard me. At least one of 'em did. Got me on a plane with all the rest and took us back."

"God. I bet you were glad to be home."

"Yep." Mr. Herron nods slowly. "It was good to be back. I found a job, met my wife a few years later, had us some kids."

"And . . ." I pause, not wanting to say the wrong thing. "And things were okay for you after that?"

He moves his eyes in my direction. "Well, I'm eighty-two years old, and I'm sitting here at my kitchen table, telling you about Randy-Kid. So you tell me."

I drop my eyes, stare at the ribboned pattern in the wood surface. There is nothing to say, no possible reply to give such a statement. What was it that James said about the things the brain chooses to remember and the things it chooses to forget? What parts of that experience has Mr. Herron left behind, whole swaths of memory that he will never admit to anyone, even himself?

"You think they'll find that guy who ran off yesterday?" I hear myself say.

Mr. Herron shrugs. "They say he's hurt. I guess it depends on just how bad."

"What do you mean?"

"Well, if he's bleedin' and don't have any medical attention, that ain't good. If he wants to live, he'll probably drag hisself to a hospital somewhere for help. So they'll find him then, I guess."

"What if he isn't bleeding all that much?" I ask. "What if he just has broken bones or something?"

Mr. Herron shrugs again. "Broken bones won't kill him. He's just gotta find someone who can set 'em. And then keep runnin', I guess."

I can't ask any more questions. It'll look too suspicious. But then, like a gift, Mr. Herron says, "You can set a bone with just about anything. My two buddies and I set a guy's leg with half a broomstick once, back in the camp."

"A broomstick?"

"We snapped it in half, pushed the sides in tight on either side of his leg, and then tied 'em up. You gotta immobilize it. Keep it straight, so's it can't move at all. Helps with the pain, too."

Another silent moment passes.

Mr. Herron rocks back and forth, while I struggle to remain upright.

"Boy, Mr. Herron, and I thought the only thing you knew how to do was plant flowers." I laugh a little, stand up again. My head feels light, like I've just sucked the contents of a helium balloon.

Mr. Herron stands up, too. "Oh, I can plant flowers," he says, nodding. "Waiting for them to bloom, though . . . well, that's a whole other story."

Chapter 18

I stop at a Lowe's Hardware after leaving Mr. Herron's, and ask the salesclerk behind the front desk—a red-haired kid with blue rubber bands on his teeth and a name tag that says JERRY—if I can have help getting two pieces of lumber.

"Sure," he says. "What size?" He's so tall that his shoulders slouch when he walks. He has big ears that stick out, and his chin is covered with red, pustular acne. I doubt he's even finished high school yet. I wonder if Randy-Kid looked anything like him.

"Um, I'm not really sure. I want to build something for my son."

"Okay." Jerry gives me a look out of the corner of his eye. "Do you know what you want to build?"

I shove my hands inside my jeans; they feel moist and clammy. "Um . . . well, really, it's just for him to build something. Mostly for knocking around, you know? He's five, he likes to pretend he's a carpenter. I just want to get him some nice pieces of wood. Let him do his own thing."

"Uh-huh." Jerry leads me down an enormous aisle flanked

with stacks of lumber. The floor is littered with dusty foot-prints; a bubblegum wrapper lies adrift on one side. There are pale wood strips as long as flagpoles, shorter, darker ones no bigger than a foot. "We have some nice furring strips I could cut down for you," he says. "I can make them whatever size you want."

"Okay. That sounds good." I wonder if he has any friends in high school. He must. All kids these days have friends, don't they? I squeeze my hands into fists, stare at the dirty tile around my feet.

"This look okay?" Jerry asks.

"Maybe a little bigger. Like, half of me?" I position the side of my hand against my thigh. "From here down, maybe?"

"So basically you're looking for a couple of two-by-fours."

"Right."

"Okay. Be right back."

I pace after Jerry disappears into a back room, cross and uncross my arms in front of me. I wonder if I'm on a hidden camera. Later, when it's all over, and the police review the tape, they will come to question Jerry. I imagine him saying something like, "You know, I *thought* she was acting weird. I couldn't put my finger on it, but she was all jumpy, talking about building something for her kid. You mean, it was for the *guy*?" I find a corner nearby, press myself inside the walls as tightly as possible.

Just in case.

"All set," Jerry says, appearing suddenly with two pieces of wood. "These look okay?"

"They look great." I step out of the corner, run my hand up the smooth sides of them. They just might actually work. "Thanks so much for your help. I really appreciate it."

"No problem." Jerry sticks a finger in his ear, starts shaking it around in there. "You need anything else?"

I need ties of some sort, soft ones to wrap the wood around James's leg. Or rubber ones, so they don't cut into his skin. But there's no way I'm going to ask Jerry for them. "I'm good, I think. I'm just going to look around."

"Okay." Jerry heads back down the aisle.

"Hey," I call out.

He turns around.

"You're really good at your job," I say. "Knowing all this stuff and everything, I mean. You're a natural."

His face brightens a little. "Yeah?"

"Yeah."

"Thanks."

I nod, duck my head, embarrassed. "You're welcome."

I LEAVE LOWE'S with the wood, six soft rubbing cloths, and three rubber strips, thin and stretchy as rubber bands. How I am going to carry all of it—plus the knapsack—into the church without being noticed is beyond me, but I'll get to that when I come to it. It's 11:20. Jane is expecting me by noon. I pull out my cell phone as I start the car, dial Jane's number.

"Hello?" She answers breathlessly, frantically. "Hello?"

"Jane?"

"Yes! Who is this?"

"It's Bird," I say, maneuvering the car slowly out into traffic. "Are you okay?"

"Oh, Bird." A sigh trembles out of her. "God, I thought it was Genevieve, calling to tell me she was feeling better and that she'd be coming in after all."

"Genevieve isn't there today?"

"No." The word comes out of Jane's voice like a wail. "And the kids are just going crazy! They won't listen to anything I say, and I can't get the baby down . . ." She stops suddenly, as if remembering who she is talking to. "Anyway. Are you calling off today, too? Please don't tell me you're calling off."

"No." I make a hard right onto North Main. "But I will be a little late, if that's all right."

"How late?"

"Not too late. A half hour, tops." As long as nothing unforeseen happens.

"Oh, that's fine." Jane sounds relieved. "That's okay. Just get here when you can, all right? I'm going to need all the help I can get today."

I ease into the parking lot of Saint Augustine's, checking for cars. There are six. Shit. I sit for a minute, just looking. That reporter Ma saw this morning could be hiding, waiting in the bushes or something. They do that kind of thing for a story— and worse. I've seen it on *Entertainment Tonight*.

I shove the rubber strips and cloths into my knapsack, tuck the pieces of wood under one arm, and get out of the car. The clouds have lifted finally, and the sky is a vivid blue, the air balmy and warm.

Just like 9/11, I think.

So clear and perfect, moments before the suicide planes dropped out of the sky.

INSIDE THE VESTIBULE, an elderly woman in a heavy green coat dips her fingers into the basin of holy water. She blesses herself, and then reaches out and touches the bare feet of the Blessed Virgin statue. When she disappears through the second set of doors, I tiptoe over to a rectangular slice of window and peer in at the church inside. There are eight people sitting in there, maybe ten. No sign of Father Delaney, though. Or that other priest who gave part of the sermon last night. All right, then. Let's roll. I take a deep breath and head for the stairs.

It's actually more nerve-wracking going up this time, mostly because everything is visible now. I can see footprints in the dust along the steps, a thread-like cobweb nestled in one of the corners. Even the wall has streaks on it, probably from a million different hands over the years, trailing their fingers on the way up. But it's the stillness downstairs that gets to me even more. With so much empty space, a cough sounds like a shout, the shift in a seat like a squeaky board. Will they be able to hear James and me up here—even if we whisper?

I look around—for maybe the first time—when I reach the top. The three tiered steps, covered in red carpet, are lined with pews the color of sand. Behind the highest step, light filters through an enormous stained-glass window bearing the picture of a white dove against a blue background. And of course the organ, big as an ox, sits in the corner.

Back when I still went to choir practice, I always sat in the very first pew, because it was only a few feet away from the balcony, which looked down at everyone below. Miss Wendell, an older woman who had never married or had children, was the choir director. She was forever yelling at me to get away from the balcony and sit down. It was high—three stories at least—and when I leaned over, it was scary, in a thrilling sort of way. Miss Wendell told me once that she had started having nightmares about me slipping and falling off the balcony. I laughed when she said that, because secretly there was nothing I wanted to do more than fall off the balcony. For some reason, I actually believed that because we were in a church, I wouldn't get hurt if I fell. Jesus or Mary or maybe even that big white dove behind us would swoop down and grab me before I hit the floor. Wouldn't they?

I get down on my hands and knees and start crawling along the floor, pressed as close to the balcony as possible. I wonder what Miss Wendell would say if she saw me up here now, using the balcony like some kind of fortress. She would probably be horrified. Or maybe she wouldn't. Maybe I was the kind of kid—even back then—who showed the early signs of going astray. After all, she had caught me fooling around with Bobby Winthrop in the tiny room that held all the choir books. "Bernadette!" she'd hissed, as if Bobby wasn't even in the room, as if I'd unbuttoned the first four buttons on my shirt myself. "What in heaven's name are you *doing*?" Bobby leapt up as if someone had stuck a pin in his backside, and disappeared with such agility that even Miss Wendell looked confused. She glanced behind her once and then again, and then finally turned her full attention on me. "Button your shirt," she said tersely. "And if I ever catch you in this room doing anything else but retrieving the hymnals, you will be sorry. Do you understand me?" I'd nodded, fastening my shirt again while getting to my feet, an endeavor that proved more awkward than anything, and almost toppled over. Miss Wendell's blue eyes narrowed even more. "You haven't been *drinking*, have you?"

"No." I shook my head, wondering how I could ask her about telling my parents. I knew Ma would be livid, but it was Dad I was more worried about. He'd be disappointed. Maybe even devastated. I couldn't bear the thought of either. "Please don't tell my parents," I blurted out. "Please. Just give me another chance. I promise it won't happen again."

Instead of answering, Miss Wendell took two large steps until she was directly in front me and bent down to sniff lightly at my mouth. Satisfied, she stood up straight and gazed at me. "All right," she said. "We will keep this between ourselves." She arched an eyebrow. "*This* time."

There wouldn't be a next time, as I'd quit the choir two months later when I turned thirteen. Getting caught with my shirt unbuttoned in the church choir loft was just the beginning, I guess. Becoming an adult with issues was my obvious lot in life, not a surprise to anyone who knew me. Maybe not even a surprise to me.

The closer I get to the organ now, the more I can feel that something's different. Misplaced, maybe, or missing. It's too quiet. Too empty. And by the time I'm all the way over next to the organ, I don't even have to look.

I just know.

James is gone.

Chapter 19

Well, of course he's gone. He couldn't stay here. He told me he was going to figure something out and he did obviously.

It's over.

I stare wide-eyed at the empty space behind the organ, panic and relief filling me.

Who helped him?

Where is he?

Evidence of his presence is everywhere—the water bottle, still capped, standing neatly next to the wall. Even the space of floor where he had been sitting is marked up with prints: narrow lines in the dust where he must have dragged himself, a handprint here, another one there. But no body. No James.

Okay, then. I guess that's it. That's all she wrote, as Dad would say. I guess I'll give the lumber to Angus after all. Let him whale away on it in the backyard. Maybe I can help him make steps leading up one side of the oak tree at the lake house, so that he can climb up into the highest branches without any problem. I'll bring the food back, line it up again inside the pantry. Ma will never notice. She might even eat the damn meat loaf tonight. Okay. So fine. I have to go anyway. Jane is waiting for me. I have a job that I have to get to, plus another one tonight, and extra work with Mr. Herron tomorrow. Money I have to make. A deadline I have to meet.

Except that I can't move. I sit there with my back pressed up against the balcony, like someone's nailed my hands and feet to the floor. Or maybe I just don't want to move. At least, not in the direction of the stairs. Not yet. I bring my knees up instead, cross my arms over the tops of them, and put my head down. I study the worn patch of carpet in the space between my feet, faded to a raspberry color, ignore the sudden, familiar pulse of emptiness that has begun to fill my chest like water. I've failed him, thrown away what will probably be the only chance I'll ever have to repay him for what he did for me all those years ago. Because that's what all this was really about, wasn't it? A debt that needed to be settled, an evening of the score? Or was it more? Had it become something else over the past few days? Something bigger?

I guess I'll never know.

THE BREAKUP WITH Charlie happened on a Wednesday. By Saturday, the loneliness arrived like an unwelcome visitor. It was not the presence of it that bothered me so much as the uncertainty of its duration. For two days, I sat on my bed and stared at nothing. The possibility of getting a cat, just to feel another beating heart in bed next to me, raised my spirits for a few hours. But when I asked the landlord, a large Italian woman with the vague hint of a mustache across her upper lip, she frowned and threatened to evict me. "I tell you early on," she said, her eyes wide as quarters inside her fleshy face. "When you move in. *No* cats. I am allergic. If I start to sneeze, you are out. Gone. *Finito.*"

If Jenny had been there, I might have opened up, even though it would have taken some prodding on her part. I'd never been a girl's girl. Never been part of the sisterhood, not even in high school, when I hung out with Tracy and the headbangers. Girls were as foreign and complex to me as boys, but boys wanted to sleep with me, which made things a little easier. As far as I could tell, most of the girls—and then later, women—I'd ever met never really articulated what it was they wanted, which left me wondering for the most part where the hell I stood with them. Jenny spent all her free time at her boyfriend's place anyway, coming home at odd hours just to shower and check her mail. The weekend hours ticked by like days, the stretch of solitude an endless sheet of white.

When I saw Charlie at work on Monday, my heart lifted and then sank. He gave me a few woeful glances, pausing once as I passed him in the dining room, and sighing heavily when I didn't acknowledge him. "Man, when it rains, it pours," he said finally, pausing as I stopped to refill an empty napkin dispenser. It was midmorning, the dining room nearly empty save for an elderly man in one corner, sipping a coffee.

"What do you mean?"

"My car broke down on Saturday." I could feel him watching me for a reaction, but I pretended to struggle with the dispenser so that I didn't have to look up.

"I'm sorry."

"Yeah, it sucks. The mechanic said it's going to cost at least two grand to have it fixed, too."

"Ouch."

"Yeah." He paused, drawing a fingertip along one edge of the table. "I had to walk to work this morning."

I looked up. I walked to work every morning, too, but I lived less than a mile away. Charlie's apartment was all the way on the other side of town, at least five or six miles from the Burger Barn. "Why didn't you just take a bus?"

"Have you ever been on one of the buses around here?" Charlie asked. "They're disgusting. They smell like piss."

I shrugged and sidled past him with the napkin dispenser. He was trying to make me feel sorry for him and I wasn't going to do it. The conversation had already gone on much longer than I wanted it to, and I was starting to feel uncomfortable. "I gotta go, Charlie," I said. "Jenny and I have to get the registers ready." I could feel his eyes on me as I walked across the room, and I knew that he would have given his left arm at that moment for me to turn around and look at him and say something, anything, to help bridge this new loneliness between us. But there had been times, I reminded myself, like the nights I sat in his window as he slept, when I'd felt lonelier with him than apart from him and that was even worse than the loneliness I felt now. This I could do, no matter how difficult it felt at certain moments. I avoided him for the rest of the day, even eating lunch in the bathroom so that he would not have the opportunity to talk to me again, and ducking out early without saying goodbye.

IT WAS GETTING late, already past nine, when the knock on my door sounded. I'd changed into my sleep sweats and favorite AC/DC T-shirt, and was getting ready to tuck into a bowl of mint chocolate chip ice cream while I looked through the Help Wanted section of the newspaper. It just made more sense, I decided, to extricate myself completely from the situation. Finding another job wouldn't be so hard, and the physical distance it provided would be the best thing for both of us.

I looked up in alarm as the knock sounded again, louder this time. No one ever came to my apartment, except maybe Ma, who stopped by every so often to make sure I was still alive. She would bring a ziti casserole with her, look around the place disdainfully, and then leave again. Besides, it was much too late for her to be coming around. She always came on weekend mornings, when she didn't have work. The knock sounded a third time, demanding, insistent. I put down the bowl of ice cream and went to the door. "Who is it?"

There was a deep intake of breath, and then a soft, liquor-laced voice. "Bird, it's me. Charlie. Let me in. I need to talk to you."

I pressed my forehead against the door. I could already tell by the sound of his voice that he was drunk. Anything that he said right now would hold little or no merit, if anything at all. And yet.

"How'd you get here?" I asked. "I thought you said your car broke down."

"I took the bus, Bird. I had to see you."

I closed my eyes again, fought against the faint little voice that swayed a little, knowing this tiny sacrifice he'd made for me.

"I just want to tell you how sorry I am for the way I acted." He spoke more quickly now, as if sensing my hesitancy. "In my office that day, when you told me you were breaking up with me, I totally overstepped my bounds, and I'm so sorry, baby." His voice cracked around the edges. "I really am. I'll never do anything like that again."

In all the time we'd spent together, Charlie had never apologized for anything. And he had never called me "baby." Not once. I liked the way it sounded. I liked the way it made me feel. Desired. Singular. I opened the door. The sour smell of beer hit me in the face as he stepped inside and gave me a quick once-over. "Wow," he said slowly. "You look great."

"I'm in my pajamas, Charlie." I eyed him warily, already realizing my mistake. I knew he was drunk, but his eyes were too bright, too, as if he'd just woken up from a bad dream. Or snorted a line of cocaine, which he'd admitted to doing on occasion.

"You look great in anything," he said. "You're gorgeous, Bird." His mouth moved awkwardly around the word "gorgeous," slurring the *g*'s and the *s*. His blue dress shirt hung loosely outside his pants and the sleeves were rolled up to the elbows, exposing a thin gold chain around his right wrist. He stepped forward and touched my cheek with the backs of his fingers. "I really am sorry," he started. "You know that, right?"

"Charlie, listen," I said, moving my head away from his hand. "You're drunk. Why don't you go home and get some sleep? Let's talk about this another time. Tomorrow, okay?"

He reached out again and ran his hand through my hair, watching dumbly as the strands fell between his fingers. "How about you let me sleep here? Jenny won't be coming back tonight, will she? Didn't you tell me she usually stays over at her boyfriend's?"

"Charlie, no." I stepped back so that his hand dropped heavily to his side. "You should go. I mean it. This is not a good time."

"It's always a good time," he tried again. "Come on, baby, don't you want me?"

For a split second, I thought about entertaining his request. About letting him bring me to bed and do his thing and then leave. It would take five minutes, ten tops. I'd have a warm body to press up against, salty skin to kiss, to brush my lips against. I could close my eyes and pretend it was anyone else. And then he'd be gone. I'd have the rest of my night to myself. But as I looked at him, standing there before me with his hooded eyes and one bad tooth, my skin began to crawl. For as much as I craved the physical contact, I knew I didn't want to spend five more seconds with this guy, let alone five minutes. And I certainly did not want to spend any of it naked.

I walked past him and opened the door. With one hand on the knob and the other hand on my hip, I stood there, waiting. He looked at me quizzically and then guffawed. "Come on, Bird."

"Get out." My voice was as firm as it had ever been with him. "I mean it."

"Get out?" He drew his head back, as if I had just spit at him. "Get *out*?"

My fingers gripped the doorknob more tightly.

He took a step toward me. "What'd I tell you about talking to me like that?"

"Leave, Charlie."

He was on me before I knew what was happening, dragging me down the hall by my hair with one hand, bending the fingers of my opposite hand with the other. There was a terrifying, inhuman strength about him that made me realize what he was going to do before it happened, but I struggled anyway, pleading with him to stop. I got a good slice in his right cheek with one of my nails before he threw me down, pinning my arms with both of his knees, nearly crushing my elbows into the floor. "You want me to get out?" he hissed above me. "Huh? You want me out, baby?" His eyes were black and spit flew out of his mouth. "Here, look. I'll take it out." He reached inside his pants and withdrew his penis, shoving it against my face. It was warm and flaccid, a thick, disgusting slug. His knees were still digging into the soft spot beneath my elbows and I turned my face, nearly gasping from the pain.

"Charlie, please!"

"Oh, it's 'please' now, huh? 'Please, Charlie'?" He shifted slightly, so that his penis rubbed against my neck, under my chin, and then bucked his hips so that it slid wildly against the side of my face. He was getting harder, the edges of him growing stiff and rigid.

"Charlie." I began to cry. "Stop."

"Say 'please' again." He leaned down and grabbed my face around the jaw, aligning my eyes with his. He was still thrusting, and the tip of his penis moved against the edge of my lips, the eye of it soft and salty and wet. "Come on, say 'please, Charlie.'"

I squeezed my eyes shut, hating the heat and stink of him against my mouth, the pain of his fingers digging into my jaw, the strength of his knees burying my elbows farther and farther into the wood, but most of all hating the helplessness of my body under his. "Fuck you!" I screamed.

For a split second, Charlie looked startled and then his face broke open into a wide, sloppy grin. "Fuck you?" he repeated. "Oh, baby. I thought you'd never ask." He moved his knees off my arms awkwardly, heavily, and straddled my hips. The sudden release of the pressure against my elbows and the new, throbbing pain in its wake was so intense that, for a moment, all my focus shifted to that part of my body. Then a sudden coldness as my bare flesh rubbed against the floor, and the re-alization of what was coming next. I began to kick as Charlie tore my sweat pants down, but the movement was futile; his weight was centered squarely along my abdomen. I shut my eyes as he ripped at my underwear. The waistband, thin and stretched with use, tore easily in his hands, and he laughed as he snatched at it again, this time splitting the crotch. I arched my back and reached for his face with both my hands, fully intending to make contact with his eyeballs. But he grabbed my flailing right hand with his and bent it all the way back. I screamed in pain and kept screaming as he forced his way inside of me. He jammed and pushed, over and over again, each time a little harder, and it hurt, but not unbearably, and I remember thinking later that maybe it hadn't really happened at all because of that fact.

And then suddenly, like a miracle, he was being lifted off me. I thought for a split second that maybe God Himself had reached down and plucked him off, thrown him like some sort of crushed insect into the corner of my room. Except that it wasn't God. It was James who was lifting Charlie by both shoulders and slamming him into my bedroom wall. There was the sound of animal grunting and shoving, and then Charlie swung blindly, somehow making contact, and sent James reeling backward across the room. A faint whooshing sound followed, as Charlie pulled a can of Mace out of his pocket and began spraying wildly. James yelled and fell back down again, and before I knew what had happened, Charlie had run down the hallway and disappeared out the door.

James stumbled past me and made his way toward my kitchen. I listened, barely breathing, as water rushed into the sink, followed by the sounds of splashing and James grunting for what seemed like hours. And in those hours I remember thinking only one thing: that Ma had been right about Charlie from the very beginning. He had been hiding something behind those eyes that wouldn't look at her. Something terrible. How hadn't I seen it? How had *she*?

I clutched a handful of blanket against me as the running water finally ceased, and listened wide-eyed as James's footsteps sounded in the hallway. He would leave now. I was sure of it. But his footsteps got closer. And then closer still, until the outline of him appeared in my doorway, filling it almost entirely. I scurried back along the floor until I was pressed up against the side of my bed, still clutching the blankets around me. Beneath them, my sweats were still down around my ankles; the space between my legs was raw and throbbing. Somehow, amid the struggle, the curtain on my window had been torn down and the unforgiving glare of a streetlight bled its way into my room.

"Bird?" James's voice floated through the dark. "Are you all right?"

"Yes." The word fluttered out of my throat, hovering there like an injured butterfly. James took several steps until he was just a few feet away from the bed. I turned my head to the wall, unable to look at him.

"Can I . . . ?" I heard him say. "Is it all right . . . to sit . . . ?"

I did not answer, did not even move, and thankfully, neither did he. The air in the room was heavy with the smell of cum and skin and beer. My elbows pulsed painfully from where Charlie had knelt on them; the skin on the rest of my body felt as tender as a pincushion.

"Bird," James said after a moment. "You have to call the police."

I thought about this for a moment, thought about the impending scenes that would arise between Charlie and me, Ma and me—and shook my head.

"No, no, you have to," James said. "Right now, Bird. I mean it. You can't let that prick get away with what he just did to you."

I turned my head from the wall. It felt like a thousand pounds. Even the space behind my eyes was heavy, as if someone opened up the top of my skull and dropped an anvil inside. Just for a moment, I pictured my heart—which was beating irregularly as if trying to keep up with the fractured rest of me—as a shred of pulsing raw ribbon, and I knew that it would never be the same again. "Get out," I said quietly.

James stared at me for a moment. The white scar along his eyebrow seemed to glow faintly in the dark, and beneath his right eye the skin was beginning to swell. "Bird," he started.

"Get out!" My voice was louder. "Get out, get out, get out! Before I call the police and tell them it was you!"

James took a step back then, the concern in his eyes turning to alarm. "Bird," he tried again. "The only reason I was here was . . ." He stopped, leaving the sentence unfinished. "I was just trying—"

I threw the pillow I hadn't realized I'd been clutching. I rose to my knees, letting the blankets drop, not caring that my lower half was bare and exposed, and swayed, bruised and light-headed, clenching my fists. "Get out!" I screamed. *"Now!"*

James left.

It was the last time I ever saw him—or Charlie—again.

Until now.

Something drops out of my eye, splashing against the heel of my boot before I realize that I am crying. Fuck. I snatch at my eyes impatiently, press the heels of my palms against my eyelids. I haven't thought about that night, haven't let myself walk through all the horrible steps of it—from start to finish—in years. Maybe not since it happened.

Why would I ever want to go back there? What would be the point? What's done was done. It didn't kill me. Finding out I was pregnant afterward—and that it was from that night, the only night Charlie had ever not used a condom—didn't even do me in. Yes, the baby had been forced into me. Yes, it would be half his, a thought which troubled me less and less as more time went by without a sign of him. But I would also have someone in my life now who loved me like no one else could.

Or ever would again. And that is how I got through it. That is how I will continue to get through it. Goddamn it.

I take a deep breath, get up to leave.

And then, suddenly, I hear it. A breathing in and out, so faint at first that I wonder if it is just mine. I pick my head back up, hold my breath, and lean toward the sound, which seems, inexplicably, to be coming from near the organ. Which is impossible, since no one's there. I scoot forward, straining to listen. Someone's definitely breathing.

And this time, I realize slowly, it's coming from inside the organ.

Chapter 20

I lean back, examining the wooden contraption in front of me. That's when I see the left side of the enormous instrument, lopsided and just slightly ajar. It almost looks like a door of some kind minus the knob.

I put my lips to the corner, where the jutted side meets one of the legs, and whisper, "James? Are you in there?"

Somewhere inside the organ, the breathing halts.

"James, it's Bird. I'm back. With more water."

Downstairs, there is a sudden slug of movement as a few people stand up and start walking toward the vestibule. I lean into the corner of the organ again, pressing my lips tightly together, as if muting any future sounds that might come out of them. The swing of doors is followed by a low murmuring as pleasantries are exchanged, afternoon details discussed. I close my eyes. Finally, there is the sound of the outside doors. Opening. And then closing. I exhale.

"James," I say again. "Are you okay?"

"I thought you said you couldn't come back." James's voice comes out from the innards of the organ. He sounds weak.

"I changed my mind." I pause. "How did you get in there?"

"Carefully."

"Where does it open?"

"On the left. It wasn't hard, really. The whole thing is falling apart."

I move my hand up the seam of the organ, gasp as it gives way slightly beneath my fingers.

"Careful," James whispers. "Don't make any noise."

Somehow, the whole side of it slides horizontally, almost like a hidden panel door, just enough so that I can finally see James sitting within its hollow insides. The space is so narrow, the height so compromised, that he is practically bent over the waist. Even with his injured leg, both of his knees are slightly raised. "Oh my God," I whisper. "You must be dying in there."

He nods grimly, his face shiny with perspiration. "I kept hearing people coming in. And then footsteps on the stairs. That's when I got worried."

"You want to get back out?"

He's breathing with difficulty again. "How many of them are still down there?"

"Hold on." I turn toward the balcony, raise myself up to the lip of it as far as I dare. If Father Delaney is sitting on the altar, I'm done for. Slowly, slowly, until my eyes are level with the hanging figure of Jesus on the cross. An inch more, until I can see the altar. There are at least a dozen bouquets of pink-and-white flowers arranged in a semicircle around the front of it. A few feet away, Father Delaney's chair is empty. Okay. Little bit higher, until the pews are in view. There's a middle-aged couple on the right. The woman has a scarf over her head; the man's coat is still on. Behind them is the older woman in the heavy green coat I saw walking in. And over on the left-hand side is a man and another woman. Both with heads bowed, lips moving silently across the knuckles of their folded hands.

I crawl back over until I can see James again, and hold up one palm, fingers spread wide. He nods. "Hold on. When they go, I'll move again."

I drag the knapsack over, take out a bottle of water. His arm is already outstretched by the time I look back up. I give it to him, go back in, and take out two peanut butter sandwiches. But he shakes his head when I slide them through the opening. "You gotta eat *something*," I say. "You'll get too weak."

"I don't want food," he says. "Just water."

"That's ridicu—"

"I've already pissed myself twice," he says hoarsely. There is a slight menacing look on his face, his eyes are flat. "I don't want to sit in anything else."

Oh my God. I didn't even think of such a thing. How could I not have thought of such a basic thing? "Oh," I say. "Right. Well, you . . . you're gonna need clothes, then. Clean pants. Underwear."

"I wouldn't worry about underwear. But pants might be good."

We both stop whispering again as the sound of people moving through the vestibule, and then the outer doors, is heard. I crawl back over to the balcony, peer over once more. Only the woman in the green coat is left; the other four have gone. She's moved closer to the front for some reason. The gold tabernacle is just a few feet away from her now; inside, a dark red flame is flickering, like a beacon. Or a warning.

I crawl back over to James. "Only one person left."

He nods. "I'm going to turn around. Then I'll need your help."

I watch him twist and squirm within the cramped confines, until I finally have to look away. He is in so much pain moving even the slightest bit, clenching his jaw so that he will not scream out, that it feels as if something inside of me will cry out on its own. This is ridiculous, I want to say. Just turn yourself in. Anything that comes next can't be as bad as this. The words are on my lips. And then I think of Mr. Herron. Of Randy-Kid, and the hole and the feeling of being forgotten by everyone, even God.

I stay silent for the ten minutes that it takes him to get in a reverse position. Finally, gasping as quietly as possible, he says my name: "Bird."

I reach under his arms and pull him out the rest of the way. It's not easy, since he is much heavier than he looks, and I am hunched over, still trying to keep myself out of sight. There is a slight dip at the edge of the organ and when I pull his feet over it and they fall heavily to the floor, James gasps audibly. We both freeze, waiting for the woman downstairs to call out, but nothing comes. Finally, James nods. I drag him over to the wall, next to the empty water bottle, and sit him up against it.

"Jesus Christ," I say, my voice hoarse. "Tell me you won't go back in there."

He closes his eyes, breathes in and out. The pungent scent of urine is apparent now, and when I look down at him, the front of his pants are wet. I'll have to bring him new pants right away. Maybe on my way back over to Jane's tonight. I can't let him sit in his own urine all night. "Listen. I brought you a flashlight so that you can see a little better up here when it gets dark. And some stuff to set your leg with."

James opens his eyes again and presses a finger to his lips. We stare at each other as a soft shuffling sound drifts up from downstairs, followed by a squeak of the vestibule door. I study his face, listening. The cut on his forehead has crusted over, but

it looks deep. It should be cleaned and bandaged. The outside
door closes softly and then it is quiet once more.

"Empty now?" James asks.

I scoot over to the balcony, peer over. The church is completely vacant, not a soul in sight. "Empty."

"It won't be for long," James says. "Someone's been here
almost constantly during this Forty-Hour thing. Just a few
hours, I think, where there hasn't been anyone." He pauses.
"You brought a flashlight?"

I nod, shrug my shoulders. "You're not insulted or anything,
are you? I was just thinking how dark it probably gets . . ."

James smiles. "It does get dark. Real dark. Thanks. What'd
you bring for my leg?"

"Just some wood and ties." I reach over for the lumber,
drag my knapsack as quietly as possible behind it. "One of my
friends told me how to do this."

"I thought you said you didn't tell anyone." Even whispered, James's voice is sharp.

"I didn't. It's an old guy, whose house I clean. He used to
be in the army and he was telling me a story about setting
some guy's leg in the war." I wrap the wood in the soft pieces
of cloth, and set them on either side of James's leg. They could
be an inch or so longer, I think, but still. It might work. He
grunts when I push the one in a little closer, and then tilts his
head back, wincing.

"Sorry, sorry, sorry," I say. "God, I'm sorry."

"I think it's broken in a few places." He's breathing hard.
"Goddamned stairs over there. I didn't even see the curve of
them until it was too late. I fell back down about ten of them.
You're gonna have to go real slow."

"Okay." I focus hard as I start again, trying not to put unnecessary pressure on any part of his leg. My face flushes as my fingers brush against the front of his zipper, but he doesn't seem to notice. Finally, when both pieces of wood are in place, I reach for the rubber ties. James's face looks slightly more relaxed; he has stopped gritting his teeth.

"Did you say you clean houses now?" he whispers.

"Yeah." I slide the first band under his heel, move it up so that it's positioned around his ankle. "Me and my mother. We sort of have a business together."

"Huh," he says. "Whatever happened to nursing school?"

I freeze when he says that, as if he is holding the flashlight directly in my face, and then drop my eyes. I can't believe he remembered. "Oh, you know. Things happen."

"You can say that again," James grunts.

"Oh, you know. Things happen." I lift my head, meet his smile with my own, and pick up the ties again. "I'm surprised you remembered I wanted to go to nursing school."

"I remember a lot of things about you." The statement is benign—and so loaded at the same time—that I feel dizzy for a moment. He's staring down at his leg, which I am still wrapping with the ties. "You're good at it," he says.

"Good at what?" I grunt, tying the last two pieces of rubber together while trying not to squeeze anything.

"This." He nods toward his leg. "Fixing me up. You shouldn't let that nursing thing of yours go, you know. It'd be a waste."

I don't say anything for a moment, until I remember something that James told me once. "What about you?" I ask. "You told me that that was your last year at the Burger Barn. And then you were leaving. Where'd you go?"

"I went out West for a year." James drops his eyes. "Made it all the way to California. And then I came back. I've been here since." He looks embarrassed admitting such a thing, ashamed even.

The next question on my lips dies as two male voices start talking downstairs. "I'm sorry I'm late, Father." The man's voice is loud, edged with excitement. "I was down at the police station, making a statement about the guy I saw running through my backyard this morning. Took longer than I expected it to."

Father Delaney's response is inaudible.

"It happened so fast," the first man responds. "But I just told them the truth. I couldn't really tell if it was him. But they're checking all leads, you know, until they find him. The whole town is looking now. I guess every little bit helps."

I'll never know all the unspoken words that travel between James and me at that moment. The only thing I remember is the new fear in his eyes—and how much more I want to help him because of it. "Listen," I say, shoving the materials back inside my backpack. "You can't stay here. You just can't. I have a bad feeling about it, with all these people coming in and out for this Forty Hours thing. I have a place I can take you. An empty house. Up at Moon Lake. You can stay there—in a real bed, with a shower and everything—until you decide what you want to do next."

"I don't want you to get involved any more than you already are," James says. "Seriously. It could be dangerous."

"Too late." I zipper the backpack as quietly as possible. "I'm already involved. I'll be back tonight with clean clothes, and then tomorrow night we'll drive up to the house together."

"It's someone's actual house?"

"It's going to be Angus's and my house. It's just the apartment upstairs. The woman who owns it lives below, but she's in Florida until next week."

James nods slowly, as if thinking it through. "Okay," he says finally. "If you're sure it'll be safe."

"I'm sure." I nod and inhale quickly.

It's probably the least sure I've been about anything in a very long time.

Chapter 21

One of Jane's four-year-old twin girls opens the door when I ring the bell. She's smaller than Angus, dressed in blue striped leggings and a pink T-shirt. With her blond hair and blue eyes, she's an almost perfect replica of her mother. "Hi," she says, arranging a socked foot against the inside of the opposite leg. "I'm Greer. Who're you?"

"I'm Bird." I step inside and glance around. Jane is nowhere in sight. Upstairs, I can hear the muted sound of footsteps, the wail of an infant.

"Bird?" Greer seems oblivious to the noise. "Like a real bird? That's your *name*?"

"Yeah," I say. "Like a real bird. Isn't that cool?"

"Sorta," Greer says. "But kinda weird, too."

I laugh. She reminds me a little of Angus. "Where's your mom?"

Greer points to the steps. "Upstairs. Are you our new nanny?"

"No, no." I head toward the bottom of the steps. "I'm your mom's cleaning lady, remember? I help her keep the house nice and neat." Greer sticks her thumb in her mouth as I talk. "Jane?" I call out. "It's Bird! Can I come up?"

Greer jerks her thumb out of her mouth again with a soft sucking sound. "I hate Genevieve. I hope she never comes back."

"You hate her?" Boy, Ma would have a field day with this kid. "Why would you hate your nanny?"

"I just do." Greer's little face is knotted in a scowl. "She's mean."

I put my purse down, take my shoes off, and line them up next to the door. Greer is close behind me as I head up the steps. "Jane?"

"She's in her room," Greer says matter-of-factly.

"Where's your brother?" I ask. "And your sister?"

"Blake's in his room playing video games and Greta's with Momma and Olivia."

Olivia's cries are getting louder as I pad down the hall-way with Greer, and the longer I go without seeing Jane, the weirder something feels. Where the hell is she? And if she's in her room like Greer said, why is the baby still screaming?

Jane's bedroom is about as big as Ma's whole downstairs. Besides the king-sized bed, there is a full couch, a glass coffee table topped with an enormous plant, an oxblood leather La-Z-Boy chair, floor-to-ceiling drapes, and two matching loveseats, the pillows of which I am required to fluff every other day. Everything is awash in pale green and cream hues; even the potted tree in the corner with its emerald-colored leaves looks like it was made just for this room.

But the only thing I see when I look in now is Jane, who is sitting on the floor next to the bed, holding Olivia. Her hair has been shaken out of its usual neat ponytail, and she is not wearing shoes. The front of her white shirt is wrinkled, the buttons incorrectly buttoned, and one of her legs is bare, the legging pushed up almost to the knee. She is crying almost as hard as the baby, her face bright pink and streaked with tears. Poor Greta—who is Greer's identical twin—is huddled in the corner, sucking her thumb, watching her mother with wide eyes.

I rush over immediately, kneel down in front of her. "Jane! What happened? Are you hurt?"

She shakes her head, squeezes her eyes tight. A thin film of snot has collected between her nose and upper lip, and she is only wearing one earring, a large diamond stud in the left ear. "I just can't . . . get her to stop . . . crying." The words stagger out of her mouth, in between gulps of breath.

I take the baby out of her arms. "Here. Let me try."

Greer walks over to her mother and drapes her little hands around Jane's neck. Greta gets up, too, and snuggles in on the other side. Jane's crying lessens just a little, her cries interspersed now with hiccups.

I hold Olivia tight, rocking her back and forth as I stride throughout the room and keep one eye on Jane. The only other thing that left me feeling as desperate as the few times I'd had to leave Angus screaming in his crib was the fact that I had no one to call. Ma wasn't an option; she'd responded to the initial news of my pregnancy with a "Well, good for you, Bernadette. I hope you're happy now." I'd stared at her for a full minute afterward, deliberating whether or not to tell her the truth about that night and then turned around and walked out of the room. For as exhausted as I was on those nights, I wouldn't have called her if someone was holding a gun to my head. And there was no one else. I know what Jane is feeling now. I do.

Olivia is not interested in being swaddled or held. She kicks and arches her back as I try to hold her close, her fists curled tight as pinwheels. Tufts of her black hair are matted down with sweat, and her pink skin, usually the shade of a rosebud, is tinged a faint purple. I put her down on Jane's bed, unwrap her from the blanket. Her yellow jumpsuit is soaked all the way through—urine or sweat, I can't tell—and her last two toes are caught in the elastic part of the jumper, the thin string of it wrapped so tightly around them that they are almost blue. I free them quickly, and massage the tiny digits as I try to catch Jane's attention from the other side of the bed. "Hey, Jane?"

She turns around, gets up on her knees, and leans against the enormous bed. Her eyes are swollen. "Do you think she's sick?"

"No." I hesitate, afraid to tell her about Olivia's toes, even though the baby's crying has lessened considerably. She might blame herself for not having caught it. "She's really wet, though. Sweaty and stuff. How about we give her a bath, cool her down a little? I think she'll feel a lot better."

Jane nods, wipes at her face with trembling hands. At the sign of their mother's sudden improvement, Greer and Greta scramble up on the bed and start jumping. Jane looks at them for a moment, her shoulders sagging.

"It's okay," I assure her. "It's all right, Jane. Let's just focus on Olivia right now, okay?"

"Right," she says, walking past the girls into the master bathroom. She moves with a slight limp for some reason, steadying herself along the wall as she goes.

I gather up Olivia, whose cries have eased even more by now and follow her. "You okay?" I ask, arranging Olivia on the rug so that I can take her out of her yellow jumpsuit. "You're limping."

"Yeah, I'm okay." Jane takes a plastic baby tub out of one of the closets and puts it in the sink. She runs her fingers under a stream of water, testing the temperature, and then stands back, watching it fill. "I have an old back injury from way back when. It acts up when I'm really stressed out." She laughs softly, embarrassed. "Or like today, when I haven't had a chance to go pick up my Vicodin."

Olivia's bare skin is pink and moist; her hair damp around the edges. I pick her up, put my mouth close to her ear. "Here we go, baby. Nice warm water." She smells like milk and baby shampoo and urine. It seems like a dream sometimes that Angus was ever this age. Like a very short, very strange dream. I place Olivia in the warm water, arranging her head against the rubber pillow, and scoop handfuls of water over her belly. Her cries are soft as a kitten's now, a faint mewing. "There we go," I say softly. "That's better."

Jane is standing next to me, leaning against the counter, just watching. I move over quickly. "Here. I don't mean to—"

"No." She puts her hand on my arm. "Please don't go. Please. I just . . ." She covers her face as new sobs overtake her, shakes her head behind her hands.

I stare at her disbelievingly, one hand still on the baby. "Do you . . ." I start tentatively, hoping I am saying the right thing. "Do you need to go to the pharmacy to get your medicine? I don't mind staying with the kids for a minute."

She takes a deep, shuddering breath. "I can't go out right now. I can't even drive. I'm a mess." She pauses, looking at me. "Would you . . . do you think you'd mind going and picking it up for me?"

I take the tiny washcloth draped over one side of the tub and lay it out flat on Olivia's stomach. It's transparent against her skin, the swell of belly barely visible beneath, like a sinking island. "Sure. Where is it?"

"Harrold's Pharmacy? On Butler Street?"

Less than a mile away. "Yeah, I know where that is." Olivia is actually gurgling now, splashing her tiny hands in the water.

"Oh, Bird," Jane says. "You don't know what this means to me. Thank you so much. Let me get my wallet. And I'll call the pharmacy now and tell them you're coming."

I TOOK VICODIN once after I had my wisdom teeth removed. It didn't do much except make me feel numb all over, which, in the long run, I guess, is exactly what it was supposed to do. I take out the drug information insert stuffed alongside Jane's prescription bottle and sit in the car and read.

> Vicodin is a pharmaceutical containing acetaminophen and hydrocodone used to relieve moderate to severe pain. Hydrocodone is in a group of drugs called narcotic pain relievers. It may be habit forming. Vicodin should not be taken by anyone who has liver problems or who consumes three or more alcoholic beverages a day. Vicodin should never be given to another person, especially someone with a history of drug abuse.

There's a lot more, but it's all stuff I can't even spell, let alone understand. The only thing I really zero in on anyway is the part about moderate to severe pain. And how little I've done to help ease James's.

I uncap the bottle, look inside. There are at least twenty-five pills in there. At five hundred milligrams each, I wonder how many Jane takes a day. She's so tiny; it can't be more than one. Which will make it a lot easier to miss a few, I think, stuffing four of the pills into my front pocket.

If she notices at all.

Chapter 22

One Sunday when I was about ten years old, Father Delaney gave a long sermon at Mass about stealing. I listened intently, taking in the information, and then promptly forgot about it. Later, however, at dinner, I brought it up again. Ma had made one of her enormous pot roasts, serving it with roasted potatoes, carrots, and turnips. There was a little bowl of horseradish sour cream, too, and a basket of bread. But I wasn't interested in any of the food; I wanted some answers.

"I know it's wrong to steal a candy bar from the store," I said. "But what if a guy's family is starving and he steals bread and peanut butter? That's not stealing, right?"

"It most certainly is." Ma put her fork down and looked straight at me. "You don't always get to choose your circumstances, Bird. But you do get to choose how you react to them."

I let this answer fly over my head the way I did with most of Ma's cerebral responses. They were so obtuse sounding that they never seemed to make any sense. "So do you really think God would punish that man for stealing?" I asked. "Even if he did it so his family wouldn't starve?"

Ma tilted her head slightly to the right, raised her eyebrows. It was her way of saying "yes" without actually saying the word.

"Well, now, I disagree," Dad said.

Ma stopped chewing. "With who?"

"With you." He pointed his fork across the table at her, the sleeve of his brown sweater drooping around his wrist. "But just with your last sentence. I think stealing is wrong, too, but I don't really think God would punish a man in that kind of situation."

My heart swelled, just looking at him. Dad always understood. He always made sense.

"Even if he *stole*," Ma prompted him.

"Yes, even if he stole," Dad said. "Because he did it for the greater good. He did it to feed his children. Don't you think God would have a harder time forgiving a man who let his family starve, than someone who had to steal food to keep them alive?"

"There are other ways," Ma said. "No one has to steal."

"What other ways?" I asked.

"Like getting a *job*," Ma answered. Her jaw was moving up and down so hard I thought she might bite her cheek. "Or going to a soup kitchen."

"What if he couldn't find a job?" Dad's tone was still light and easy. There was no reason for this to segue into an argument; it was just a family discussion around the dinner table. We could agree to disagree. "What if the guy was injured? Or what if he was in between jobs? What if he was supposed to start something in a day or two, but in the meantime his family was starving?"

"And he had little babies," I piped in. "What if he had little babies, Ma? They need milk, you know."

We were both looking at her now, waiting for her to answer.

I expected her to come back again with some other retort, or even recite something that Father Delaney had told her about mortal sin. For Ma, things always came back to sin. Always. But instead, she set her fork and knife down on either side of her plate and stood up. "Why are you doing this, Bill?" Her voice was barely audible, but so venomous that if she had screamed, it would not have had the same crushing kind of impact.

"Doing what?" Dad was aghast.

"Putting me on the spot like this!" Ma was blinking back tears now. "Making me out to be the monster of this discussion!" She glared at me. "*Babies*, Bird? Really?"

And then she left the room.

As badly as I felt, that day was a turning point for me. Because I realized that the real root of Ma's frustration was that she had run out of answers. That, at least in this particular situation, she didn't know what the right thing to do was. It was my first foray into the world of gray. An introduction to the possibility that maybe it wasn't all as black and white as Ma always held it up to be. Dad's way of seeing things *could* work, despite the insistence of Ma's nagging rebuttals.

Now, driving home from Jane's, I remind myself of that every time I think of the Vicodin in my pocket. They are painkillers that I have stolen, yes. But they are for a man who is in unbearable suffering. They will ease the torturous state he is in for at least a little while.

They are for the greater good.

EVERYONE AT AFTER care—the kids, Molly, Miss Annie, and Carol—is pressed up against the big glass window in the back when I come for Angus. I watch Jeremy, who is elbowing Angus a little, trying to get a better view of whatever it is they're looking at, and then step forward. "Hey, guys! What's out there?"

Angus turns immediately at the sound of my voice. "It's a bad guy, Mom! The cops are looking for him!" His eyes are button-sized; there is a dried ketchup smear along his chin.

Molly tears herself away from the window, walks briskly toward me. "There's a bunch of policemen across the street." Her voice is low, brimming with excitement. "They're searching those two big office buildings over there next to the movie complex. Someone said they got a tip. You know, for Rittenhouse."

"Oh." My heart skips a beat. Is a church considered an office building? Will they go to the rectory, ask Father Delaney to lead them through any unused rooms?

"You can't see them now; they just went into the bank." Molly clutches my elbow, points to the window. "But the kids were all excited when they saw the lights."

I look in the direction Molly is pointing until I can see the cars myself. There are four of them—plain Buicks painted to read NEW HAVEN POLICE DEPARTMENT on the sides. Two of them still have their lights on; the cubed blue-and-red flashes swirl around methodically, turning the sides of the building a pale red. My mouth feels hot and much too dry.

"Okay, well, thanks." I look away from the trucks, back over at Angus. "Come on, Boo! We gotta go!" But he and Jeremy have gotten involved in some sort of tussle. Jeremy's got Angus around the neck, bending him in half, almost to his knees. Angus's arms are out straight on either side of him, flailing uselessly. I'm over the two of them, yanking Jeremy off Angus in two seconds, leaning my face in close to his.

"Don't you touch him!" I know my voice is too loud, the harshness of it unacceptable for a child this age. But I don't care. "You stay away from Angus from now on, do you hear me? I don't want you to be his friend. I don't even want you to say hi to him anymore." Jeremy takes a step back, stares up at me defiantly. "Do you under*stand* me?" My voice is on the edge of a shriek, my eyes bulging. Jeremy breaks finally under my crazy-lady stare and starts to cry.

Molly, who has been standing next to him, gathers Jeremy up in a hug, holds him close against her. Jeremy wraps his small corduroy legs around her waist, shoves his face into her shoulder. "Mrs. Connolly," Molly says.

"*Miss* Connolly." I grab Angus's hand.

"Miss Connolly." Molly's cheeks flush pink. "I know these two have been having some issues, but there's really no need to speak to a child like that."

"Well, someone has to." And before Molly can say another word, I pull Angus out of the room, down the hallway, and into the car.

ANGUS GETS IN the backseat very carefully, fastening his seat belt without being told, and folds his hands neatly in his lap. His steady gaze along the nape of my neck feels like a heavy necklace settling around the top of my spine. I put the key in the ignition, start the car, and then put my head down on the steering wheel and sob.

"Mom?" Angus lets himself out of the seat belt again, climbs over the seat until he is next to me. "What's the matter?"

His questions make me cry harder, and I bury my face into the side of his neck, right where the bottom of his hair curls.

But my onslaught of tears is abruptly curbed when I feel Angus's tiny hand patting my shoulder. *No, no, no. He shouldn't see me like this. I'm the mother. He's the child. Pull yourself together, Bird.* I sit up, smear away my tears with the heels of my hands.

"I'm sorry, Angus. I didn't mean to scare you like that. I've just had the worst day."

Angus studies me for a moment, his mouth slightly ajar, just the tips of his tiny teeth inside peeking out. Behind him, a large forsythia bush is clotted with straining yellow buds. "Wanna go see Dopester?" he asks. "Just you and me?"

I nod, smooth my hand over the curve of his head. "Yeah," I say. "Yeah, let's go see Dopester."

Chapter 23

We sit in the car for a few minutes, both of us leaning out the driver's side window, staring at the little gnome. He is the very last one in the row, all the way on the other side of the lawn, but it is easy to see his wide, sail-like ears sticking out on either side of his cherubic face and his purple hat drooping down low over his forehead. "Why do you like Dopester so much?" I ask Angus after a minute. "I mean, there's seven of those little guys there. What is it about him that you like the best?"

Angus wiggles in a little more tightly against me. "His shoes," he says finally.

"His shoes?" I lean out the window a little farther, trying to make them out. All I can see is a pair of brown slipper-like things, exactly like all the rest. "They all have the same shoes, Boo."

"No." Angus shakes his head solemnly. "Dopester's are different. They're smaller."

"They're *smaller*?" I squint, visoring my eyes with the side of one hand to see more clearly. "How can you tell?"

"'Cause he's the smallest dorf," Angus says.

"Dwarf," I correct him.

"Dorf."

I let it go. "So you like him the best because he's the smallest?"

Angus nods. "And because he has the smallest shoes. Which makes them magical."

"Ah." I tuck a curl behind his ear. "Kind of like your magic shoes?"

"Yup."

"Well, no wonder he's your favorite, then. That makes perfect sense."

Angus rests his chin on the backs of his hands, which are holding on to the bottom of the window, and smiles.

"Hey, Boo?"

"Yeah?"

"You want to go see a favorite thing of mine?"

He turns his head without lifting his chin. "Where?"

I PULL MY car into the circular driveway, a carpet of pine needles and soft dirt crunching lightly beneath my tires. The hollow drilling of a woodpecker echoes in a tree above me; the scent of pine is thick as smoke. I inhale deeply. Moon Lake is only a ten-, fifteen-minute drive outside of New Haven, but coming out here always feels as if I've landed on another planet, complete with oxygen, white-pebbled yards, and cedar decks high as trees. Even the light out here is different—softer somehow, with a pale, fluid quality, as if filtered through water.

And here, not fifty yards ahead of me, is the white bilevel house that Angus and I will soon be calling home. Someone (probably Mrs. Vandermark) has replaced the rosebud wreath with a green chinaberry one; and the heavy deck furniture sits like shadows behind the screen of the enclosed side porch.

Even from the back it is impossible not to glimpse parts of the enormous oak tree on the front lawn, the new buds that are just now starting to turn green. A lone branch, thick and solitary as an arm, reaches out above the water, as if trying to glimpse its reflection below. After we move in, I am going to hang a tire swing from that branch for Angus. I'll stand on the doorstep every evening as the light drains from the sky, and watch as he sails out over the lake, dark hair rippling, his shouts carrying over the wind.

I took note of where Mrs. Vandermark left a spare key the very first time she showed me the apartment, hidden inside the swirled crevices of a conch shell just behind the first step. I realize that what I'm about to do could technically be considered breaking and entering, but it's not really. I've already paid Mrs. Vandermark the first and last month's rent, which is two-thirds of what I owe. Which means, at the very least, that the place is already two-thirds mine. I turn the shell over in my hand, let the key drop out, smile at Angus. "Come on. I want to show you something."

"Whose house is this?" he asks, already climbing the steps.

I trudge up behind him, holding a cardboard box filled with kitchen items, which has been in the back of my car for over a week now. "It's gonna be ours, Angus. This is gonna be our new home." I hold my breath, the way I always do whenever the front door opens, as if we are stepping into Disney World. It's not Disney World, of course, but you wouldn't know it the way Angus runs into the living room, flushed and wide-eyed, hollering at the top of his lungs. "Echo!" His voice bounces off the empty white walls, scuttles along the hardwood floor, and down the tiny hallway that separates his bedroom from mine. "Echo!" he yells again. "Echo, echo, echo!"

I put the cardboard box down on one of the kitchen counters and run up to him quickly. "No yelling, Angus. That's gonna be one of the rules when we move in, too, okay? You can't yell."

Angus ignores my reprimand, pointing to the large, Buick-sized window on the other side of the room. "Look! You can see all the way to the other side, Mom!" The last time I'd been here, it had been raining, and so foggy that I couldn't see halfway across the lake, much less to the other side. Now, as we walk over to the glass together, my eyes are riveted on the opposite shoreline. It is barely visible, almost a smudge; a house with a red roof appears the size of a toy. In between, the water is vast and dark, a heavy, cloudy blue. A wind is blowing tiny whitecaps across the surface; the sky is the color of cream. I can feel my breathing slow, the beat of my heart settling back down to a normal, steady rhythm. Maybe it will have the same effect on James.

Angus disappears down the hallway, into the room where we will put his bed and dresser and his Buzz Lightyear comforter. I stand in the middle of the living room for a moment, trying to envision where I will put James tomorrow. It would probably be safer to hide him away in one of the bedrooms, but maybe he can stay out here—at least until Mrs. Vandermark returns next week—so he can look out the window. Enjoy the view. I'll get blankets and sheets, arrange a bed of sorts on the floor here, right next to the window, so he can get comfortable and lay down flat and look out at the water.

I open up the red cupboards below the kitchen sink, slide my few dented pots inside one, a colander, three bowls, and four plates inside the other. One of the drawers gets the plastic silverware tray, and I separate the forks and knives and spoons carefully into its wide partitions. Afterward, I withdraw one of

the pots from the cupboard again, fill it with water from the
sink, and set it on top of one of the stove burners. Tomorrow
night, after I bring James here, I will boil the water and pour
in some tube pasta. I'll buy some fresh vegetables and fruit,
too, maybe some bread and cheese. I will have to get soap
and shampoo, so that he can use the shower properly. Toilet
paper. Some clean towels, a toothbrush, toothpaste. And water.
Lots more water. Hadn't he told me some other statistic once?
Something about the Three Threes when it came to survival?
Humans could go three minutes without air, three hours in
extremely harsh weather, and three days without water. After
that, your chances of survival plummeted by the moment. Yes,
I would be sure to stock up on water.

Angus comes running out of his bedroom. "I just saw a blue
jay, Mom! Right outside the window! It was sitting in the tree,
and I was watching it and then it flew away! What do blue jays
eat? Do they eat blue food?"

I put my arm around my boy, kneel down next to him. "I'm
pretty sure they just eat worms, like all the other birds."

Angus's face falls. "Not even blueberries?"

"Maybe blueberries." I stand back up, press my hand against
my chest hard, as if to quell the banging of my heart beneath it.

It'll be okay, I tell myself. It will. Angus will not have anything to do with this. James just needs a place to stay for a few
days until he figures out what to do next. And then he will go
to wherever he needs to go, disappear again as quickly as he
appeared.

That's all.

Chapter 24

"Can we go to Friendly's?" Angus suggests on the way home. "They have the best French fries and they make those ice cream sundaes with the chocolate cookie ears for dessert, and besides, I'm *starving*."

"You got it." I am straining to make my voice cheerful, still forcing myself to act normal; anything to put aside the fact that tomorrow I will be housing a criminal, that less than an hour ago I broke down in front of my four-year-old son like a little girl. Not to mention the monster-mom mask I put on at day care, dealing with Jeremy. Maybe I'll get a phone call from his mother tonight: "Who do you think you are, screaming at my son like that? What's your problem?" I wouldn't blame her, I guess. I'd do the same thing if some woman came in and freaked out on Angus.

Ma's in the kitchen, frying chicken in a heavy cast iron pan. The little TV next to the stove is on, turned to the five o'clock news. Headline: James and the police search downtown. I turn it off, reach over, and give her a kiss on the cheek. "C'mon. I'm taking us to dinner. Angus wants to go to Friendly's."

She looks at me surprised, and then turns off the heat under the pan. "Well, all right. That sounds lovely actually. Let me just put some lipstick on."

FRIENDLY'S IS CROWDED, even in the back where Angus likes to eat. Ma and I settle in on the red bench by the front doors, watching people come and go as we wait for a table. Angus runs over to the gum machine in the corner, and gets down on his knees. He starts fiddling with the dial, hoping to dislodge a loose piece, even though I've told him he can't have any gum before dinner. A man and woman—both wearing Red Sox baseball hats—brush past us.

"Oh, I'd bet the farm he's still local," the man says, standing back to let the woman through the door. "Someone that stupid wouldn't have enough sense to go anywhere else. Besides, he's injured. Someone said he got shot in the foot. He's probably holed up somewhere like a scared little rabbit."

I bring my hand to my mouth, start biting my nails.

"Don't," Ma says, swatting gently at my hand. She tucks a piece of hair over my shoulder. "How was work?"

"It was okay. How about you?"

"Not bad. Violet had me take everything out of her kitchen cupboards today and wipe them all down."

I turn to look at her, my mouth slightly ajar. "C'mon, Ma. You're not supposed to be doing stuff like that."

She shrugs. "Oh, it wasn't *hard*. Afterward, we had a cup of tea together. She told me about the day she met her husband at a county fair in Georgia. He won a blue ribbon for having the biggest pig." She chuckles. "She was the one in charge of pinning all the ribbons on. Isn't that cute?"

I smile a little, too, although I wish she didn't have to clean people's cupboards out, wipe down the grease and dust they accumulate over the years. It's beneath her, is what it is. It's beneath anyone. People should clean up after their own damn selves. "You're not too tired, then?"

She shakes her head, tucks her purse in against her chest. "I'm fine. How was Mr. Herron today? And Jane?"

"They're okay." I tell her about Jane's situation with the baby, how I helped calm her down. Ma looks alarmed when I get to the part about the bath, and when she starts shaking her head, I finally stop. *What?*

"You shouldn't be doing things like that, Bird."

"Like what? The baby was hysterical. Jane was in pain or something, because she didn't have her medicine . . ."

"What medicine?" Ma asks.

"She takes Vicodin for back pain or something. I don't know. I didn't really ask too much about it."

"*Vicodin?*" Ma repeats. "How can she be taking care of four children if she's on Vicodin?"

"I don't know. Normally Genevieve's there. She takes care of the three older kids. But she called out sick today, so Jane was on her own."

Ma's shaking her head. "I don't know about that woman."

"What don't you know, Ma?"

"Well, she shouldn't even be *having* all those children if she's got some sort of back problem, for one. And two, Vicodin is a pretty strong drug. I'm sure it alters her ability to mother decently." She turns to look at me. "Don't you think?"

"I have no idea. I try to stay out of it." I think back to yesterday, when Jane asked me if I liked being a mother. What was really underneath that question? Did *she* like being a mother? Or was Ma right—that being on a pain medication like Vicodin fuzzed her maternal abilities? Maybe being on Vicodin fuzzed *most* of her abilities.

Our waitress calls our name then, leading us through the restaurant to one of the round booths in the back. She's an older woman, about Ma's age, with bleached blond hair, teeth the color of overripe banana peels. Her orthopedic shoes and support hose look odd under her Friendly's uniform, but strangely complementary, too. The embroidered name on her shirt reads MARJORIE. Angus and Ma both order the same thing: grilled cheese with bacon and extra French fries, while I get a 7-Up, a double cheeseburger with a fried egg on it, and a side of coleslaw.

"A fried egg?" Angus asks incredulously, getting up on his knees. "On a burger? That's gross, Mom!"

Marjorie laughs. "Lots of people put eggs on their burgers," she tells Angus. "It's actually very good."

I hand Marjorie our menus, look at her hands as she collects them. Thick, worn around the tips. Scraped pink nail polish. "Thank you," I say, making sure she sees me smile. What the hell is she doing working the night shift at Friendly's? She should be home in bed with her feet up, having a cup of tea, goddamn it.

"Sit down correctly, Angus," Ma says, tapping the table in front of him.

"I *am* sitting," he answers.

"On your bottom." Ma raises her eyebrows.

Angus uncrosses his knees and sits back down. I bite the inside of my cheek, slide the coloring book and small packet of crayons in his direction. God, it will be nice not to have to share the parenting anymore.

"Listen," I say to Ma, keeping my voice low. "I have to go to Jane's tonight to help her with the play set. She's expecting me around seven. And then after that, I thought I would . . . Well, would you mind staying with him for a little while longer tonight? Just for another hour or so?"

"Of course." Ma folds her hands, raises an eyebrow. "Where are you going after Jane's?"

"Well . . ." I squint, pick at a piece of loose skin around my thumb. "I thought I'd go sit again for a while. At the church. You know, for that Forty Hour thing."

Ma's hands fall open loosely as she sits back against the red seating. "You're playing with me, Bernadette."

"No." I shake my head. "I'm not."

"You want to go back?" Her lips part the slightest bit. "Really?"

"Yeah. I don't know. Not to *do* anything . . ."

"Just to sit."

"Yeah." I shrug away the guilt I am feeling, scratch the top of my forehead. It's for the greater good. The bigger picture. "Just to sit."

Ma pats my hand conspiratorially. "All right, then."

"When does it end anyway? The Forty Hours, I mean?"

"Tomorrow morning," Ma says. "Father will have a Mass of Deposition and then he'll close up the tabernacle."

Perfect. I'll have time to bring James clean clothes before I go to Jane's tonight, and then go back up to the choir loft tomorrow, right after I finish up at Mr. Herron's, so that I can grab him and throw him in the car before the church locks up for the night.

Marjorie brings our drinks over—white milk for Angus in a kiddie-cup with a straw, coffee for Ma, a 7-Up with lemon for me. "There you are," she says, giving Angus a wink. "And your meals will be right out."

Maybe Ma will end up like Marjorie when Angus and I move out to the lake. There's no way she'll be able to keep up with this whole cleaning thing for much longer. It's too much. The work is getting too strenuous for her body, whether she wants to admit it or not. She's worn out. Maybe she can get a part-time job here at Friendly's; she and Marjorie can take their breaks together, slipping into a corner booth in the back, settling their stockinged feet along the fake red leather. They'll split a piece of the coconut cream pie with their coffee, exchange stories about their grandchildren. It wouldn't be so terrible, spending her last working days like that, would it? Wouldn't it be better than working herself into the ground, breaking her back along someone else's floor?

I look up, startled suddenly as someone says my name. "Bird?"

Mrs. Ross is standing in front of our booth, next to a man with dark hair. "Hi, hon!" she says. "I thought that was you!"

"Oh, hi!" I reach out and shake her hand, hoping she doesn't notice the sudden flush along the side of my neck. "Um, Ma, this is Mrs. Ross." I pause. There's really no other way to say it. "From the probation office? Mrs. Ross, this is my mother. And my son, Angus."

Mrs. Ross shakes Ma's hand, smiling widely. She's dressed up as usual—a gray camisole with delicate lace edging under a pink-and-white cardigan, sharply ironed black pants, heels. Her hair is down, cascading in waves around her shoulders, and she is wearing long earrings punctuated with pink-and-white stones. "It's wonderful to meet you, Mrs. Connolly. You must be so proud of Bird. She's worked so hard."

Ma glances over at me, smiles a little. "I am. Thank you."

"And, Angus!" Mrs. Ross turns toward him, shaking his hand as well. "I've heard so much about you! But your mother never told me you were so handsome!"

Angus grins and ducks his head.

"This is my husband, Tony," Mrs. Ross says, putting her arm around him. "Tony, this is Mrs. Connolly, Bird, and Angus."

Tony grins, shaking hands all around, including with Angus. He's really good-looking. Tall, dark hair, great teeth. An excellent dresser, too, in a green-and-white checkered shirt, caramel-colored leather jacket, nice pants. I wonder if Mrs. Ross picks out his clothes. Ma used to pick out Dad's, bringing home stuff from JCPenney and Sears. He couldn't dress himself if his life depended on it. "Great to meet you all," Mr. Ross says, and then, looking directly at Angus: "You know, Angus was my grandfather's name."

Mrs. Ross draws her head back a little, staring at her husband. "You never told me that!"

Mr. Ross nods. "Great name," he says. "It's Celtic. It means 'one choice.'" He looks directly at me. "But you probably already knew that, didn't you?"

I nod, laugh lightly. *Pleaseleavepleaseleavepleaseleave.*

Mrs. Ross tucks an arm into the crook of her husband's elbow and smiles out at us. "Tony's a historian over at the college. He loves things like the meaning of names."

"'One choice,'" Ma repeats slowly. She's looking sideways at me, her left eyebrow arched into an *A*. I wait for her to say something about me not knowing anything at all about the meaning of Angus's name, let alone that it had anything to do with a choice, but she just sits back again and folds her hands.

"What about Mom's name?" Angus is up on his knees again, gazing at Mr. Ross with big eyes. "What's it mean?"

"I'm not sure," Mr. Ross says, shaking his head from side to side. "Bird's a first for me actually."

"Oh, Bird's just a nickname." Ma is looking up at Mr. Ross intently. "Her real name is Bernadette. As in Saint Bernadette. The one who saw the Blessed Virgin? At Lourdes?"

"Yes, of course," Mr. Ross says. "I think the French interpretation is 'strong bear.' Or maybe it's 'brave as a bear.'"

Thedoorisrightbehindyoupleaseturnaroundandleavenow.

As if reading my thoughts, Mrs. Ross laughs lightly, and runs a hand through her hair. "Well, it certainly was fun running into all of you. Bird, I'll see you shortly to wrap things up and send you on your way!"

Mr. Ross puts his hand lightly around Mrs. Ross's back as they turn around, and keeps it there as they walk down the aisle. I wonder briefly where their children are. Maybe the two of them are on a date, the kids home with a babysitter. Mrs. Ross is definitely the kind of woman who would insist on date-night with her husband.

"She's certainly cheery," Ma says, dragging a French fry through a puddle of ketchup. "You never mentioned anything about her before."

"She's my probation officer, Ma." I keep my voice low. "What am I supposed to tell you?" I glance over at Angus, who is eating only the middle part out of his grilled cheese. He will discard the crusts, banish them to one side of the plate the way he always does. I let him, more in direct defiance to Ma, who forced me to eat every-single-crumb-children-are-starving-all-over-the-world, than for any other reason. He looks up at me, catches me looking at him. "Can I call you Mama Bear now?" he asks.

I laugh.

So does Ma.

Chapter 25

A few months after Angus and I moved in with Ma, I went up to the attic to get some extra bedding for Angus's crib. Ma had told me where to look—all the way in the back, just under the eaves—and she was right. What she hadn't told me, though, was that right next to the bedding were two large boxes, each marked neatly with masking tape. They were labeled BILL—CLOTHES.

I lifted the cover off the box, staring down at the pile of Dad's neatly folded shirts. There was the camel-colored one he wore to work, usually under a black vest. It was soft and nubby, the collar worn a little at the edges. Under that was the dark blue one with the bleach stain on the pocket that he wore on Saturdays, when he puttered around the house. There were a few of his T-shirts, too—the old ratty ones, with holes in the bottom, and faded yellow stains under the arms. I was confused at first, not that Ma had saved his clothes, but that she had saved such crappy ones. There was the horrible black cardigan he'd liked to wear to church even though Ma begged him not to, the overly pilled V-neck sweater, even a faded bathing suit he'd worn to the beach one summer.

And then I smelled it. Old Spice aftershave, mixed with coffee and the lingering, almost indecipherable trail of pipe smoke. The scent drifted out from in between the materials, faint as air, strong as a fist. It made my knees buckle, the skin along my cheeks prickle with heat. I gripped the pile of T-shirts I was holding so hard that my hands turned white, and sat there for a long time, surrounded by the clothes and the smell of Dad, until Ma called up finally and asked if I was okay.

Now, when we get home from Friendly's, I put a movie in for Angus, and head up to the attic. I haven't been back up here since that day. But as I lift the box top, digging deep toward the bottom where Dad's pants are, the smell hits me again—so hard this time, and with such insistence, that I stand up straight as if someone has just grabbed me around the shoulders. I can't do this. What the hell am I thinking—taking my dead father's pants to give to an escaped criminal hiding in a church? Even if it is James? *What is wrong with me?*

I reach down instead, and take the camel-colored shirt in my hands. I bring it to my face, close my eyes, and breathe in as deeply as I can. "Dad." My voice breaks inside the shirt, lost among the folds, hidden deep against the buttons. "Oh God, Dad, what should I do?"

I honestly don't know what happens next: maybe it is the familiarity of the smell again, or maybe I just want to believe that he's around somehow. But something lifts inside, having said that, and a vague realization, as if he has heard me somehow, wherever he is, settles across my shoulders. A few moments later, it occurs to me that Dad wouldn't mind if I took his pants right now and gave them to James Rittenhouse, who is sitting in a puddle of his own urine at the top of Saint Augustine's Church.

That maybe, just maybe, he would do the exact same thing.

FATHER DELANEY IS straightening a pile of prayer booklets next to the statue of the Blessed Virgin when I walk in. He turns immediately, his lean face brightening. "Bird!" His voice is hushed as he walks toward me, his right arm outstretched. "How wonderful to see you here again!" He touches me lightly on the elbow and drops his hand again.

"Thanks." I smile tightly. "I just thought I'd, you know, maybe sit and hang out for a while." I adjust my backpack casually, hoping he doesn't mention it. People bring backpacks to church, don't they?

"Oh, of course, absolutely!" Father Delaney shoves his hands into his pockets, peers in at my face as if he hasn't just seen me yesterday. "So how *are* you? How are things going?"

Oh God. Now he wants to chat. Couldn't he have said something yesterday, when we were all leaving after the service? I step on my foot, clear my throat once, sharply. "Things are good. Thanks for asking."

"What is it that you're doing now?"

"Oh, just working." I shrug. "You know, cleaning houses with Ma."

"Wonderful. Wonderful. I'm sure it's a huge help to your mother, having you on board like that."

"Yes."

"How about just for you? What're you doing these days for yourself? For fun?"

Is he serious? What is this, some kind of therapy session? I wonder briefly if Ma has put him up to this, the way she got him involved in the sweater fiasco. "Um, you know. I get out. Meet up with friends and stuff."

"Good friends?" The priest's mouth is crooked into the tiniest of smiles; if it didn't look so genuine, I'd probably ignore the question altogether.

"Good friends," I concur. "Don't worry, Father."

He pats me on the back. "I'm not worried."

"Well, you can tell Ma not to worry, then."

He grins, deepening the lines on either side of his face. "I'll do that. Go on in. I don't mean to keep you."

He's an all-right guy, I think, sliding into one of the back pews. He was nice enough to Angus the other day. And there's something to be said for sticking by Ma all these years—even if it's just because he's as crazy a Catholic as she is. Of course, he probably has no idea that it was him, more than anyone or anything else, who turned me away from this place. How, when he said at Dad's funeral mass that Jesus was right there with him in the car when he died, I almost leaned over and threw up. It was an insult, really. A slap in the face, trying to comfort us with some bullshit line like that. I mean, think about it: Catholics believe that Jesus is God. And God is all-powerful, all-knowing, the creator of the universe. He can do anything. *Any*thing. And this guy is going to stand up in front of a church full of people and tell me that this being, this deity who created atoms out of dust, who breathed life into the stars, sat by and *watched* as my father got his skull crushed against the dashboard of his car?

After that, I wanted nothing more to do with the whole crazy business about God. Besides, when I really sat down and thought about it rationally, who was to say there even was one at all? There were a million stories out there about Him, but no one had proof of His existence. No one had ever seen Him, had ever sat down and had an actual conversation with Him. There was no telling that we went up to some puffy-clouded heaven after we took our last breath here on Earth, or that some white-bearded divinity was going to meet us there when we did. If anything, it seemed it was people who had created their own version of God, stories that fit their lives somehow, gave meaning to their desperate, unanswerable questions. I was pretty sure that when all was said and done, the real truth was that no one really knew anything about any of it at all.

Out of the corner of my eye, I can see Father Delaney walk up the opposite side of the church. I watch his dark head move under the stained-glass windows—a moving comma against a sheet of color—until he disappears through a back door.

Then I stand up.

James is waiting.

Chapter 26

Somewhere in the distance a clock chimes once, alerting the quarter hour. Six-fifteen already. I told Ma that I'd be home by ten, but maybe it will be even later. I might even be late getting to Jane's. There's no telling how long any of this is going to take. Will James need help changing into the new pants? And if so, will it take long to do, the way it did to extract him from inside the organ? I'll definitely have to untie the wood around his leg so he can redress, which means it will need to be set again afterward.

I don't feel as frightened creeping up the stairs this time, but I'm not sure why. Yes, there are still things to worry about—James being found, me getting into trouble—but maybe now that I'm involved, now that I've decided to go down this road, it's taken some of the edge off. It's kind of like when I first found out I was pregnant. Aside from the way it happened, everything else about it scared the shit out of me, too: being too young, the inevitability of pushing something the size of a watermelon out of a hole the size of a lemon, having another human being around that I was going to be responsible for.

I'd thought about having an abortion, sat with the possibility of it for two whole days. It was easiest when I thought about that night, when I let myself dwell on the reality that half of the baby's genes would belong to Charlie, and that even if we never crossed paths again, this tiny new life would create an inextricable link between us. Still, I couldn't stop thinking about the other set of genes, the part that belonged to me, that I had somehow gone and created despite the horror of the situation. I couldn't bear to erase what might turn out to be the best part of me. The funny thing was that once I realized I was going to keep the baby, that this was going to be the next real step in my life, some of the fear dissipated. It was almost as if making the choice itself had lifted some of the burden.

James is in his usual spot behind the organ, clutching the gun. When I appear, the vein cords in his neck relax again, his wide eyes soften. "Sorry," he whispers softly. "I just never know."

"Still just me." I settle in a little against the wall and dig inside my pocket. The smell of urine is stronger now; the front of his pants saturated. Every few seconds, his body shivers around the edges, and then settles again. "Listen, I brought you something." I take out the pills, hand him two of them. "It's Vicodin. I thought it might help the pain in your leg."

"You take Vicodin?" James looks at me curiously.

"No."

"Where'd you get it, then?"

"It's my mother's. She has a bad back."

James tosses both pills into his mouth, grabs the water I hand him, and gulps. "Thanks. To your mother, too, I guess."

I grab my knapsack, pull out a handful of the lavender-scented wipes that Jane gave me, and set them in a little pile. Then I take Dad's pants, shake them out, smooth the wrinkles along the creases in the legs. "These pants'll probably be too big on you, but at least they'll be dry. And I brought some wipes so you could . . . you know . . . clean yourself off." The air is charged with embarrassment, but it has to be said. "Unless you . . ." I pause. "Do you want me to . . ."

"No." He cuts me off quickly. "I'll do it."

"Can you? With your leg and everything?"

"I'll figure it out. Besides, now that you've given me the Vicodin, maybe the pain won't be so bad."

"Okay." I point to the other side of the choir loft. "I'll wait over there until you're finished. Just tap on the side of the organ to let me know you're done."

I can feel him watching as I crawl away, and for some reason just then, I remember that he almost killed someone in a bar. It's not that I've forgotten this fact exactly; more like stored it away, I guess, in the back of my head somewhere. But now it's front and center again. Blaring, like some kind of neon sign: HE PUT SOMEONE IN INTENSIVE CARE. I turn around, sit up. "James."

He jumps a little, hands at his waistband, where he has been working the button on his pants. "What?"

"The guy. That you hurt? He isn't dead."

Even from this distance, I can see the color drain out of his face, a twitch in his left eye. "He isn't?"

"No."

"Is he in the hospital?"

"Yeah. I don't know all the details, but I think he's in critical care. And he might need surgery."

James nods, his eyes moving across the floor in between us, as if following a mouse. "Okay. Thanks."

I settle myself at the top of the steps, stare down at the gaping mouth of it below. It's impossible to read James's reaction just now. Is he disappointed? Relieved? Or just numb? I wonder if he really meant to kill the person. He couldn't have. For as little as I've actually spoken with James, I would still bet my life that he did not mean to kill anyone. Maybe he just got drunk and then went crazy. But if so, why? What could anyone in a bar have possibly done to drive him to such a state?

A faint tapping sounds behind the organ. I lean back, catch sight of James's hand knocking lightly against the side of it, and crawl back over. The rubber ties and pieces of wood are lying next to him. His dirty pants are crumpled down around his knees, and he is covering the front of his underwear with Dad's clean pants. "I just need help getting the pants all the way off," he whispers, motioning with his hands. "I can't reach. Will you pull the legs?"

I arrange myself at his feet, pull gently until the pants slide off. He bites down hard on his bottom lip when his right leg is exposed; an awkward bulge is visible just beneath the hair and the skin, a horrific, misaligned bone under the thin layers. "James." I shake my head, lean forward to examine it more closely. "You have to go to a doctor. You're never going to be able to walk on this leg again if you don't get it fixed the right way."

He squints, as if my words are causing him pain, and not his leg. "I will. Eventually. Listen, I'm going to need help with"—he pauses, clears his throat—"with my underwear, too. Will you go back over to where you were? I'll call you when I'm decent."

I sit just behind the organ this time, listening to the series of barely audible gasps that come from the other side as James struggles to remove his underwear. I try not to think of the surreal aspect of the situation, how gruesomely bizarre the whole thing has gotten. And yet I feel so tenderly toward him that he is embarrassed. That night when I rose up on my knees and screamed at him, not caring that the blankets had fallen around me, or that he could see my naked lower half, it was an act of defiance. An *I dare you to come any closer; I dare you to hurt me, too* kind of scream. But of course, that is not the situation now. James is struggling just to move his legs a few inches. Just to retain a little bit of dignity while moving without crying out. I will be as respectful and impassive as possible, maybe even pretend that I am a nurse. Nurses see it all, don't they? Penises, blood, shit, urine, vaginas. All of it. They can't afford to be squeamish, can't let their emotions get the best of them. Well, neither will I.

A tap sounds on the organ once more.

James's breathing is visibly labored, his soiled underwear in a wilted clutch around his knees, his hands cupped around his groin. We avoid each other's eyes as I remove the under-wear, working around the obvious humiliation of the situation. I move as quickly as possible, angling the hole around his right leg without touching it until they are all the way off. Wrap-ping the soiled clothing into a ball, I stuff it into the bottom of my backpack, and push a handful of the wipes in his direction. "Here. Use these. Just clean off as best you can. I'll wait behind the organ again until you're done."

"I can't." His head tips back, and he sags backward, ex-hausted. "It's fine. Just leave it."

"You'll feel so much better if you just . . ."

"Can you?" He lifts his head an inch or two. "I mean, if you don't mind?" He leans all the way back slowly, so that he is stretched out on the floor. "I just . . . I just can't."

I move toward him, extricating one of the lavender wipes out of the package. The scent, bracingly clean and woodsy, drifts up between us as I move the cloth carefully over the tops of his thighs, in between his legs, and then down around the sides of his buttocks. His hands do not move from the cupped position they are still in, but his eyes are closed, his breathing has slowed. I use three more wipes, moving them as softly as possible over his skin, marveling at the little whorls of hair above his belly button, the smooth slope of his hip bones, the slick band of muscle above each one like a cord. I've never looked at a man's body in such a way, not once. Who knew it could be so beautiful?

"Does that feel any better?" I ask, finishing up.

James nods, but doesn't answer.

"Okay, now pants."

He lies still as I move the pants over his legs, gasping once when I brush against the injured one, only to fall silent once more. It takes me over ten minutes, literally moving inch by inch, until my father's pants are finally around his waist. They are much too big, bagging and slouching against James's narrow frame, but I safety pin them on one side and roll the band over twice so that they sit comfortably along his hips.

"Okay, I think we're done."

He raises himself onto one elbow and looks down at himself, regarding my work. "Wow," he says. "Thank you."

"You're welcome." I glance down quickly at my watch: 6:25. It will take me at least eight minutes to get to Jane's, which means I have to get out of here in a little under nine minutes.

"I think the Vicodin is kicking in," he says. "It didn't hurt nearly as much to pull the pants on."

"That was fast." I grab a handful of wipes, move over to the spot he was sitting in, and start rubbing the floor.

"Don't do that," he says, stretching one arm out. "Please."

"Do what?"

"Clean up after me. You've already done so much. Please. I'll do it later, after you go." He smiles wryly. "It'll give me something to look forward to."

But I continue to rub the cloth over the floor. "It's nothing. Really. My God, I do this kind of thing in my sleep."

"Stop." His voice has changed; it has an edge, a vague bitterness to it that I haven't heard before. "I mean it, Bird. Don't do any more."

"Fine." I sit back then, uneasy, embarrassed. "Whatever."

He watches me for a moment without saying anything. Then: "Why're you doing all this anyway?"

I don't answer right away. So much has happened in the past twenty-four hours that I can't even remember anymore what made me come back in the first place. Until I do again. "You helped me once," I answer finally.

James's eyes rove over the floor, my hands, the rag, but do not meet mine. I wonder if he is thinking about that night, too. About the terrible things I said to him after he pulled Charlie off me. What must he have thought when I threatened to accuse him? He had to have known I didn't mean it. Didn't he?

"So if I was just some stranger up here stuck in the same situation, you wouldn't've come back?" he asks.

"I don't think so."

James nods, as if deliberating my answer. "It's kind of nuts, isn't it? You being here the same day that I dragged myself up these steps? I mean, what are the odds?"

"Yeah." I think about this all the way through, maybe for the first time. I'd been so annoyed about it earlier, but what if Ma hadn't asked me to go back for her sweater? Or someone else had heard James that day and come up to the loft to investigate? What then?

Who's to say what course a life takes, how it steers one way and then another? Ma would say it's all part of God's plan, that the things that happen are directed by His hand, but I like to think of happenstance as some kind of ship at sea, leaning this way into the wind and then in the opposite direction when the wind blows again. You get lucky sometimes, is all. Or you don't.

I stuff the dirty wipes into my backpack and sit back on my heels. "Can I ask you a question?"

"Sure."

"Why'd you shave your head?"

James squints at the question, and for a moment, I wonder if I've overstepped my bounds, if maybe I've gotten too personal. "You just used to have all that *hair*," I say. "It was so . . ." Beautiful, is what I want to say. Beautiful and lovely, like him. "I mean, there was just so much of it."

He runs a hand over the top of his head, as if to remind himself that he is indeed still bald. Then he shrugs. "It was just something I wanted to do. I needed a change. Something different."

Something about his answer doesn't sit right, but I let it go. It's not important anyway. "Okay," I say. "How about otherwise, then? I mean, how've things been going for you?" James grins at the absurdity of the question. I can feel my face flush. "I mean, aside from the obvious. You said you still live in New Haven, right?"

"Yeah. Still here. I have a place over on the east side. Machell Avenue."

Machell Avenue. That's less than two miles from where Ma and I are. Surreal that he's been there all this time, without me knowing. A ship on a parallel course, perhaps. Or maybe just one completely lost at sea. "What do you do? For work, I mean?"

"Carpentry, mostly," James says. "Or at least I did."

"Oh, that's right. My mother said that you had worked on her house a few summers ago. Something with the roof."

"You told your mother?" James's left eye twitches.

"She saw you on the news, James." I reach out, touch the tip of his foot gently. "It was on the news. I haven't told anyone. I promise."

"Okay." Beneath his shirt, I can see his rib cage rise and then fall again. "Yeah. All right. I keep forgetting." He smiles faintly at me, blinks a few times. "Where's your mom's house again?"

"Andover Street. Right on the corner. The one with the little metal shed out back?"

"That was your mother, huh?"

I nod. It occurs to me suddenly that he must not have known my last name back then. I don't think I ever got around to telling him. Actually, if he hadn't been on the news for the last three days, I might not have remembered that his last name was Rittenhouse.

"Yeah, I think I remember that one," he says. "It wasn't a big job. Just a patch-up around the chimney, mostly, where it was starting to get thin. I was only there for a day, maybe even just an afternoon. Your mother brought me a glass of lemonade, just before I finished. Left it right at the foot of the ladder, so I could get it when I came back down. Paid in cash, too, if I remember." He shakes his head. "Still, that was a while ago. She remembered me, just from the TV report?"

"My mother has a memory like an elephant. She can recognize anyone from anywhere, no matter how long ago they first met."

"That's amazing." James stares at his boots sitting off to one side. The laces are loose, the soles caked with dried mud. "You know, I'll never climb up on a roof again," he says softly. For a second, I think he is referring to his leg injury. And then I realize that he is talking about the possibility of spending the best years of his life in prison. That maybe the only work he'll ever do in the future will be in the laundry room of a heavily locked basement, with other orange-suited men like him.

"You never know." My voice is faint.

He shakes his head. "I know."

"God, James, what happened? What . . . what did you do?"

James's eyes change when I ask him that, almost like a shade has been pulled down over them. He stares at me for so long without blinking that I wonder where he's gone inside his head. Suddenly, in the background, the clock chimes six forty-five. "Never mind." I grab my backpack, slide it in between my shoulder blades. "It's none of my business anyway. I'm sorry. I have to go."

"Where do you have to go?" James asks.

"I have another cleaning job I have to get to tonight. Across the river. It'll take me about ten minutes to get over there, and I can't be late."

"You work nights, too?"

"Well, not usually. I'm just pulling some extra shifts now because I need the money. For that apartment I told you about. I still owe them the security deposit."

"Where're you living now?"

"With my mother." I raise an eyebrow. "Which is another reason why I really, really need that money."

"Ah." He nods, a flicker of recognition in his eyes. "When are you coming back?"

"Well, I have to go home after work tonight. My little boy likes me to tuck him in. But I'll be here tomorrow. We'll drive up to the lake and then figure out what to do next." I shift the backpack more comfortably along my shoulder, slide over against the wall.

"Hey, Bird?"

I stop. "Yeah?"

"What's your little boy's name?"

"Angus."

James grins. "Really? Like Angus Young of AC/DC?"

"Yeah. Exactly."

A moment passes, filled with everything that's been lost, and for this single, tiny thing that has been found again.

"Don't be late tomorrow." James's voice is soft. "And, Bird?"

I look up.

"Thanks for coming back."

Always. The word flits behind my eyes, a small glimmer of light.

"No problem," I say instead. "See you tomorrow."

Chapter 27

H i!" Jane says a few minutes later, opening the door for me. "Come on in!" I step inside cautiously, wondering where the borderline-hysterical Jane from this afternoon disappeared to. Dressed in a purple velour sweat suit, new sneakers, and no makeup, she looks much more rested now. Relaxed, even. Her hair has been twisted and anchored at the nape of her neck with a plastic clip; both earlobes are bare. Maybe she took a whole handful of those happy pills I brought back for her earlier.

"Sorry I'm late." I take off my shoes immediately, aligning them inside the front door. "I ran into a little traffic on the way over."

"Oh, please," Jane says. "It was five minutes." I follow her into the kitchen, stand uncomfortably at one corner of the butcher block as she opens a cupboard. "I was just about to have a glass of wine. Richard got back from Napa Valley last week, and he brought me two bottles of sauvignon blanc from a really terrific winery. It's my favorite. Would you like some?"

Here is another perfect example of why a relationship between Jane and I would never work. If I were to have a drink, it would never be wine. Not even remotely. I prefer something stronger, with a little guts: maybe a finger of single malt Scotch, or a highball, straight up. At the very least a very, very good vodka and soda. Wine is for sissies. "No thanks," I say. "Not while I'm working."

"Working?" Jane sets two wineglasses on the butcher block. The stems are as thin as pens, the mouths wide as softballs. "We're not working! We're going to be putting together a play set! Come on, have a glass of wine with me!" She takes a green bottle out of the door of the refrigerator, twists the cork out. It's already half-empty; the label on the front is a picture of a gold peacock. She pours the pale gold liquid into the glasses, filling each a little more than halfway, and then slides one over in my direction. Raising her glass to her lips, she pulls it away suddenly, and then lifts it into the air. "To motherhood!" she says.

I lift my own glass, clink it against hers obligingly. "To motherhood." I take a small sip. It's not Jameson, but it's not terrible either. "Where are the kids? Everyone asleep?"

"All the girls are asleep," Jane says. "Blake's upstairs, playing video games. He tries to stay up every night until Richard comes home, but he always falls asleep, poor baby." She stares into the mouth of her glass, runs a finger around the edge of it.

"Richard works late?"

"Oh, yes." Jane sips again. "Partly because of the job, and partly because of Richard, who's obsessed with everything that goes along with the job. He never gets in before midnight on weeknights. Ever."

I take another sip of wine. "Wow. That is late."

"It is." Her voice is soft. "Well, should we get to work? I've got everything all set up in the back for us, including the directions. Now, let's just hope you can understand them, because I don't."

Jane turns on the lights, illuminating the yard in a pool of yellow. Off to the left, beneath an elm tree, she has laid out a blue tarp. The surface of it is covered with enormous puzzle-shaped pieces of thick plastic, each one stacked according to shape and size: the red ones are on the right, the blue on the left, the green and yellow in the middle. We walk over together, stand there for a moment, just looking at the flattened display. "Holy cow, Jane. How long did it take you to do all this?"

"Oh, not long." She looks pleased by my compliment. "I thought it might help if we had things in order before we started."

"You got that right." Still holding the glass of wine, I sink down to my knees and pluck out the instructions, which have been tucked under a corner of one of the red pieces. "We're going to need a screwdriver and a hammer. And a wrench, too."

Jane points to a red metal toolbox opposite the tarp. "That was one of Richard's Christmas presents last year. I don't know a hammer from a wrench, but I'm pretty sure it's got everything inside."

I drag the toolbox over, open the lid. A thin film of plastic is still stretched across the top of it, the tools inside untouched. "Um . . ." I hesitate, closing the lid a little. "Do you have anything that's not so . . . new?"

"Oh, no, use it! Please!" Jane shakes her head, gulps her wine. "Just because Richard doesn't have time to fiddle with it doesn't mean we have to let it go to waste." She pulls out a small key from the pocket of her purple sweat suit, and cuts a deep slit into the plastic covering. "There! Now dig in. Use whatever you want."

We work side by side for over an hour—Jane holding the necessary pieces upright while I screw them in and tighten the bolts. She works harder than I thought she would, pushing the sleeves of her sweat shirt up to her elbows, getting down on her hands and knees next to me to study the directions. She goes inside only once to refill her wineglass and check on Blake, and when she reappears, she is holding a plate of cheese and crackers. Around the edges, like a fan, are thin slices of green pear. "I don't know about you," she says, holding out the plate, "but I always get hungry at night."

I eat a piece of cheese and a slice of pear, and then excuse myself to use the bathroom. Afterward, I wash my hands with some sort of pink liquid soap, and use the tiny embroidered hand towel to dry off my hands. I lean in toward the mirror, examining the tiny lines around my eyes, and then open it and look inside. There are nose hair clippers, a box of Band-Aids, two bottles of Benadryl, and a thin orange bottle of medicine. I reach for the orange bottle automatically, turn it around until I see the word *Vicodin*. The other pills helped James so much. Dramatically. I slip two more inside my jeans, recap the bottle, and shut the mirror again.

Later, Jane and I stand back and survey our progress. Only the roof needs to be attached; the rest of the structure, which is significantly larger than its initial appearance on the tarp, has been screwed and bolted into place. "Well, what do you think?"

"It looks amazing," Jane says. "But different somehow from the picture on the box, don't you think?"

I study the picture on the box: a boy in green shorts sitting atop the small red slide on the right, while a pigtailed girl wearing a blue sundress peeks out from the side window, her small hands resting on the plastic sill. I shift my gaze back and forth between the picture and the playhouse in front of me until suddenly, with a sinking feeling in my chest, I see the difference. "Oh, shit. We put the window and door in backward."

Jane's eyes bloom wide over her wineglass. "We did?" She giggles. "Are you sure?"

I move closer to the playhouse, peer at the details of the smooth plastic pieces. The windowsill is on the inside of the house, the hole where the doorknob will be attached on the left instead of the right. It will take hours to disassemble the house again and put it back together correctly. "Shit," I say again. "I can't believe we just did that."

"Oh, don't worry about it." Jane plops down on the grass, cradling her wineglass between her palms. "Nothing ever turns out exactly the way they say it will. Besides, we got the bulk of it done. We can fix it tomorrow. Or maybe we'll just leave it. I doubt the kids'll even notice." She stretches out against the grass, balancing the stem of her glass against her breastbone.

"Oh, I don't want to leave it. You're paying me to do this, Jane. And you said you wanted to surprise the kids. I want to do it the right way."

"All right." She twists her head, looking up at me sideways. "But we'll do it tomorrow, okay? Come sit down. Relax a little." She repositions her head, looks up above her. "Do you ever come outside and just look up at the stars? I used to do that all the time, but I never think to do it anymore. I'm always so busy with the babies . . ." She sighs heavily, rearranges her fingers around the wider part of the glass. "They're like little headlights up there, don't you think? Or like eyes, glowing."

I sit down next to her, drawing my knees into my chest, and wrap my arms around them. A heavy impatience is growing inside my chest—a combination of screwing up the playhouse, and just wanting to get out of here. But Jane is still talking, and I don't want to be rude. There is a chill in the air I hadn't noticed before, probably because I was so immersed in the task at hand. Now, the tiny hairs on my arms prickle; my earlobes feel cold.

"Did you know that stars are in constant conflict with themselves?" Jane asks.

I look at her over my shoulder, wonder briefly if she is drunk. "What?"

She sits up, pouring the rest of her wine into the grass, staring at the thin stream of it. "They're constantly pushing and pulling against themselves. Technically, it's because the gravity of all the mass of a star pulls it inward, while all the light photons, which are already inside the star, are pushing against it, trying to make it to the outer edges, but I like to think it's because they're kind of like little kids, not knowing what the hell to do with everything they've got. *Push? No, pull! No, push!*" She smiles. "It's amazing though, isn't it? How something in such a state of unrest can be in perfect balance like that at the same time?"

"Yeah," I say, thinking that the really amazing thing is that Jane knows such a thing. "How do you know all that?"

"Oh, I studied astronomy in college." Jane plucks a blade of grass from the lawn, inserts it between her lips. "I love all that stuff. Always have." Her voice has taken on a forlorn quality, the tone of someone remembering, wistfully.

"So then are you a . . ." I stumble, not knowing what the exact word is. "Like a scientist?"

Jane withdraws the blade of grass from her mouth, studies it for a moment. "No. I didn't even graduate. I met Richard, got pregnant at the beginning of my senior year, and dropped out."

"Oh."

She lowers her head behind her arm; only her eyes peek out.

"Maybe someday I'll go back. Finish. Although there wouldn't really be any reason to now."

"Why not?"

She lifts one hand, encompasses her house and everything inside it with a flutter of her fingers. "Because this is my life now."

I don't say any more, mostly because I don't want to get into a long, extended conversation with Jane about her personal life. But the other part of it, I realize later, after I say goodbye and get back into the car, is that the ache in her voice sounds familiar. Like an echo of something I might have said—or at least thought—and then pushed away, deep down, so as not to remember again.

Chapter 28

I take a left on South Main Street after leaving Jane's and drive for a while, just looking at the neighborhood houses with their half-shaded windows, dirty even beneath the harsh glare of the streetlights. The green digital clock in the car says nine-fifteen, but it is so dark as to be almost midnight. A multitude of stars, glittering haphazardly against an inverted bowl of black, look as though they've been scooped up and flung without forethought. What was it once that James had told me about stars? That when you looked at them, you were literally looking back in time? Something about the light from the star taking millions of years to reach the Earth, which meant that the star you glimpsed on any given night was not the present image you held in your mind's eye, but literally how it appeared thousands of years ago. What if the same thing could be said of us? What would change if the images we held of one another weren't actually the ones we saw, but fragments of ourselves from another time? How would I look at James if I knew the face he showed me tonight wasn't really him, that it was, in fact, just a part of him from long ago? The child he used to be, perhaps, or the teenager whose mother had vanished suddenly from his life?

I pull the car over and take out my phone.

"Ma?"

"What's wrong?"

"Nothing. I just want to stay a little while longer. Is that okay?"

There is a pause. "You mean at the church?"

"Yes. At the church. I ran into Father Delaney and—"

"You did?" Ma breaks in excitedly. I close my eyes, hating the fact that I am lying to her again. "You're talking, then? The two of you?"

"Yeah. Sorta. Anyway, I'll be home later. Can you put Angus on the phone?"

"Of course."

"Mom?"

"Hi, Boo. Listen, I'm calling to say good night, okay? I won't be home to tuck you in tonight."

"Why not?"

"I have to stay at the church for a little while. Just to see about something."

"What do you have to see about?"

"Oh, nothing important."

"The incense?" he asks.

"No." I draw a line around the steering wheel with my finger. I will not lie to him. "Not the incense."

"Then what?"

"Just some big-people things. I'll tell you about them later, okay?"

"Okay," Angus says.

"I love you. I'll see you in the morning, okay?"

"Okay. Oh, and, Mom?"

"Yes?"

"Can we go see our new house again tomorrow?"

"Maybe." I bite my lip, wondering if Ma is nearby, if she's overheard him. Maybe Angus has taken it upon himself to tell her about our visit; he tells her everything anyway. A stab of guilt as I think about bringing James there tomorrow. "We'll talk about it tomorrow, Boo, okay? See you in the morning. I love you."

"Love you, too. Night, Mom."

THIS TIME, WHEN I climb up the stairs, I hear a single, faint click behind the organ. And even though I have never even seen a gun up close until two days ago, I know for a fact that the click is the sound of a gun being cocked. James doesn't know it's me, I realize. He thinks I've gone for the night, that I won't be back for him until tomorrow. And he's ready to shoot whoever else comes up here. Again.

I lean in close as I dare and hiss loudly. "It's Bird."

James looks physically deflated when I finally get over to him, as if all the air has just rushed out of the top of his head. "I'll tell you what," he says. "I'm gonna end up shooting your goddamned head off if we keep going like this. We need a signal or something."

"Okay." I scoot in against the balcony and stare at the gun, which is still in his hand. It's metal-black and shiny, darker along the handle, and eerily compact. I wonder how heavy it is, if a charred smell of some sort comes out of it after it fires. "How about a whistle?" I say. "Like three of them in a row or something?"

"Too risky," James says. "Someone's bound to hear it. What else?"

I think for a minute. "A couple taps? Maybe one, then a pause, then two more quick?"

"Try it," James says.

I knock lightly against the linoleum, watching for James's reaction. One. Pause. Twothree.

James shrugs and then nods. "Okay."

I look back down at the weapon in his hands. "You wouldn't really shoot anyone, would you? I mean, after everything that's already happened?"

James turns the gun to one side, examining the barrel. "I don't think so. But you never know. I'm in pretty deep here. I wouldn't really have anything left to lose."

I keep quiet when he says that, watch as he slides the gun back into his place against the wall. What would something like that feel like? I wonder. To not have anything left to lose? Is such a thing really possible?

"I don't *want* to shoot anyone." He's looking at me with a peculiar expression, searching my face, it seems, for some kind of approval. "You know that, right? Or do you think I'm already gone?"

I look up. "Gone?"

"You know. Past the point of no return. Finished."

I uncross my legs, shift uncomfortably against the balcony. "You mean because of what happened in the bar?"

"Yeah, because of what happened in the bar. Because of what I *did* in the bar. And because I escaped on my way to prison and stole a sheriff's gun, which I have no idea whether or not I would use if someone found me here just now and came to take me away. I've crossed a line in your world, haven't I?"

My world? As opposed to who else's exactly? "I don't know

what you're talking about." Except that I do know what he's talking about. I know exactly what he's talking about. And the truth is that part of me does think he's gone. There's no arguing that what he's done—first in the bar, and then in the police car—is pretty serious stuff. But I've done bad stuff, too, deliberately cheating the system the way I did. And not just once, but four times. Then, just a few hours ago, I stole pills from a client. For the second time in one day. And last but certainly not least, I am here, willingly aiding and abetting a criminal, which, even if I wasn't on probation, could very well land me in jail. Who's to say that my sins weigh less than James's? And who gets to determine whether or not that weight classifies someone as gone?

James raises his eyes, looks at me. "Well, I guess if you really thought I was such a terrible person, you wouldn't be here, would you?"

"I don't think you're a terrible person." I wonder if he believes me. I wonder if I believe myself. Maybe, deep down, we're both terrible people. "Why'd you run?" I ask suddenly. "Why'd you take the gun?"

James shakes his head, stares at something on the floor. "I panicked," he says finally. "I was literally having a fucking panic attack in the backseat of that cop's car, thinking about being shut up in some cell. I just . . ." He bites his lower lip. "Remember that time when I told you I was afraid of the dark? Well, I'm afraid of small spaces, too. Of being locked up. It was something my father used to do to me when I was little. Throwing me in the coat closet in the hall and locking the door was his idea of punishment. He'd force my mother out of the house so she couldn't help me, and then come back an hour, sometimes three hours, later—I never knew how long it was going to be—and let me out again. One time, he kept me in there for two days. Two fucking *days*. I cried for so long and so hard that I literally passed out." He pauses, his face slick with sweat around the edges. "Anyway, small spaces—small, dark spaces—make me crazy. I knew I'd lose it once they locked that jail door behind me. And I didn't mean to take the gun. It fell out of the holster when the guy and I were wrestling, and I . . . I just grabbed it."

I don't say anything. What is there to say? Does knowing these new details about him make his actions any easier to understand? To forgive? Or am I just looking for excuses?

A noise downstairs causes us both to freeze. Soft footsteps are followed by the squeak of a pew, a heavy sigh.

"How many of them are still down there?" James asks.

I peek over the banister slowly, scan the emptiness below. There are four figures huddled in the front, a few feet away from the tabernacle. Red candles flicker against the walls, throwing tongue-shaped shadows along the floor. I turn back around, raise four fingers. "They might not stay too long," I whisper. "Father Delaney—the priest here—told me the other day that they have to lock up the church between midnight and five A.M. because of security issues."

"Ah." James nods. "That explains those big chunks of silence. Although you never know. My mother used to go to these services. She'd stay all night sometimes. Literally hours."

"Your mother?" I repeat. "She was Catholic?"

James nods. "I think that's why she never left my father, even though he was such a bastard. The Catholic Church is pretty hard on divorcees. They won't let them remarry, for one. And they can't even receive Communion afterward. Like they're tainted or something. Too dirty now, to receive the Host."

"Are you a Catholic?"

"Me?" James smiles. "No. I don't know what I am exactly, but I definitely know what I'm not."

"Me either. My mom raised me Catholic, but I haven't believed in any of that stuff since I was a teenager."

"So what do you believe in now?" James asks.

"Nothing."

"Nothing at all?"

"Not unless you can prove it to me."

James grins. "Still a doubter."

I shrug, feeling a little embarrassed, although I'm not sure why. "It's not a bad thing to doubt."

"No," James agrees. "But I don't know if I feel the same way about not believing."

"In what?"

"In anything." His forehead creases. "Don't you think it's better to believe in something than to go through life not believing in anything?"

"What's there to believe in? Religion is all the same bullshit. Catholics, Muslims, Jews, Protestants. They all think they have the only answer, and that their answers are the only ones that are right. How can you believe in things like that?"

"I wasn't talking about religion," James says.

"Then what are you talking about?"

He shrugs. "How about one of those facts I used to throw at you? You could try to believe in one of those."

I cock my head to one side, study him carefully. "Those facts were interesting. But honestly, James, they were useless. I still don't know if any of them were ever proven and neither do you. That book could have been written by some crackpot, for all I know. Besides, what's the point of believing in whether or not a heart beats 100,000 times a day or not? I mean, who really cares?"

"But why *wouldn't* you believe in something like that?" James presses. "Just for the hell of it? To take it on face value."

"It wouldn't hurt, I guess. But it wouldn't *do* anything either."

"It might make you look at your heart differently," James says. "Which might make you feel better about things in general."

"You think because I decided to believe that my heart beats over 100,000 times a day I'm going to feel *better* about things?"

"Our hearts weigh less than a pound," James says. "And despite that, it does the most physical work of any muscle in our whole body during a lifetime. It beats 100,000 times a day, Bird. That's seventy-two times a minute. Three and a half million times a year! Isn't that extraordinary? Doesn't knowing that make you look at yourself—or at least that little muscle inside your chest—in a whole different way?"

"Not if it's not true."

"But what if it *was*?" He leans forward, a new sense of urgency laced throughout his whispering. "What if it was true? Wouldn't it be amazing?"

"Maybe." I look down, pick at the edge of my shoelace. "*If* it was true."

"I think it's true," James says. "And I think my life is better because I do."

"How is it better?"

"I don't know. I guess because it makes me think about other things that are kind of miraculous."

"Like what?"

He hesitates, but only for a moment. "Like the size of our universe. Have you ever stopped to think about how big something like that actually is?"

"Not really."

"You couldn't do it," James says, shrugging. "It's almost impossible to comprehend, really. The only way scientists can get some kind of semblance of it is by measuring it with light."

"What's that mean?"

"It means that the universe is so big that even light hasn't had time to cross it." He pauses dramatically. "In fourteen *billion* years."

I try to consider this for a moment, but he's right. It is impossible to grasp, like trying to imagine eternity, which was something I did constantly as a kid after Ma told me that heaven was a place without end. It drove me crazy that I couldn't fathom it, made me feel as though God was playing a trick on me. "That's impressive," I offer. "But how can you consider something you can't even comprehend to be miraculous?"

"Okay, how about something smaller?" James offers. "The hummingbird, for example."

"The hummingbird?"

"Some of them are the size of my thumbnail." He holds up a hand, splaying his thumb to one side. "But they have the biggest brains of any bird on the planet, something like four percent of their whole body. They're smart, too. They can remember which flowers they've already sipped the nectar out of, and how much time they have to wait before they can go feed again."

I give James a look that says I'm not buying it.

He pushes on, undeterred. "They can fly forward or backward, hover, and even fly upside down, and they do it all so fast that we can't even see it. Bird, they beat their wings between seventy and two hundred times per *second*!"

I raise my eyebrows, watching him. Listening to him. The urgency in his voice is nearing desperation. What is it about this stuff that is so important to him? And why does he feel the need to keep sharing it with me?

James is still talking. "You know, it's interesting that of all the facts I told you back then, the one you remember is about the heart."

"Why is that interesting?"

He shrugs. "I must've told you at least one hundred facts back then. Stuff about animals, space, plants, food. But you remembered the one about the heart. About all the work it does in a single day." He's looking at me so intently that I drop my eyes, feel my pulse beating inside the soft part of my wrists.

"Yeah." I cross my arms. "So?"

He's smiling. "You don't find that interesting?"

"No. Not really."

"I do."

"You already said that."

"I'm saying it again."

"Well, stop." I'm fighting the playfulness between us, but I'm not sure why. "You're getting a little weird on me here, if you want to know the truth. Let's just drop it, okay?"

"Okay." James reaches up, pulls hard on one of his ear-lobes. He adjusts the front of his pants, smoothing down the new creases that have formed along the insides of his legs. "So why did you come back again tonight? Did you forget something?"

I shake my head.

"Then what?"

Thoughts dart in and out of my head, flashing this way and that, like so many brightly colored fish. *This. For this. To sit with you a little while longer and hear you talk to me the way you used to.* No, God, no. Too much. I'll sound pathetic. Ridiculous.

"I just . . ." I start, and then I remember the Vicodin in my pocket. "I brought you some more Vicodin. I thought it might help. "

But James is shaking his head. "Thanks, but I can't."

"Why not?"

"I'm pretty sure you're supposed to take that stuff with food. I almost passed out last night from the stomach pains I got from it."

"Oh my God." I slide the pills back inside my pocket. "I'm so sorry. I didn't know."

"How could you?" James smiles a little. "What about Angus? Didn't you say you had to go back home and tuck him in?"

"I called him on the phone. He's with my mother. He's okay. We said good night." James is staring at me with a knowing expression, and I am so afraid of his next question that my hands literally start to shake.

"Can I ask you something?" His voice is gentle, soft as rain. I nod and drop my eyes. "Is Angus . . ." he starts. "I mean, was he from the—"

"Yes," I answer. "He is."

The silence between us is charged with so much emotion that I can feel it humming like a blue electricity. Why do I feel so ashamed suddenly, now that James knows this? What has transferred the horror of that night into a guilt that is blurring my vision, making the soft spots beneath my elbows ache?

"Did you ever call the police?" James asks.

I shake my head.

"Does anyone know?"

My head moves back and forth again. The inside of my mouth is dry; my stomach feels weighted.

"What about your mother?"

"My mother?" I raise my head. "My mother will never know. She would have been the last person on Earth I would have told something like that to, and I still plan on keeping it that way."

"Why? She would've helped you, wouldn't she?"

"Yes. She would have helped me. She would have called the police and taken me to the hospital and done all the right things. But she would have blamed me, too. Especially since I dated him. And because I opened the door that night. Even though I knew he was drunk. Even though I knew I shouldn't have."

A long silence passes between us.

"That wasn't your fault, you know."

I move my hand brusquely, as if brushing away a fly. "Oh, I know."

"Do you?" James is leaning forward a little, away from the wall. He is peering at me, trying to gauge my expression, I guess. Trying to figure out if I am really telling him the truth.

"Yes." I deliberately hold his gaze for a moment and then look away again. "And I don't want to talk about it."

A moment passes. "How about Jenny?" James asks. "Did she ever talk to you about it?"

"Jenny?"

"She was your roommate, right?"

"Yeah. But we weren't close. She was never there anyway. And she moved into her boyfriend's place a few weeks after it happened."

"But she was there," James says.

"Where?"

"At the apartment. That night. That was how I found out what was going on actually. The door was open and she was right inside, just standing there with her hands over her mouth.

I started to ask her something, and then we heard you scream again and she turned and ran back down the steps." He pauses. "You already know where I went."

My heart is racing, sweat breaking out along the back of my neck like small goose bumps. "I . . ." It's the only thing that comes out, the only sound I can make at the moment.

"She must have come back for something," James says. "And heard you. She had to have heard you. Maybe she was just too scared to go back there."

I nod, swallow. That must have been it. Would I have felt the same way, if the roles had been reversed? Is it possible that I would have stood there, listening to my roommate scream as a former boyfriend raped her in the bedroom we shared? I would like to think that the answer is obvious, that I would have run back there with a bat, or a frying pan, anything to knock him out cold, get him off her.

But the honest answer is that I don't know what I would have done.

"You look so freaked out," James says softly. "I shouldn't have told you. I'm sorry."

I shake my head, pick at the hem of my jeans. "It's just . . . weird," I get out finally. "I just . . . I never knew she was there."

"Are you angry? That she didn't help you?"

"Yeah." I look down at the floor. "Well, not really. I don't know." Neither of us says anything for a moment. I occupy myself by drawing a wayward line through the thin film of dust, as if it might lead me to my next thought. "Why *were* you there that night?" I ask, looking up suddenly. "I never got the chance to ask you that."

James gazes at me for a moment and then drops his eyes. "I was on my way to the movies," he says. "I love the movies. I used to go all the time, two, three times a week, just by myself.

Get a box of Junior Mints and a Coke with extra ice, and sit in the last row, happy as a clam. And I don't know, that night . . ." He shrugs, letting his voice trail off.

"That night, what?" I don't realize I've been holding my breath until I exhale.

"That night I didn't want to go by myself."

"No?"

"I wanted to go with you. In the worst possible way. Ever since that day when we'd kissed . . ." He pauses, ducking his head. "Anyway, then I heard you and Charlie had broken up, and it was all I could think about, every day at work. Having you with me at the movies. Right there next to me. For two whole hours." He smiles. "I was nervous about asking you, too. I walked up and down the sidewalk in front of your apartment for about twenty minutes trying to work up the nerve. When Jenny showed up, I almost left, but then we started talking and she actually came right out and asked me if I was there to ask you out and I told her that I was thinking about it, and she was so nice about it—she said everyone at work had been waiting for me to do it—"

"Wait," I interrupt, "what do you mean everyone had been waiting for you to do it? How?"

"I'm not sure." He shrugs. "I guess some people knew that we used to talk out back."

"Who?" I'm genuinely shocked. "No one was ever around."

"I don't know. I didn't really ask her. But you know how people are. How they pick up on things, make their own as-sumptions. Especially about situations like that." He looks up at the ceiling, his eyes roving over the length of it. "Lionel said something to me about it once."

"Lionel? The other cook? What'd he say?"

"Something about me losing my concentration whenever

you were in front, working the register." James shrugs. "I hadn't even noticed that I'd been distracted. But he was right. Every time you were up there and I could see you through that little window, it was a little like being at the other end of a telescope. Everything else around me just sort of faded away. The only thing I could see was you." He inhales lightly. "Anyway, that's why I was there. That night. The rest, as they say, is history."

"The rest . . ." My brain is moving so fast that I feel breathless, light-headed. What if Charlie hadn't come around that night? What if I had opened the door to find James standing there instead, hopeful and nervous, stammering over a request to accompany him to the movies? Would I have gone with him? And what might have happened as a result? Where else could we have taken things?

"Tell me about Angus," James says suddenly. "What's he like?"

Angus. My heart skips a beat. There would be no Angus if things hadn't happened exactly the way they did that night, down to the last horrifying detail. Angus. Something inside me swells at the thought of him, momentarily tempering the rush inside my head. "Oh God, he's sweet. He's got black hair and real wide blue eyes. He's kind of small for his age—he's five—but he's the shortest kid in his preschool class."

James nods. "He'll grow."

"He's really into his shoes. He thinks they're magic. They're just these goofy kid sneakers that we found last summer at Sears, but he's obsessed with them. He wears them every day, even though they don't fit. It makes me a little crazy, because I know his toes are all squished up in there, but I've stopped trying to get him to wear anything else. He used to go nuts when I did."

"Why does he think they're magic?"

"I have no idea. He honestly believes that they can make him run faster and jump higher."

James smiles.

"I don't know what's going to happen when he tries to put them on one day and he can't get his foot into them. Or when they just fall apart completely and we have to throw them away. He's going to be devastated."

"You don't have to throw them away."

"Well, yeah, of course I do. They've already started to smell. And they'll be—"

"Let him keep them," James says. "Even if he just puts them under his bed. Or in his closet. He needs to have something like that."

"Like what?" I laugh softly. "A pair of old shoes sitting around, smelling up his—"

"Something he can believe in," James interrupts. "Even if he doesn't know why just yet."

A slim chorus of voices drifts up beneath us. *Our Father, who art in heaven . . .*"

I press myself more tightly against the banister, look at James as I hold my breath. "They're just saying the rosary," he says. "They did this last night, too. When they're done, they'll leave."

"Hail Mary, full of grace . . ." I close my eyes, lean my head back against the balcony. The women's slow, muted voices have an almost soporific effect on me, weighting my eyelids, slackening my jaw. I used to say this prayer every night, right before bed. I don't really have anything against Mary, per se. When I was younger, in fact, I thought she was one of the loveliest women I had ever seen, with the crown of stars set just above her long, serious face and her blue robes. I'd even imagined her

as a real mother of sorts, looking out for me from afar. Now, though, she's just another part of that same dubious Catholic-icon category: beatific, ethereal, anything but real. Anything but here.

"Does Angus like preschool?" James asks.

I open my eyes again. "Yeah. Pretty much. There's one kid, though . . ."

"A bully?"

I wince, thinking of my shameful tirade against Jeremy. "It's kind of hard to tell if he's actually a bully. They've been best friends for the last year. Angus is crazy about him. But lately . . ." I shake my head. "I don't know. They haven't been getting along."

"Does he pick on him?"

"It's more of an attitude." I pause, searching for the right word. "What's it called when you don't give a shit anymore about someone? When they could shrivel up right in front of you and disappear and you wouldn't care?"

"Apathy," James says. "He's apathetic."

"Exactly. That's what Jeremy is. Apathetic. When it comes to Angus anyway." I shrug. "He *is* only five years old. I could just be coming down the tiniest bit too hard on him. I don't know. I guess you want everyone to love your kid the way you do. All the time, no matter what happens."

"It doesn't work that way." James's voice is gentle.

"Yeah, I know. It sucks."

"*Glory be to the Father, to the Son, to the Holy Spirit . . .*"

"You're a good mother," James says out of nowhere.

I lift my head. "What?"

"You heard me."

"How do you know I'm a good mother? You've never even met Angus."

"I don't have to. I can tell just by listening to the things you've said about him."

I look down at my jeans, rub a finger along one of the denim creases. No one's ever told me such a thing before. Not even Ma.

"You don't think you are?" James asks.

I shrug, blink back tears.

"But how could you not be? You love him so much."

I nod. My jeans are blurring under my eyes; a tear drops down on the dark blue material, splattering slightly.

"Bird." He reaches out, brushes his fingers over my leg. "What is it?"

"I don't know." And it's the truth. I don't know. It's just that sometimes when I think of Angus stuck with me, I feel like I could cry and never stop. He deserves so much better. So much more.

The Hail Marys start again, amid a series of soft sighs. I wipe my cheeks with my fingers, try to laugh a little. "They sound like they're falling asleep," I whisper, motioning backward with my thumb.

James nods, still watching me. His face is somber, as serious as I've seen it tonight. "He'll be okay, you know. With you. Even if you screw up sometimes."

I look over at him, my eyes still leaking a little around the corners. I don't know if I've ever wanted to believe anything more in my entire life.

"All he needs to know is that you love him. If he knows that, he'll be okay. No matter what else happens."

Below us, the faint chorus of voices begins chanting the Hail Holy Queen prayer, signaling the end of the rosary: *"Hail holy queen, mother of mercy, our life, our sweetness and our hope . . ."*

We sit silently, listening to the prayer and, as it ends, the shuffle of people as they rise, collect their things, and make their way out of the church. There is the heavy sound of the front doors closing a final time, and then a clicking from somewhere in the back. Slowly, the red lights go off, one after the other, like a series of traffic lights, until the only thing visible in the whole building is the pool of yellow light hovering over the Eucharist in the corner.

Then complete silence.

Chapter 29

J ames." I move closer to him, reach out and touch the tip of his sock. Dad's sock. "Tell me what happened the other night. In the bar."

There is a long silence, and for a minute, I regret that I've asked such a question. That I've gone there again. I withdraw my fingers, sit back again against the wall. I must be imagining this light familiarity that I feel between us. It isn't real. Or maybe it used to be, but it isn't anymore. Now, it's just the memory of the thing; an old coat thrown on casually, without thinking about how tightly it fits in the shoulders. I bite my lip, get ready to apologize, to retract my statement. Except that James starts talking.

"These last couple years, I've just been taking care of my dad." His voice is weary, as if anticipating the first step of a long journey. "He was sick when you and I first met, but then he took a turn for the worse. That's why I came back from California. The doctors said he had a rapidly progressive form of Alzheimer's, and he probably wouldn't last much longer. One of them said a year, and that was what I let myself hang on to.

One more year, and then I was gonna leave again." He leans his head back against the wall, stares up at the ceiling. "Except that the bastard took his own sweet time to die, just like he did with everything else."

"And you took care of him? While you were working and everything?"

"Well, he was already in a nursing home when I got back from California because he couldn't take care of himself anymore. There were nurses there, tending to him around the clock, so I didn't have to worry about the basics. But I came at night. To sit with him. To read to him."

"What'd you read to him?"

James starts to say something and then stops. "Let me go back a little. Before he went into the nursing home, when we were both working at the Burger Barn, he was already starting to get a little fuzzy around the edges. He lived alone, but when he called me—which he did every so often—I noticed that he'd forget some people's names or what certain foods were called. I didn't think anything of it, really, but it made him crazy, not being able to remember things. It infuriated him. Anyway, one day he asked me to come over to his place, and when I did, he showed me a pile of books he'd gone and checked out at the library. They were all these science books about the planets and atoms and space and all that. He was a carpenter all his life, but he'd always loved anything having to do with science. Said if anything had a right to make him feel small, it was the universe. Anyway, he sat me down after showing me all those books and he told me something that I've never forgotten. He said he was at war."

I arch an eyebrow. "At war?"

"With himself," James finishes. "He said he was fighting a battle to keep his mind intact and that he'd be damned if he was going to lose it. Then he said he needed my help, which, I'll tell you, almost made me fall out of my chair."

"Why?"

"He'd never asked me for anything," James answers. "Half the time, I wasn't even sure he knew I was alive. Except when I got in the way, of course. Or was trying to pull him off my mother." He rubs one eye. "Anyway, he said he needed my help, that every afternoon after I got off work from the Burger Barn, he wanted me to drop by, give him three facts from one of the science books, and then quiz him the next afternoon to see if he remembered them. I was a little hesitant about the whole thing, I guess because it was just such an odd thing for him to ask, and I asked him why he couldn't just do it himself." A small smile escapes James's lips. "He said he'd cheat, that he needed someone else around to keep him honest."

"Is that why you were always reading the fact book at the Burger Barn?" I ask, marveling silently at the situation's new context. And to think I'd thought he was a freak, leafing through all those random statistics at six o'clock in the morning. A weirdo!

James nods. "We ran out of the science books in a few months, so I went and got a few of my own, one of which was that *Curious Facts and Data*. He *loved* that one—there were things in there that made him chuckle. Anyway, I liked to check up on the new things I would tell him, go over some of the questions he might ask me afterward." He bites his lower lip with his teeth and holds it there for a moment. "He'd get so excited when he remembered. God, you would've thought he won a gold medal or something the way he'd explode when I told him he was right, hopping a little in the air and pumping his fists." A vague smile fades. "But then the opposite was true, too. It was awful when he couldn't remember. He'd curse

and throw something, even spit sometimes. And then after the
anger passed, he'd get so down on himself, slumping around
the kitchen, pulling his hair. He'd tear so hard at it sometimes
that it came out by the roots." He flicks his eyes up at me.
"That's when I started to realize that maybe his mental state
was really starting to go."

"Because he pulled his hair?"

James smiles sadly. "Remember all that hair I used to have?"

I nod. How could I forget?

"I got it from him. Like, exactly. Same color, thickness,
even the same two cowlicks in front. When I was real little, he
used to say that if I hadn't had the same hair he did, he'd have
to be convinced we were even related." James shakes his head,
purses his lips as if tasting something bitter. "He took serious
pride in his hair, getting the part right, always slicking it down
with this wide, perfectly arched swoop in front. For him to
pull at it like that—to leave *bald* patches all over his skull—was
another indicator that he was starting to lose it. Sometimes I'd
lie to him about the answers, just to make him think he was
right, because I couldn't bear to see him so desperate."

"It's amazing that you were able to do that. To make up with
him and everything. Especially after all he put you through as
a kid."

"Who says I made up with him?" James studies his nails,
lifting the edge of one thumb to his mouth.

"You didn't?"

"I was just there because I promised my mother." James's
hand falls away from his mouth. "It was the last thing she asked
me to do before she died."

"To stay with him?"

"To forgive him." James's voice quavers around the edges.
"And I tried. I really did. I stayed right there." His jaw clenches,

the edges of his nostrils flare. "I showed up every night and waited. For three more fucking years."

"Waited for what?"

"For him to say something! About everything that had happened. I wanted him to acknowledge all the terrible things he'd done to my mother and me so that I could, too, and then maybe we could move forward. After a while, I realized I didn't even need it to be an apology, which was what I thought I wanted. It could have just been a kind word. A glance. Anything that said that he had fucked up when I was a kid, but that deep down he loved me because . . ." He pauses, shrugging. "Because I was his."

"Did you ever bring it up?"

"Once, in the nursing home. He was pretty well gone by then. I don't know why I even tried. He was upset about something, but I can't remember what it was. Maybe it was a Tuesday. Who the hell knows? He'd gone and thrown something across the room. The remote, I think, or maybe a coffee cup. Anyway, it broke, whatever it was, just split apart as soon as it hit the wall, and I went over and picked it up and he yelled at me and told me to leave it where it was, that he didn't need some pansy-ass cleaning up after him. So I went over and sat down on the chair next to his bed for a minute, and then I asked him why he was so angry all the time." James furrows his forehead. "He acted like he didn't know what I was talking about, like I was speaking Russian or something. He kept saying things like, 'Angry? I'm not angry. What're you talking about?' And I said, 'Yeah, Dad, you're angry. You've been angry my whole fucking life and I want to know why.'" James leans his head back against the wall and stares up into the inky space above. "Stupid, to ask him then. So stupid. I don't know what I was expecting. But, God, he was such a shit about it. He just turned on me. Practically sneered in my face. 'You gonna get psycho-analytical on me? Huh, Mr. Freud? Ask me ten million questions about how I *feel*, how I should do things? Huh?'"

I fold one of my hands over the other, resisting the urge to reach out for James's arm.

"He just wouldn't meet me halfway. Ever." James raises both hands over the wide span of his face and rubs at the edges of his temples. The tips of his fingers turn white; his knuckles are calloused and worn. "And you know, I realized something that night. That when my mother had asked me to forgive him, she'd meant that it was something *I* had to do, for myself, without expecting anything in return. But you know what? Still, even after realizing that, even after sitting with it and mulling it over, I couldn't make myself do it. I wanted—I just *needed*—him to say something first." He lifts his eyes. "Do you think that makes me a terrible person?"

"No," I whisper.

"Maybe just a selfish one."

"You're hardly selfish. My God, look at all the time you gave him. Especially before the nursing home."

"It wasn't real time." James shrugs the suggestion away. "We both hated each other through the whole thing."

"No, you didn't. I can't speak for your father, but you wouldn't have agreed to give him those three facts every day and then come back and quiz him on them if every part of you hated him."

"Well, I guess that makes me a sucker, then, doesn't it?" James stares hard at me. "Or just an idiot."

"I don't think it makes you either." I reach out and touch the toe of his sock again. "I think it makes you human." I close my fingers around the soft material. "I think it makes you good."

"Good." James snorts, spitting the word back out at me. His face twitches suddenly, and he winces, reaching up to brush the cut on his forehead.

I sit forward quickly. "Are you bleeding?"

"No. It just itches."

I reach for the backpack, pull out the bottle of hydrogen peroxide and the small plastic bag filled with cotton balls, Q-tips, and gauze that I took out of the medicine chest at home. James watches silently as I saturate the cotton ball with peroxide, and closes his eyes as I press it against the cut on his head. But after a few seconds, he pulls back, out of reach. "Please let me," I say. "Otherwise, it'll get infected." He relaxes again, letting me clean the wound. It's so deep that I can see flesh inside the cut, the pale striations of fat and muscle within the skin. I keep wiping, then arrange a square of gauze over the cut, bite off a section of tape.

"He died two weeks ago, just before everything happened at the bar." James's voice floats up from under my hands. I sit back down, a little closer to him this time, the circle of tape still in my hands. "I was so stunned when I came into the nursing home that night and they told me he was gone that I literally just stood there for about five minutes without moving. Then I left. I walked around the city for hours. It was so cold that I couldn't even feel my feet after a while, but I couldn't stop walking. I couldn't believe it was over. I just couldn't believe it. I think somewhere, deep down, I'd really convinced myself that he would break through that goddamn wall he lived behind and look at me. *See* me, you know? As someone. As his son.

"But it didn't happen. And I didn't know what to do with that fact. I didn't know how to make sense of it, or how to make it better. So I went down to Dugan's and sat on a stool and started drinking. I remember when I got home that night, I went into the bathroom. Stared at myself in the mirror." He winces. "Maybe I was just drunk as shit, but the longer I looked at my reflection that night, the less I recognized the person looking back at me. I had this crazy thought that maybe my father had had that same experience, that when he looked at me, he didn't recognize anything. That maybe *that* was why he didn't love me, because he couldn't see anything of himself in me except for a fucking head of hair. And so I opened the medicine chest, and took out the razor and shaved it all off." He shrugs. "Maybe it was a 'fuck you' to him; maybe it was the booze; hell, maybe it was just me starting to go off the deep end. I don't know." He inhales deeply, the edges of his nostrils turning white. "Anyway, I did the same thing the next day. And the day after that. Went to Dugan's. Drank. Walked and walked in the freezing, bitter cold. Went home."

He looks at the floor, nods as if accepting something. "It was my fault. I was two sheets—hell, I was *eight* sheets—to the wind by the time Charlie walked in."

"Charlie?" I gasp involuntarily, lean forward a little. "Wait, is that who . . ."

James nods. "It wasn't what you think, though, Bird. I wasn't out to settle any kind of score or anything. I swear. He was just there with some girl." James looks past me. "Some young kid, probably not even old enough to drink yet. He was all over her, whispering in her ear, playing with her hair, and then at one point he got up to go to the bathroom. We locked eyes and he froze, and I swear that whole night in your apartment passed between us in a second and then he blinked and said, 'What the hell you looking at, dirtbag?' I just looked away, but I could feel something starting to build inside, and then on the way back from the bathroom he bumped into me.

I knew it wasn't an accident, and I told him to watch his step—that was it, I swear to God, Bird—and he stopped for a minute and said, 'What'd you say to me?' And I repeated myself, although I think I threw in a few expletives this time, and before I knew what was happening, he had reached out and grabbed me, right around the face." James demonstrates with his hand, reaching up to grab the hollows above his jawline.

"He started to stay something, but he didn't get to finish. It was like someone threw a match inside a bowl of gasoline. I just erupted." James leans his head back against the wall. His eyelids are so heavy now as to be almost closed, his mouth slack and drawn. "It was terrible. Like choking the life out of a puppy. Even before they pulled me off him, I knew I'd gone too far. He was just . . . laying there, so still. I couldn't even tell if he was breathing. I hadn't meant to take it to that level. Shit, I didn't even know I was *capable* of inflicting that kind of damage on anyone. It was just . . . everything. Him, what he'd done to you. Getting *away* with it. My father. Not being able to forgive him. All of it." He lifts his eyes, searching mine for a moment, and then drops them again. "So. You asked what happened that night in the bar. That's what happened."

A long, silent moment passes. The faint scent of incense lingers in the air.

"And now you're here." My voice is a whisper.

He nods, rubs the side of his neck. "If you want to go, I understand."

My brain is whirling with the new information I've just been given, but it's not lingering on the details about Charlie. It's stuck on James, walking miles and miles in the bitter cold every night with freezing feet and no hair. With a broken heart and no one to give it to.

"I probably should." I reach out slowly, put my hand over

his. "Except that I want to tell you something first." I move in closer, until my leg is barely touching his. An old longing winds its way through me like a plant tendril searching for light; I have to struggle not to cup the edge of his jaw in my palm, to keep my face away from his. The faint traces of lavender and urine hover in the air, the barely there scent of peroxide. Through the dark, only the outline of his lips is visible—the slight wave formation along the upper one, like a small *W,* above the rise and swell of the larger bottom one.

"Maybe you showing up every day and quizzing your father on those facts *was* a way of forgiving him. Even if you didn't know it at the time." I take my index finger, run it gently around the edge of his lips, then duck my head, brushing my cheek against his. His skin feels like a petal, the heat coming from inside his mouth a tiny furnace. I lift my head again, gaze at his scar, trace the scythe-like shape of it with my index finger. "And maybe him asking you for your help was his way of apologizing. Even if he didn't know it at the time either."

James looks at me for so long that I swear I can see a flurry of thoughts moving around behind his eyes, tiny birds flying high in some nameless sky, their feathery wings beating against the pull of the wind. The only thing that moves is his breathing, which sounds ragged around the edges, as if something has torn inside. "Maybe you're right," he whispers finally. "I never thought of it like that."

This time when I touch his face, I use my lips, retracing my steps between the space of his eyebrows, then farther down along his nose where the skin is ridged and puckered, and finally against his cheek where the scar ends. A muscle pulses along his jawline as I hover there, my lips barely touching his skin, and then he turns, pressing his mouth against mine. His lips are dry, rough, almost metallic tasting. I hesitate, but James leans into me, cupping the back of my head with his hand. He kisses me hard, insistently, but edged now with something that tastes like terror. Or maybe the terror is mine. I start to pull away, but he reaches up with his other hand and caresses my cheek with his knuckles.

I study him for a moment, the small specks of gold inside the green of his eyes, the burst of black inside the pupil. And then I lean in. We kiss and kiss and there is nothing in the world that exists in that moment but this. His tongue is gentle against mine, his lips like warm sponges now against the planes of my face, the wide space of my forehead. He takes his thumbs at one point and, cupping my face in the rest of his hands, draws them around the edge of my hairline. "You're beautiful," he whispers. "God, I've always thought you were so beautiful."

I wrap both of my arms around his head as he leans into my chest, bury my nose against the stubbly growth of hair along his skull. His skin smells faintly of salt; the tiny hairs are rough against my skin. "Do you remember what you told me that day just before you kissed me on the step?"

"That you smelled like rain," James murmurs.

"Rain after a long stretch of hot, dry weather." I kiss the top of his head, lower my face until it is in front of his. "Do you know what that's called?"

James kisses the tip of my nose. "Is there really a term for it?"

"There is. I looked it up that night."

"You did?" His eyes light up. "What's it called?"

"Petrichor," I answer. "'Petra' from the Greek, meaning 'stone,' and 'ichor,' which is what they called the fluid that flowed through the veins of the gods."

"Petrichor," James says slowly. "The veins of God. I never knew that." He kisses me again. "But then I never knew anything until I met you."

I kiss him again and pull back, my lips lingering against his. "Actually, I think I like your definition better."

"My definition?"

"Relief," I remind him. "Liberation."

His lips curve into a smile and he nods, pressing his cheek against mine. "Yes," he whispers. "Yes, I have to agree."

Chapter 30

The air outside is cool against my face, a sudden breath. I'm sweating a little under my shirt; the back of my neck is damp. I hadn't realized how warm it could get upstairs, how quickly dead air collected, as if trapped in a bottleneck. It's well after midnight, the sky above newly strung with stars. I'd gotten up finally, when James insisted I leave, his finger lingering along my eyebrow. "People will worry," he said. "The ones who shouldn't. Go home and get some sleep. I'll see you tomorrow."

Large forsythia bushes have started blooming by the front stairs; in front of them are the tulip plants pushing their way out of the dark earth, their buds still swollen tight. I get in the car, start the engine, think briefly of Mr. Herron's tangerine parfaits. The streets are empty at this hour, deserted as a Sunday afternoon. I drive slowly, my fingers barely touching the wheel. I feel the way I do when I have drunk too much beer—outside of myself, fuzzy around the edges. My skin is hot to the touch and my fingers are trembling. At a stop sign, I close my eyes, remembering his mouth against mine, the way he lingered over the edge of my jaw, buried his face in the hollow of my neck. The way he'd said I was beautiful. The way he'd *looked* when he said I was beautiful, as if all the facts and statistics he'd given me over the years were nothing if I would only believe this.

Me, beautiful!

I tip my head back against the seat, holding the novelty of it in my chest. It's big and warm and like nothing else I've ever felt before in my life. I'm afraid to move, as if doing so might disturb it, a pebble thrown into still water. But I know I have to get home. I have rooms to clean, beds to make, laundry to wash. A child to hold.

After a long time, I open my eyes again and step on the gas.

THE HOUSE IS dark when I let myself in finally, drained and bleary-eyed. The light in the living room is still on, the curtains open. I am hanging up my coat when my name floats softly down the steps: "Bird?"

"Yeah, Ma. It's me."

She appears in the hallway, dressed in her flannel nightgown with the pink wildflower print and her big purple slippers. Her hair is askew—flat on one side, still puffed and teased on the other—and the hollows under her eyes are as large as quarters. "What time is it?"

I shrug, glance down at my watch: 1:10. "Late."

"Where were you?" Ma asks. "You haven't been talking to Father Delaney all this time, have you?"

"No. I was just driving around."

"Driving around?" Ma repeats. "What does that mean?"

"It means exactly what you think it means, Ma. I was in the car, driving around the neighborhood."

"Just wasting gas?" Ma presses. "Jeez, Bernadette. Gas is so expensive now. What's the point of that?"

"I needed to think." I head up the steps, past my senior year portrait that Ma still keeps on the wall, and pause for a moment, struggling to recognize anything inside the vacant expression and dimmed eyes. I lean in closer. It's my reflection I'm staring at, the eyes looking back at me now that I don't recognize.

"What'd you have to think about for so long?" Ma whispers the question. And then more vehemently: "Bernadette. Do you have to speak to me with your back turned?"

I whirl around then, glaring, ready to tear into her. Except that the expression on her face is so full of worry, so etched with concern, that I feel everything inside start to drain out of me, a slow leak. And then I am crying, hard, something that has come from a dark corner, a sudden, forceful release of feeling. It surges out with such intensity that my legs give out beneath me; I am seated on the step, leaning against the wall, weeping as though I have just learned how to do such a thing, the sounds coming out of my mouth a language all their own.

MA HELPS ME back down the steps, shushing me softly, steering me toward the kitchen table under one arm. She lets me cry as she busies herself around the kitchen, putting a flame under the copper kettle, taking out two mugs, arranging tea bags neatly inside each one. She fills the sugar bowl and then the creamer, and takes out a package of butter cookies, fanning six of them on a small saucer. When the kettle whistles, she pours the boiling water into the mugs, sets one in front of each of us. Then she folds her hands. Sits forward. "All right now," she says. "Tell me."

I reach down and pick up the string of my tea bag. "Ma. I really need you to listen to me." My voice is cracking. I clear my throat, pull a tissue out of the box on the table, and blow my nose.

"I'm right here, Bernadette." Ma takes a bite of cookie, dabs the corner of her mouth with her ring finger. "Go ahead."

"It's about the day I got pregnant."

Her whole face tightens, first with confusion, then with alarm, a sudden defense, as if someone has just pulled a fire alarm. She blinks once, twice. Picks up her teaspoon and fills it with sugar. Both of us watch the granules pour from her spoon, white sand dissolving in a tiny, scalding ocean. "Oh, Bernadette," she says finally. "I really don't think it's necessary to get into—"

"Ma." I wait until she looks at me. "I didn't just get pregnant. I was raped."

She stares at me without saying anything, the cookie frozen in her hand. Outside the house, the swish of tires rolls by along the street; a bird cries in the distance.

"Who?" she says finally.

I bite my lip, stare down into my teacup, wish I could somehow immerse myself beneath the dark liquid. "Charlie."

"Charlie?" She sits back in her chair, another blow. "But you . . . you were *dating* Charlie. You told me you were . . . with him."

"I know, Ma."

"So how could he—"

"He just did. He pushed his way into my apartment one night, and"—I bite the inside of my cheek so hard that I can taste blood—"he just did, okay?"

"Bernadette." Ma leans forward, her head tilted a little to one side. "Are you sure that's what happened?"

"Am I *sure*?"

"Yes. Are you sure?" She is floundering now, having been dragged into some kind of strange territory that she does not know the way out of, but refusing to admit it. "I mean, back then you were drinking and carousing, and . . ."

"And what? Drinking and carousing gives someone a license to *rape* me?"

She rests her elbow heavily on the table, brings her fingers to her forehead. "Well, of course not. But . . ."

I am trying to think logically. I am trying to give her the benefit of the doubt. I know she has a right to question my choices back then. The few times she came to my apartment, she'd seen the bottles of booze, the crushed joint in the seashell ashtray. Still, alluding to that behavior of mine right now as a justification for Charlie raping me hurts so much that I have to reach down and grab hold of the chair I am sitting on so that I don't take a swing at her.

Suddenly Ma lifts her downcast eyes. "What did Father Delaney say about all of this?"

"Father Delaney?" I run my tongue over my bottom lip. "I didn't talk to him about this."

She arches her back, raises an eyebrow. "But I thought that's why you said you wanted to stay later. To talk to him."

"Ma, I wouldn't talk to Father Delaney—or any priest—about that night if you paid me a million bucks." I drain the last of my tea, even though it's scalding, and set my cup back down on the table. A numbing sensation fades from the middle of my tongue, followed by an immediate stab of heat, which pools and then settles like a lily pad along the rough surface.

"Now why would you go say something like that?" Ma looks as if I've punched her in the gut.

"You want to know why?" I pull my chair in a little closer

to the table, lean on both elbows. "Because Father Delaney would say the same bullshit about it as he did at Dad's funeral. That God was *right there next to me* the whole time. And I don't want to hear it—or anything about God—ever again."

"Father Delaney's words are not bullshit," Ma says, whispering the last word. "And don't you speak of God like—"

"You know what, Ma? *Fuck! God!* If He thinks it's enough to sit next to someone and hold their hand while their brains are being splashed against a windshield, then fuck Him! If He thinks He's got it covered, whispering in my ear while some guy holds my arms down and shoves his *dick* into me, then fuck Him, again! Okay, Ma? Do you hear what I'm saying? Do you?"

Ma claps her hands over her ears, squeezes her eyes shut. She's moaning a little, swaying side to side. Then she stops. Opens her eyes. They are piercing. "I want you out, Bernadette." Her voice is shaking. "You can leave Angus here with me until you move in at the lake, but I want you out by tomorrow. You are not welcome here any longer."

"I've never been welcome here." I grab the cow-shaped saltshaker off the table, clench it tight in one fist. "It'll be my pleasure to leave."

The shaker goes hurtling out of my hand, smashing against the wall and splintering into four small pieces before crashing to the floor. I turn to leave but not before noticing the severed cow head as it skitters into one corner and then rolls to a stop, one lone eye staring up at Ma.

Chapter 31

Upstairs, I pause outside of Angus's room, stare at the back of his sleeping head, waiting, I guess, to start crying again, or even for my eyes to fill up, but nothing comes. It's as if a stone has planted itself in the middle of my chest, a weight of enormous proportions siphoning off my breath. I slump against the doorframe, realizing suddenly just how long I've been waiting to tell Ma what happened that night, and how long I've deluded myself into thinking that she would find a way to be kind or maybe even compassionate about it when I finally did. I'd come close only once before, when Angus was just a few months old. He'd been in the middle of a crying jag, a prolonged period of bitter wailing that went on for over three hours. I'd already checked all the basics; he was not hungry, he was not wet or dirty, and he was not, as far as I could tell, in any physical pain. Desperate, I put him in a warm tub, the water momentarily startling him into silence, and pulled him out again as he reclenched his fists, arched his tiny back, and screamed even more furiously. I swaddled him burrito-style, the way the nurse at the hospital had shown me, and unwrapped him again as his face turned scarlet with rage.

"What?" I cried helplessly, sinking down on the bed next to him. "What do you *want?*" His doll-like limbs, fingers and toes so small as to be almost imaginary, jerked at the sound of my voice, and as I watched him holler anew, it occurred to me that maybe he was just very, very angry, that somehow far back in the crevices of his baby brain, he knew exactly how he had been brought into this world and it did not sit right with him. A swell of my own rage followed, and I got up on my knees, glaring down at him. "Yeah, well, guess what, buddy? I'm pissed off, too. I didn't ask for this to happen. I didn't want any of this shit, including you." I could barely get the last few words out; they stuck in my throat like burrs, and I choked on them, realizing how much I actually meant them. The truth in that moment was that I didn't want anything to do with him ever again. He was the product of the single worst night of my life, forced into me against my will. His DNA was meticulously and miraculously half mine— and half Charlie's. Charlie, who had grabbed me around the face and twisted my arm behind my back and dug his knees into my elbows so hard I thought they might snap like dry tree branches. Charlie, who'd told me to say "please," whose eyes had turned black above me, who tore my underpants to shreds. Charlie, who'd taunted me when I begged him to stop. Charlie, who pinned me, helpless as a child, beneath the weight of him and violated me. Again and again and again.

I still don't know why the screams coming out of Angus shifted abruptly just then. And there is no way to comprehend how or why they seemed to move from a place of anger to one of deep sorrow, almost as if he knew that nothing in this world could ease it. They went on and on, an endless, forlorn sobbing, and as I recognized my own voice within them, I fell to the floor and wept. I needed my mother. I needed to tell her what had happened to me, and why, because of my shame, I had denied it ever happening, even to myself. I needed her arms around me and her soft voice in my ear, assuring me that I was not to blame and that no matter how ugly the details surrounding his existence, Angus was still mine, that I could still love him if only because of that fact.

I reached for the phone, dialing her number with shaking hands. Behind me, Angus bawled, with no indication of slowing down. I plugged my other ear with one finger as the ringing sounded in the other. Two. Three. Four.

"Hello?"

Only a tenth of a second to realize I'd made a mistake. She sounded exhausted, the familiar irritation creeping around the edges of her voice. "Hello? Who is this? Hello?"

"Ma." *(I need you.)*

"Bernadette?" A rustling on the other end; was she in bed? Or had she fallen asleep on the couch and was righting herself? Patting the corduroy throw pillow with the zipper down the side to get more comfortable? "Bernadette, is that you?"

"Ma." *(Please listen to me.)*

"What's wrong? What's that crying in the background? Is that the baby?"

"Yes."

"Is he okay? What's the matter?"

"I don't know."

"Well, is he hungry or wet?"

"No."

"Oh, Bernadette, he probably has gas again. You're just going to have to walk around with him and keep patting his back. It's the only way it'll come up."

"Ma." *(Please. He's not the only one screaming.)*

"*What*, Bernadette? If you think for one second that I'm coming over there . . ." She inhaled angrily. "You've made your bed, young lady. Now it's good and time for you to lie in it."

I was as numb that night as I feel right now. How could I have let myself believe that Ma would have any other reaction to the admission I just made? And what does it mean now that it hasn't come? Where does that leave me, what else can I do?

I walk across the room and stand over Angus; his blankets are flung to one side of his bed, one bare foot dangles over the edge. I rearrange his leg along the mattress, draw the sheets and blankets up around his shoulders, and tuck them lightly under his chin. He wrinkles his nose and turns away from me. I run my fingers absently through the curls on the back of his head, and then lay down, arranging myself around his tiny form, and hold him tight inside my arms.

Hours later, sleep arrives, an unexpected mercy.

THE SOUND OF voices from downstairs wakes me with a start. I'm still in Angus's bed, but he is missing. I look down at my watch. Eight-thirty. Shit. I have to get Angus to preschool by nine. And then I have to get everything ready to take James up to the apartment. I might as well just stay there with him, now that Ma has thrown me out. No one has to know. And Angus will be safe here with her—at least until I can figure out what to do next with James. My unconscious brain takes over, moving my legs, propelling me down the staircase. The couch in the living room is empty, but I can hear the sound of Angus shouting in the kitchen. "I can get dressed by myself!"

"Now you listen to me, young man . . ."

I bound into the kitchen, breathless, frightened. Ma startles at the sight of me, and then runs out of the room, snatching at her eyes. "Everything okay?" I ask Angus, who is sitting on the floor, clad only in his Ninja Turtle underwear and one red sock. "Why're you getting dressed in the kitchen?"

"Nanny made me. She said she wanted some company while she made breakfast." He yanks a green sock up along his other leg, but makes no move to touch the pile of other clothes sitting in a heap next to him.

"Oh, okay." I sit down in the chair opposite him, and rest my arms against the table. "You all right? It sounded like you were yelling a minute ago." Angus ignores my question a second time, deliberately extricating his blue cargo pants from the pile and tugging on one leg at a time. "Angus?" I'm getting annoyed. "What's going on here?" He stands up, plucking his shirt off the floor, and comes over to me for help. I pull it over his head, and kiss the top of his hair when it emerges through the opening. But he yanks it away, turns around so that his back is facing me.

"Angus?" I say softly. "Please tell me what's wrong."

He stands very still and lowers his head.

I come around to the front of him, kneel down so that I am at eye level with his face. When he was a baby, Ma used to say that he had ocean eyes, because they were blue and green with a little gray mixed in there, too. Now, they look like a storm above the water, a splitting of clouds over the sea. "Tell me, Boo. What is it?"

He stares at the floor. Lets a tear drop out of his eye without moving to wipe it away.

I lean down, maneuvering my head under his, so that I am staring up at his face. It is pink, his eyes squeezed tight. "Are you mad at me?"

He nods, lifts his head finally. "You were mean to Nanny," he chokes out. "I heard you last night. I was only pretending to be asleep when you laid down with me." I can tell by the way his nose is wrinkling that it hurts to say this to me. "You make her cry all the time. The other night, before we went to the church. And then last night, too. I don't like it when you yell at her. I don't like it when Nanny cries. I love her!" He throws his arms around me, hooking his tiny chin over my shoulder. His sobs are long and forlorn sounding.

I let him cry for a moment, and then pull back so that I can look at him. "Listen to me, Angus. Nanny and I have a hard time getting along sometimes. And lately it's just been harder than usual. But when the two of us move into our new place up at the lake . . ."

He takes a step back, pulling his hand out of mine as if I have just burned him. "Just you and me?"

"Just you and me," I say, trying to make my voice happy and light.

"Not Nanny?" Angus asks.

"Well, no. She'll stay here, Angus. This is her home."

"I don't want to go, then!" Angus tips his head back and hollers.

I grab both of his wrists—too hard—and yank him forward. "She can visit, Angus. As much as she wants. We can have her—"

"Noooooooooooooo!" Angus screams. "I don't *want* to leave Nanny!"

"All *right*!" I hiss, although it is the wrong thing to say. It's misleading, and I know it. Most of all, though, I don't want Ma to know that he is freaking out about leaving her. The slightest bit of ammunition on her end of things right now will just make it worse between us. If that's even possible.

The screaming halts abruptly. "All right?" he repeats.

"I'll think about it."

"What does you'll 'think about it' mean?" Angus asks. His face is blotchy from the screaming, his blue eyes wet around the edges.

"It means exactly what you think it means. I will *think* about it. Now put on your shoes. We have to go, or you'll be late for school."

I'm almost out the door when I notice Angus kick one of his magic sneakers under the table. "No magic sneakers today?"

He shakes his head, reaches silently for a pair of tan bucks that I bought him a few months ago. They have a large Velcro strap over the top of each, orange rubber soles.

"The magic sneakers are too small for you now, huh?" My hand is on the door. Well, I knew the day would come. Eventually.

"No." Angus's face transforms into a grim map of determination as he slides his foot into one of the suede shoes. "They're not too small. They just don't work anymore. And they're stupid."

I TURN THE radio to a news station on my way over to Mr. Herron's, keep it on WALL, even though it is in the middle of a commercial jingle. I think back to Ma this morning after the scene with Angus was over, how she avoided my eyes as Angus and I took a seat at the breakfast table, leaning in close to Angus for a kiss instead. I waited for the little twinge, some small thread of remorse, to snake its way through me for the things I said last night, but I felt nothing at all. Maybe I'm cut from the same cloth as James, I think, making the turn onto Mr. Herron's street. Or even James's father for that matter. Maybe the Rittenhouse men and I have more in common than I ever thought possible.

Angus hadn't said anything more on the way to school either—at least, not until we got into the parking lot. Then I
turned around, looking at him over the back of the seat until
he raised his eyes. "Angus. Listen to me, okay? I've been thinking about the situation with you and Jeremy."

"What's a 'stitch-u-a-tion'?" he asked.

"The whole thing going on between you guys. You know,
with him not being so nice to you lately."

He dropped his eyes again, staring down at his suede bucks,
and chewed the inside of his cheek.

"It was wrong of me to yell at him the way I did yesterday.
You can always come to me for help if you need it, but I'm not
going to interfere like that anymore."

"What's 'interfere'?"

I sighed, closed my eyes. "Butt in. I'm not going to butt in
again if it's something I think you can take care of yourself,
okay?"

Angus still hadn't moved. Not a blink, not a breath, except
for the inside of his mouth, which was working his cheek like
a piece of gum.

"But listen to me, Boo. If Jeremy bothers you, I want you
to stand up for yourself, okay? Don't let him push you around.
Don't just sit there and take it. It's okay to fight back. Okay?"

Still nothing.

"Angus!"

Finally, his eyes flitted up again, meeting mine. He looked
frightened.

"Are you listening to me?" I asked softly. "Did you hear
what I just said?"

He nodded and slid over sideways, opening the car door. "I
just want to go to school now," he said. "Bye, Mom."

IT'S MIDMORNING, BUT the sun is still hovering behind a shroud of clouds, deciding whether or not to come out. The air feels lighter, as if a warm front is moving in, and I roll down the window, rest my arm on the sill. Up ahead on the right is the Owen Street bakery with the green-and-white striped awning out front. Maybe I will stop, buy five or six of the big cinnamon rolls that Ma and Angus like so much. We can heat them up in the oven tonight after dinner, drizzle them with the plastic cups of vanilla icing the bakery provides for such purposes. Ma will put on a pot of hazelnut coffee; Angus will smear the frosting off with his fingers and lick them clean. My heart swells a little at the thought of it—until I pull into the parking lot and stare at the front of the store. Who am I kidding? Cinnamon rolls and coffee? Do I really think that is going to help anything?

I steer the car in the direction of Mr. Herron's house, turn up the volume on the radio: "*. . . who beat the victim at a local bar last Wednesday, is still at large. Police are saying they have a few leads, but are still asking the public for their assistance. It is imperative that anyone who sees Mr. Rittenhouse call the New Haven Police Department immediately as he is still considered armed and dangerous.*

"*It has also been confirmed by the New Haven police that the victim has been moved out of the intensive care unit at General Hospital and is expected to make a full recovery.*"

A sudden thought: now that Charlie is recovering, James won't be charged with murder. Assault, yes, but still. There's a big difference.

Years of difference.

And then, like a light, something comes to me. I step on the brake as it does, my body jerking forward from the abruptness of the movement, and just sit there in the middle of the street, breathing hard.

Mr. Herron's street is at the next stop sign on the right. There's no telling what he will say if I call him now and say I'll be late. Especially since I'd had to leave an hour early yesterday. He'll definitely have my paycheck adjusted. Maybe he'll fire me. Or maybe he won't.

A car horn beeps behind me. "Hey!" a guy yells. "Let's move it!"

Yes, I think to myself. *Let's move it. Right now.*

Quickly, before I change my mind, I make a hard left.

Chapter 32

The large hospital is all the way on the other side of town, the towering ten-story structure rising like a mountain over a sea of trees and houses. Wide glass doors appear as I get closer, the word EMERGENCY splashed across the front in red. They are flanked with small, neat bushes, a bordered path of unopened tulips. Behind the glass there is only the dimmest of lights, and a stillness I know belies an unseen panic somewhere inside.

I park the car on the street, a hundred feet or so from the front doors, and just sit for a minute, my hands on the wheel. Am I really going to do this? There is nothing to be gained by going in there. I can't change what happened any more than I can force what will happen in the future. Instinctively, I reach inside my pocket, pull out a cherry ChapStick. I run it along my lips, once, twice, a third time. It tastes faintly of James, and something stirs deep in my belly. Capping the ChapStick, I throw it on the seat, push open the door, and, propelled by some unnamed force, get out of the car.

THERE IS NO one at the information desk; all the chairs in the waiting room are empty. I guess it's still too early for visitors. Or maybe even patients. I stand in the middle of the enormous room for a moment, just looking around dumbly. A huge portrait hanging above the waiting room chairs looks like something Angus did once a few years ago with finger paints; across from it is a picture of Monet's *Water Lilies*. The carpet is a navy blue color, and the odd, combined scent of antiseptic and mashed potatoes lingers in the air.

"Can I help you?" I startle at the voice, spin around frantically. "Over here." A woman has appeared behind the information desk. "I'm sorry," she says. "I just went back to refresh my coffee. What can I do for you?" She sits down in a small blue chair, gives me a cursory look with a flick of her eyes. Next to her computer is an empty Styrofoam coffee cup ringed with pink lipstick and a half-eaten box of chocolate glazed doughnuts.

"Um, actually, I'm looking for someone." I lean over the small lip of the counter, lower my voice. Am I going to regret this for the rest of my life? Will an alarm go off if I say his name? "Charles Wilkins? He's been here for a few days. Do you know what room he's in?"

"Charles Wilkins . . ." The woman leans forward, punching a few keys in the keyboard. She studies the screen, her flamingo earrings swaying lightly. Both birds have one leg propped up under them and large, yellow beaks. "Hmm . . . It says here he was in the ICU for two days, but then . . ." She taps the keyboard, glances at the screen once more. "Apparently, he was transferred to another floor. Yesterday, as a matter of fact, at three P.M. He's on the fifth floor now, room 512."

"Thanks. Can you tell me where the elevators are?"

"Down the hall to your left." The woman sits up straighter

in her chair. "But you can't go up there now. Visiting hours don't start until noon."

"Oh, I know." I nod obligingly, and hightail it down the hallway. "I'm just going to duck into the gift shop. Thanks for all your help."

THE ELEVATORS OPEN directly in front of the nurses' station, a wide, brown semicircle filled with charts and chairs and two nurses in uniform. Both of them look up as the elevator bell dings, and the larger one, who is wearing a lab coat covered with SpongeBob characters, frowns as I step out. "Can I help you?"

"I'm just here to drop something off for my coworker." I lift my purse, praying that they don't ask me to take anything out. Inside is a wallet—which contains my driver's license, two dollars and seventy-eight cents, a coupon for a free Happy Meal with the purchase of one Big Mac—my keys, a tube of Blistex, four of Angus's Matchbox cars, and a few more of those lavender wipes from Jane. Nothing even remotely related to Charlie. "It's just some papers from the office that he asked for. It'll only take a second."

The large nurse raises her eyebrows. "Patient?"

"Charlie?" I try to make my voice light. "Charlie Wilkins?"

The smaller nurse takes a step forward now. She's wearing a long, white cardigan, and her hair is pretty, kind of a goldish-red color, half of it pulled up with a clip. "You can leave them with us," she says. "We'll make sure he gets them."

"Oh." My eyes sweep the floor around her white clogs. "I was kind of hoping to give them to him myself."

The nurse looks at me skeptically. "You're not family?"

"Well, actually, I'm his cousin. We grew up together. That's sort of how Charlie got me the job in the first place. You know, 'cause we're . . . close."

Shit. Where the hell did *that* come from?

The two nurses exchange a glance. "All right," the smaller one says. "Just for a few minutes. And if he's sleeping, please don't wake him up. He needs his rest."

"Absolutely."

Room 512 is all the way down past the nurses' station at the apex of the curve around the hall. Charlie's door is ajar, the linoleum inside a pale gray color, speckled with bits of blue. The walls are white with blue trim, the left one centered by a red leather chair. An empty bed, stripped of sheets, peeks out from behind a dividing curtain; beyond it is an enormous window only partly shrouded with dark blue drapes. Through the space between them is an enormous span of rooftops, and for a brief moment, standing there looking out at a faint thread of smoke winding its way up from the chimney of one, an ineffable loneliness fills me. Far above the roofs a band of white sky stretches out, thin as cotton, pale as silk. No sun or clouds in sight. Emptiness.

Slowly, I turn my attention to the rest of the room. Another bed on the opposite side of the curtain is not empty. My heart speeds up as I catch sight of a pair of feet forming narrow tents beneath a white hospital blanket. I take another step inside the room, silently regarding the outline of knees, a hollowed stretch of thigh, and then, suddenly, like something from a dream, the rest of him.

Charlie is lying on his back, his face turned toward the window, eyes closed. He looks smaller than I remember, shorter, too. One of his arms, resting atop his chest, is in a sling; just the tips of his fingers peek out from the hardened plaster cast. Beneath the swath of sheet around his torso, I can make out more gauze and tape plastered mummy-like up to his nipples. A brown bandage the size of a playing card covers the left side of his throat, and above it, his ear looks singed, the now blackened cartilage dented somehow, maybe even torn. Above the damaged ear, his whole head has been wrapped in white; tufts of hair peek out here and there like small black weeds.

There is a chair at the foot of his bed, a brown makeshift table next to it. I take another step toward the chair, somehow miscalculating the distance, and when I bump into it, the chair skids noisily across the floor. I hold my breath as he stirs, hang on to the foot of his bed as he opens his eyes. He blinks for a few seconds, as if trying to decipher me underwater. I turn, ready to flee, but he struggles to sit up, yelps something from the back of his throat. "Hey!"

I rush toward the door, three steps away, until I'm out in the hallway. The nurses at the other end of the hall are standing next to each other, pointing to a chart.

"Hello?" Charlie's voice hurtles out behind me. "Who was that? You want something?"

What do I want? I don't know what I want. Sitting there at the stop sign ten minutes ago, the thought had occurred to me that I might confront him, offer him a deal: *I won't ever say anything about the rape if you drop charges against James.* Now it sounds ridiculous, like something a kid might say on the playground: "I'll give you my blue marble if you give me your purple." Who am I kidding? Life doesn't work like this. People can't bargain their crimes away! Or am I just looking for an excuse? I hadn't considered that seeing Charlie again might start an involuntary trembling throughout my body. Is that the reason I won't go through with it? Or can I get a handle on things, tell myself in no uncertain terms that I am the one in control now?

I look away from the nurse, smooth the front of my shirt down with a shaking hand as I walk back into the room. Charlie is busy trying to sit up, but whatever part of his torso is injured makes it impossible. He does not see me yet, as he is otherwise occupied, grabbing two of his pillows and ramming them impatiently behind his lower back. Finally he stops and lifts his head, startling a bit as he catches sight of me again.

His face pales as his eyes meet mine, the fear in his eyes fleeting, like a deer running across the road. "I thought that was you." His voice is hoarse. "What do you want?"

"I . . ." The words are lodged in my throat; my knees are shaking.

Charlie's hands dart across his blankets, pulling them up around his waist. He looks at me steadily, sensing my fear. "You have something to do with this? You get him to do this to me?"

"No."

He peers at me curiously now, as if I am an insect under a microscope. "No, huh? Just a happy coincidence? After all these years?"

I shake my head, try to shrug. My shoulders feel like weighted stones. It is not difficult to reconcile the broken and battered body before me with the memories from that night. Nothing about Charlie's eyes have changed. They are still dead. Still empty.

"I've been watching the news," he says. "I know he ran outta that cop car. And now you're here. You think I'm s'posed to believe that you two weren't in on this? Together?"

I shake my head.

"You here for money?" Charlie asks suddenly.

"Money?"

"Yeah. Are you here for money or something? I don't have anything."

"What would I want money for?"

He studies me for a moment, his jaw tightening. "Oh, I get it. You're here to tell me you're gonna press charges. Is that it? Go tell the cops what I did? Five years later?" He snorts. "You've been waiting a long time for this day, I bet." He's crouched over a little, one hand clutching the sheet, a tiger ready to spring. *"Say something!"*

He laughs when I jump, his front dead tooth displayed like a dirty shell as he opens his mouth, and for some reason the sight of it sends a new wave of fear through me. I take a step backward, Charlie watching me like a caged animal. Another step. His eyes flatten until they are almost black, and a sac of spittle rests in the corner of his mouth. Two more steps. No. I can't do this. Not even for James.

"Hey, if you could prove anything, maybe I could share a cell with Rittenhouse." Charlie chuckles as I reach the doorway. "Wouldn't that be sweet? You could come visit. Do the whole conjugal thing. With both of us."

I walk quickly, moving on legs I do not feel as Charlie's taunts follow me down the hall: "You got anyone else out there? The sheriff or someone? Should I be expecting any more visitors today, Bird? Huh?"

The nurse with the SpongeBob jacket looks at me as I rush past the desk, then leans over and says something to the smaller one. They exchange a few words as I stand in front of the elevator, and then the smaller one heads back toward Charlie's room. My insides are churning like a washing machine; a rush of roaring static is filling my head.

But it is not until the doors open, letting me inside the four metal walls with a flickering overhead light, that I start to retch. Over and over again, until the contents of my stomach splash against the silver walls, congealing in a heap inside one of the corners. For a moment, it feels as though I am choking on my own tongue, and I flail wildly at the sides of the elevator with my arms, gasping for breath.

Finally, I slump down in a corner of the elevator. The closeted air is putrid; my arms are trembling. The white buttons on the wall glow *three, two, one*. The doors open again, and even though I can see the wide EMERGENCY door and the neat trees and hydrangea paths that will lead me out to the sidewalk and back to my car, I do not move.

The doors close again, and then open.

Close, open.

Close, open.

Chapter 33

It's a terrible thing to do, but I leave my mess in the elevator. It's a hospital, not a funeral home; vomit on the floor is not an anomaly. Someone will clean it up. Besides, I can't bear the thought of rushing around, looking for a bathroom with paper towels, or worse, having to ask someone to find me a janitor; it's all I can do to drag myself outside and move in the direction of my car. The light, sharp as glass shards, hurts my eyes, and my legs are still trembling. I swallow over and over again, trying unsuccessfully to dissolve the sour knot in the back of my throat and then lean forward until my forehead touches the steering wheel and close my eyes.

Charlie's face leers at me, his eyes little slits, the warped, twisted mouth. *"Maybe Rittenhouse and I can share a cell. You could come visit. Do the whole conjugal thing. With both of us."* His face had looked like that that night, only worse—the eyes black and glossy, the mouth like an angry slash above me, spitting saliva, epithets, hate. I squeeze my eyes tighter, willing the tears to stop, but they come anyway, hard and fast and furious.

And then suddenly, like a faucet being turned, *I* am furious. I am more furious than I have ever been in my life, even toward Ma and Father Delaney. Maybe even toward God. The rage feels like a living thing inside me, an octopus with long, sticky arms, filling the recesses of my belly, pushing out the sorrow. I clench my fists as a scream emerges from the back of my throat, long and howling, and I open my eyes and lean forward and beat my fists against the steering wheel over and over and over again until it dwindles down and I am dizzy with grief. There is no more sour taste in my mouth. No more tears.

Behind the windshield, the white sky looms.

The day waits.

I slide the key into the ignition and start the car.

MR. HERRON IS ON his hands and knees out in the garden, feeling around again in the dirt. Same pressed pants, cardigan over a white T-shirt, soft moccasin slippers. Same tiny plot of ground, muddy, rutted yard. Nothing changes, I think. Until one day, when everything does.

"Mr. Herron!" I call from the back door.

He gets up on his knees, turning his face toward me, as if sniffing the wind. "Bird?"

"Yeah, it's me. I just wanted to let you know I'm here. I'm a little late, but I won't leave 'til I finish everything. I'm just gonna get started inside, okay?"

"Hold on a minute!" Mr. Herron beckons with one hand. "Come here! I want you to see somethin'!"

A low growling sound catches in the back of my throat as I walk across the yard. I've already wasted enough time with the whole debacle in the hospital; I just want to get my work done so that I can go over and see James for a few moments before heading over to Jane's. I don't have to go see him, of course, but I want to tell him about seeing Charlie in the hospital. I can't imagine what he'll say, but the need to share it with him feels overwhelming. The need to share everything with him feels overwhelming, as if I have been waiting to do exactly that for a very long time.

I look down at the spot of garden Mr. Herron has been tending. There are several small shoots coming out of the earth, little fingertips of green. "Oh, they're growing!" I try to muster a little enthusiasm in my voice. "That's great, Mr. Herron."

He ignores my comment, pointing to a tallish green plant in the back. It has wide, thick leaves, and a few pointy buds. Set apart from the other plants, it looks regal nonetheless, proud. And weirdly familiar looking, too. "Look," Mr. Herron says. "It'll bloom soon, too. I'm countin' on it."

"What will?" I lean in, peering at the glossy leaves, then stand back up. "Hey, is that the big ugly thing from your kitchen? What is it?"

"It's called a bird of paradise," Mr. Herron says. "And it ain't ugly, thank you very much. I've just replanted it. It's my very first one. I've taken care of it all winter, and now I'm going to see what it can do out here."

"Bird of paradise?" I repeat. "That's the name of the plant?"

"Uh-huh."

"Tangerine parfaits, birds of paradise. Who comes up with this stuff?"

"Well, the tangerine parfaits are called that because they're orange. And the bird of paradise was named for the way the flowers look when they bloom. Kinda like big cranes. All orange and blue. Spectacular." Mr. Herron nods his head. "Hard keepin' 'em, too. They don't like it here much. They're tropical flowers. Native of South America. They need lots of sun. Warmth."

"Well, they're never going to make it, then." I glance at my watch. "April's almost over and it's still freezing!"

"Just has to be above fifty," Mr. Herron says placidly. "Long as we don't get some freak freeze one of these nights, they'll be okay."

"Well, good luck with it. I have stuff to do inside." I turn to go back in. "I'll talk to you later."

"Bird?" Mr. Herron sits back on his heels, scratches the nape of his neck with a gnarled hand. "You got a minute?"

Shit. Here we go. The speech he didn't give me earlier for being late today. "Sure."

"I been thinkin' about what you told me th'other day. 'Bout leaving your mother. Gettin' a new place and all that?"

"Uh-huh." I cross my arms, waiting. He's probably going to fire me now. Tell me he doesn't need me, since I'm moving, that Ma needs the money more. Well, let him. He's right anyway.

"Where you goin'?" he asks.

"Moon Lake. I found a little place right on the water. For Angus and me. It's really nice."

Mr. Herron nods. "Why so far?"

"It's not so far. Less than twenty miles. And I've always wanted to live on the water."

He nods again, a thoughtful expression creasing his face. "You gonna clean houses up there, too?"

"Maybe. I don't know yet. I'm still looking around."

"That what you want to do with yourself, Bird? Clean other people's houses?"

The question is so blunt that for a moment I am taken aback, stung as if slapped. "There's nothing wrong with cleaning houses, Mr. Herron."

"Didn't say there was. I asked you if that was what you wanted to *do*."

I suck in my top lip, press down on the soft earth with the

toe of my sneaker. What's he getting so nosy about, anyway? What does he care?

"You don't have anything else you been wantin' to do? Something on hold that you waitin' to get to when the time's right?"

"Maybe," I let myself say, because what do I have to lose, telling this guy about my old hopes and dreams? He's just shooting the breeze. Killing time.

"Maybe what?" he asks.

"I always thought I'd make a pretty good nurse."

He nods slowly, a soft smile spreading across his face. "You'd make a good one. 'Specially if you learn them hospital corners on the beds."

I grin, despite myself, shove my hands deep in my pockets.

"Yoo-hoo! Mr. Herron!" A female voice floats across the yard as Mr. Herron and I turn around. "Hey there, angel baby! It's Lucille!" She waves at him as if he can see her, puts one hand on a meaty hip. "I know I'm early today, but I have some things going on this afternoon that I absolutely can*not* get out of. Will you come in, sweetie pie, so I can check your insulin and blood pressure?"

Mr. Herron struggles to his feet, cursing under his breath. "I get tired of her talkin' to me like I'm some kind of infant. I ain't senile yet, goddamn it."

I let him hook his arm through mine as we walk back across the yard; he leans against me as we ascend the steps, his feet feeling each one. Lucille waits for us inside the door, smiling broadly. She is a short woman, overweight in a matronly sort of way with crazy black hair that sticks up all over her head as if she inserted one of her fingers into an electrical socket. Her skin is pale and soft like bread dough, and her eyebrows have been drawn on with a pencil. "And how are you, dear?" she asks, looking at me. Her sweatshirt has a large painted pumpkin on the front of it, little black beads for eyes.

"I'm fine, thanks." I sidle a glance at Mr. Herron and move toward the sink to get my bucket and sponges.

"How's your mother?" Lucille inquires. "I haven't seen her here in a while? Has she retired?"

"Oh, no. She's still working."

"Are you—"

"I'm *waiting* here," Mr. Herron interrupts loudly, still standing in the doorway. "You just pulled me outta my garden and now you're gonna make me stand here listening to you gab? I don't got all day, you know."

Lucille laughs gaily, taking Mr. Herron's elbow and guiding him into one of the kitchen table chairs. "You like to keep me an honest woman, don't you, William? I'm sorry, punkin. I know you love to do your gardening early in the morning, and I'm sorry I have to tear you away from it. But I've just joined a folk group and we're going to have our first practice later on today. I can't miss it, since I'm one of the soloists."

"A folk group?" Mr. Herron repeats.

"Yes!" Lucille giggles. "How about that? I bet you didn't know your nurse had a singing voice, too, did you?" She pauses, withdrawing a tiny stick from inside a blue vinyl case and tapping the wiry point with her thumb. "All right, gimme that first finger of yours so's I can get a drop of blood."

Mr. Herron's face darkens as he turns his index finger over and rests it flat on the table. "Not so hard this time," he says. "It hurt like hell when you did it yesterday."

"It hurt?" Lucille looks wounded. "Land sakes, I've never had anyone say that I *hurt* them. Was it the other finger? May I see it?"

"Nah." Mr. Herron taps the table with the extended knuckle. "Come on, let's just get on with it. I got work to do outside."

I reach under the sink, pull out the pine-scented cleaner and three sponges.

"So, what's a folk group?" Mr. Herron asks. "You meet up with a bunch of folks?" He grins, turning his head to gauge my reaction.

"It's a singing group." Lucille's voice drops from its nasal pitch. "We sing folk songs. You know, like Peter, Paul and Mary. Or Simon & Garfunkel." She clears her throat, trills a scale.

"Never heard of 'em." Mr. Herron winces as Lucille stabs his finger gently with the little stick. A small drop of blood surfaces on the pad of his finger.

"You never heard of Simon & Garfunkel?" Lucille's mouth turns into a little *o* shape. She grips Mr. Herron's finger firmly with two hands and squeezes the drop of blood into the well of a plastic instrument. Another few seconds and his sugar reading will pop up at the top of it. "How about Peter, Paul and Mary? 'Puff the Magic Dragon'?" She clears her throat, attempts another verse. It comes out warbled and slightly off-key.

"Yeah, yeah," Mr. Herron says, waving her off. "Okay, I've heard of that one."

"Well, I should hope so." Lucille leans in, examining the electronic number on the sugar reading. Her face brightens. "Eighty-six," she announces. "Perfect. You're right on the money."

I spray Mr. Herron's eggshell-colored countertops, sponge them down until the streaks disappear. As annoying as Lucille is, I'm kind of glad she's here. It means I don't have to keep answering Mr. Herron's questions. About my future, or anything else for that matter. It's embarrassing, him quizzing me like that. And I'm ashamed of myself, when you get right down to it. Ashamed that I've gotten myself into the kind of situation where someone like Mr. Herron has to even think of asking me such questions. He knows I can do better. And so do I.

"All right," Lucille says. "Let's check your blood pressure next, I'll give your eyes a little peek, and then you can get right back out into that garden, all right? How does that sound?"

I head upstairs, setting the blue bucket down in the hallway as I move into Mr. Herron's bedroom. It's Friday, which means that his sheets need to be stripped and thrown into the dirty clothes hamper. I gather his sheets in a large bundle and start back down the steps.

". . . at Saint Augustine's," Lucille is saying gleefully. "In that old choir loft."

I stop on the third step.

"Why you practicing there?" Mr. Herron asks.

"Well, Tyrone, who's in charge of the group, is real good friends with Father Delaney, who's the pastor at Saint Augustine's. And since we don't have a place big enough to practice in yet, Father Delaney said we could use the loft at his church. They haven't used it in years apparently. Isn't that sad? A big, beautiful choir loft like that, just abandoned? We're going to head over this afternoon after lunch to wipe it all down, clean it up a little. Then we should be all set." Lucille makes a clucking sound with her tongue. "I'll tell you what, I can hardly wait!"

My hands are clutching Mr. Herron's sheets so tightly that my fingertips hurt.

"Maybe I should ask Bird what kind of cleaning supplies are best for a job like that," Lucille continues. "You know how dust can accumulate. I'm sure there are just layers upon layers of it up there. I wonder what the best kind of wood cleaners are. And dust cloths, too. I can't even imagine how many cob . . ."

Her words trail behind me as I streak for the front door, leaving Mr. Herron's dirty sheets in a pile at the foot of the steps.

"Bird?" I can hear Mr. Herron shout behind me. "Bird girl, where the hell you *goin'*?"

Chapter 34

I'll have to take him to the apartment on the lake right now. It's only ten o'clock, but there's no way I can risk Lucille's stupid folk group people showing up early. He won't even have time to get inside the organ again, let alone find a way out of the loft by the time he hears any of them on the steps. My head is spinning. I'll take him there now and then go back up tonight. Okay, then. That's what we'll do. I step down harder on the gas, curse as the light up ahead changes to red.

Inside my pocket, my cell phone rings. I have a mind to ignore it until I remember that it could be the preschool. I take the phone out of my pocket, glance down at the number. I don't recognize it. Shit. I don't know the preschool number by heart. It could be them. I flip it open, press it to my ear. "Hello?"

"Bird?"

"Yeah?"

"This is Mrs. Ross. From the probation office?"

I can hear someone crying in the background. My heart starts pounding in my ears. "What's wrong?"

"You need to come home, Bird. Right this minute." Mrs. Ross's voice is devoid of her usual perkiness.

"Wait, what?" I pull over to the side of the road, throw the car in park. "Why? What's going on?"

"I'll explain it to you when you get here." Her voice softens a little. "Just come home, hon, okay?"

"Home? Why home? Are you at my *house*?"

"Yes. I drove out this morning to see you about a situation that's just come up."

The crying in the background is getting louder.

"Is that my mother?" I explode. "In the background? Is she *crying*?"

Mrs. Ross clears her throat, muffles the mouthpiece with something. I can hear an exchange of words, but they are far away, as if under a blanket.

Then: "Bernadette?" I barely recognize Ma's voice it is so clotted with grief.

"Ma." I am shaking with rage and fear. "Why are you crying? Why aren't you at work? What the hell is going on?"

"I didn't go to work today." Her voice is edged with embarrassment. "I didn't even go to church. I was too tired . . . after everything that happened last night. Please just come back to the house. Mrs. Ross is here. She said the whole situation could probably be cleared up if you just sit down and—"

"*What* situation? What happened?"

My brain is racing. Did Charlie call someone? Is that what it is? Am I in trouble because I went to the hospital?

"I don't know." Ma starts crying again. The sound is killing me, snatching the breath out of my chest, turning the sun into a blinding pinpoint through the windshield. "Please, Bird," Ma croaks. "Just tell Mr. Herron you have to go. That it's an emergency. Please just come home and fix this. Please."

"You wait right there. Don't you move, Ma. I'll be there in two minutes."

I snap the phone shut again, throw the car back into gear. There's no way in hell anyone could have found out so quickly that I was at the hospital this morning. Besides, I didn't do anything. I barely even spoke to the guy. It's got to be something else, some ridiculous triviality regarding my case. Did I forget to sign something? Is there some document I've overlooked regarding my payment schedule, some glitch regarding my last disbursement? Who the hell does Mrs. Ross think she is, coming to my house? She can pick up the fucking phone and call me from her office if that's the case, just like anyone else would. I'm going to report this; I swear to God I am. That woman'll end up with her ass in a sling.

I give the rearview mirror a quick glance as the car speeds away from Saint Augustine's. Jutting out from the skyline is the silver tip of the steeple, the glint of the crucifix at the very top. I can still do this. I'll go home, fix whatever *situation* has arisen, and then drive back over to the church and get James out of there, once and for all.

I keep my eyes on the steeple as I press down on the gas, watching as it fades slowly from sight.

MRS. ROSS AND MA stand up simultaneously from their places on the couch when I burst in. Steam is still rising from the mugs of tea on the coffee table, and for some inexplicable reason, Ma has set out a plate of sliced oranges.

"Bernadette." Ma's still in her robe, clutching the edges of it under her chin with pinched fingers. Her face is dry, but I can see the salty tear tracks along her cheeks. "My God, how did you get here so fast?"

"I drove fast." I glare at Mrs. Ross, who is wearing a navy

pinstriped suit and a bright red necklace with stones so large they look like eggs. "Probably over the speed limit. Now, can you please tell me what this is all about?"

"Have a seat, Bird." Mrs. Ross looks at me with a sympathetic expression. Her hair is long and loose around her shoulders; tiny pearl earring studs dot her earlobes.

"I don't *want* to have a seat. I have to get back to work. What do you need, a signature? A paper? What?"

Mrs. Ross blinks. "We got a call this morning from the police station, hon."

"From the police station?" My heart skips a beat. "Why?"

"Apparently, a Mrs. Jane Livingston went down and filed a report a few hours ago. Against you, Bird. She said that you stole some of her drugs after you offered to go to the pharmacy and pick them up. Her Vicodin. Do you know anything about that?"

Can floors sway beneath you? Or do your knees somehow just unbuckle themselves and set you down? Both happen to me now, and I stagger over to the blue armchair in the corner so that I don't collapse in a heap.

"Bernadette?" Ma says my name so softly that I have to bite down hard on my tongue to prevent the tears. "You didn't take any of Jane's Vicodin, did you?"

How did I honestly think I could get away with this? Of course Jane counts her pills. She's neurotic about everything; why wouldn't she be completely anal about the number of Vicodin capsules her cleaning lady brings back from the pharmacy? I wonder briefly if this is what the beginning of the end looks like; if the really big things in life, the ones that knock you completely off your axis, start off in your own living room, across from your mother, who is still dressed in her fluffy green bathrobe.

"Bernadette?"

I look up. "No. I didn't take any of Jane's Vicodin."

"Why would she say that, then?" Mrs. Ross licks her pink-coated lips.

I shrug. "No idea."

"She said she called the pharmacy first, Bird, to make sure they hadn't miscounted. She said the pharmacist was one hundred percent positive that he put twenty-five pills in there, and when she counted them later, there were only twenty-one. Then later, after you left a second time, there were two more pills missing."

"I don't know what to tell you. I didn't take any kind of drugs." I glance over at Ma. "I swear to you, Ma. I didn't."

Her face has softened some, but her shoulders are still tight, bunched up stiffly around her neck. "They need to look, Bernadette." She motions toward Mrs. Ross with her head. "That's why she's here. She has to search your room."

"Go ahead." I am in full defense mode. Where the fuck are the jeans I wore last night? Did I throw them on the floor? The bed? Are they in the laundry hamper? How could I have forgotten about them there in my pocket? *Jesus.*

Ma steps back as Mrs. Ross crosses in front of her, then trots a few feet behind. Mrs. Ross turns as she gets to the foot of the stairs, looks at Ma kindly. "I should probably do this alone."

Ma's face withers; her shoulders sag finally.

"Come on, Ma." I head for the kitchen. "She's not going to find anything anyway. I didn't take them."

Ma follows, leaning heavily against one of the counters for a moment, just watching me. Her eyes are already lined, but now they look as if Angus found a pale purple marker and scribbled on the thin skin under them. She's released the front of her robe; pink flannel peeks out from inside like a splash of spring lilac. I sit down at the table, pick up the lone ceramic pepper shaker, and put it back. It looks ridiculous there without its mate, in an awkward, solitary world of its own now, thanks to me. I crack my knuckles one at a time, and tilt my chair backward. Still, Ma doesn't say anything. "You want some tea?" I let the chair fall back down heavily and stand up, moving toward the stove.

"No." Her voice is as heavy as a stone.

"Ma."

"Why, Bernadette?" Her face crumples in on itself and then, as if thinking better of it, straightens again.

"*Why what*, Ma? I haven't done anything!"

Except that I have. I've done everything. And then some. I've done so much that, right now, thinking back on all of it—especially the last three days—I can hardly believe it myself. But I want so much to not have. Or, more accurately, I want so much to have done it all—and, somehow, still be good. To have her look at me with a tenderness I know she does not feel, maybe has not ever felt.

"You're lying." Ma is nowhere near tears anymore. She is on fire. Ma the Maelstrom, as Dad used to call her sometimes. She could get like a hurricane when she got that mad, a tempest. "I can always tell when you're lying because of the way your chin moves."

"My *chin*?"

"Yes." She gestures toward me with one hand. "It quivers, right at the bottom there. It always does when you lie. Even when you were younger."

"Oh, yeah?" I take a step forward. "Is it quivering right—"

"Excuse me, ladies." We both whirl around as Mrs. Ross steps into the kitchen. She's pinned her hair up for some reason, fastening it at the nape of her neck with a small plastic clip, and her heels make a light clicking sound against the linoleum floor. Without a word she walks over to the kitchen table and deposits the other two Vicodin, white and diamond-faceted, on the tablecloth. Then she looks at me.

"I don't know where those came from." I know I'm just making things worse, but I can't help it. I'm drowning, begging for a life preserver, scrambling for a rope. Anything, anywhere.

Ma's eyes are like coals across the kitchen, searing into my flesh.

"I'm sorry, Bird," Mrs. Ross says. "But you're going to have to come with me now."

Chapter 35

W ait, you're not taking her to jail, are you?" Ma hangs on to Mrs. Ross's sleeve, her eyes pleading.

Mrs. Ross puts her free arm around Ma's shoulders, pats her gently. "No, Mrs. Connolly. She's not going to jail. But I do have to take her down to the probation office. Bird's going to have to prepare a statement in accordance with the evidence I've discovered in her room, and then give us a urine sample. She'll be charged with an initial probation violation because the drugs were found in her room, but if the urine comes up hot . . . I mean, if any trace of Vicodin shows up in it, we'll have to charge her with another two counts as well. After that, it's up to the judge."

Ma clutches at the neck of her bathrobe again, as if pinning it to her throat. "I'll get Angus," she says, looking at me.

"You don't have to get Angus. They're not going to find anything in my *urine*, Ma, which means all they're going to do right now is draw up some paperwork for finding Vicodin in my room. It isn't going to take long." I look at Mrs. Ross. "Right?"

She reaches up and fiddles with an earring. "Let your mother get Angus, Bird. I really don't know how long things are going to take."

I lick my lips. Inhale deeply, while holding Ma's eyes in a vise-like grip. "Don't you say a word to him. I mean it, Ma. Not one single word."

"Well, of course I'm not going to *say* anything," Ma scoffs, as if the possibility of doing such a thing would ever enter her mind.

"Okay, then," Mrs. Ross says. "Let's go."

I grab for my keys and then pause. "I can take my own car, can't I?"

Mrs. Ross hesitates, her eyes roving over my face, as if trying to find a shred of veracity somewhere in there. "No," she says finally. "I think you'd better come with me."

The ride over to the probation office takes less than ten minutes, but every red light, every stop sign, feels like a barrier. I look out the window, purposely avoiding Mrs. Ross's eyes, which skitter in my direction every few minutes, and set my jaw. Her car smells like hairspray and cherries. A rubber air freshener in the shape of a lemon hangs down from the knob of her CD player, and next to my feet is an extra pair of heels. Blue leather, with a gold buckle. I kick them to one side, pretending not to notice as Mrs. Ross shoots me a look, and stare out the window. I still can't believe Jane ratted me out. Yes, it was her medicine, and yes, the fact that I took them means that I am not to be trusted (God knows what else I must've taken), but going to the *cops*? Couldn't she just have confronted me herself? Fired me, the way I'd deserved to be fired, maybe shut the door in my face, called me a few nasty names? Maybe I'm an idiot, but I thought the little bit of time we spent together—especially last night, talking about things, *real* things, not just the logistics of the house, or where I needed to clean, but her life, herself—might've tempered her decision. I'm not saying she should've let me off the hook, but couldn't she have given me some slack? Just a little bit?

Inside the office, Mrs. Ross holds the front door open, stepping back to let me in.

"Don't forget," I say, striding past her. "I'm still innocent until proven guilty in this country."

"I saw what I saw." Mrs. Ross stalks on ahead, the muscles in her calves bulging with each step.

Screw you. You don't know anything.

But I know that's a lie. Even worse, I know she's got the evidence of what she saw hidden in some Ziploc bag inside that gigantic purse of hers. Still, it's not like she can prove that I took them from Jane. No one can, really, when it comes right down to it. Vicodin is Vicodin. I could've gotten it anywhere, from anyone. And my urine will come back clean, which is going to throw an even bigger wrench into the situation. By the time this whole thing is over, Mrs. Ross won't know which end is up. She'll have to let me go, and I will. There's an eleven-thirty bus that comes to the corner right across the street. I'll ride home, get my car, and hightail it the hell over to the church. If there is a God somewhere, I'll have just enough time to still get James out of the loft before the folk group people get there and drive up to the apartment.

"Have a seat," Mrs. Ross says abruptly as we reach the door outside her office. "I'll be out to get you when I'm ready." She slides some sort of credit card thing inside a little black box and then yanks open the door when it beeps.

There's only one seat available in the row against the wall. The other two are occupied—fellow probation violators, I guess. Or newbies, maybe, just like I was eighteen months ago.

I sit down in between a guy wearing a leather jacket and sweat pants, and a woman who looks as though she hasn't eaten a meal in at least a year. Even her ankles, which stick out from the bottom of a pair of yellow cropped pants, are the size and width of chicken bones.

I glance at the clock above the door: 10:36. As long as Mrs. Ross doesn't drag her feet, I'll still have a little less than an hour to go over and get James. Although how long it's going to take me to get him down all those stairs is beyond me. And that's assuming no one will be hanging around the vestibule or inside the church itself. I don't have to worry about the time afterward, since going to Jane's is out of the picture—so that's one good thing. If I can just get James out of the loft, put him in my car and—

"Who do you see?" The guy in the leather jacket elbows me. His belly is so enormous that the bottom of it, jutting out from beneath his orange T-shirt and stretched taut with white-and-purple striations, reminds me of a marbled piece of meat. He's wearing heavy work boots with the laces undone and white socks. Black stubble darkens the lower half of his face and his nose is pocked with deep pits.

"What?"

"In there." He points his chin toward the door. "Who's your probation officer?"

"Oh." I cross my arms over my chest. "Mrs. Ross."

"Uh-huh." He nods, as if he knows her personally. "I got Billings. He's a total dick."

I stare straight ahead, hoping that he will get the hint that I am not interested in having even a small discussion about our probation officers.

But then the anorexic leans forward, tucking her white sandals under her chair. "I have Billings, too. And I agree. He *is*

a dick. He doesn't give me a break for anything." There is fine
hair growing on the tops of her arms, like chick fuzz, and she
runs her palms over it lightly as she talks. "He yanked me in
here again 'cause he says he saw me 'hanging out' with some
of my old friends at the movie theater, which isn't even true.
There was one girl in the group that I used to know from
before and I wasn't even talking to her. I was there to see a
movie and that was it."

"You can't hang out with your old friends?" the man asks,
his eyes skittering up and down the length of her. "What're
they, trouble?"

"The one girl's a druggie." The anorexic shrugs. "I used to
buy stuff from her. But I wasn't even *talk*ing to her. It was total
coincidence that she was even there. When I knew her, she
barely ever left the house."

"You mean total coincidence that *he* was there," the man
says. "Or just bad luck." He grunts sympathetically. "He wrote
me up 'cause I was ten minutes late getting home last night.
Didn't matter that I was up at the mall, buying my kids *shoes*.
He didn't want to hear it. Just kept saying, 'Rules are rules,
buddy-boy. Rules are rules.'"

"He calls *me* buddy-boy!" The anorexic sits back, folding
her toothpick arms over her chest. "Like I'm some kind of fucking Boy Scout." She shakes her head. "What an asshole." She is
wearing a thin white sweater with no sleeves, even though it's
barely warm enough for a T-shirt. The tops of her shoulders
stick out like knobs. She sits forward again suddenly, opening
her legs, draping her elbows along the bones of her thighs. "He
treats us like kids. Like we'll never grow up or get it right, you
know?"

The man nods, draws his fingers down the stubble along his
face. "They're all like that. Every single one of them."

Like we'll never grow up or get it right. I wonder if this is how Ma sees me. Stuck perpetually at fifteen, still kicking and screaming about missing Dad. Still deliberately making the wrong choices, although I know better. And how about Mrs. Ross? Am I just another one of her clients who lets her down, a typical self-centered brat with tunnel vision? Have either of them ever really believed in me, or have they just been holding their breath all this time, waiting for me to screw up?

Mrs. Ross appears then, a stack of files in the crook of her elbow. She pushes open the door, gives me the same dour expression as before. "Okay, Bird. Let's go."

"Good luck," the man says behind me. "Don't let them push you around."

I can hear the two of them snickering as the door closes behind me.

The second hand on the clock ticks forward: 10:46.

I FOLLOW MRS. ROSS's legs back down to her cubicle, sit down in the empty chair next to her desk before she has a chance to tell me to. She slides into her own chair, arranging her legs just to the right of the desk, and, without giving me a glance, starts typing. Her fingers move quickly and then speed up, flying so forcefully at one point that the keyboard starts sliding around the desk. She doesn't seem to notice, her eyes set firmly on the screen, until finally, with two deliberate smacks against the keys, she sits back in her chair and turns her head. A long moment passes as she hooks a finger over one of the strawberry-sized beads in her necklace and glares at me.

"What?" I ask finally.

"Don't 'what' me, Bird," she says. "You know very well what."

"But you're freaking out for no reason. You don't even *know* anything and you're just jumping to conclusions."

"First of all, I am not *freak*ing out." Mrs. Ross spits the word back out at me, as if the thought of using such vocabulary would never occur to her. "I'm just incredibly disappointed. And secondly, I am not jumping to any conclusions." She leans forward, lowering her voice. "I found the drugs, Bird. In your pants pocket."

"But that doesn't mean *I* took them. Or that they even belong to me. Or Jane."

Mrs. Ross straightens up again in her chair. "Well, what would it mean, then, Bird? Why don't you tell me? Do you have some kind of secret life on the side that I should know about? Have you started popping Vicodin suddenly for some phantom illness? Or are you conducting a little extra business on the side?"

"Don't talk to me like I'm an idiot." I can feel a latent anger starting to catch, a flame lighting. "I'm not a . . ." I pause, the word "child" sitting on the end of my tongue, and swallow it back down. Not because it's the wrong word. Because it's the right one. I'd bet any amount of money that those idiots out in the waiting room know it, too. For some reason or another, we are all still acting like kids, every single one of us in this place, making stupid, thoughtless decisions that we don't take the time to think all the way through. But why? It can't be as simple as being selfish, can it? Have all of my actions, from writing that second bad check to deciding to help James, really just been about me?

"I don't think you're an idiot," Mrs. Ross says. "I'm pretty sure I know you by now, Bird. Which is why I know you're hiding something from me about those Vicodin."

"I'm not!"

"Okay." Mrs. Ross shrugs, neither agreeing nor disagreeing with me. "Explain it to me, then."

"It just means you found two Vicodin in my pants pocket. They could've been there for years. Or maybe I was holding them for someone. Maybe I even—" Why can't I stop lying? What is it that keeps me from getting out of my own way? Maybe some of us don't ever grow up. Maybe some of us will never get it right, no matter how much we want to.

"Bird." Mrs. Ross cuts me off, leaning forward again. "Stop it, okay? You're insulting my intelligence and yours. You and I both know where the Vicodin came from."

"No, you don't! That's what I'm trying to tell you. You have no idea—"

"I do." Mrs. Ross's voice is soft, her blue eyes edged with glossy mascara. "And you do, too. I don't know why yet, and maybe you don't either, but we're going to figure out why you would go and do something like that when you're *this* close to getting off probation." She holds up her fingers, spaced an inch apart. "When you're days away from moving into that apartment on the lake you want so much for you and Angus. Why do you think, Bird? Why would you go and sabotage something that you want so much, that you've worked so hard to get?"

Something flashes through the back of my head then when she says that, but it doesn't have time to register because the sudden roar of sirens outside makes us both jump. There is a flurry of movement around me as various probation officers stand up, and the sizzle of static from the police scanner on the wall.

"All units to Saint Augustine's Church on Maple Avenue," a flat voice says. *"Repeat. All units to Saint Augustine's Church on Maple Avenue."*

I leap up as if someone has just lit my chair on fire. "What did they say?"

The crackly voice over the intercom gets louder. *"CODE 217. ALL UNITS TO SAINT AUGUSTINE'S CHURCH ON MAPLE AVENUE. REPEAT. THIS IS A CODE 217."*

"Bird?" Mrs. Ross is looking at me strangely. "Sit back d—"

But I'm already running blindly through the cubicle's rat maze, heading for the exit. "Bird! Where are you going? Bird, wait!" Mrs. Ross is yelling behind me; somewhere in the distance, I can hear footsteps. They may be hers or someone else's, but I'm not sticking around to find out. "Bird!" she screams again, just as I turn a corner and swerve to avoid slamming into a cubicle wall. "Sawyer! Philip! Get her!" I backtrack quickly, spinning around just as enormous hands grab me from behind, pinning both of my arms tightly against my sides.

"No!" I scream, my heart plummeting as the hold around me tightens. The guy's big, with arms like trees. I'm sorry to have to hurt him. I kick back, aiming low, feel a sudden release as the man grunts and then stumbles forward, dropping both of us to the floor. I look up; the door to the outside is ten feet away. I scramble to my feet and lurch for it, even as bodies seem to fall out of the heavens, from every direction, pinning me against the rough blue carpet.

"No!" I scream again. "I have to go! Let me go! I have to get him! Please! He's waiting for me! Let me go get him! He needs me! He needs me!"

Mrs. Ross appears suddenly, getting down on her knees as two men hold my arms on either side. Her eyes are wild, the skin around her lips pale and tight as she leans her face in close to mine. "Who are you talking about, Bird? Who do you have to get? *Angus?*"

My brain crackles like lightning. Yes, of course, I'll tell her it's Angus. She loves Angus. I'll tell her he's sick. And then, when she lets me go, I'll take the back route, past North Main, down all the one-way streets. I can do it. I know I can. I'll get there before the police cars and fire engines and God knows who else they're sending to bring him down. And I can . . . I can . . .

As if to mock my thoughts, the scanner sputters again: *"Shots fired at Saint Augustine's Church. Repeat. Shots fired."*

No.

Who fired the shot? James? The police? Both?

"Who, Bird?" Mrs. Ross asks me again. "Who do you need?" She reaches out, touches my face. Everything feels as if it's slowing down around me. "Who, hon?"

"Officers moving in."

And just like that, I know it is over.

I know that our time has run out, that there is no way, no possible way anymore, that I can save him. Something in my body takes over then, and I kick and scream as if possessed, writhing and twisting my limbs like airplane propellers. I bite and scratch, fighting for my life. For his. For us. For the life we will never have, at least not in this world.

"Suspect down."

"Nononononononono!!!!"

The shriek in my ears is the last thing I remember before lurching a final time and hitting my head on the floor.

Afterward, black.

Chapter 36

I wake up in a hospital bed, a white sheet draped over my clothes. I open my eyes slowly, staring up at a white ceiling. My shoes are gone and someone has fastened a plastic band around my wrist. The space I'm in is tiny, bordered by one of those blue-and-white striped shower curtain sheets that slide around on a thin metal strip. A dull pulsing behind my eyes feels like fists beating the back of my head. *Boomboomboom*. The ache is enormous, spreading down behind my ears and into my neck. My arms hurt, too, just under the armpits, as if someone pulled on them.

Suddenly, I remember the probation office. James. Shots fired. Suspect down. My God. What happened? Where is he? I sit up with a start, clutching at the sheet.

"Hey." Mrs. Ross gets up from a plastic chair at the foot of my bed and clicks her way over to me. Her suit jacket is off; she's pinned her hair back up. "How are you feeling?"

"I'm fine." I yank the sheet off, slide sideways off the mattress. My head feels like it's going to explode from the inside out, but I force myself to keep moving.

"Whoa, whoa." Mrs. Ross reaches out and grabs my shoulder, pushing me back down. "You have to stay in bed for a little while. At least until the doctor comes back. You hit your head pretty hard back there at the office. You were out for a while."

"I don't need a doctor." I wince as the pain in my head spreads down the front of my face. "I'm fine."

"It won't take long." Mrs. Ross sits down on the bed and crosses her legs. "He'll be back in a few minutes. He said it might be a mild concussion, but he wanted to run a few tests once you were awake to be sure."

"I don't need any tests either." I push past Mrs. Ross, pulling the long silver arm attached to a television on the wall until the screen is close to my face. "I need to know what happened at the church. At Saint Augustine's. Do you know? Does anyone know?" I flip impatiently through the channels. Soap operas. *Family Feud*. More soap operas.

"Bird."

"I'm just looking for the news." I keep flipping. "Okay? Am I still allowed to watch TV?"

"Bird."

I stop then, my hand going limp. I can tell by the expression on her face that she already knows, but I don't want to hear it from her. I can't. "What?"

"Did you know he was up there?"

I stare at her, a plate of pain widening behind my eyes.

"There are a lot of things being said right now, but the big one is that someone helped James Rittenhouse while he hid in that choir loft." She rubs the bottom of her chin. "Was that you?"

I don't even blink.

"They found food and water and his leg had been set. With the injury he suffered, there's no way he could have done that himself. He had clean clothes, too. Pants at least. And baby wipes so he could keep himself clean." She inhales deeply. "Is that who you were talking about in the probation office? Is that who you wanted to go see?"

A long moment passes. I know she's waiting, but I can't bring myself to say it. I can't bring myself to say anything. Not about this. Not about him.

"Do you know what harboring a fugitive means, Bird?" Mrs. Ross gets up off the bed finally, arranging her arms in a neat little package across her chest. The softness in her voice is gone; the little lines around her eyes have begun to crease. "Do you understand what can happen to you if you're found guilty of something like that? If you're on probation and you're found guilty of something like that?"

My voice is still lodged in a rock eight miles away. Where is he? Is he here, in this hospital? In an operating room?

"It can be classified as a felony, Bird. A *felony*! Do you know what a felony is? It means that you could go to jail for two years! Maybe even longer! Do you understand what I'm telling you?" Her eyes are snapping under the fluorescent lights. "*Do* you?"

I don't know if I have ever been so terrified in my life. And yet, somehow, there is something even bigger to be scared of. Something that pushes the voice out of the back of my throat, and out into the space between us. "Did they shoot him?" I whisper. "Is he dead?"

Mrs. Ross's shoulders sag. She has the same defeated look on her face that Ma had earlier in the kitchen. Then she points to the television behind me. "Look for yourself."

I turn around.

And all of a sudden, there he is.

Or there *some*one is, lying on a gurney, covered in a sheet, being wheeled into the back of an ambulance. It doesn't mean it's James. It could be anyone. A police officer, a fireman, maybe even Father Delaney, God forbid. Police officers stand around as the body passes, watching as the EMTs fold the metal legs and roll it inside the cavernous vehicle. I lean in slowly, turn up the volume.

". . . *the body of James Rittenhouse, who was involved in a bar fight a few days ago and then managed to escape while in police custody.*"

I bring my fingers to my mouth. They are trembling.

"*Police are currently saying that Rittenhouse provoked the ultimately lethal response by pointing a gun at the three officers as they entered the building, leaving them no choice but to defend themselves. Further investigation is pending.*"

I want to move. I do. I want to put my fist through the television. Rip the volume knob off. Throw the whole fucking thing through the window. Or better yet, at Mrs. Ross.

But I can't.

There's nothing left inside.

Nothing at all.

THE NEXT TWO days are a blur of quiet, clipped activity. It turns out that I do have a mild concussion, just as the doctor suspected, and so I have to lie still, keep away from the TV, and avoid any loud noises. This is not hard to do, since both Ma and Angus tiptoe around outside my room, talking in whispers and letting me sleep. I am not sleeping, of course. I doubt I will ever sleep again, although I have no choice but to lay there with my eyes closed since it hurts too much to keep them open. Still, the pictures inside my head torment me. I play the final scene between James and the cops a thousand different times, from every possible angle, but each one ends the same way. My eyes fly open just as the bullet hits him (in the chest, not the head) and I lay there panting, tears leaking from both sides of my eyes.

On the third day, Ma comes into my room and tells me that I am wanted down at the district attorney's office. "I can tell them you're still not feeling well," she says, standing in my doorway, rewrapping the edges of her cardigan around her waist. I don't know if I've ever seen the look on her face before; it's a mix of terror, rage, and maybe a little bit of apathy, which frightens me the most. "Do you want me to call them back?"

"No." I push the covers off, inhale a stale stink. "I just want to get this over with. I'll go down."

"Take a shower first," Ma says. "I'll drive you."

I sit in the back with Angus, who reaches for my hand as soon as he climbs in and rests his head against the side of my arm. No one says a word as Ma drives to the courthouse, and despite the warmth of his little hand in mine, I can't help but wonder what Ma has told him, or if he'll ever talk to me again.

Inside the DA's office, I follow directions woodenly, sitting in a brown chair behind a long glass table, staying quiet until I am spoken to. I tell the truth, too, when they start firing questions at me, because honestly, I'm too afraid at this point to keep lying. I'm scared they'll take Angus. I answer everything as succinctly as possible, even though it feels as if I am under-water, as if someone else is doing the talking for me:

"No, I didn't take James to the church."

"Yes, I accidentally ran into him after heading up to the choir loft."

"Because I heard a noise up there, and I thought it was Father Delaney."

"No, Father Delaney did not know anything about it. At any time. Ever."

"Yes, I brought him food and water and the equipment to set his leg with."

"Yes, I brought him clean pants and baby wipes, too."

"No, we weren't romantically involved." I'm not giving them that, as small as it was. No how. No way.

"No, we did not have sex in the church choir loft."

"Yes, I knew him from before."

"Yes, he told me what led up to the bar fight."

The district attorney sits up a little straighter when I answer this last question, and flicks his eyes over at the guy across the table who has loosened his tie, and has one finger on the tape recorder. "He talked about the bar fight?"

I nod.

"Even though you weren't romantically involved? Even though, according to everything you've just told us, there was absolutely nothing at stake for him—or for you—to make such an admission?" The district attorney is a tall man with a squarish face and large, wide hands. When he talks, he thrusts both of them forward, as if such movements are necessary to get the words out.

I look down at the surface of the table, study the swirled patterns of maple and caramel beneath the glass veneer.

"He left a note, you know."

I look up.

"Well, not a note exactly," the DA says. "More of a . . . I don't know what you would call it, really. One of our men found it inside the organ, where he managed to get himself inside as our men were coming up." He watches me carefully while sliding a torn piece of paper across the table. "Doesn't mean anything to us right now, but maybe it might ring a bell for you?"

Everything still feels foggy; the note itself looks like a raft of some kind, afloat in a body of very dark water. I can see the faint marks of words printed inside, the swoop and scrawl of ink. I reach for it with trembling hands, open it slowly. There in shaky script are James's last words:

Fact #346: The heart will continue to beat even when separated from the body as long as it has an adequate supply of oxygen.

I read the words once quickly, and then again, more slowly. Something in my chest fills like water. Had he heard noises? Voices? The slow ascent of footsteps on that terrible, circular staircase? Had he known he wouldn't make it out of there alive and, in his last moments, reached for a piece of paper, a pen? Where had he found a pen? Had I brought him one? Or had he seen one in my bag, slid it out while I wasn't looking? Oh, James.

James, James, James.

I close my eyes, thankful to be sitting. If I was on my feet, my legs would give out from under me. When had he found this particular fact? How had he known exactly the right moment to use it? And what does it mean when someone you love knows more about you than you do?

"Miss Connolly?" The district attorney clears his throat. "Does it mean anything?"

I shake my head.

The two men exchange a look. "How about this, then? Do you have any idea why James Rittenhouse beat that man in the bar?"

"Does it really matter now?" I run a fingertip over the word "Fact." The ink is smeared along the capital *F*, blurring the top line. "He's dead."

Another glance exchanges between the two men. "We'd still like to know what he told you." The district attorney runs his fingers over the point of his chin.

I end up telling them the story about James's family. I tell them how awful James's father was to him growing up, how James read the fact book at his father's bedside for two years, waiting for the man to extend a single shred of humanity to him before he died. And I tell them how James went on a bender afterward, how he got drunk and ended up in a fight with a mouthy guy who insulted him. "It was just a perfect storm," I hear myself finishing. "All those things coming together at the same time . . ." I shrug, my shoulders like anvils. "He just went a little crazy, I guess."

The district attorney looks at the tape recorder guy again. He sighs deeply, loosening a button on his suit jacket. "Well, then, I guess that's about all we need from you right now."

I stare down at James's note, watch as the letters swirl before my eyes. "Are you going to press charges against me?"

"The fact that this guy is dead doesn't negate your actions." The district attorney rubs an eyebrow. He has a map of red veins threaded across the top of his nose, a few gray hairs in his eyebrows. "Do you realize that what you've done is a felony?"

I nod without looking at him.

"Our police force wasted innumerable hours over these past three days because of the assistance you provided to James Rittenhouse. I had people working overtime—double, triple shifts—to get this guy behind bars. Do you know how much money it costs to keep a system going during a crisis like that? Do you have any idea?"

The *y* in the word "oxygen" is long and narrow; the *g* has a little dip at the top of it, like a lopsided apple. I'd never seen his handwriting before; nothing we'd ever shared had been written. Now it seems like something miraculous, a singular trait all its own, just like one of his factoids, a small perfect thing, right there on the page.

The district attorney is waiting for me to answer. I look up, shake my head again.

"A lot," he says. "It costs a lot of money, young lady, and a lot of manpower."

"So you are going to press charges, then?"

"We still haven't decided. But I'll tell you what." He stops here, lifts a thick finger to point at me. "The fact that you're already on probation isn't going to do you any favors."

I swallow, look back down at the note.

All I see this time is the word "heart."

Chapter 37

If there is ever a time to be thankful that Angus can't read yet, it's now. The two local newspapers continue to run a front page piece about James and me for the next week. It's sordid stuff, too, with the kind of gossipy headlines people love. "Escaped Con Assisted by Woman," and "Church a Hideout for Former Lovers?" Awful stuff that makes me scowl and Ma cringe. The TV people are all over the place, too. Or at least they try to be. Someone got a shot of me as I was walking into the probation office, but Ma and I haven't been outside since, especially since they started parking across the street from our house. Neither of us has been back to work yet, and Angus hasn't gone to preschool. When he asked me why, I told him he just didn't have to, that we all just needed a little break. "Okay," he said, looking around the room. "You wanna play Connect Four?"

The district attorney decided to go ahead and press charges after all. Now I will be facing two charges when I stand in front of the judge again: violating my original parole by being in possession of illegal drugs (whether or not they can prove I stole them) and harboring a fugitive. According to Mrs. Ross, there is no telling what is going to happen at the hearing. Each count will be charged separately, dealt with according to its own set of circumstances. The worst possible scenario will be an extended jail sentence; I could get six months just for violating my parole, thirty days for the Vicodin, and then two or more years on top of that for helping James. The best-case scenario would involve having my probation revoked and getting resentenced only according to the crimes I have committed. It would mean probation for a long time, maybe even house arrest, but at least I wouldn't go to jail. I wouldn't be taken away from Angus. I can deal with losing the house on the lake. I can come to terms with the fact that Angus will have to go a little while longer without a tire swing. I just can't lose him. No matter what.

It's a limbo period, this part of things, a hell all its own as we wait for the press to leave and, more importantly, for word from Mrs. Ross, who will call to let me know when my appearance in court will be. But then, my whole life up to this point has been a limbo period, hasn't it? Waiting and waiting, and waiting some more. For what, I don't even know anymore. All I do know is that it hasn't worked. I'm tired of it. It's time to try something else.

Ma and I barely speak at all, if we even look at one another, and I stay in my room most of the day anyway, playing board games with Angus. Ma's been making coconut cookies, which are Father Delaney's favorite, and which she will probably bring over to him in person when all of this dies down as some kind of humble peace offering. She's called all her clients and told them she'll be back next week, which I know has been humiliating for her, but I think the thing that pains her the most is not being able to go to Mass every morning. Saint

Augustine's is still shut down because of the investigation and no one knows when it will reopen. I snatch sightings of her moving from room to room, clutching her rosary, mumbling the words under her breath, but I know it's not the same thing. It's not Father Delaney and her morning novena crew. It's not the Holy Eucharist.

Missing James is the hardest of all. Now that the shock has worn off, it hurts to breathe. When his face flits across my mind's eye, I have to press my knuckles against my lips so that the sound behind them doesn't escape, and I cry so many times during our fourth game of Candy Land that Angus finally closes the board and crawls into my lap. Holding him is the only thing that eases some of the ache; feeling his warmth against me is like a salve.

Nights, though, are the worst. I lay in bed and replay the time in the loft—every minute, every second—until I have to get up, and flick on the lights so that I don't start screaming. Sometimes I go into the bathroom, undress, and then sit under the shower, letting the hot water pummel my skin, leak into my ears. It's the only thing that will stop the shaking, the only thing that will drown out my cries. Sleep comes, but only in spurts, and when I wake up again, it is James I think about first, the memory like a sledgehammer coming out of the darkness and smashing me to pieces all over again.

WHEN THE PHONE rings on Friday morning, exactly one week after James has died, Ma and I lunge for it at the same time. We are in the kitchen, silently preparing our separate breakfasts: coffee and half a grapefruit for her, peanut butter toast and orange juice for me. She gets to the phone first and drops her eyes as she presses it to her ear. "Oh, hello, Mrs. Ross. Yes, she's right here."

I grab the phone. "Hello?"

"Hi, hon," Mrs. Ross says. "I have some good news."

A heart flip-flop. "What?"

"I went to talk to Jane Livingston yesterday. And she told me she wanted to drop the theft charges against you."

"Oh my God, really?" Pause. "Do you know why?"

"Apparently, her husband was the real motivator behind the charges, not her. She said he pushed her into doing all of it."

"Wow. And she . . . she knows about James and everything?"

"Yeah," Mrs. Ross says. "She does. So that's really good news, Bird. We'll be able to put that on the record, and tell the judge when we go for your sentencing hearing. He'll take that into consideration when it comes to deciding everything else."

"Okay. All right. Well, thanks."

"You doing okay?" Mrs. Ross asks. "Hanging in there?"

"Um, yeah."

"Back to work yet?"

"Monday."

"Okay. Hang tight, hon. I should be getting a hearing date any day now. I'll call you as soon as I do."

Ma's waiting for me by the counter when I hang up, sipping cautiously from her coffee.

"Jane dropped the Vicodin charges," I say.

She raises one eyebrow, presses her fingertips against the mug until they turn white. "Why?"

"She told Mrs. Ross her husband kind of forced her into it." I shrug. "I guess it wasn't something she wanted to do herself."

"Really." It's a statement, not a question.

"Yes, Ma. Really."

She shrugs, looks down into her mug.

"It's a good thing, Ma. Mrs. Ross said that they'll tell the judge at my sentencing hearing, and that it might help him take things into consideration."

She nods, runs her thumb along the curve of the handle.

"Do you *want* me to go to jail?"

"Of course not, Bernadette. And don't shout, please."

I shove my hands inside my pockets, as if that might somehow prevent the rage from rising inside of me. "Then why're you acting like you're disappointed that Jane's not going to press charges against me?"

She looks up. "I just want you to take responsibility for what you've done."

"Oh, Ma," I groan, letting my head fall back between my shoulders. "Come on. I'm not standing in front of the pearly gates here. It's not heaven or hell, okay? Besides, don't you think I'm trying?"

"I don't know what you're doing anymore. I really, honestly don't. Has it even occurred to you to pick up the phone and call Father Delaney?"

"Father Delaney? What would I call him for? Guidance?"

"For what you did to his church!" Ma bellows. "Desecrating it like that!"

"*Dese*crating it? How did I—"

"You vandalized a holy place, Bird! Letting that . . . that . . . *person* stay up there. Harboring evil like that. Changing his *under*wear!"

"Oh, Ma." I drop my eyes, shake my head. "He wasn't just a person." I start to tell her and then pull back again. What good will it do?

"Don't you 'oh, Ma' me."

"Just stop it." I push by her. "Leave it alone, for God's sake. Let me go."

"I let you go a long time ago, Bernadette." Her voice has

that steely quality to it. "You're the one who's still hanging around, if you hadn't noticed."

I stop in my tracks. Catch my breath in the back of my throat. That one stings. Deeply. But I toss my head, inhale through my nose. "Does that mean you're finally giving up on the whole Monica and Augustine routine, then?"

Ma looks mortally wounded. "It was never a routine, Bernadette," she says. "Not once."

LATER THAT NIGHT, after Ma has fallen asleep, I head upstairs to the attic. It's the farthest I can get away from everything, since I'm not allowed to leave the house, and the only room that doesn't smell like Ma's coconut cookies. The rafters overhead are splintering with age; the scent of mildew and cedar hovers lightly in the background. I sit for a long time next to Dad's box of clothes, but I don't open it. Behind it is a stack of old Easter baskets, a few leftover tufts of plastic grass. When I was little, Ma used to fill my Easter basket until it overflowed— solid chocolate bunnies, pink-and-yellow marshmallow chicks, piles of jelly beans, and peanut butter eggs. She did it after Dad died, too, at least for another year or two. One year, when I was sixteen and had started smoking pot pretty regularly, she tucked in a gigantic bag of ranch-flavored Doritos, which, she said, I'd started eating "like a crazy person."

A few feet past the Easter stuff is another box, a smaller one, the top taped shut. I glance over at it, and then look again as Ma's writing jumps out at me: BERNADETTE—SCHOOL. I pull the box out, peel the tape off impatiently. My Wonder Woman lunch box with the pink handle is on top. Ma bought it for me at the beginning of third grade, back when I loved Wonder Woman more than anything. It still has the dent on the left side from the time I cracked it over Donna Lewis's head after she called me a beast. Wonder Woman's boots are scuffed at the toes, her lasso nearly rubbed off completely, but she still looks as invincible as she looked back then.

Beneath the lunch box is a stack of papers—some thick, some thin, a few lined, mostly unlined. The majority of them are drawings I did at one time—several boats floating on small, cresting waves, brightly colored fish weaving in and out of finger-shaped pieces of seaweed, even a pirate ship, complete with a skull and crossbones flag, a gigantic cannon on deck. All of the pictures have my name at the bottom, written in my large, scrawling handwriting: BIRDIE CONNOLLY. I haven't been Birdie Connolly in forever, I think, running my fingers over the letters. That's what Dad used to call me, when I was first born. He said I'd had eyes like an owl's, a voice like a song. Little Birdie. She is someone I will never be again.

Under the drawings is another piece of paper, this one worn around the edges, a faint circular stain in one corner. It's written again in my handwriting, titled *My Family, Birdie Connolly, Grade 2-B*:

> My family is the best. My dad goes to work. He plays hide-and-seek with me when he comes home. My ma makes me peanut butter pancakes. She loves me, even if I do gross things. Like pick my nose. My family is special. My family is the best!

The words unravel me completely. Who was this little girl who used to be so confident, who used to believe in something bigger than herself? Who used to believe at all? What was it that James had said that night in the choir loft: *Wouldn't it be better to believe in something than to go through your life not believing at all?* Well, I *had* believed. Back then, I had. I'd believed in my family, the circle the three of us made. I'd believed in the love in the middle. Had it made me any happier? Had it made any difference?

I cry harder, already knowing the answer.

Maybe all those days James spent next to his father's bed, believing that something might happen, was what made them bearable. Maybe it gave him something to live for the next day, kept him coming back. Could it really be that despite all our differences and bickering and downright loathing for one another Ma and I have managed to forge ahead simply because we still believe in what we used to have? Was Mrs. Ross right? Have I needed Ma so much—still, after all this time—that I have unconsciously thwarted every outward effort of mine to leave?

And if so, what does that make me? A child, still?

Or perhaps only this: a woman in constant conflict, pushing and pulling at the same time, trying with all her strength to someday burn bright as a star?

Chapter 38

Jane calls the next day, completely out of the blue. It's Saturday morning around ten. Thankfully, since Ma is in the bathroom, I get to the phone first this time, and then nearly drop it when I realize who it is.

"Bird?" She says my name cautiously, as if it might pop like a balloon. "It's Jane. Jane Livingston?"

My face flushes hot at the sound of her voice, humiliated and horrified at the same time. "Yeah. Hi."

"Listen, I was wondering if you would have time to meet with me . . . maybe for some coffee? Or tea?"

"Today?"

"Well, yes. I was thinking maybe in an hour or so?"

I pull one of the curtains back and lean in, looking down the street both ways. No news cars in sight.

"There are some things I was hoping we could talk about," Jane says quickly, as if sensing my hesitation. "And maybe clear up."

There are a few things I'd like to tell her myself. Like *I'm sorry.* And *Please don't hate me.* And *If you would just let me explain . . .* "The thing is, I'm actually not allowed to leave my house right now . . ." I let the words trail off, knowing how awful they sound, but not wanting to explain any further.

"Could I come there?" Jane says the words in a rush. "I mean, if it's okay with you, of course. I don't want to impose."

"Um . . ."

"Yeah, maybe that's not the best . . ."

"No, no." I'll ask Ma to take Angus to the movies or something. She hasn't been out in weeks and, considering the situation, I think she'll be reasonable. I give Jane the address and hang up.

MA'S LEERY ABOUT going out with Angus, but when I tell her about the phone call with Jane, her face softens a little. "What do you think she wants?"

"I'm not sure, really."

"Are you going to apologize?"

"Of course I'm going to apologize."

"All right," she says. "But don't let her stay too long. I get nervous being out there right now. Especially with Gus. People know who we are. And they're . . . you know, still talking."

"Oh, they'll talk about this one forever, I bet."

"It's not funny, Bird."

"I'm not laughing, Ma."

I pull on clean pants and a light V-neck sweater, brush my hair, and hold it back with a wide headband. There's no reason why Jane shouldn't see me in my usual scrub uniform, but for some reason, I don't want her to. Something's changed between us; I can feel it.

Whatever it is, I want to be ready.

IT'S A STRANGE sensation to have Jane on the other side of the doorstep when she rings the bell. She looks a little weird without Olivia in her arms, but no, that's not it exactly either. She's dressed differently, in khaki pants, a soft blue cowl neck sweater, small gold hoop earrings. She's put on a little makeup, too—some black eyeliner, a little concealer under her eyes, peach blush. She looks . . . good. Rested.

"Hey," I say, letting her in. I can barely make eye contact; it is so painful. "I have some tea set up in the kitchen."

"You look nice," Jane says, sliding her feet out of her shoes and arranging them neatly inside the door. "I've never seen you in anything but your sweats."

I smile, wondering why I'd been so quick to assume all this time that her "no shoes inside the house" rule had only been meant for me. "Yeah, well I'm not really working right now."

She drops her eyes and follows me into the kitchen where I've set up Ma's china teapot, white with pink roses, and matching cups and saucers. In the middle of the table is a small plate of Oreos, which were the only cookies I could find in the pantry and which, in traditional Ma fashion, I have spread out like a fan.

"Oh, how sweet!" Jane says, sitting down in one of the chairs. "I hope you didn't go to too much trouble."

"No, it's fine." I sit down opposite her, and immediately reach for the teapot, grateful for the diversion. Neither of us says anything as I fill her cup and then mine with the steaming liquid. I put the teapot back down and pick up the saucer of cookies. Jane takes one and smiles at me. I drop my eyes and replace the saucer. "God, Jane, I'm just so sorry." The words come out in a squeaky rush.

Jane leans forward. "I didn't ask to see you so that you could apologize, Bird. Although I'm glad you did, and I accept."

I inhale, shuddering faintly.

"Mrs. Ross came to see me yesterday," Jane says. "And she told me a lot about you."

Oh, I can only imagine.

"She thinks the world of you, you know. As a mother, a woman."

I lift my head, blink.

"She does," Jane says, as if sensing my skepticism. "She said those exact words to me. And I agree with her. I do. I think you're a really good person, Bird, who made some bad choices."

"That's generous of you," I say, and I mean it. "Thank you."

"It might be generous," Jane says. "But I think it has more to do with the fact that I know what it's like to make a few bad choices myself." She laughs lightly, picking up her teaspoon and stirring her tea. "Actually, you might say I'm the Queen of Bad Choices."

"Yeah, well. No one's perfect."

"True." Jane nods. A moment passes. "You know, before I got married, I was a drug addict." I freeze in my seat, stare across the table. Maybe Ma was right about her. "Pills, mostly," she continues, "although honestly, I'd do anything I could get my hands on. I was a total mess. And then I met Richard, who changed everything. I've never loved someone the way I loved him." She shrugs, as if such a thing is perfectly understandable. "I literally forgot about everything except being with him. Including the drugs. Plus . . ." She looks at something out the window, past my head. "Well, you know, he would've never loved me back if he knew I was a drug addict." She blinks. "But it was easy, giving them up. For him. To be with him. To be his wife, carry his children. It was all I'd ever wanted. All I'd ever dreamed." She looks down at the table, runs the tip of her finger around the edge of her Oreo. "Except that for the last five years, there hasn't been a single day when I haven't thought about taking them again."

"But you didn't?"

"No, I did." She nods. "A few times. Once, after the twins were about a year old, and then again, a few years after. But it was just Amytal—sleeping pills—and even though I was popping a lot of them, I got it under control pretty quickly. I had to. I had little kids I was taking care of now, whose lives were my responsibility. Plus, we go to La Jolla for a month every summer, and to Paris for two weeks in the winter. Richard's always counted on me to take care of things and get those trips in order." She pauses, lifting her teacup to her mouth and taking a shaky sip. "But something changed after Olivia came. I could feel it in my bones a few days after I delivered her, which sounds so awful, I know, because the only thing you're supposed to be thinking about then is your new baby and how much you're in love . . ." Her voice trails off as she shakes her head. "But it was there, right in the middle of my chest, as big and awake as a . . . a storybook monster."

"What was?"

Jane blinks. "That thing," she says slowly. "That absolute, unequivocal, don't-even-try-to-argue-with-me *thing* inside me that said 'this is not my life,' and 'this isn't what I wanted,' and 'no one even asked me if I wanted to have kids in the first place!'" Her voice gets incrementally louder with each word until, on the last one, she is almost shouting. She brings her hand to her mouth quickly, embarrassed, but I shake my head.

"It's okay," I tell her, because it is okay. "I get it."

"Yes. I kind of knew you would." Her voice is full of wonder, looking at me. "I really did. Isn't that funny?" She takes a sip of her tea again. "Anyway, it wasn't something *I* understood. Or I guess I should say I understood it, but it made me feel so terrible, you know? Like I was just an awful mother, a terrible, disgusting person. And it definitely wasn't something I could have brought up with Richard." She sighs, and I can hear the weight of it. "Overnight practically, I went back to popping Vicodin like they were candy. The fact that I wrenched my back just gave me an excuse to take more of them. By the time you came around, I was so addicted again that I was literally watching the clock until I could take another one. Plus, I started counting them—incessantly—to make sure I had enough." She shrugs, looking up at me. "That was how I caught the missing ones. You know, that you took."

Wow. Ma used to say that you never knew what was behind closed doors and damn if she wasn't right. *Jesus.* Jane Livingston, a drug addict. You could've knocked me over with a feather. But why is she telling me all this? Aside from counting out her pills and figuring out that I took them, what does all the rest of the story have to do with me?

"So . . ." I look down at my tea, wondering what to say. "Are you okay now?"

Jane shakes her head slowly. "I'm leaving for a treatment program tomorrow. I'll be gone for thirty days. I've never been to one, can you believe that?" She picks up her Oreo, studies the chocolate lettering on the front. "I've always just had the willpower to make myself stop. Or maybe it was fear . . . I don't know. But I know I can't this time. This is too big. What I'm feeling inside is too big. I want to be there for my kids, but I need help."

"That's incredible . . . I mean . . . that you know that."

"I don't know how incredible it is." Jane smiles. "But I do think it's treatment or nothing. And if I choose nothing, I'm pretty sure I'll lose." I hold her gaze for a few seconds when she says that and I know she means it. "You know, I might've gone along like this, counting and popping Vicodin for another ten years, if something hadn't happened. I don't know what it is exactly," she says slowly, fiddling with the neckline of her sweater. "But I think it had something to do with you."

"Me?"

"Don't get freaked out." She smiles, embarrassed. "But I've been watching you. Not in a stalker kind of way or anything. More like a 'how does she do it?' kind of way. It's just . . ." She fumbles for a moment, groping for words. "I know how much you have on your plate. I know what happened to your family. With your father. And now you have Angus, and you work so hard cleaning other people's houses, just to make ends meet. And then that day that I was a mess because I didn't have my pills, you were so kind to me, Bird. You were so wonderful with Olivia, putting her in a bath, getting her all calm again. You didn't have to do that." She shakes her head, uses a fingertip to press a tear from the corner of her eye. "It just got me thinking, you know?"

"About what?"

"About how little of my life I was living. And how much life you always seemed to be squeezing out of yours. It made me want to be more like you, Bird. To be that kind of person."

I am aghast. Mute. Who's to say what kinds of things people see in one another? Even if they are the very things that we never glimpse in ourselves?

Jane laughs, a short burst of nerves. "I don't have it all wrong here, do I? You do try to live your life well, don't you? Or is that my Vicodin daze?"

I stare at the table, shake my head slightly. I *want* to live well. Maybe on the whole I do. Except when life gets in the way. Then I don't do very well at all.

"Well, I don't think I am wrong." Jane sits up a little straighter, takes a gulp from her tea. "I think you're pretty amazing."

"Is that why you dropped the charges against me?"

She nods almost imperceptibly. "Like I said, I know what it's like to make bad choices. But I don't want either of us to have to live with this one for the rest of our lives."

"I . . ." My head shakes on its own. "I just don't know what to say. I . . . I just hope someday I can return the favor."

"Maybe . . ." Jane looks up at me cautiously, shyly. "Maybe you could come visit me. At the treatment center. It's in Reading, which is only about thirty minutes away."

I look at her. And for the first time, I see her the way I saw myself up in the attic last night—a little girl inside the woman, still lost, still trying to figure it out. How is it that I feel such shame when I glimpse that part of me, and yet sitting here, realizing the same thing about Jane, all I feel is empathy and compassion? Maybe the answer isn't pointing fingers or tallying our wrongs. Maybe the answer is holding out a hand and steadying one another until we figure out how to walk again.

"You know, now that I've told you all this," Jane says, "I may as well just tell you everything. I've wanted to be your friend for the longest time, Bird. I mean, from the minute I met you, I thought you were funny and interesting and capable. I know it must sound pathetic, a thirty-four-year-old woman saying something like this, but I don't really have friends. At least not here in New Haven. All my friends from college moved away a long time ago. And it's hard to stay in touch when the kids come and you have so much on your plate, you know? It just gets so . . . lonely."

I reach across the table, put my hand over hers. "I'll come visit. At the treatment center."

Jane looks up, her eyes rimmed with tears. "You sure? I mean, you don't have—"

"I will," I say. "I promise."

Chapter 39

Father Delaney opens the door to the rectory when I ring the bell. "Bird." He says my name softly, making no move to hide his surprise. "Come in." He's dressed in his usual black pants and sneakers, a soft black vest sweater over a T-shirt. No collar. He takes a seat in a chair in the corner, indicating the other with a nod of his head. The room is small and white; a copper crucifix is attached to the wall behind him. "How have you been?" he asks. "How's your mother? And Angus?"

"We're okay." I sit down carefully, sliding my hands under my thighs. "I just wanted to come by and . . . apologize."

"What is it that you're apologizing for?" Father Delany clasps his hands.

Ma's words ring in my ears. *"For desecrating a holy space! For letting evil in! Changing his underwear!"*

"For . . . you know, for helping . . . James." I pause for a moment, shake my head. "Well, no, actually, I'm not really sorry for that part." I glance up. "I mean, I apologize if that offends you, but that's just how I feel. I really don't think I did anything wrong by helping him."

"What, then?" Father Delaney's voice is gentle.

"Well, I guess I'm sorry I was dishonest. About the whole Forty Hours thing and using that to pretend that I was coming back to church and all that." I tuck my legs beneath my chair self-consciously. "I feel really bad about not being straight with you. About being misleading."

"I appreciate your apology," Father Delaney says. "Thank you."

He rests one of his ankles over the other knee, and I study the outline of his black sneakers for a moment. The tracks on the bottom are coated with dried mud; one of the laces is loose.

"Did you know him?" Father Delaney asks suddenly. "The man in the loft?"

"Yeah, I knew him." And then, in a rush: "I loved him actually." I take a breath when I say this, realizing for the first time that I have never admitted such a thing before to anyone, not even myself, but that the admission has opened something in me, let something in. I sit up straighter, feel my breathing start to slow.

"So you knew him well, then."

I blush, feel my lower lip start to tremble. "No, actually. I didn't know him very well at all. But he saved me once, and . . ." I drop my eyes, fumbling for words. I can't go there. I just can't. Not with him. "What happened in the choir loft, Father, I mean, you've gotta know it just happened. Out of nowhere. I don't know if was fate or coincidence, or what. But I came to the church that morning to pick up Ma's sweater—you remember—and I heard a noise in the loft, and there he was." My voice cracks, remembering. "At first I just ran, you know? I was so scared. I didn't know what to think. But then I started thinking about all these parts of himself he'd given me a long time ago when I didn't even know I needed it, and how they were right there in front of me again when I needed them more than anything. And that's why I went back. That's why I helped him. I'm sorry." I bury my face in my hands, let them fill with my tears. "I'm so sorry, Father."

He's in front of me suddenly, crouched down on one knee, one arm draped around my shoulders. I let him hold me as I cry.

"No one's ever loved me like that before." It's as if I've forgotten to whom I'm talking. Or maybe it's the small weight of his hand on my shoulder, which feels like a release of some kind. Whichever it is, words are staggering out of me, pulled by an invisible line. "And it did something to me, you know, him loving me. It opened me up, Father. I hadn't even known how closed I was, how tightly I'd shut myself to everyone and everything until I met him. Until I started loving him, too. It changed everything. Everything! It was like I hadn't understood anything at all about myself until I saw myself through his eyes. He told me I was beautiful, Father. That I smelled like petrichor."

"Petrichor?" Father Delaney cocks his head.

"Yes." I nod. "It's the smell that comes out of the earth when it rains after a very long dry spell."

"Ah." Father Delaney nods.

"I miss him so much. Oh my God, I miss him." Sobs overtake words, and still they push their way through. "There's nothing I can do to bring him back, nothing at all, and some days when I think of going through it without him for one more second . . . I just . . . Oh my God, I don't know. I'd do it all over again, every single part of it, even though I know it's wrong, if I could spend one more day with him. One more hour."

My shoulders hurt, and my back, too, by the time I am done, and still Father Delaney hasn't moved. Finally, when I raise my face, stained and leaking, he gets up and grabs a few tissues off his desk. I take them gratefully, clean myself off, sit back with a shudder. I can tell he is getting ready to say something. He's got that look in his face that he used to get when I went to confession as a kid: a sort of perplexed, thoughtful expression, as if gathering up all his thoughts and laying them out in front of him, like playing cards. He's probably going to give me a speech, inform me in no uncertain terms of all the missing spaces in my life that can be filled only by God.

Instead, he says this: "I'm sorry it hurts so much. And that it's been hurting so much for so long." New tears spill over, running down my cheeks. "But let me tell you this, Bird. When you do something with great love, it can't possibly be wrong. God says that—"

"I don't believe in God," I interrupt, still sobbing. "I don't, I don't!"

"But you believe in love." Father Delaney reaches out, clutches my shaking hand in his. "You believe in love now, Bird, don't you?"

I nod slowly. "I do."

Father Delaney smiles. "Then if you believe in love, you believe in God. They're the same thing."

I stare at him disbelievingly. It's so simple as to be ridiculous. So small as to be miraculous. So factual as to make perfect sense, just like the oxygen a heart needs to continue beating outside the body.

I CAN'T SLEEP at all the night before the hearing. Mrs. Ross has called twice, to go over things with me, but it hasn't done anything to ease my anxiety. For all I know, I could be going behind bars tomorrow—for a long time. Now, I hold Angus close beneath the covers, slip my fingers through his silky hair. We're watching *E.T.* on the television—for probably the eighth time—and eating popcorn. It's the end of the movie, where E.T. and Elliott have to say goodbye, and Angus is riveted. Even the popcorn, which he has up until this point been stuffing voraciously into his mouth, is forgotten to one side. A figure appears in the spaceship, the strange shape glowing in the doorway, and Angus says immediately, the way he always does, "That's E.T.'s mommy."

I think how amazing it is that he thinks such a thing without any hesitation. The figure could be anyone: E.T.'s brother, a sister, an aunt, an uncle. But it makes the most sense to Angus that it is E.T.'s mother standing there, come back to get him after so much time away, and when the plaintive, honking sound comes out of the figure's mouth, calling for E.T., I look at him again, in wonder.

After the movie, while we are lying in bed talking, I gaze at his features, as if trying to memorize them. Which, for all I know, I might have to do. I haven't even broached the topic of Angus coming to visit me in prison, but even if it's allowed, I don't know if I want him to. What would that do to him, going to see his mother behind bars? How much further back would that set him?

"Hey, Boo," I say. "Can I ask you a question before you go to sleep?"

"Uh-huh."

"Remember those magic sneakers you used to love wearing all the time?"

"Yeah."

"Why'd you stop wearing them?"

"I told you," Angus says. "They don't work anymore."

"What do you mean? You can't jump in them anymore? They don't help you run?"

"Yeah." Angus scowls. "And they're dumb."

"Why're they dumb?"

"They just are. They didn't really do anything."

"Because Jeremy said they didn't? Or because you think they didn't?"

Angus wrinkles his nose. He rolls over so that his back is facing me, shoves a piece of hair out of his eyes. "I'm going to sleep."

I tuck an elbow behind my head, watch the shadows sift lightly across the wall. Behind the curtains, the shy eye of a half-moon looks in on us; stars wink like a handful of scattered diamonds.

"I don't like Jeremy very much." Angus's voice is very small.

"No?"

"He's not a good friend. He makes me feel bad. A lot."

His little voice quivers on the last word, and I lean over just as he starts to cry, and wrap my arms around him. "I love my magic sneakers," he says after a moment, pushing me away. "And I *miss* them, too."

"I bet they miss you." I fling the covers back. "Let's go get them. Right now. You can put them on and wear them while you sleep."

"In bed?" Angus sits up, his tears forgotten.

"In bed," I say. "All the time if you want."

"Forever?"

I nod. "Forever, Boo. Forever and ever."

I GET UP early, before the sun rises, and head downstairs to put some coffee on. I don't know what coffee is going to do, except make me even more jittery than I already am, but I've got to do something to kill time. Ma's sitting in one of the chairs at the kitchen table, wrapping the tea bag string around the tea bag, squeezing every last drop into her cup. The exhaustion on her face is visible, the muscles limp beneath her papery skin. She blinks when I come in, sets her spoon down on the table next to her.

"Can't sleep either?" I ask.

She shakes her head, rubs a thumb along the inverted part of the spoon until it makes a squeaking sound.

I take out the tin of coffee and the filters, insert one into the coffeemaker. Even in the dark, I can make out patches of green in the tiny yard outside the window, Ma's clothesline hanging loose and slack between the metal poles. It looks like a discarded jump rope now, a forgotten toy that hasn't been used in years. The single window in Dad's toolshed is coated with grime, the small door in front edged in rust.

"Sometimes," Ma says, "I miss Dad so much I wish I had died along with him that day."

I freeze, my hand still inside the coffee filter, as something inside me breaks . . . and then reattaches once more. "I know," I say. "Me, too."

I can hear her turn slightly in her chair, feel her eyes along my back. "Except that I'd never leave you, Bernadette." Her voice cracks when she says my name. "Never."

I turn around as she gets up out of her seat. "I'm sorry I wasn't there for you the day . . ." She drops her eyes, struggling to get the words out. I have stopped breathing. "That . . . that day. When that man hurt you."

"Ma." My voice is shaking, hanging on by a cobweb thread. "You couldn't've . . . I let him in . . ."

She's staring at me, the lines on either sides of her eyes creasing so deeply that her eyes have almost disappeared. I hold my breath again, wait for her to say *I told you so, Bernadette. All those years ago, I told you so.*

Instead, she takes a shaky step toward me. Reaches out with a trembling hand. "Oh, Bird," she says. "Oh God, I love you so much."

She closes both of her arms around me, and when she does, when I feel the solidness of her hands gripping my shoulders, when I smell the familiar scent of coffee and lemon oil behind her ear, it feels as if something I have been waiting for has finally slipped back into place, the final note in a song, the last, single beat.

I close my eyes, and hold her tight.

IF MRS. ROSS LOOKED good before, now she looks like she's about to walk the runway in a Miss America pageant. The woman is glammed up to the max: black silk suit jacket, knee-length skirt, heels with tiny silver buckles on the front, dark red lipstick. She's rolled and twisted her hair into some kind of chignon, knotted a loose string of pearls around her throat.

"Your kids must love having a mother that looks like you," I say. We're waiting in front of the courtroom, making small talk before we have to go in. I am trying not to vomit.

"I don't have kids," Mrs. Ross says.

I turn to look at her. "You don't? What about those pictures in your cubicle? You know, the one of you and the two kids in the pool?"

"That's my niece and nephew," Mrs. Ross says. "Tony and I do a lot of things with them. I can't have children."

"Oh." I sit back, wondering how many other things I've automatically assumed about people will turn out to be wrong. "I'm sorry."

"You don't have to be sorry," Mrs. Ross says. "That's life. That's just the way it goes. I have other things that make me happy." She looks over at me. "You nervous?"

"Horribly."

She leans over, pats my knee. "Remember, it's all up to the discretion of the judge. The district attorney's office has pressed charges against you, yes, but it's the judge's call as to what to do next."

"Right." I smooth my hands over the front of my new pants, run them down along the sides of my hair. "Okay."

A short man with white hair and thick stubby fingers opens the courtroom door. "Connolly!" he yells.

Mrs. Ross stands up quickly, adjusts the pearls around her throat.

"Okay," she says. "Let's go."

It's a long hearing. Testimony is given, taken, and made record of. I watch the stenographer's fingers pushing the strange little keyboard in front of her whenever someone says something aloud, stare at the elderly man sitting off to one side, discreetly trying to pick his nose. When I am asked to take the stand, I walk up on sea legs, holding on to the sides of the little brown box they tell me to sit in as if it is the railing of a ship. Mrs. Ross goes up, too, reading a letter that Jane has written on my behalf, and answering questions about my previous behavior, followed by the police officer who found James's note inside the organ. The judge is an older man with soft white hair that curls around his ears and a long, pointed nose. He lifts the sleeves of his black robe often, as if adjusting his arms inside, and arranges his fingers into a tent whenever someone starts talking. He doesn't look at me. Not once.

And then it's over. The judge asks me to stand. Mrs. Ross stands up with me. The judge says that because he doesn't believe I acted maliciously, and because James is dead, he is going

to roll the aiding and abetting charges into my probation violation charge and issue a single, final sentence.

I hold my breath, balance myself against the table with my
fingertips.

"Two years' probation," the judge says. He looks at me for
the first time and points his gavel directly at my face. "You're
getting another chance here, Miss Connolly, because a lot of
people seem to believe in you. Turn it around now." He bangs
the gavel once off a small piece of the desk and looks out at the
rest of the room. "Hearing adjourned."

Mrs. Ross hugs me for a long time afterward. I don't pull
away. Besides, she smells good. "You know I'm one of those
people the judge was talking about," she says finally, picking
an invisible piece of lint off the front of her suit jacket. "I really
believe in you. Always have."

"Really?" I feel shy suddenly.

"*Yes*, really." Mrs. Ross squeezes my hand again.

"Why?"

"Because you're a good person." Mrs. Ross studies me carefully. "You're a good mother, a good daughter, and a really,
really good woman." She shrugs, as if that's all there is to it.
"That's why."

I give her hand a squeeze, resisting the urge to throw my
arms around her neck. "Thank you."

"You bet your duppa," she says. "Try not to worry so much
about everything else, okay? Just put one foot in front of the
other. Starting now. Today."

Chapter 40

Later that night, I riffle through the phone book in bed, paging through the *L*'s. My heart is pounding so hard I can hear it in my ears, and my index finger, which I draw down the list of names I come across, is shaking. It's a long shot. But I have to try. I won't be able to live with myself if I don't at least try.

"Hello?" She picks up on the third ring.

"Is this . . ." I clear my throat. "Is this Jenny Locke?"

"Yes." A pause. "Are you selling something? Because if you're selling something, I'm not interested."

"No, I'm not selling anything."

"Who is this, then?"

I swallow hard, force my voice to steady itself. "This is Bird, Jenny. Bird Connolly? From when we shared the—"

"I 'member." She cuts me off, inhales sharply. Starts to say something, and then retreats, as if collecting her thoughts. Then: "I saw you on the news. With James and all that."

"Yeah."

Silence. I press my fingers against the wildflower print on

my quilt, as if the blooms themselves will bleed courage into my skin. "I know it's been a long time, Jenny. And this might seem really crazy, bringing it up after so many years, but James told me some things that I was hoping to talk to you about."

Silence.

"Jenny?"

"Yeah."

"It's about that night," I say. "When Charlie came over?"

"Listen, I really didn't see anything. Actually, I thought you guys were just having make-up sex." She says this so quickly, an edge of defense so apparent in her voice, that I almost hang up. But then I remember James's words: *Maybe she was just too scared to go back there.*

I want to move past this. I do. But the only way I can move past it is to force Charlie to take responsibility for his actions. To stand up for myself the way I should have that day in his hospital room. Or even in the district attorney's office, when they were asking me for the real story behind James and Charlie. After I come clean, I can move on. After that, I think I can forgive.

"Okay," I say slowly. "But you did hear me screaming, didn't you, Jenny? You did hear me saying 'no' over and over again. Didn't you?"

Silence.

"Jenny?"

Silence.

"Jenny. I don't blame you for not doing anything that night. I was too scared to do anything either. I let it go because I felt guilty that I even let him inside in the first place, because I knew he was drunk and I didn't even really want to see him. I didn't call the police, I didn't report it. I didn't do anything because I blamed myself. I had a baby, and I never told anyone that he came from a rape. But I'm not the same person that I was back then, Jenny. And I want to hold Charlie accountable now for what he did to me. I want to press rape charges against him. My probation officer told me that there's a ten-year statute of limitations when it comes to rape charges in our state. So I still have time. But I need your help. James is the only other person who witnessed what happened that night, and he's gone. You're all I've got, Jenny. And I'm asking for your help. I'm asking you to help me make things right. For me. And my son."

There is a soft intake of breath, tremulous and frail as a cloud. "You know, I've been waiting for five years to run into you somewhere," Jenny says finally, "to see you across the street, or in the Laundromat. I guess in the back of my head, I always knew this day would come. It's like what they say: what goes around comes around."

"I'm not trying to punish you, Jenny. Really, I'm not. That's not what this is about here. I just can't do it without you."

"I was just going to pop in that night," she says. "Literally. For, like, two seconds. And then I ran into James just as I was about to head upstairs to the apartment to grab something, and he looked like a nervous wreck so I stayed there for a minute and talked to him, and he told me he was trying to work up the nerve to go ask you out."

I close my eyes, thinking of it.

"I told him he had to do it, that we all knew he was crazy about you . . ." Jenny's voice fades a little; she knows the futility of going down this road, too. "Anyway, he said he would, and I ran upstairs. James knew my boyfriend, who was sitting there in the car, waiting for me, so he stayed downstairs for another minute to talk to him."

I bite my lip, close my eyes, pray for her to finish.

"Anyway, I opened the door, and I heard . . ." She inhales shakily. Clears her throat. "I heard you screaming. I did. Oh God, Bird, I'm so sorry. I heard you saying 'no' and . . . I don't know what happened. I mean, I knew what was happening, or at least I thought I did, but I just couldn't move." Her voice rises to a whine on the last word, and then breaks into a sob. "And then James came up. . ."

"I know." I nod, all the pieces fitting together suddenly. All of it making sense. All of it culminating, finally, into something I can hold on to. Something I can believe in. "He told me."

"He pushed past me as soon as he heard you . . ." Jenny says. "And I was so relieved that someone else was there, that he'd come, that I just bolted." She cries quietly. "I've thought about it every day since it happened, Bird. I'm so sorry. God, I'm just so sorry."

"Thank you."

"You tell me when and where," Jenny says. I can hear her blowing her nose over the phone. "When and where, Bird. I'll be there."

AN UNUSUAL WARM front blows in at the end of May, getting so hot at certain points of the day that it is uncomfortable to be outside for long periods of time. Ma puts fans in all the downstairs windows and lets them run all night long. I pull out Angus's summer clothes and, much to his delight, allow him to sleep in his underwear. The air is still thick with humidity when I visit James's grave for the first time, and it hovers over everything like an evaporating skin. By the time I reach the corner of the cemetery where the groundskeeper directed me, my arms are slick with perspiration, the small hairs on my neck damp as seaweed.

His headstone is smaller than I expected, just a rough, rect-angular slab, flush with the ground. My heart speeds up as I kneel down next to it and sit back on my heels. It is still unfath-omable that he is gone, still just as painful. His absence is like a physical hole in the world.

I reach out and trail my fingers over the engraved letters: JAMES WILLIAM RITTENHOUSE. Once, and then again. And then, because it is what I would do if he were sitting next to me, I stretch out on my back and tell him about Angus's magic sneakers, and how he wears them to bed at night. I tell him about the last, nearly miraculous conversation with Ma in the kitchen, and the phone call with Jenny and how, despite my nearly suffocating fear of the impending trial, I am going to push through, see it all the way to the end, no matter what happens. And I tell him that because he loved me, I am a dif-ferent person now. Stronger. More hopeful. A woman.

It is not until I get up to leave that I feel the first few drops of rain. The wind is blowing, too, and the leaves overhead make a soft rustling sound. I inhale deeply as the earthy, metal-lic scent drifts up from the ground and close my eyes. It will be difficult, continuing on without him. And I will miss him every day.

But he will not be so far.

He will be here, in every stir of the branches before a rain, inside all the tumultuous fallings from heaven thereafter.

Chapter 41

Late June.

I am in Mr. Herron's garden, helping him replant some of his flowers. My arms and elbows are covered with dirt, the knees of my jeans clotted with mud. The warmth in the air is palpable, the breeze like a breath against my skin. Tomorrow I will go down to the district attorney's office again, rehearse the many questions he will ask me when the trial against Charlie starts next month. I feel sick to my stomach when I think about it. It will be opening another door, looking deep into the mouth of another dragon. Mrs. Ross is coming with me, though. And Jenny, too, who is also going to be put on the stand, and will testify to what she heard that night. It might not be as hard as I think with both of them there. It might be possible after all.

"Here?" I ask, moving Mr. Herron's hand farther to the right. He is on his knees next to me, trying to "see" where he wants his plants positioned.

"Too far." He frowns, stretching his hand in the opposite

direction. "They can't be too close to the parfaits or they just shrivel up and die."

Last week, Mr. Herron called me at home and asked me to come over. He said he had something he wanted to discuss with me. Something of utmost importance. I was nervous going over. It was going to be bad, whatever it was. He probably had a speech planned, something about how he respected Ma, but that he just couldn't have a criminal working in his house anymore. I drove too fast on my way over, sped through a stop sign on his street.

He was sitting in the kitchen when I came in, a plant on the table in front of him. Next to the plant was a small envelope, the back of it sealed shut.

I sat down at the table, put my hands in my lap. "Hey, Mr. Herron. I'm here."

Instead of answering, Mr. Herron moved the envelope toward me.

"What's this?"

"It's for you," he said. "Open it."

I opened it, sure I would find a final check, maybe with a little extra added on so that we could part without any hard feelings. Instead, I caught my breath as a sheaf of one hundred dollar bills fell out. It was at least five thousand dollars. "What's this?"

"I told you," Mr. Herron said. "It's for you."

"But I didn't earn this money. There's no reason—"

"You gonna earn it." Mr. Herron sat forward slightly. The edge of a leaf brushed his cheek; his unseeing eyes roved over my shirt. "You gonna use it for school. For nursing school. It's just to start off, now. Get you rollin'. You know, an old man like me don't get very many opportunities to do something again for someone who needs it."

"You think I need it?"

"Yeah. You bust your butt every day, taking care of your mother and your son. I know it ain't easy. I've heard you upstairs, crying a few times."

I looked down at the table.

"Nothin' to be 'shamed of," Mr. Herron said. "Nothin' at all." He nodded. "It's not the cryin' that bothers me. It's the being stuck. Not being able to do nothing about it. You hear me? I can do something about this, Bird. I can help try to make things a little easier. 'Sides, I want to see what you can do with yourself, girl, once you get planted. Just like that bird of paradise." He grinned broadly, turning his head in the direction of the plant. It was still upright and, somehow, despite the rains and the forty-degree temperatures, a single bud was perched on the end of one stalk. "I's lookin' forward to seein' you bloom, girl. I really, really am."

Now, I watch as Mr. Herron's papery fingers press the dirt around his parfaits, wonder why, out of all the ways he could spend his time, he chooses this. Dirt, and seeds. Flowers and stems and roots and weeds and sometimes even flowers.

"How about over here?" I ask again, maneuvering his hands toward the left.

He shakes his head.

"Where, then?"

"Hold your horses, missy. I's *trying* to map it out."

I sit back, study the small flowering bush in my hand. It's some kind of zinnia, according to Mr. Herron. A hardy plant that won't require too much attention. I look at the petals, the perfect, spiraling formation of them, how the leaves along the stem follow a staggered pattern, one beneath the other, so as not to block the sunlight. And I think about all the moments happening right now in the world, the strange, beautiful dichotomy of them: a star spinning in space, a child pulling on a winter hat. The transparent wings of a bumblebee, the cut of a knife, a mother gazing at her newborn baby. Silence after screams, and the kindness of a stranger. The beating of a heart, and the stopping of another.

How brave we are to continue loving each other among the ruins; how strong a choice to decide to go on when death has seemed the only option.

"Okay, right here." Mr. Herron taps the ground exactly where I previously placed his hand. "Here's the place. Start diggin'. And then put that puppy in real gently. Nice and soft, y'hear? Like a baby."

"I got it, Mr. Herron." I pick up the shovel, stick it into the rich earth. "Don't you worry. I got it."

THERE'S NOTHING REMARKABLE about my drive home afterward. I wind through the same familiar streets, brake at exactly the same stop signs I've been looking at all my life, even pause at the same spot on the bridge, so that I can look out and see the water. But when I pull into the little apartment on Vine Street, six blocks away from Ma, and hear Angus shrieking in the backyard as she pushes him on his brand-new tire swing, it feels remarkable suddenly.

Extraordinary, even.

Acknowledgments

Thanks to my editor, Emily Krump, who believed in this book from the beginning. And to the loves of my life, my children, Sarah, Sophia, and Joseph, who sustain and lift me up every day. Thank you, angels.

About the author

About the book

Read on . . .

Insights,
Interviews
& More . . .

Meet Cecilia Galante

Herbert W. Plummer

CECILIA GALANTE, who received an MFA in creative writing from Goddard College in Vermont, is the author of eight young adult novels and a children's chapter-book series. She has been the recipient of many awards, including an NAIBA Book of the Year, and an Oprah's Teen Read Selection for her first novel, *The Patron Saint of Butterflies*. She lives in Kingston, Pennsylvania, with her three children. ❧

Behind the Book

Although I drew from various experiences in my life while writing this novel, including single-motherhood and a volatile mother-daughter relationship, the one that stuck out most vividly was something that had nothing to do with me at all. In October of 2003, a convicted felon from our neighborhood, accused of murdering two drug dealers and then burning and burying their bodies in his back yard, escaped from prison. According to reports, he and another man somehow managed to tie their bedsheets into a rope of sorts and then lower themselves out of a seventh-floor jail cell window. The accomplice, who went first, slipped and fell halfway down, fracturing both hips. The murderer, who tossed a mattress out the window, made it safely all the way down and, without a backward glance at his injured cellmate, disappeared into the night.

The police believed that the felon would try to return home, so for three day our little town was gripped with fear while he was on the loose. My own dreams were haunted with images of running into this man, and my daily activities, which I'd used to embark upon without a second thought, were colored within a whole new context. I imagined stumbling into him on my morning run or while headed to the local mini-mart for milk. What if he appeared suddenly while I was filling the tank ▶

of my car with gas, or when I was stopped at a red light? He would most likely be exhausted, filthy, starving, maybe even injured. What would he say? What would he *do*?

It was that three-day pocket of possibility that I remembered most vividly when I decided to center my next book around a woman who accidentally found herself enmeshed with an escaped prisoner. The sheer panic of that time period came back full force as I began to craft scene after scene around the two characters. And then of course, the writer's imagination took over and I allowed myself to go deeper. What if the main character actually knew the escaped convict? And what if she knew him through some vividly shared past experience that she felt indebted to him for? Would such a thing motivate her to help him get away? Or wouldn't it matter?

One of the reasons I write is to try to understand how people's minds work, why they do what they do, especially in certain unusual situations. Why might one person choose to go right, while someone else opts for left? Why not up? Or down? And how much of how we were raised and what we were taught influences those decisions?

I think the history I gave Bird, including a dead father and a critical mother, not to mention her rape and resulting child, played a huge part in her decision to do what she did. But I also think that becoming James's accomplice had less to do with the idea of repaying a debt than it did with wanting to be with someone who, maybe for the first time in her life, saw her for who she was and loved her anyway. I think really seeing someone might be the biggest gift we can give one another in this lifetime.

Including ourselves. ∾

Have You Read?
More from Cecilia Galante

THE INVISIBLES

Brought together by chance as teenagers
at Turning Winds, a home for girls,
Nora, Ozzie, Monica, and Grace quickly
bond over their troubled pasts and form
their own family, which they dub The
Invisibles. With a fierce loyalty to each
other, the girls feel that they can
overcome any obstacle thrown their way.
Though the walls they've built around
themselves to keep out the rest of the
world are thick, they discover one night,
when tragedy strikes, that there are
cracks in their tight-knit circle.

While Ozzie, Monica, and Grace
leave after graduation to forge a fresh
start, Nora decides to stay behind in
Willow Grove. Now, fifteen years later,
she's content living a quiet, single life
working in the local library and
collecting "first lines"—her favorite
opening lines from novels. But when
Ozzie calls out of the blue to let her
know Grace has attempted suicide and
is desperate for them to reconvene,
Nora is torn between elation at seeing
the women who were once her most
cherished, trusted friends and anxiety
over the unresolved conflicts that will
most certainly surface.

As the women gather and reminisce,
the truth about their lives comes to ▶

light. And when The Invisibles decide to take the road trip they always dreamed of, they will be forced to reveal their deepest secrets and confront the night that changed them forever.

"With heart, wisdom, and a quartet of unforgettable protagonists, Cecilia Galante deftly examines the ways in which the sense of community created by profound friendships can act as a salve on even the deepest of wounds. Gripping and heartrending, *The Invisibles* will—warning!—keep you up into the wee hours, hungry for just one more page."

　　　　—Meg Donohue, *USA Today* bestselling author of *All the Summer Girls* and *Dog Crazy*

Discover great authors, exclusive offers, and more at hc.com.